MILLS & BOON®

Medical
romance™

*Emotions and passions run high,
lives are on the line and sexual
tension is in the air!*

*Working together, seeing each
other day after day, when you're
attracted, it's hard to resist…*

EMERGENCY: LOVE

Three exciting romances
based in the fast-paced world of A&E

EMERGENCY: LOVE

Containing

A Wife for Dr Cunningham
by Maggie Kingsley

Dr Mathieson's Daughter
by Maggie Kingsley

Snow Emergency
by Laura Iding

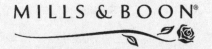

MILLS & BOON®

*MILLS & BOON and MILLS & BOON with the Rose Device
are registered trademarks of the publisher.
Harlequin Mills & Boon Limited,
Eton House, 18-24 Paradise Road, Richmond, Surrey, TW9 1SR*

EMERGENCY: LOVE © by Harlequin Enterprises II B.V., 2006

A Wife for Dr Cunningham and *Dr Mathieson's Daughter* were
first published in Great Britain by Harlequin Mills & Boon
Limited in separate, single volumes.

A Wife for Dr Cunningham © Maggie Kingsley 2001
Dr Mathieson's Daughter © Maggie Kingsley 2001
Snow Emergency © Harlequin Books S.A. 2005

Standard ISBN 0 373 06313 X
Promotional ISBN 0 373 60493 9

122-0806

Printed and bound in Spain
by Litografía Rosés S.A., Barcelona

A WIFE FOR
DR CUNNINGHAM

BY
MAGGIE KINGSLEY

Maggie Kingsley lives with her family in a remote cottage in the north of Scotland surrounded by sheep and deer. She is from a family with a strong medical tradition, and has enjoyed a varied career, including lecturing and working for a major charity, but writing has always been her first love. When not writing she combines working for an employment agency with her other interest, interior design.

CHAPTER ONE

DR ROBERT CUNNINGHAM groaned as he stared down at the file on his desk, the file with its neatly typed label proclaiming that Dr Hannah Blake had been appointed to St Stephen's Accident and Emergency Unit as its newest member of staff.

He didn't need this, not right now. Right now what he needed was sleep—hour upon hour of dreamless sleep— not some junior doctor straight out of med school, hanging onto his coat tails wanting guidance and advice.

If he'd only had his wits about him he would have attempted to persuade Mr Mackay, the consultant in charge of A and E, to allow Elliot to take care of this Hannah Blake. Taking care of women was the blond-haired, blue-eyed SHO's speciality, whereas he—

Don't think, his mind warned. Don't remember. Quickly he pushed the file to one side and reached for his morning mail, only to discover it was the usual boring collection of advertising circulars and bumph. The usual uninspiring selection sent to every special registrar in the country—except for the catalogue at the bottom. The catalogue addressed to Dr Laura Cunningham.

Sudden tears filled his eyes as he gazed down at it.

A year.

It was almost a year since Laura died and yet just the sight of her name on an envelope was enough to remind him of her laughter and vitality. A year, and yet simply seeing his wife's name in print was all it took to prod the still raw wound inside him.

Angrily he crushed the catalogue between his fingers.

What right had companies to send out mail to people long since dead and buried? What right had they to remind relatives of the loved ones they had lost? Did they think he needed reminding? Did they think he'd ever forget?

And did his boss honestly believe he was the right person to wet-nurse a new member of staff? he wondered bitterly as his eyes fell on Hannah Blake's file again. The A and E department of St Stephen's Hospital in London was one of the busiest in the city, and certainly no place for any inexperienced girl.

Grimly he got to his feet and strode out of his office and down the corridor. Well, he'd give this new girl the facts of A and E life, but that was all he would do. The last thing he needed right now was a babysitting job.

Or Little Miss Muffet in a white coat, he groaned silently when he opened the staffroom door and saw the girl standing by the window.

'Dr Blake?' he asked, hoping he might be wrong.

'Yes, I'm Hannah Blake.' She nodded, turning eagerly towards him. 'And you are…?'

Old, he decided, as he stared at her elfin-shaped face and mop of curly golden-brown hair cut into a short bob. He'd just turned thirty-four the previous month, and yet suddenly he felt old, and tired, and jaundiced.

'I'm Robert Cunningham, special registrar,' he said quickly, seeing the eagerness in her face beginning to turn to uncertainty as her eyes took in his crumpled brown corduroys and shirt, and his dishevelled black hair.

Her smile returned and she held out her hand. 'I'm very pleased to meet you, sir.'

He ought to have told her that everyone called him Robert—he should have done—but all he could think as he continued to stare at her was that once, a very long time ago, he must have looked like this—optimistic, eager, keen. Once he must have believed the world was full of endless possibilities, and suddenly all he wanted to do was stamp on that youthful vitality, crush that idealism and enthusiasm, which seemed somehow to mock him.

'OK, there are four things to remember when you're working in A and E,' he declared, deliberately ignoring her outstretched hand. 'Anything you don't know, or aren't sure of, ask me or our SHO, Elliot Mathieson. Keep out from under my feet at all times, always erase the name of the last patient you've treated from the white board immediately, and everyone contributes fifty pence a week towards the cost of our coffee and biscuits, whether they take them or not.'

And with that he sat down, put his feet on one of the coffee-tables and pointedly closed his eyes.

'That's it?' she said faintly. 'I mean, I expected.... I rather hoped—'

'For a guided tour?' he said, opening one cold grey eye. 'A brass band—a welcome to St Stephen's buffet?'

A deep flush of colour stained her cheeks. 'No, of course not, but—'

'Dr Blake, according to your CV, you're a doctor. Unless that CV lied, I suggest you go away and do some doctoring and leave me to get some sleep in peace.'

And without waiting for her reply he closed his eyes again.

Well, her special registrar was a real charmer, and no mistake, Hannah decided as she walked out of the staffroom, only just resisting the impulse to slam the door behind her. Of course she hadn't expected a welcome mat but a little bit of civility wouldn't have cost him anything. A little bit of kindness wouldn't have killed him.

And she'd thought he'd looked quite nice, too, when he'd first opened the staffroom door. Not nice as in handsome—his features were far too sharp and angular for that—but nice as in approachable, understanding, and then he'd virtually told her to get lost.

A prickle of tears welled in her throat and she pulled a handkerchief from her pocket and angrily blew her nose. She hadn't cried since she was six years old and she wasn't about to start now because of one rude man with a shock of untidy black hair and a pair of cold grey eyes.

So what if Robert Cunningham clearly considered her the lowest form of medical life? And so what if the St Stephen's Infirmary looked even more dilapidated now than it had done when she'd come for her interview two months ago in June?

She'd wanted a junior post in London, in a hospital as far away from Edinburgh as she could get, and she'd got one. It was up to her to make a success of it, and everyone in this hospital couldn't be as rude as the special registrar.

They weren't.

The minute she stuck her head round the treatment-room door, a plump girl with thick black hair caught up into a high ponytail under her cap smiled a welcome. 'Can I help you at all, Doctor?'

'I hope so,' Hannah replied fervently. 'I'm Hannah Blake.'

The girl gazed at her blankly for a second, then clapped an apologetic hand to her forehead. 'Oh, cripes! Our consultant, Mr Mackay, did tell me you were starting on the 4th of August but I'm afraid I completely forgot. Jane Halden,' she continued, holding out her hand. 'Senior Sister in A and E for my sins. Flo, come and meet Dr Blake,' she called, beckoning to the tall, striking-looking black girl who had emerged from one of the cubicles. 'Dr Blake, this is Staff Nurse Floella Lazear, one of the best staff nurses in the business.'

'Flattery will get you nowhere, Jane!' The girl laughed. 'Nice to meet you, Doctor.'

'Please, call me, Hannah—both of you,' she insisted. 'Would either of you know where I might find Dr Mathieson? I really ought to introduce myself to him.'

'He's in cubicle 3 at the moment with Kelly Ross, our student nurse, examining a possible perforated appy,' Floella replied, 'but I wouldn't worry too much about introducing yourself to Elliot. Our SHO has a built-in homing device when it comes to new female members of staff.'

'A built-in homing device?' Hannah repeated, bewildered.

The staff nurse's deep brown eyes danced. 'Dr Mathieson may not be mad and bad, but he's most definitely dangerous to know, Hannah.'

'Oh, come on, Flo,' Jane protested. 'Elliot's great to work with…'

'And thirty-two-years old, blond, blue-eyed, and absolutely gorgeous,' the staff nurse grinned. 'Unfortunately he's also divorced with absolutely no intention of ever settling down again, so—'

'St Stephen's is littered with broken hearts,' Hannah finished for her with a laugh.

'Too right.' Floella nodded. 'If you're wanting fun with no commitment, Elliot's your man, but a long-term relationship? Forget it.'

If the staff nurse intended her comment as a warning, Hannah didn't need it. Being a useful member of the team was all she was interested in, and after what had happened with Chris… No, she didn't need any warning about handsome male doctors.

'You'll have met our consultant—Mr Mackay?' Jane queried.

Hannah nodded. 'I met him when I came for my interview. He seemed very nice.'

'He is,' the sister agreed. 'Though you probably won't see very much of him unless it's something really serious.

Robert Cunningham—our special reg—pretty much runs the show on a day-to-day basis, and—'

'I met him this morning,' Hannah interrupted. 'He seemed…he seemed a little tired when I saw him,' she said, determined to be charitable.

'Exhausted, more like.' Jane grimaced. 'God knows when that man last ate a decent meal, or had a good night's sleep. He practically lives in the department, and has done ever since…'

The rest of what Sister Halden had been going to say died on her lips as the doors to the treatment room suddenly banged open and two paramedics rushed in, pushing a trolley.

'Stabbing incident! BP 60 over 40, GCS 3-3-4. No breath sounds on the left side, so we tubed him, Doc!'

Doc.

He meant her, Hannah realised as Floella and Jane instantly slipped into their professional roles and began cutting off the young man's clothing and attaching him to a ventilator. He meant she should do something, and do it quickly. And why shouldn't he think that? She was the only one wearing a white coat, and she was the only one doing nothing.

'Do we know his name—age—anything?' she asked with a calmness she was very far from feeling.

'He's Ian Simpson, according to his wallet,' the paramedic replied. 'And at a guess I'd say he's between twenty-three and twenty-six.'

Quickly Hannah placed her stethoscope on the injured man's chest. The paramedic had been right. There were definitely no breath sounds on the left side. The young man's left lung had collapsed, and blood and air were seeping into his chest cavity.

'IV lines, Floella?' she asked.

The staff nurse glanced up at the drip bags containing

the saline solution which was temporarily providing a substitute for the blood Ian Simpson was losing. 'Open and
running.'

'BP, Jane?'

'Still 60 over 40,' the sister replied as she connected the
injured man to the cardiac monitor.

Sixty over forty was much too low, and Ian Simpson's
GCS—his score of consciousness on the Glasgow coma
scale—wasn't a whole lot better.

'Hannah?'

Jane Halden was gazing at her anxiously. The heart monitor was showing an increasingly uneven heart rhythm.
With blood and air seeping into his chest cavity, Ian
Simpson's heart was having to beat much too fast, trying
to get enough oxygen to his brain, and if they didn't insert
a chest drain—and fast—he could have a heart attack.

'Do you want me to page Robert?' the sister continued,
clearly sensing Hannah's indecision.

And have him think she couldn't cope? Have him
think—as he all too obviously already suspected—that she
was useless? She'd watched a chest drain being inserted
many times, had even performed a couple herself under
supervision. Well, now was the time to find out whether
she could do one alone.

'Chest tube and scalpel, please, Jane,' she said firmly.

The sister handed them to her and quickly Hannah made
an incision into the upper right-hand side of Ian Simpson's
chest, then carefully inserted a plastic tube directly into his
chest cavity. With the tube hooked up to the suction line
the excess air and blood was removed in seconds and the
lung began to reinflate.

'Well done,' Jane murmured as Hannah let out the breath
she hadn't even known she'd been holding. 'You'll be
wanting six units of O-negative blood, a chest X-ray and
a CBC?'

Hannah nodded. Type O blood could be given to any patient, buying them time until their blood samples had been tested. The X-ray would show whether she'd positioned the chest tube correctly, and the CBC—the complete blood count—would tell them just how much blood the patient had lost.

'OK, folks, what have we got here?'

Hannah spun round, startled, momentarily lost her balance and fell nose first against a broad, muscular chest. A broad, muscular chest which she was mortified to discover belonged to none other than Robert Cunningham.

'I'm so sorry, sir,' she began, whipping her hands quickly away from his chest. 'I didn't know you were there.'

'So it would appear,' he observed irritably. 'Perhaps I should wear a bell round my neck in future if you're as jumpy as this.'

Jumpy? She wasn't jumpy, but, then, neither had she expected to find herself noticing that, up close, the special registrar had eyes she was sure could smile if only he'd let them, and a mouth that looked just made for laughing if he'd only give it the chance.

'I'm sorry, what did you just say?' she asked, pulling her scattered wits together as she suddenly realised that Robert Cunningham had asked her something.

'I asked what was wrong with your patient,' he said tightly.

'It's a—a pneumothorax,' she stammered, wondering why on earth she should start wondering what the special registrar would look like if he smiled, 'but I've inserted a chest drain.'

His black eyebrows rose. 'You've done what?'

'You told me to go and do some doctoring so I have!' she retorted without thinking, only to flush deeply as his eyebrows rose. 'Dr Cunningham—'

'Have you remembered to order six units of O-negative, a chest X-ray and a CBC?'

Her chin came up at that. 'Of course.'

'Then, assuming you've inserted the chest drain correctly—'

Well, thanks a bundle for the vote of confidence, Hannah thought grimly.

'And assuming he doesn't have an unusual blood group, all you have to do now is to tell his family he's survived your ministrations. Where are they?'

'Th-they?' she faltered, her heart catapulting to the pit of her stomach as she realised the implication of his words.

'You did remember to ask the paramedics if anyone came in with him, didn't you?' he asked, his eyebrows snapping down.

The colour on her cheeks darkened to crimson. 'I... We... Everything was happening so fast, you see, and I...I...'

Her voice trailed away into mortified silence and Robert groaned inwardly. That was all he needed this morning. A new member of staff who not only looked as though she should be still at school but who was inefficient into the bargain.

'And how, may I ask, do you propose to discover if your unfortunate patient was accompanied by anyone?' he demanded, his voice ice-cold.

'The paramedics—'

'Will be long gone by now,' he snapped. 'Which means we'll either have to go out into the waiting room and ask everyone there if they came in with a stabbing incident, or perhaps you favour the more direct approach—an announcement over the Tannoy?'

Hannah's cheeks reddened even more. 'I'm sorry. I didn't think—'

'A fact that is all too blatantly obvious!' he retorted, and Jane Halden cleared her throat awkwardly.

'Robert, Hannah only arrived half an hour ago. Don't you think you're being a little harsh?'

Of course he was but, damn it, he didn't have time to babysit anyone. He'd never had to babysit Laura when she'd been his junior. She'd always known what to do. She'd—

'BP 60, neck veins swollen, no heart sounds!' Floella suddenly yelled.

Robert whirled back to the trolley. 'The pericardium— the sac round his heart—must be filling with fluids.'

'Will I page the chest surgeon?' Jane asked, reaching for the phone only to see Robert shake his head.

'This guy will be dead before the chest surgeon gets here.'

'Then what are we going to do?' Hannah asked, but Robert wasn't even listening to her. He'd already snapped on a pair of latex gloves, grabbed a scalpel from the trolley and, without a second's hesitation, made a wide incision across the young man's chest, slicing through the muscles to the ribs below.

He's going to do a thoracotomy, Hannah thought in amazement when he then took a large metal rib spreader, inserted it between two of Ian Simpson's ribs and spread them wide enough apart to get his hands into the chest cavity. It was a last-ditch effort, but if he pulled it off…

'BP now, Flo?' he demanded after he'd cut into the sac round Ian Simpson's heart and the trapped blood gushed out.

'Still falling!'

It shouldn't have been. Hannah could see the patient's heart beating more forcefully beneath Robert Cunningham's fingers so the blood pressure should have been going up, not down.

'There's a hole in his heart!' she exclaimed, suddenly seeing it. 'Lower right side. The knife must have pierced it when he was stabbed!'

Without a second's thought Robert inserted his finger into the hole and the flow of blood stopped instantly.

'BP now, Flo?' he asked.

'Eighty over sixty…ninety over seventy… You've got him, Robert!'

'Theatre ready?'

'On standby,' Jane replied.

'OK, Flo, let's go!'

And with Robert's finger still lodged in Ian Simpson's heart, Floella Lazear swiftly guided the trolley out of the cubicle and down the corridor, leaving Hannah gazing wistfully after them.

She would have liked to have gone, too. She would have been even happier if Robert Cunningham could have conceded she wasn't entirely useless, but he hadn't even glanced in her direction before he'd left.

'If you're hoping Robert will ever say "Well done", I'm afraid you'll wait until hell freezes over,' Jane murmured, clearly reading her mind. 'He's not being rude, it's just that he's always so focused on his work it never occurs to him to give praise.'

'He's good, isn't he?' Hannah sighed. 'At his job, I mean?'

Jane nodded. 'Brilliant. Unfortunately he can also be lethal if he thinks you're not pulling your weight, as poor Dr Jarvis discovered.'

'Dr Jarvis?' Hannah queried.

'Your predecessor. He only lasted two months with us before he handed in his resignation. He just couldn't cope, you see,' Jane added as Hannah stared at her in dismay. 'I don't think he realised how stressful working in A and E was going to be, and not everybody is up to it.'

Hannah fervently hoped she was. Robert Cunningham quite clearly was. She'd never seen anyone approach a thoracotomy as casually as he had done, for all the world as though he'd been doing nothing more exotic than removing someone's tonsils.

'Robert is one of the best in the business,' Jane continued, as though she'd read her mind. 'You'll learn a tremendous amount from him—we all have. I just wish...' She sighed and shook her head. 'I just wish he'd ease up a bit. He virtually lives at the hospital.'

'He's a workaholic, then?' Hannah suggested.

'He was always a very dedicated doctor, but ever since his wife was killed last year he virtually eats and sleeps A and E.'

'Had they been married long?'

Jane shook her head. 'Two years, that's all. Laura was a junior doctor in the department, and she was knocked down by a car right outside the hospital. Actually, it was pretty awful. Robert was on duty when they brought her in.'

'But that's dreadful,' Hannah gasped, truly shocked. 'He must have been devastated.'

'He was—is.' Jane nodded. 'And the trouble is, he won't let any of us help him. He won't talk about it or discuss it. All he does is work, and everybody knows that doesn't solve anything.'

Sometimes it did, Hannah thought pensively. Sometimes work could be a panacea for your troubles, as she knew only too well. 'Jane—'

'Hey, what's a nice girl like you doing in a place like this?'

Did every male doctor in this department walk like a cat? Hannah wondered as she turned to find herself gazing up into a pair of deep blue eyes. Deep blue eyes that were set in the handsome face of a man with blond hair. Elliot

Mathieson, she decided. It just had to be, and Jane Halden confirmed it.

'Elliot, that has to be the oldest chat-up line I've ever heard,' she protested, and he grinned.

'Fair's fair, Janey. I've been up to my elbows in a perforated appy for the last forty minutes. What did you expect—originality?'

'Something a whole lot better than that hairy old chestnut,' she said with a laugh. 'Hannah, this—if you haven't already guessed—is Elliot Mathieson, our SHO. Elliot, meet Hannah Blake, the latest recruit to the madhouse.'

'Pleased to meet you,' he declared, shaking her outstretched hand. 'Lord, but either I'm getting old, or you look terribly young.'

'I'm ageing by the minute, believe me,' she said with feeling, and he chuckled.

'Rough morning?'

'Not too bad,' she replied, but Elliot wasn't fooled for a second.

'Had a run-in with Robert already, have you?' he said shrewdly. 'Stand up to him, love. If you don't, he'll walk all over you.'

She squinted over her shoulder at her back. 'I think he already has.'

He laughed, then a slight frown appeared in his deep blue eyes. 'Hannah Blake. *Hannah* Blake? Look, I know this is going to sound really corny but could we possibly have met before?'

Oh, but she didn't need this, she thought, not on her first day. The department's consultant, Mr Mackay, knew who she was, and eventually—inevitably—everyone else would find out, too, but she'd hoped to have established herself, to have proved she was good at her job, before that happened.

She cleared her throat awkwardly but to her relief Jane unwittingly came to her rescue.

'You're right, Elliot. That was corny, and clichéd, and undoubtedly the *second* oldest chat-up line, I've ever heard!' she groaned.

The SHO stuck out his tongue at her. 'I'm trying my best, Janey.'

'In that case, maybe you should give up flirting,' she retorted, and Elliot winked at Hannah.

'She's secretly madly in love with me, you know.'

'Yeah, right, and I'm also six feet tall with a figure like a supermodel.' Jane laughed. 'Come on, Hannah. Elliot clearly needs time to think up some new chat-up lines, and you and I have work to do.'

Hannah chuckled as Jane bore her away, but her laughter died when she reached the end of the treatment room and glanced back to see that Elliot was staring after them, a decided frown on his forehead. How long would it be before the SHO remembered why her name sounded so familiar? A month—maybe less? And he would remember. She had no doubt about that.

But at least not today, she thought ruefully as the rest of her shift sped by in an exhausting and bewildering round of casualties. Nobody would have time even to think today, far less remember.

'Doesn't it ever ease up?' she protested when Floella stripped the cover off the examination trolley and replaced it with yet another one in preparation for the next patient. 'I've lost count of the number of casualties I've seen.'

'Wait until you do nights,' the staff nurse replied. 'Days are a picnic in comparison.'

Jane had told her earlier that weekends were a nightmare, and now Floella was saying that nights were murder too. Terrific, Hannah thought, trying and failing to ease the ache in her shoulders and back. She could hardly wait.

'Who's next?' she asked.

'A fifty-two-year-old homeless man, complaining of trouble with his leg. He's been living rough for the past ten years, so I'd better warn you—he's pretty ripe.'

Ripe wasn't the word Hannah would have used to describe the smell that emanated from the man Floella helped into the cubicle. Putrid was closer to the mark.

'I understand you're having bother with your leg, sir?' she said, trying unsuccessfully to hold her breath when the man clambered awkwardly up onto the trolley.

'I keeps falling over, ducks, and it ain't because I'm drunk.' He cackled, revealing a row of broken, discoloured teeth. 'Leastwise, not always.'

Hannah frowned as she took his blood pressure, pulse and temperature. His pupils were slightly dilated and his heart rate was unsteady. He might be only fifty-two, but he looked at least seventy, and unsteadiness on his feet could mean a stroke, or even heart problems.

The safest thing was to give him a complete examination. It would have been a task made considerably easier if he hadn't appeared to be wearing every stitch of clothing he possessed, but what really puzzled Hannah was why, with every layer she and Floella removed, a strange, unidentifiable aroma should become stronger.

'What *is* that smell?' she murmured out of the corner of her mouth as Floella gingerly placed yet another layer of filthy clothing on the cubicle floor.

The staff nurse shook her head. 'Beats me. Some new aftershave called City Streets, perhaps?'

It wasn't. When they finally removed the last of the homeless man's clothing the cause of the stench became all too horrifyingly clear. His leg was one huge, ugly, suppurating sore.

'Dear God!' Floella whispered, taking an involuntary

step back, and it took all Hannah's self-control not to run straight out of the cubicle.

'I...I'm afraid I'm going to have to send you up to one of our wards, sir,' she began. 'Your leg...' She took a deep breath and immediately wished she hadn't. 'It requires a lot more expert attention than I can give. I'll get a porter...'

'You mean I'm going to have to stay, ducks?' the man asked, his faded brown eyes lighting up. 'I'll have a bed for the night? So every cloud does have a silver lining!'

Hannah wondered where her particular silver lining had gone when she turned to summon a porter and saw Robert Cunningham watching her.

She hadn't seen him for at least a couple of hours, and something about the way he was leaning against the cubicle wall, his arms folded across his chest, told her she didn't want to see him now.

'Is there something wrong?' she asked as soon as one of the porters had wheeled the homeless man away.

'I won't insult your intelligence by asking if you've kept your tetanus and hepatitis shots up to date,' he observed, 'and you've at least remembered to put on latex gloves...'

'But?' she said stiffly.

'You didn't put a mask on that patient and he was coughing.'

She gazed at him in disbelief. 'Dr Cunningham, the man's leg was plainly gangrenous, and you're worried in case he might have a *cold*?'

He unfolded his arms and straightened up. 'I am, if it means he has TB.'

'TB?' she echoed faintly.

'Patients bring germs into A and E, Dr Blake. Hepatitis, HIV and TB, to name but three. We have a vaccine for hepatitis, and if you remember to wear gloves you should be safe from being accidentally infected with HIV, but TB is endemic amongst the homeless. Putting a mask on a patient who is coughing is the best—perhaps the only—way of preventing yourself from exposure.'

She opened her mouth, then closed it again. Even a third-year medical student would have remembered the dangers of TB. How could she have forgotten? How could she have been so stupid?

And Robert knew she had been stupid, and yet an unwelcome flicker of sympathy stirred inside him as he gazed down at her.

How old was she? Twenty-three—twenty four? She looked considerably younger with that ridiculous mop of hair, and it was clear from the redness of her cheeks that she didn't need another lambasting. What she really needed was someone to give her a hug, to tell her they'd all made mistakes at the start of their careers. Well, the hug was a definite no-no, but he could at least provide some encouragement.

'Look, Dr Blake—' he began gently, only to spin round as a piercing scream split the air. 'What the—?'

'The waiting room!' Hannah exclaimed. 'It sounded as though it came from the waiting room!'

It did, but as they ran through the waiting-room doors together Hannah came to a horrified halt when she saw the reason for the disturbance. Two drunks were fighting by the tea and coffee dispenser, while a third was casually urinating against the reception desk.

'Shocked, Dr Blake?' Robert murmured, hearing her sharp intake of breath.

Of course she was shocked, he thought as he gazed down at her white face. Only a man like him who had long since lost all feeling wouldn't have been, and Hannah was plainly sensitive. Sensitive and vulnerable with her big brown eyes and golden brown curls, and suddenly, inexplicably, he knew that he didn't want to see A and E destroying her freshness and enthusiasm. Didn't want to watch her becoming hardened and cynical as he knew she must to survive.

'This is child's play compared to what you'll have to face in the future, Dr Blake,' he continued as two security guards manhandled the drunks away and their receptionist began calming the waiting casualties. 'Fifteen—even ten years ago hospitals used to be regarded as sacred territory, but not any more. Now, doctors, nurses and porters are routinely threatened or attacked by gangs, disgruntled patients and psychotics.'

She glanced up at him. 'Are you trying to frighten me?'

His grey eyes held hers. 'Am I succeeding?'

She lifted her chin a notch. 'No.'

'Then you're a fool,' he said bluntly. 'The NHS doesn't award medals for bravery, and the staff who survive in A and E are the ones who possess a healthy sense of fear.'

Oh, she possessed a healthy sense of fear all right, Hannah thought ruefully, but it wasn't fear for her own safety. It was fear that in an emergency she might not be able to cope. In a crisis she might be found wanting.

And you're going to tell Robert Cunningham that, are you? a little voice asked at the back of her mind as she watched him walk back into the treatment room. You're going to tell him you're scared you'll fail?

Unconsciously she shook her head. No, she couldn't tell him that—she simply couldn't—but she also realised something else as she stared out over the still crowded waiting room.

It wasn't only the special registrar's good opinion that mattered. It was the people sitting there. The people who were in pain, the people who were unhappy, the people who were looking to her to help them.

Nobody had ever said this branch of medicine was easy. Nobody had promised it would be a bed of roses. She had chosen to specialise in A and E, and somehow—some way—she was going to have to cope. She had to. To be able to look Robert Cunningham in the eye, and maintain her own self-respect.

CHAPTER TWO

IT COULDN'T be anyone else, Hannah thought with dismay as she came to a halt in the middle of the pavement. The broad shoulders, the shock of unruly black hair, the way he was walking with his chin hunched deep into his shoulders. Robert Cunningham. Robert Cunningham walking so slowly that unless she made an immediate detour she'd catch up with him.

So, catch up with him, her mind urged. Since you came to St Stephen's a fortnight ago the man's scarcely said two words to you. Maybe he'd welcome the opportunity to talk. Maybe he only appears distant and aloof because he's still hurting over the death of his wife last year.

Yeah, right. And maybe this was really an incredibly bad idea, she decided when she quickened her pace and he greeted her cheery 'hello' with all the enthusiasm of someone stuck at a party with the world's biggest bore.

'I didn't know you lived around here,' he observed, managing to make his comment sound like an accusation and a condemnation at the same time.

'I've got one of the hospital flats in Leyland Court,' she replied, pointing to the drab grey building behind her. 'It looks a bit grim from the outside but the flats themselves aren't too bad.' Actually, they were dreadful. Minimum furniture, minimum comfort, maximum dreariness. Their sole advantage was their close proximity to St Stephen's. 'I understand you live in Wellington Place—in fact, we're practically neighbours—'

'Aren't you far too early for your shift?' he interrupted. 'Or has my watch stopped?'

'I always come in early. There aren't any private kitchens in the flats, you see,' she added as his eyebrows rose. 'And as the communal one gets a bit frantic in the morning I usually just pick up some coffee and toast in the canteen before I start work.'

'I see.'

'St Stephen's… It does the best breakfast in London.'

And why the heck was she bothering? she wondered when her voice trailed away into silence and he said nothing. He didn't want to hear about her eating habits. He obviously didn't want to hear anything she had to say, full stop. The best thing she could do was to make herself scarce, fast.

'I'd better go…'

'How are you settling in at the hospital?' he asked unexpectedly.

Was she supposed to think he cared? 'Fine, thank you.'

'No problems, then?' he pressed.

Lots. Like never seeming to get enough sleep. Like knowing she was surviving each day in A and E on a wing and a prayer. But the main problem at the moment, she thought ruefully, was Robert Cunningham obviously suddenly deciding he ought to talk to her. 'No problems, thank you, sir.'

'It's Robert,' he said irritably. 'Everyone calls me Robert.'

She knew that, but now didn't seem to be the time to point out he'd never actually told her to call him by his first name. 'I really ought to go—'

'Do they still serve fried bread in the canteen?' he interrupted.

'F-fried bread?' she stammered, then nodded.

'Then what are we waiting for?' he asked, surprising her for a second time. Hannah's surprise was as nothing to the total bewilderment Robert felt when he found himself standing in line at the hospital canteen.

What in the world was he doing here? he wondered, all too uncomfortably aware of the number of pairs of curious eyes fixed on him. Normally he just had strong black coffee for breakfast. Normally he avoided any kind of social contact with his colleagues like the plague.

It was all Hannah Blake's fault, he decided, glancing irritably across to where she'd found them an empty table by the window. If she hadn't looked so ill at ease talking to him. If he hadn't found himself suddenly feeling guilty for the way he'd been ignoring her since she'd come to St Stephen's...

And was it any wonder he felt guilty? Little Miss Muffet who looked as though a puff of wind would blow her away. Little Miss Muffet with her snub nose, too-large brown eyes and skin so pale he suspected a kiss would bruise it.

Not that he ever had any intention of finding out. Good God, no. He wasn't looking for a relationship, and, even if he had been, cradle-snatching had never been in his line. He simply felt sorry for her, he told himself firmly, as he would have for any junior doctor new to A and E. And someone had to make sure she was starting an eight-hour shift with something more substantial than a cup of coffee and some toast in her stomach.

'That isn't what I ordered,' she protested when he arrived at the table carrying two heavily laden plates of the St Stephen's special.

'You need feeding up.'

'But—'

'Eat,' Robert ordered, putting one of the plates down in front of her.

'Aye aye, sir,' she muttered, but he heard her.

'Insubordination, Dr Blake?'

That was very nearly a joke, she thought in amazement,

and sure enough, when she glanced up at him, there was actually a ghost of a smile playing round his lips.

'Mutiny, more like,' she observed wryly. 'If I eat even half of that I'll be comatose by eleven.'

'Not with our workload, you won't. Look, Dr Blake—'

'My name's Hannah,' she interrupted, 'and if you're worried in case I'm either too poor to buy myself breakfast or anorexic, you can relax. I've never eaten much for breakfast and I've always been thin.'

Skinny would have been a much more accurate description, he thought critically. Skinny, and pale, and he'd bet money those dark shadows under her eyes weren't smudges of mascara.

'Hannah, nobody can work a sixty-hour week and study at the same time if they're not eating properly,' he insisted, then bit his lip. He was beginning to sound like her mother. He'd be asking her next if she was getting enough sleep, remembering to wrap up warm. 'And we're short-staffed enough in A and E as it is, without you suddenly going off sick,' he added brusquely.

The smile that had been lurking in her eyes died. 'I'm sorry,' she murmured, picking up her knife and fork. 'I'll try my best not to inconvenience you by becoming ill.'

Which was all he was interested in, he told himself, so why did he suddenly feel like a complete and utter heel? And he did as he watched her silently beginning to eat her breakfast. She hadn't asked him to join her—he'd invited himself—and what had he done? Supplied her with a breakfast she didn't want, and made her feel guilty into the bargain.

'Look, are you really settling in all right in A and E?' he asked before he had time to consider the wisdom of his question.

'Of course I am,' Hannah began brightly, then sighed a little wryly when his eyebrows rose. 'OK—all right—I'll admit it's a lot more immediate than I'd expected. One minute you're dealing with a splinter in somebody's finger, the next it's a possible heart attack.'

'And with no medical records to go on, "What's wrong with the patient?" can all too quickly become "What did the patient die of?"' He nodded. 'The trick is to become very skilled at asking the right kind of questions.'

'Yes, but even asking someone "How badly does it hurt?" doesn't help a lot when pain is such a very personal thing,' she exclaimed, forking some egg into her mouth. 'I mean, what you might find quite bearable, I could say was excruciating.'

Robert doubted it. She might look as though a puff of wind would blow her away but now that he was looking at her—*really* looking—he could see a hint of stubbornness about her jaw despite her apparent fragility, a determination in her large brown eyes he hadn't noticed before. Miss Muffet had backbone. The big question was whether she had enough.

'I think the best advice I can give is always think the worst,' he observed, taking a sip of his coffee. 'Rule that out first, then you can safely move on to investigate other possibilities.'

It was good advice. What amazed her most was that it was Robert Cunningham who was giving it. Robert Cunningham, whose habitual response to any question she'd asked since she'd arrived at St Stephen's had been a brusque, 'Ask Elliot.'

He looked different, too, today, she decided, though she couldn't for a moment figure out why. His faded green shirt was just as crumpled as all the other shirts he normally wore, and though his corduroys were black this morning instead of brown, that hardly explained the difference.

It was because he was smiling, she suddenly realised. OK, so it wasn't a full-blown, right-up-to-the eyes effort, but it was still a smile and she'd been right when she'd thought it would change him. It made him look considerably younger and quite unexpectedly attractive. His hair badly needed cutting, of course, and his shirt could have done with an iron...

And you need your eyes tested if you think this man's attractive, her mind protested. Elliot Mathieson's an attractive man. Robert Cunningham's a mess. Yes, but a mess with a very nice smile when he chooses to use it.

'And don't ever be afraid to ask for help,' Robert continued, clearly taking her silence to mean just that. 'Nobody expects you to be an expert when you're first starting out.'

Kindness, understanding from Robert Cunningham? Wonders would never cease, she thought in amazement. In fact, if he was going to be this accommodating perhaps she might actually be able to start relaxing at St Stephen's.

And then again, perhaps not, she thought, her heart skipping a beat when he suddenly added, 'According to your CV, you were born in Edinburgh, and did all your training there. What brought you to London? I mean, wouldn't it have made more sense to look for your first post in your home town?'

'I wanted a change of scene,' she replied lightly, 'and as I used to come to London a lot for holidays when I was a little girl, I thought, why not?'

It had been the answer she and Mr Mackay, the consultant in charge of A and E, had agreed upon, and none of the rest of the staff had ever queried it, but, then, none of them, as she quickly discovered, was Robert Cunningham.

'You have relatives here, then?' he pressed. 'If you came often when you were a child...?'

'Not relatives, no,' she floundered. 'My father...he just happened to like London.'

A slight frown appeared in his dark grey eyes. 'It still seems rather a long way to come on the strength of holiday memories. Personally, I'd have thought starting a new job was enough of an upheaval without uprooting yourself as well.'

'Like I said, I wanted a change,' Hannah declared, striving to sound casual, dismissive, only to feel her cheeks heating up under his steady gaze. Why, oh, why did she always have to blush at the most inconvenient moments? It was a childish habit she should have outgrown years ago. 'And it seemed the right moment to make the break.'

'Yes, but—'

'Good grief, is that the time?' she interrupted, getting to her feet. 'We'd better go, or we'll be late for the start of our shift.'

She was right, they would, but Robert's frown deepened as he followed her out of the canteen and into A and E. Hannah Blake wasn't telling the truth about why she'd come to St Stephen's. She had a secret—a secret she didn't want discovered—and he didn't like secrets, never had. Secrets meant guilt. Secrets meant complications, and A and E had no room for either.

'Hannah, about this decision of yours to come to London—'

'RTA on the way, Robert!' Jane called. 'ETA five minutes.'

'Injuries?' he demanded, instantly focused.

'One female aged twenty-nine with minor cuts and bruises,' the sister replied, 'and a six-year-old girl with chest and head injuries. I've alerted the chest surgeon in case we need him, told Theatre to be on standby, and Jerry's on his way down from radiology.'

Robert started towards the treatment room door, then glanced back at Hannah. 'Would you like to assist me on this one?'

She gazed at him, open-mouthed. Did he mean it or

was he joking? The question was academic. Robert Cunningham didn't joke. 'You bet!' she breathed.

'Just remember—'

'To keep out from under your feet at all times.' She nodded. 'I haven't forgotten.'

A faint smile appeared in his eyes. 'Actually, I was going to say, if we need to intubate the little girl would you like to tackle it?'

'Oh— Right— Of course,' she replied, mentally kicking herself. 'I thought…when you said—'

'Hannah, will you relax?' he said gently. 'I'm not an ogre, you know.'

Perhaps not, she thought with a sigh as the ambulance arrived, its siren wailing, but he certainly could give a pretty good impression of being one at times.

'The kid and her mother are in London for a few days' holiday,' one of the paramedics announced as he and his colleague transferred the little girl from the stretcher onto the trolley. 'They were coming down The Mall when some maniac sideswiped their car, then took off.'

'Wonderful,' Robert commented dryly as Floella began inserting more IV lines to carry the O-negative blood which had already arrived, and Jerry Clark wheeled in his portable X-ray machine. 'Jerry, I'd like X-rays of her chest, pelvis and cervical spine. Hannah—'

'Get ready to intubate.' She nodded.

The little girl's head might be covered in blood, and her kneecap protruding at a grotesque angle through her skin, but the first priority was to regulate her breathing. At the moment it was ragged and uneven, and if they didn't alleviate it her brain would start to swell because of the reduced oxygen it was receiving.

'Are you ready, Hannah?' Robert asked, after he'd inserted a catheter into the child's urethra to drain her bladder and given her an injection to temporarily sedate and paralyse her.

She nodded. Once Robert opened the front of the cervical collar round the little girl's neck, and pressed down firmly on the cricoid cartilage so her stomach contents couldn't reflux into her airway, they'd have to work fast.

'I'm ready,' she said.

'OK, let's go,' he ordered.

Swiftly Hannah inserted the laryngoscope blade into the girl's mouth and suctioned away the blood and saliva obscuring her vocal cords. Then very gently she eased the endotracheal tube past her vocal cords and down into the child's trachea.

'Everything OK, Hannah?' Robert murmured.

It felt all right, it seemed all right, and she placed her stethoscope on the child's chest and listened. Bingo! She was breathing deeply and evenly without effort.

'Everything's fine,' she replied with relief.

'Is the haematocrit back on those blood samples yet?' Robert demanded. Floella held out the results to him, but to Hannah's surprise he waved them towards her. 'What have we got, Hannah?'

Quickly she scanned the results. 'Red cell count very low. How's her BP?'

'Stable,' Floella called.

'X-rays of the chest, pelvis and cervical spine are ready, too, Robert,' Jerry declared, but again, to Hannah's bewilderment, the special registrar nodded towards her.

'Any problems, Hannah?' he asked, snaking an orogastric tube into the little girl's mouth, past the endotracheal tube and into her oesophagus to empty her stomach.

'Two broken ribs—pelvis fine, cervical spine fine. On the evidence of these I'd say she should probably have a CT scan to check out those head injuries before she goes to Theatre, but..'

'But?' Robert prompted, his eyes fixed on her.

'To be perfectly honest, I'm not sure,' she admitted. 'It's her stomach, you see. It looks very firm to me, and it also seems slightly distended.'

'So?' Robert pressed.

Hannah took a deep breath. If she was wrong, so be it. If she looked like an idiot, she'd survive.

'I think the haematocrit result is too low for the amount of blood the child seems to have lost. I think she could be bleeding into her stomach and I'd send her to Theatre right away.'

For a moment Robert said nothing, then he smiled—a real, honest-to-goodness smile. 'So would I. Well done.'

He'd praised her, she thought in amazement as Floella and one of the porters wheeled the little girl out of the cubicle. She couldn't believe it, but he'd actually praised her.

'If your smile was any bigger I'd say you'd just won the lottery,' Jane observed, meeting her as she made her way to the white board to erase the child's name. 'Care to explain why?'

Hannah's smile widened as Robert strode past them and into cubicle 3 to talk to the child's mother. 'Would you believe hell just froze over?'

'Hell just…?' Jane gazed at her in confusion, then shook her head. 'Insanity. Normally it takes two to three months for people working in A and E to succumb—'

'Succumb to what?' Elliot asked curiously, overhearing her.

'Insanity,' Jane declared. 'Poor Hannah here. Right as rain two weeks ago and now…' She sighed and shook her head mournfully. 'Completely nuts, like the rest of us.'

Quickly Elliot clasped Hannah's wrist between his fingers and consulted his watch. 'Pulse rate fast and erratic, silly smile on her face… Yup, it looks like insanity to me, but I'd have to make a full examination to be sure. How about my place, tonight, eight o'clock?'

'Elliot, I said the girl was nuts, not stupid!' Jane exclaimed and Hannah chuckled as the sister hurried to answer the phone.

'I think I'll give the examination a miss, Elliot.' Hannah smiled.

'Do I look like the sort of man who'd take advantage?' he protested, his blue eyes wide and innocent.

'Elliot, you look like the man who wrote the book on how to!' She laughed.

'Too true,' he teased with a wickedly handsome grin. 'So your mother warned you about men like me, did she?'

Her smile became a little crooked. 'My mother died when I was born so she didn't have time to warn me about anything.'

His own laughter died instantly. 'Hannah, I'm sorry...I didn't know—'

'It's OK,' she interrupted. 'I never knew her, and people keep telling me you don't miss what you've never had.'

'And people who make observations like that deserve to be hung, drawn and quartered,' he declared, putting his arms around her and giving her a hug. 'Extremely slowly.'

She chuckled but she didn't move out of his arms. He was hugging her with sympathy and understanding, and she accepted the gesture in the spirit it was given.

Robert clearly didn't. In fact, judging from his thunderous expression when he emerged from cubicle 3 and saw them, he didn't appreciate the gesture at all.

'I think we'd better get back to work,' she murmured, quickly extricating herself from Elliot's arms. 'The boss doesn't look too happy about us wasting time.'

Elliot glanced over his shoulder at Robert and an amused smile curved his lips. 'Oh, I don't think that's what's bugging him, sweetheart.'

'You don't?' she said, puzzled, and he shook his head.

'It's jealousy, love,' he whispered. 'Pure, unadulterated, green-eyed jealousy.'

A splutter of laughter came from her as Elliot strolled away. Robert Cunningham *jealous*? If Elliot believed that then insanity wasn't simply common in A and E, it was endemic, but, judging by Robert's grim expression as he began walking towards her, now wasn't the time to discuss it. Now was the time for a very swift retreat, and Paul Weston in cubicle 6, with acute back pain according to the white board, fitted the bill perfectly.

'I feel so stupid, Doctor,' the young man declared the moment he saw her. 'I was helping my sister move some furniture yesterday, and now I can hardly move.'

'Which part of your back actually hurts?' Hannah asked, pulling up a chair to sit level with him.

'Down near the bottom—sort of to the left. And I'm feeling a bit sick, too.'

Warning bells went off in her head immediately. Nausea coupled with back pain could mean pyelonephritis—an inflammation of the kidneys—or even chronic kidney failure.

Robert had said she should always think the worst, she remembered, and she fully intended to.

'Have you been passing less urine recently, Mr Weston?' she asked, quickly taking his pulse.

'Yes, but—'

'Felt feverish at all—lethargic—as though you were coming down with flu?'

'Doctor, I only came in because I pulled a muscle in my back,' he protested.

Maybe he had. His pulse rate wasn't high, and his temperature and blood pressure were near normal, too, and yet…

'I'd like to do a few tests, Mr Weston,' she declared, getting quickly to her feet. 'Just as a precaution.'

'If you say so,' he murmured reluctantly, 'but could you give me something for this pain while I wait? I'm in absolute agony.'

A painkilling injection wouldn't affect the results of any tests she performed so swiftly she administered one, then went to phone the lab. Speed was of the essence if Paul Weston was suffering from chronic kidney failure, and she wanted to ensure there'd be no delay over any samples she took.

'Something wrong?' Jane asked, seeing Hannah frown as she put down the phone.

'Could be. Look, are you free right now, Jane? I need to take some blood and urine samples.'

'No problem.' The sister nodded. 'Where's your patient?'

'Cubicle 6.'

Jane stopped in mid-stride. 'Cubicle 6's empty. The guy who was in there left a couple of minutes ago.'

'But he can't have left,' Hannah protested, bewildered. 'He could hardly walk!'

'Believe me, that guy could have qualified for the next Olympic games, judging by the speed he left the treatment room,' the sister declared. 'What were you treating him for?'

'Back pain.'

Jane rolled her eyes heavenwards and groaned. 'And you gave him some painkiller. Oh, Hannah, drug addicts always insist they're suffering from either back pain or migraine because they know damn well there isn't a lab test or X-ray in the world which can disprove it. It's one of the oldest tricks in the book.'

Known to everybody but me, Hannah thought wretchedly. It had never occurred to her—not even for a second.

'Look, forget it,' Jane continued, seeing her expression.

'We've all been conned at least once in our professional careers.'

Not Robert Cunningham, Hannah thought as she suddenly saw him and realised he must have heard every word. Robert Cunningham had probably never been conned even when he'd been a student doctor.

He would think her so stupid and naïve. She felt both as she miserably erased Paul Weston's name from the white board. And Paul Weston probably hadn't even been his real name. That would be as fictitious as the symptoms he'd given her.

'Hannah—'

'You don't have to say anything, Robert,' she said, turning to him quickly. 'I know I've been a fool—'

'The first drug addict I ever treated told me he had kidney stones,' he interrupted. 'He had every symptom right down to blood in his urine. I sent a sample off to the lab, but the poor bloke was in such pain I gave him morphine while he waited. When the lab report came back there was blood in his sample all right. Chicken blood.'

'*Chicken* blood!' she gasped. 'But your patient—'

'Disappeared, having got what he came for. It's happened to all of us, Hannah, so don't lose any sleep over it.' He turned to go, then a slight smile curved his lips. 'Oh, by the way, I've just had word back from Theatre. You were right about that little girl who came in. She *was* bleeding into her stomach, but she should be all right, thanks to you.'

Why on earth had she ever thought him aloof and arrogant? she wondered as he walked away. He was kind and nice, and when he smiled like that, and his dark grey eyes didn't have those lurking shadows in them, he could be very nice indeed.

It was the single bright moment in a day that turned into

an unremitting round of chest pains, broken limbs, and accidental poisonings.

'Thank God we've only got another half-hour to go,' she told Floella as she binned yet another pair of latex gloves. 'I'm absolutely shattered.'

'Snap,' the staff nurse said laughing. 'And I'm afraid it looks like we've got another big one. Thirty-six-year-old male, very bad gash on his right hand, according to Reception.'

To Hannah's relief, however, the wound looked considerably worse than it actually was.

'It only needs a few stitches,' she told the plump, florid-faced, middle-aged man after she'd examined him. 'I'll get Staff Nurse Lazear to clean it for you, then I'll insert some sutures.'

'No.'

'You won't feel a thing, honestly,' she said reassuringly. 'I'll give you something to deaden the pain—'

'I'm not bothered about the pain,' he interrupted with irritation. 'I just don't want that black touching me.'

Hannah paused in the middle of filling her syringe and turned slowly to face him. 'I beg your pardon?'

'That black. I don't want her touching me. I want somebody else.'

'Well, it may surprise you to learn that this is not a supermarket where you can pick and choose,' Hannah said tightly. 'Staff Nurse Lazear is one of our most experienced nurses—'

'I don't care how experienced she is,' the man snapped. 'I want somebody else.'

'And perhaps you'd prefer to bleed to death!' Hannah flared.

The man levered his not inconsiderable bulk upright and Floella tugged quickly at Hannah's sleeve. 'Look, I really don't mind asking Jane to help you—'

'You'll do no such thing!' Hannah exclaimed. 'He'll have his hand cleaned by you, or he can leave right now!'

'You can't do that,' the man protested. 'You doctors have taken a…a hypocrite's oath to help people.'

'Our Hippocratic oath requires we help members of the human race, sir,' Hannah threw back at him. 'And right now I don't think you come even close to qualifying!'

The man's florid face reddened alarmingly. 'Why, you stuck-up little bitch! I'll teach you—'

'OK, what's going on in here?' Robert demanded, throwing open the cubicle curtains, his eyes cold, his face taut.

'This…this gentleman—and, believe me, I'm using the word extremely loosely,' Hannah replied icily, 'seems to have a problem with our nursing staff.'

'I don't have any problem,' the man exclaimed. 'I just don't want any black treating me.'

Robert stared at him silently for a second, then stepped out into the treatment room and beckoned to Elliot. 'Could you take over in here for Dr Blake, please, Dr Mathieson?'

'Now, just a minute,' Hannah protested as the SHO nodded. 'This is my patient—'

'Not any more, he's not,' Robert declared, gripping her so firmly by the elbow that, short of kicking his shins, there was nothing she could do but accompany him out of the cubicle and down the treatment room.

Which didn't mean she had to like it, and when he released her she turned on him angrily. 'You had no right to do that!'

'I'm the special registrar—I can do whatever I like,' he said calmly. 'Now, why don't we go to the staffroom, have a nice cup of tea—'

'I don't want a cup of tea!' she stormed. 'I want to know why you pulled me out of there. Why you let that jerk get away with what he said!'

'I did not let him get away with it.'

'You sent in Elliot—'

'And did I ask Flo to leave?' he demanded. 'Did I?'

'No, but—'

'Hannah, that man was going to hit you, and the only way to defuse the situation was to send in somebody with a much cooler head.'

She bit her lip. Robert was right. She'd lost her temper, and she shouldn't have.

'OK, I admit I handled the situation badly,' she muttered, 'but I don't need protecting. I can take care of myself.'

Dear God, he thought, if she believed that, then it wasn't a babysitter she needed but a bodyguard. 'Hannah, London isn't Edinburgh—'

'And Edinburgh isn't some quaint Highland village where we all leave our front doors open and never lock our cars,' she exploded. 'We have Aids, a huge drugs problem—'

'Which didn't help you when you met a real drug addict, did it?'' he retorted, then sighed when she coloured. 'Look, as you clearly have a very volatile temper, I think it might be better if I restrict you to treating female patients for a while until you learn how to control it.'

Her jaw dropped. 'You can't be serious!'

'My decision, Hannah,' he declared. 'And it's non-negotiable,' he added in a tone that brooked no opposition.

She opened her mouth, then clenched her teeth together until they hurt. She'd been right the first time. He wasn't nice. He was arrogant, and obnoxious, and stupid, but much as she longed to say so she knew she couldn't.

'Very well, *sir*,' she said instead. 'May I go now?'

'Hannah—'

'I've still got five minutes of my shift left, and with any luck I might be able to find some frail little old lady or a five-year-old child, you think I can safely treat!'

'Hannah, wait—'

But she didn't wait. She simply strode past him, her cheeks red, her back ramrod stiff with anger, leaving him gazing impotently after her.

'Everything OK now, boss?' Elliot asked as he emerged from cubicle 2, and Floella escorted Hannah's clearly very chastened patient back to the waiting room.

'*OK*?' Robert repeated. 'Elliot, that damn girl is going to get herself killed!'

'Yeah, she's feisty enough.' The SHO grinned.

'*Feisty*? Of all the knuckle-headed, irresponsible—'

'And you're always Mr Calm, are you?' Elliot observed, but Robert didn't smile back.

'She says she can take care of herself,' he fumed, as though the SHO hadn't spoken. 'She says she doesn't need protecting!'

Elliot's blue eyes became suddenly thoughtful. 'Ah.'

'Standing up to a bully like that—good God, Elliot, he must have outweighed her by at least fifty kilos!'

'Stupid.' Elliot nodded. 'Definitely stupid.'

Robert thrust his fingers through his black hair in exasperation. 'What am I going to do with her, Elliot? When I think of what could have happened, what undoubtedly *will* happen…'

The SHO's mouth turned up at the corners. 'Yeah, she is kinda cute, isn't she?'

'*Cute*?' Robert spluttered. '*Cute*?'

Desperately he tried to think of something swingeing, sarcastic, to retort but failed miserably—and to his acute irritation was reduced to walking away in disgust, much to Elliot's obvious amusement.

'What's so funny, Elliot?' Jane asked as she came out of the office and saw him laughing.

'Nothing yet, Janey. But in a couple of months' time, maybe less…' His blue eyes sparkled. 'I think life around here could get really interesting!'

CHAPTER THREE

'I HATE afternoon shifts,' Floella grumbled. 'Starting at three, finishing at eleven. By the time I get home my husband and kids are in bed, and I'm too exhausted to do anything.'

'I hate nights,' Hannah observed, following her and Jane across the street towards the entrance to St Stephen's. 'Trying to sleep during the day, all the drunks to look forward to at night—'

'Yes, but afternoon's—'

'Hey, will you two lighten up?' Jane protested. 'It's a beautiful September afternoon. There's not a cloud in the sky...'

'And not a window in A and E for us to admire it from,' Floella pointed out. 'I want to win the lottery and never have to work again. I want to travel the world and meet people who wouldn't recognise a stomach pump if they fell over one, far less know how to use it.'

And I want Robert Cunningham to get off my back, Hannah thought irritably as they walked through the treatment-room doors and she saw him deep in conversation with Elliot.

Ever since the SHO had quite rightly pointed out that the department couldn't function properly if they restricted her to treating female patients, Robert had been like a bear with a sore head. Nit-picking, carping, hovering about her if she got anywhere near a male casualty, and it was driving her slowly and completely mad.

So talk to him, her mind urged. Tell him you're not an

42

idiot, that you know what you're doing, and you won't take unnecessary risks.

Yeah, right, she thought ruefully as she hung up her jacket and turned to see Robert watching her, a deep frown pleating his forehead. Frankly, cutting your own throat would be an easier and far less painful way of solving your current problems.

'You know, once—just once—I'd like to come to work and find the waiting room completely empty,' Floella grumbled, glancing through the stack of notes which had come through from Reception.

'Not a hope, I'm afraid,' Jane sighed. 'Any priority?'

'The fourteen-year-old in cubicle 3, I'd say,' the staff nurse observed. 'Complaining of shortness of breath. History of asthma, according to his mother, and none of his usual medications seem to be working.'

They weren't. The teenager was gasping and gulping for air, and his fingers and lips were blue, a clear sign of cyanosis.

'How long has he been like this?' Hannah asked the boy's mother after she'd sounded his chest.

'About an hour,' the woman replied, panic plain in her eyes. 'I phoned our doctor and when I told him how drowsy he was, not seeming to know where he was—'

'Pulse 130 over 65,' Floella murmured.

Hannah turned to the teenager's mother with what she hoped was an encouraging smile. 'Wouldn't you be a lot more comfortable in one of our private waiting rooms? There's tea, coffee—'

'I want to stay with my son.'

'I know you do,' Hannah said soothingly, beckoning to their student nurse, Kelly Ross. 'But there's really nothing you can do here, and I promise we'll let you know what the situation is as soon as we can.'

The boy's mother reluctantly allowed the student nurse to lead her away.

The drowsiness and disorientation she'd noticed in her son, coupled with his rapid pulse rate, meant that too much carbon dioxide was building up in the boy's blood. They needed to take a pulse ox. to determine how much oxygen was left in his blood, and though the procedure wasn't a frightening one—it simply involved slipping a small plastic clip onto his finger containing an electrode which could read the oxygen content directly through his skin—the results would determine just how ill he was.

And with a pulse ox. of 82 he was very ill indeed.

Swiftly Hannah reached for an endotracheal tube to ease the teenager's laboured breathing. Once—oh, it seemed like a lifetime ago now—she would have approached this particular procedure with trepidation, but not any more. Now it was all too unfortunately commonplace.

'You'll be wanting a chest X-ray, CBC and a coag. panel?' Floella said, once the tube was in place and she'd set up an IV line and attached cardiac electrodes to the boy's chest to monitor his heartbeat.

Hannah nodded. The chest X-ray would reveal if there was any damage to the boy's lungs. The CBC would tell them how many red and white blood cells there were in his blood, and the coag. panel would test his body's ability to clot.

'Everything OK in here?'

Hannah gazed heavenwards with disbelief. Good grief, didn't Robert Cunningham trust her to treat even teenage boys now?

'Everything's fine, thank you,' she replied curtly.

'BP 160 over 95, pulse 140,' Floella announced.

Well, perhaps not exactly fine, Hannah amended mentally. The teenager's heart was working much too fast, trying to compensate for the low level of oxygen in his blood, and they had to stabilise him quickly.

'OK, Flo, I want epi. and solumedrol intravenously, and albuterol through the ET tube,' she declared.

The staff nurse nodded. With luck the epinephrine—the adrenaline—would regulate the boy's blood pressure and pulse, while the solumedrol and albuterol should ease his breathing.

'I presume you've taken samples for a CBC and a coag. panel?' Robert observed.

'You presume correctly,' Hannah replied, trying—and failing—to keep the edge out of her voice as Jerry Clark appeared with his X-ray equipment. 'Chest X-rays only, please, Jerry.'

'Anything for you, Hannah, love,' he replied, then added with a knowing leer, 'and I do mean *anything*.'

Of course he did, the little creep, but she managed to smile back. Slapping the smirk off his face would have been infinitely more preferable, but she'd very quickly learned that if you were a junior female doctor at St Stephen's, and wanted your X-rays processed fast, you had to put up with Jerry's clumsy attempts at flirtation.

Robert obviously didn't agree with her. In fact, judging by his icy expression, Jerry was lucky not to be sailing out of the cubicle by the seat of his pants.

Which would have suited Hannah just fine until she noticed Robert was throwing her a glance of equally arctic proportions. Did he think she actually *liked* toadying to an odious little creep like Jerry? She wouldn't have touched the X-ray technician with a bargepole, but as she was neither a male doctor nor a special registrar she couldn't afford to be antagonistic.

'His BP and pulse are coming down,' Floella murmured. 'I think he's stabilising, Hannah.'

The teenager was. His fingers and lips weren't nearly so blue, and his breathing was a lot less laboured.

'Are the coag. panel and CBC results back yet, Flo?' she asked.

The staff nurse handed them over to her. There was nothing in them to suggest anything other than a very severe asthma attack, neither did the teenager's X-rays show any sign of lung damage, but the quicker he was in Intensive Care the happier Hannah would be.

'That must be our fourth asthma case in the last three days,' Jane commented as Floella and one of the porters wheeled the teenager out of the treatment room on his way to IC.

Hannah nodded. 'I was reading an article the other day that said asthma was on the increase because so many of our houses are centrally heated. That, coupled with wall-to-wall carpeting—'

'And when the two of you have quite finished discussing interior design you might remember that we have a full waiting room of patients out there!'

Hannah's jaw dropped as Robert strode past them, his face tight and angry. She and Jane had taken a five-second breather. Five miserable, measly seconds to discuss what might cause asthma. There had been no need for him to be so rude, no need at all.

'I'd keep out of Robert's way for the rest of the afternoon, if I were you,' Jane murmured, clearly reading her thoughts. 'And if you need any help, ask Elliot.'

'Too damn right I will,' Hannah said tartly. 'Honestly, Jane, that man—'

'Hannah, his wife was knocked down and killed exactly a year ago tonight.'

'Oh, God, no,' Hannah gasped, turning quickly in time to see Robert disappearing into cubicle 8. 'No wonder he's being so difficult. Is there nothing we can do—nothing we can say—that would help?'

'Just keep out of his way,' Jane declared. 'Believe me, he won't thank you for anything else.'

Perhaps not, Hannah thought as their shift sped by. She followed Jane's suggestion, consulting Elliot if she needed any advice, closing her ears to the sound of Robert's snapped, caustic orders, but her heart went out to him every time she saw him.

How must he feel today? How would she feel if it were her? Desolate, shattered, bitter. There had to be something she could say that would help ease his grief, but any conversation she attempted was met by such a vehement rebuff that when a Miss Sheila Vernon came in shortly after ten o'clock with severe stomach pains, Hannah's heart sank into her boots.

'I don't suppose you could manage on your own, could you?' Floella grimaced when she asked her to go and get Robert. 'I know Elliot's all tied up with that OD, but Robert's on such a short fuse tonight, and asking for help…'

There was no alternative, Hannah thought grimly. She couldn't see inside Sheila Vernon's stomach to confirm or rule out anything, so palpation was the first line of investigation, and she knew she didn't possess the necessary skill to do it. She'd have to ask Robert for help, and if he chose to make her look ridiculous for requesting it, she'd just have to grit her teeth and bear it.

To her amazement, however, Robert neither took the opportunity to slip in a sarcastic comment about her lack of ability nor subjected her to withering scorn. In fact—if she hadn't known better—she could almost have sworn he was pleased to help her when she admitted her problem.

'The secret of successful palpation is never to rush,' he explained. 'The slower you press into the stomach, the more chance you'll have of seeing the patient ''guarding''—trying to push your hand away when you press on a particularly sensitive area—which can help pinpoint the source of the pain.'

Hannah nodded.

'People who come into A and E with severe stomach pain always think they have appendicitis,' he observed as he began pressing gently across Sheila Vernon's stomach, 'but it's actually quite rare—less than four per cent of all cases—and Miss Vernon quite clearly doesn't have it or we'd be scraping her off the ceiling by now.'

Floella smothered a chuckle but Hannah, he noticed, didn't even smile.

He wasn't surprised. After his earlier jibe at her for wasting time she was hardly likely to be feeling very charitable towards him, but how she could tolerate the slimy overtures of a man like Jerry Clark was beyond him.

Laura wouldn't have tolerated it for a second. Laura would have drawn herself up to her full five feet nine and given Jerry one flash of her violet blue eyes, and if that hadn't intimidated the scumbag, she'd have hit him.

'Pulse and BP both dropping, Robert,' Floella warned.

'OK, get me a urine analysis, a guiac test on her stools and a liver function test, a.s.a.p.,' he ordered.

So why on earth had Hannah put up with it? he wondered as he began palpating the lower left quadrant of Sheila Vernon's stomach. OK, so she was only five feet two, but she'd stood up to that man who hadn't wanted Floella treating him last week and he'd been twice the size of the puny X-ray technician.

Which could only mean that incredibly—inexplicably—she was actually attracted to the creep.

Was she insane? he wondered, risking a quick glance across at her. God in heaven, she could do so much better—deserved so much better—and the thought of her in Jerry

Clark's arms, of him holding her, touching her, making love to her...

'How much longer are you going to be with those damn urine and guiac tests, Flo?' he snapped, taking his anger out in the nearest available person. 'I could have had them flown to America and processed in the time it's taken you to do them!'

The staff nurse blinked, but her voice when she spoke was calm, even. 'There's no blood in the urine, and the guiac and liver function tests are normal, too.'

Without a word he strode through the cubicle curtains, indicating with a jerk of his head that Hannah should follow him.

'You're absolutely certain she's not pregnant?' he demanded the minute they were safely out of Sheila Vernon's earshot. 'Ectopics can cause severe abdominal pain if the foetus is hiding in the liver, or under the bowels, and if the foetus grows into a blood vessel and ruptures it...'

The results could be catastrophic. Massive internal bleeding would occur, and if it wasn't detected in time, a patient could die.

'The blood test was definitely negative,' Hannah assured him.

His frown deepened. 'At twenty-nine she's too young for diverticulitis...inflammation of the colon...'

'What about pelvic inflammatory disease?' Hannah suggested. 'Or endometriosis?'

'It could be,' he murmured. 'But did you notice how swollen her stomach was, and yet she was otherwise quite slim? I think we're looking at a ruptured ovarian cyst here, and I'd like to get the consultant down from Gynae.'

Hannah wasn't about to argue with him. She was much too relieved to have him take charge. But there was something she wanted to say, and she waited until he'd replaced the phone to say it.

'Something wrong?' he asked, seeing she hadn't moved.

She shook her head. 'I just… I only wanted to say thanks for helping me in there.'

'It's what I'm paid for,' he replied dismissively, but as he turned to go she put out her hand to stop him.

'Perhaps it is, but…' She came to a halt. Robert was staring down at her hand on his arm and she withdrew it self-consciously. 'I still… I felt I ought to say thank you, and…' She took a deep breath and met his gaze. 'I'm very sorry about what happened to your wife.'

She had disappeared back into cubicle 2 before he could reply. Which was just as well, he decided as he stared after her because he was too busy wondering why—when he'd gazed down at her small hand on his arm—he'd been seized with the quite bewildering and totally inexplicable desire to grab hold of it and never let go.

It was crazy, ridiculous. She was just a skinny kid with a snub nose and a mop of curly short hair. A skinny kid he heartily wished he could transfer to some other department.

No, he didn't really wish that. She might be relatively naïve and inexperienced at the moment, but in time he knew she could be a real asset to A and E.

And she wasn't really skinny either, he was forced to admit when she reappeared at the cubicle curtains and beckoned to Kelly to join her. She was slender. Slender, but with curves in all the right places. Slender, with a tiny waist, and fine, delicately boned legs. The kind of legs which would wrap themselves around a man, holding him, while he…

'Everything OK, boss?' Jane asked curiously as she passed him.

Hot colour flamed across his cheeks. 'Fine—great.'

But it wasn't fine, and it wasn't great. He didn't want to

find Hannah Blake attractive. He didn't want to find *any* woman attractive, ever again.

And certainly not a woman who could be interested in a jerk like Jerry Clark, he thought grimly as the X-ray technician came through the swing doors with the gynaecological consultant.

'All I can say is this had better be an ovarian cyst and not plain old indigestion, Robert,' the consultant said with a grin. 'I'll have you know I was enjoying coffee with Gorgeous Gussie Granton in Paediatrics—'

'Well, pardon me for interrupting your social life!' Robert snapped as Hannah joined them and he saw Jerry wink across at her. 'I was under the impression this was a hospital, not a dating agency!'

The consultant's smile vanished in an instant. 'Now, just a minute, Robert—'

'I don't have one,' he retorted. 'Unlike you, I have neither time for cups of coffee nor for socialising. I have work to do!'

And before the consultant could reply, he'd walked away, leaving Hannah staring after him in stunned dismay.

Oh, God, but what was he doing? He'd asked the consultant to come down—specifically requested his help—and then to walk out on him...

Awkwardly she cleared her throat, all too aware that the gynaecological consultant was fuming beside her. 'I... We—we're very busy tonight, sir.'

'Are you, indeed?' he replied tightly. 'Well, personally I've never believed that being busy excused rudeness, and I can only hope your boss has acquired a set of better manners by the time I've finished examining his patient!'

He hadn't, not even when it was confirmed that Sheila Vernon was, indeed, suffering from a ruptured ovarian cyst. In fact, at eleven o'clock the whole A and E team sent up a collective prayer of thanks that their shift was over.

'I, for one, hope I don't have to put in another shift like that in a hurry,' Elliot observed ruefully as he accompanied Hannah out of the hospital. 'Talk about stressful!'

'I'd rather not remember it at all,' Hannah sighed, noticing Robert had come out of the hospital, too, and was standing watching them, his face cold and impassive. 'In fact, all I want to do is go home and go to bed.'

Elliot wiggled his eyebrows at her. 'Sounds good to me. Fancy some company?'

She shook her head and laughed. 'I'll see you tomorrow, Elliot.'

'Look, why don't I take you out for dinner?' he pressed. 'Cheer both of us up a bit. I know this really nice little place—' He swore under his breath as his pager suddenly went off. 'No, don't go,' he insisted. 'Give me five minutes to find out if this is urgent, and then at the very least let me take you for coffee.'

She laughed again as he disappeared back into the hospital, but her laughter died when she saw Robert striding across the hospital forecourt towards her, his face even grimmer than before.

'Look, whatever it is, can't it wait until tomorrow?' she said quickly to forestall him. 'I'm really tired—'

'I'm not surprised!' he thundered back, his grey eyes ice-cold. 'First it's Jerry Clark, and now it's Elliot. Frankly, I'm surprised you can find the time to treat any patients when you're so busy organising your social life!'

She stared up at him, open-mouthed. 'I beg your pardon?'

'As well you might, but I'm not here to judge your morals—or, indeed, apparent lack of them!'

'My lack of—'

'My job is to ensure that A and E functions to the best of its ability. A task that is not being made any easier by a junior doctor who seems incapable of resisting the temptation to flirt with anything in trousers!'

It was the injustice of his remark that cut her to the quick. She didn't have a social life, not after working an eight-hour shift each day then going home to study for her exams. And for him to suggest she was some sort of raving nymphomaniac...

She gripped her hands together tightly, and when she spoke every word sizzled like hot oil. 'I don't know why I should even dignify your comments with an answer, but for your information I think Jerry Clark is a creep.'

'A creep whose attentions you don't appear to find particularly distasteful!'

'Only because I can't afford to!' she retorted. 'If you were a woman doctor at St Stephen's, you'd know that if you want your X-rays processed quickly you have to put up with Jerry's crude innuendoes, and touching, and pawing.'

He looked truly horrified. 'That's sexual harassment—'

'Too damn right it is, so think yourself lucky you don't wear a skirt and have to endure it!'

'Hannah—'

'And as for your suggestion that I flirt with Elliot!' She dug her fingernails deep into the palms of her hands and struggled to keep calm. 'I talk to him. I laugh with him. It's called making conversation with friends, Dr Cunningham. Something you quite obviously neither recognise nor subscribe to, so I'm not surprised you haven't got any!'

He whitened then reddened in quick succession. Never had she seen him quite so angry, but to her dismay there wasn't just anger in his face but pain, too. Conscience-stricken, she took a step towards him. 'Dr Cunningham... Robert...'

He didn't even wait to hear what she'd been about to

say. He simply wheeled round and strode away, and she bit her lip when she heard Elliot's deep groan behind her.

'I went too far, didn't I?' she mumbled unhappily, turning towards him.

'The words "a little" and "over the top" certainly spring to mind,' he said with a sigh. 'I don't know what it is with you two. Five minutes together, and you're at each other's throats.'

He was right. She wasn't normally so quick to anger—in fact, it was usually quite the reverse. Only her father had ever managed to rile her quite so much, and she didn't want to think about her father, not tonight, not ever.

'I've got to go, Elliot.'

'But what about dinner—coffee?' he protested.

'Maybe some other night,' she said gently, seeing his disappointment. 'Look, I wouldn't be good company—not for anyone.'

He nodded reluctantly, but as she began to walk away he suddenly came after her. 'Hannah, about Robert...'

'What about Robert?' she demanded.

'Apologise to him. Look, it doesn't matter who was at fault,' he added when she opened her mouth to protest. 'You've got to work with the guy, and...well...I know it's no excuse, but today—with it being the anniversary of his wife's death—it must have been really hellish for him.'

Elliot was right. It didn't excuse what Robert had said to her tonight, but it might explain it, a little.

And if she was going to apologise she might as well do it now, she decided, hitching her bag higher onto her shoulder. Wellington Place was only a couple of streets away. A quick detour on her way home and it would be done.

Or at least it would have been if she hadn't arrived in Wellington Place to find Robert's ground-floor flat in total darkness. Either he'd gone out, or gone to bed, and it didn't require the brains of Einstein to figure out he wouldn't exactly be thrilled if she woke him up simply to say she was sorry.

With a sigh she began retracing her steps, only to come to a sudden halt. From somewhere inside the flat she was sure she'd heard the sound of breaking glass. Could he be ill? Could he have collapsed? Could he be so eaten up with grief that he'd done something really stupid?

She ran back to the front door, put her finger on the doorbell and kept it there. Five minutes. She'd give him five minutes to answer, and if he didn't—

'Will you get your damn finger off that bloody doorbell before you wake the whole neighbourhood?'

Robert wasn't ill, she realised with dismay as she gazed up into his furious face. He was angry. Angry at being disturbed, angry with her for being there, and then suddenly she noticed something else. Blood was trickling down from his wrist onto his shirt cuff, staining it black under the fluorescent streetlight.

'Oh, my God, what have you done?' she gasped in horror.

'Done?' he repeated blankly.

'Your wrist... Have you any SteriStrips—antiseptic—in the house?' she asked, pushing past him into the flat. 'I'll need water, towels, too. Oh, Robert, I know you're upset—unhappy—but to do something like this...'

'Something like what?' he protested in obvious confusion as he followed her. 'I simply tripped and fell when I was carrying some glasses, and some of the glass went into my wrist and arm.'

'Then you didn't— I mean, you weren't trying to...' She coloured furiously under his puzzled gaze. 'Look, where's your bathroom?'

'Over there, but—'

'You'd better take off your shirt,' she ordered, slipping off her coat and throwing it over the chair in the hall as she led the way into the bathroom. 'If you've cut your arm as well as your wrist, they're both going to need attention. Lacerations can cause infection—'

'Hannah—'

'What on earth were you doing, stumbling about in the dark in the first place?' she demanded, taking refuge in anger when what she really felt was acute embarrassment at having so clearly jumped to the wrong conclusion. 'Saving on electricity—checking your night sight?'

'Hannah—'

'And as for this little lot,' she continued, shaking her head in disbelief when she opened his bathroom cabinet and scanned its contents, 'most of this—'

'Should have been thrown out years ago. Yeah, I know.' A rueful smile curved his lips as she turned angrily towards him, then appeared to forget what she'd been about to say. 'There's no need to look quite so shocked, little Hannah. The whisky's purely for medicinal purposes.'

It wasn't the glass of whisky in his hand that had made her bereft her of speech—though, heaven knows, he should have known better. It was the sight of his bare, broad, muscular chest. A bare, broad, muscular chest covered with an intriguing pattern of glistening dark hair. A bare, broad, muscular chest which for some inexplicable reason seemed to be doing the most amazing things to her heart rate

'I...um... You don't appear to have any sterile dressings,' she spluttered, swinging back to his bathroom cabinet. 'I...I'll have to make do with lint and Micropore.'

'Whatever,' he said dismissively. 'But could you get a move on before I freeze to death?'

He was lucky, she thought, letting out her breath in a rush. Hot flushes were her problem at the moment. Mega-hot flushes.

And it was crazy, ridiculous. This man was her boss. She'd worked with him for over a month and never once thought of him as a man. OK, so when he'd smiled at her that one time, she might have thought he had a very nice smile, but she'd never thought of him as A Man. And yet now…

Now she was all too aware of him. All too aware of the rapid rise and fall of his chest, and her own skittering heart-beat.

'Could you…?' Her voice had come out in a squeak, and she took a firm grip on herself. 'Could you sit down on the edge of the bath for me, please?'

He nodded absently, but a frown creased his forehead when she began cleaning his arm with some lint. 'Forgive my appalling memory, but did I actually invite you round here tonight?'

The colour on her cheeks darkened to crimson. 'I came to apologise. I was very rude to you earlier—'

'Water off a duck's back,' he interrupted dismissively, wincing slightly as she dabbed at his wrist and arm with antiseptic. 'If everyone I'd been rude to during the day came round to my flat to apologise, there'd be a queue stretching back to St Stephen's.'

There probably would be, she thought wryly, leaning over him to retrieve the Micropore. 'OK, I think I've got all the glass out, but I'm afraid your arm and wrist are going to be pretty sore tomorrow.'

They were pretty sore right now, but that wasn't what was making him twist uncomfortably on the edge of the bath. It was the feel of her warm breath against his throat as she bent over him, the caress of her hair against his cheek as she tilted her head in concentration.

God in heaven, what was the matter with him? he wondered, gritting his teeth as he felt his body unmistakably stirring in response. He scarcely knew this girl. His traitorous body shouldn't be responding to the rapid rise and fall of her small, high breasts. His hands shouldn't be trembling with the urge to reach for her, to slide her onto his lap, to…

'I really don't think you should drink any of that,' Hannah protested as he reached for his glass of whisky and took a gulp from it.

She was right, he shouldn't, but because he didn't know how to deal with the conflicting emotions her nearness was provoking, he took refuge in the simplest—anger.

'What I choose to drink is none of your damn business!' he retorted, getting to his feet so abruptly that she banged back against the bath.

'I know it isn't, Robert, but drinking isn't going to solve anything. I know about your wife—'

'You know *nothing* about my wife!' he roared, making her jump. 'What do you know about love, and loss, and heartache? Little Miss Muffet with your big brown eyes and bouncing curls. Little Miss Muffet who's probably never been properly kissed by a man, far less been made love to by one!'

Hot colour flooded her cheeks. He was wrong, but she wasn't about to tell him about Chris. She wasn't about to tell him anything.

'I think I'd better go.'

'Running away, Miss Muffet?' he mocked.

'Will you please stop calling me that?' she protested.

'But that's what you are,' he said, his voice brutal, biting. 'Little Miss Muffet, who thinks she has the answer to everything. Little Miss Muffet without a care in the world.' He leant towards her, his gaze suddenly sharp. 'But you do have a care, don't you? Or more precisely a secret. What's your deep dark secret, Hannah? Come on, let's trade. I'll tell you why I fully intend to get blind drunk tonight, and you can tell me what made you leave Edinburgh.'

She stared up at him silently. She wished she hadn't come. She wished she'd waited until morning to apologise like any other sensible person. But most of all she wished she didn't feel the quite ridiculous urge to reach out, take him in her arms and somehow comfort him.

Quickly she retrieved her handbag. 'I think I should go home.'

'Go on, then—run away!' Robert jeered, and she would have done if the bathroom hadn't been so small, and he hadn't been so big, and she hadn't tripped in her haste to get past him.

And he would have let her go if she hadn't stumbled straight into his arms and the touch of her hands on his bare chest hadn't sent a jolt through his body like lightning.

For a second he froze. Let her go, his mind urged, get her out of the house, but his body wasn't listening to his mind. His body wanted her. Wanted to bury itself in her soft sweetness, and forget at least for a time the bleak emptiness that lay inside him. And he surrendered to those demands.

His lips came down on hers with a bruising intensity, his arms crushed her to him, and a groan escaped him as he felt her small high breasts against his chest, a groan of desperate, desolate need.

God, but he wanted her, wanted her so much. His head was spinning with desire as he covered her face and throat with searing kisses. His body was hard, aching, desperate for release as he slid his hands up her sides to cup her breasts, and the result would have been inevitable if the wailing sound of an ambulance siren in the street outside hadn't suddenly penetrated his brain and brought him to his senses.

What was he doing? he wondered as he shuddered and drew back from her to stare with inward horror at her flushed face, her swollen lips and dazed eyes.

'I'm sorry,' he muttered thickly. 'So sorry. What I just did... Unforgivable... Completely unforgivable—'

'Robert—'

Her eyes were dark, confused, bewildered, and jerkily he grabbed her by the elbow, thrust her coat and bag into her arms and propelled her to the front door. 'Go home, Hannah. Go home now.'

'But, Robert—'

He couldn't bear to hear any more. Couldn't bear to even look at her and realise what he'd almost done. With a muttered oath he shut the door, and leant his forehead against it, and heartily wished that he'd never been born.

CHAPTER FOUR

'I CAN quite understand why you thought he might have gallstones,' Robert observed as he accompanied Hannah out of the cubicle. 'The acute pain in his upper abdomen, his extreme pallor and nausea—'

'And all he's got is plain, old-fashioned indigestion,' she interrupted, completely mortified.

'Stomach pain is one of the hardest things to diagnose, Hannah,' he said gently. 'There can be so many reasons behind it, and I did advise you to always think the worst. Just remember in future not to become so convinced you've got a zebra that you forget all about the donkeys.'

'The donkeys?' she repeated, puzzled, and he smiled.

'It's something one of my old professors used to say. In medicine we can all too easily become so hung up on our own knowledge that we can forget the commonplace, and go looking instead for the exotic.'

'And you certainly can't get much more commonplace than dyspepsia,' she sighed ruefully. 'I feel like such an idiot.'

'Don't. It might well have been gallstones, and you were right to ask for a second opinion.'

She nodded without conviction. 'Thanks for helping, and I'll remember what you said about the donkeys and zebras.'

He smiled again, and she fully expected him to go, but to her surprise he didn't.

'It's very quiet in here today,' he observed, glancing round the treatment room.

She supposed it was if you considered thirty patients still waiting out in Reception a quiet day.

'In fact,' Robert continued, 'for a Thursday, it's quite amazingly quiet.'

He glanced down at his watch, adjusted his name tag, then to her acute dismay he cleared his throat awkwardly.

Oh, no, he was going to talk about what had happened in his flat. He was obviously trying to get up the nerve to do it, and it was the last thing she wanted. What could she possibly say in reply? Forget it? It meant nothing? Men are always kissing me?

'Hannah—'

'Did you hear about the homeless man I sent up to ward 12—the one with the gangrenous leg?' she said, beginning to edge casually away. 'They had to amputate eventually.'

'Did they?' he murmured, following her.

She nodded. 'I don't know how he's going to manage. Life on the streets is hard enough for someone fit and healthy, but for a man with one leg…'

'If you're really worried about him, why don't you contact the hospital social services department?' he asked. 'They might be able to find him hostel accommodation, though I've got to say that many men who've lived rough for years can't bear to have a roof over their heads. They feel shut in, trapped.'

'Do they?' She risked a quick glance up at him, decided it was a very bad idea and transferred her gaze to his shirt buttons instead.

'Hannah—'

'I didn't know so many people slept rough until I came to London,' she told the shirt buttons, knowing perfectly well that she was babbling but wishing only that he would go away. 'We have homeless people back in Edinburgh, but nothing on this scale.'

'I suppose not. Hannah—'

'It might be quieter today than normal, but there are still

quite a few people waiting to be seen, and I really should—'

'Get back to work,' Robert finished for her, his voice oddly flat.

Idiot, her mind whispered as she peeped over her shoulder in time to see him disappearing into the office. He probably hadn't even been going to talk to you about what happened in his flat at all, and now he thinks you're some sort of lamebrain half-wit. Good grief, it happened three days ago, and as he hasn't even hinted about it before, the likelihood of him doing so now—in the middle of the treatment room—is pretty remote. In fact, considering he told you that he had every intention of getting blind drunk, he probably doesn't even remember.

But she remembered.

Oh, yes, she remembered. Remembered the bruising intensity of his kisses. Remembered how her initial surprise had quickly given way to desire. How she'd wanted him to keep on touching her with those unbelievable hands, to satisfy a hunger she hadn't even known she'd possessed.

And it was crazy. She couldn't possibly be attracted to Robert Cunningham. No woman in her right mind could possibly be attracted to a man who in the space of five short weeks had ignored her, clucked round her like a manic broody hen, then suddenly kissed her with a desperation that had taken her breath away.

No, she wasn't attracted to him, she told herself firmly. She felt sorry for him—who wouldn't? And that night she'd been a bit low herself. Low, and a little bit lonely, and as for Robert...

He'd been lonely, too, grieving for his dead wife, and his solution to his loneliness had been sex. Sex with anyone, and she'd just happened to be there, available. She mustn't read any more into it than that. If she did she'd only be hurt again, and that was the last thing she wanted.

'You seem a bit preoccupied this afternoon, Hannah,' Jane observed after they'd arranged for a porter to take the elderly man in cubicle 4, who had fractured his forearm, to the plastering department. 'Something troubling you?'

'I was just thinking about Elliot,' she lied, gesturing towards the SHO who was quite mercilessly teasing their student nurse.

'Dangerous occupation, that,' the sister declared, her grey eyes sparkling. 'Thinking about Elliot.'

'I know.' Hannah laughed. 'And there's no need for you to get worried. I mean, I like him—I do—but...'

Jane rolled her grey eyes expressively and nodded. 'It's an awfully big but, isn't it?'

'Do you think he'll ever settle down with just one girl?' Hannah asked.

'Not a hope, I'm afraid. The trouble with Elliot—though you'd never ever get him to admit it—is that with one failed marriage behind him he's terrified of being hurt again and so he simply flits from girl to girl. Some men are like that. Others, like Robert, fall in love once, and can't ever fall in love again.'

'Can't they?' Hannah said, wondering why she should find that opinion so deeply depressing.

Jane shook her head. 'It's quite sad, really. Robert was never a great lady's man—in fact, we all thought he was married to his work—but when Laura joined the department he fell for her, hook, line and sinker. Mind you, so did every other red-blooded male in the hospital,' she added with a chuckle.

'She was very pretty, then?' Hannah murmured, her eyes following Robert as he came out of the office.

'And how. Think Marilyn Monroe but with red hair. And clever! Boy, was Laura clever. Top grades at med school, a gold medal prizewinner in obstetrics and physiology. She was consultant material for sure.'

Hannah sighed inwardly. Nobody had ever said she was consultant material. Nobody had ever said she looked like Marilyn Monroe either—with or without red hair. Minnie Mouse perhaps, but not Marilyn Monroe.

'Jane—'

'If that's Admin on the phone again about those requisition forms, I swear I'll rip the damn thing off the wall,' the sister groaned as the phone in the treatment room began to ring. 'Honestly, Hannah, you'd think we had nothing better to do with our time than fill in bits of paper!'

Hannah laughed, but she felt anything but amused later that afternoon when Elliot caught her by the arm and hustled her to the side of the treatment room after she'd finished treating a young girl with a dislocated shoulder.

'Elliot, this had better be important,' she protested as he gazed down at her, his blue eyes gleaming. 'The waiting room's filling up again—'

'And I've just realised I'm an idiot!' he exclaimed.

'I thought Jane had already told you that,' she responded, torn between irritation and amusement. 'In fact—'

'I should have recognised your name immediately,' he continued. 'Charles Blake, the eminent Edinburgh gynaecologist. Charles Blake, whose wife Hannah tragically died in childbirth. Hannah, you're *Charles Blake's* daughter!'

'Elliot, will you keep your voice down?' she cried, glancing nervously round in case anyone had heard him.

'But your father's written more award-winning books on gynaecology than I've had hot dinners! He's a legend in his own lifetime. He's—'

'Absolutely wonderful,' she finished for him tightly. 'Yes, I know. And I'm just his plain, ordinary daughter instead of the brilliant, prizewinning son he always wanted.'

Elliot gazed at her uncertainly. 'Hannah, you're not plain, and you're anything but ordinary—'

'Yeah, right,' she said cynically. 'So what are you wanting? An autographed copy of my father's latest book—an introduction to him?'

'I don't want anything,' he protested. 'Look, I'm sorry if I've upset you—'

'Of course you haven't upset me,' she said with spurious brightness. 'Why should I be upset because you admire my father? Everyone admires my father.'

Including Chris, she remembered with an unwanted shaft of pain. Chris who'd said he loved her, and she'd believed him, until she'd found out he'd only wanted to marry her to fast-track his own medical career.

'Hannah—'

'Please, don't tell anyone about my father,' she begged. 'I know everyone will find out eventually, but—'

'What do you take me for?' Elliot exclaimed, clearly deeply hurt by her suggestion. 'Of course I won't tell anyone.'

'Thank you,' she murmured, but as she turned to go he touched her arm sympathetically. 'Hannah, love... I'm really sorry. I thought...well, I assumed you'd be thrilled to bits, so proud—'

'So does everyone,' she said with a slightly crooked smile, and neither of them noticed Robert watching them from across the room, his eyes bleak, his hands bunched tightly by his sides.

Why had he done it? Why had he kissed her? Even now he could neither understand nor explain his behaviour. OK, so he'd been deeply unhappy, remembering the good times he and Laura had shared before it had all gone disastrously wrong, but if that ambulance hadn't gone by, if its wailing siren hadn't brought him to his senses...

He closed his eyes tightly. What must Hannah think of him? All too vividly he could remember the concern in her deep brown eyes, her belief, he now realised, that he'd been attempting to slash his wrists. And how had he repaid her kindness?

He wanted to apologise to her again. He desperately wanted to apologise again, but what good would it do? She was already tiptoeing around him, clearly deeply uncomfortable in his presence. Better by far that she believed he couldn't remember what had happened than resurrect an incident she so obviously longed to forget.

But he remembered.

Yes, he remembered all too vividly the feel of her body against his. Her tiny waist, so small his hands could span it, the gentle curve of her breasts, surprisingly full under his fingers, and the odd little cry she'd given when he'd crushed her to him—the cry he'd echoed with a groan, wanting her, wanting her so much.

His lips twisted bitterly. Wanted, not loved. Lust. An old-fashioned word, but an accurate one, he thought as he gazed across at her, and felt his groin tighten as he saw her smile at something Elliot had said. And as an adult, mature male he had to deal with it, conquer it.

But that didn't mean he had to stand by and watch Elliot talking to her so intimately, he decided, striding grimly across the treatment room before he had time to rationalise his thoughts.

'Care to tell me what's so important that it's had your heads together for the past ten minutes while we have patients waiting?' he demanded, his eyes flicking coldly from Elliot to Hannah.

'I...um... It wasn't really that important,' Hannah muttered, all too aware that the blush she could feel creeping across her cheeks suggested otherwise.

'Then if you've both finished whatever world-shattering topic you've been discussing,' Robert snapped, 'I suggest you get yourselves back to work!'

And with that he strode away, leaving Hannah staring unhappily after him.

'I really seem to have the knack of making him angry, don't I?' She sighed.

'He's not angry with you, love,' Elliot said thoughtfully. 'Maybe *about* you, but not *at* you.'

'You mean, he heard what we were talking about?' she said with dismay.

He shook his head. 'If Robert had heard you admitting to being Charles Blake's daughter, half of London would have heard his roar.'

'But he doesn't know my father—'

'He doesn't need to. Robert's parents had to make a lot of sacrifices to put him through med school, and he's got no time for the children of rich consultants pulling strings to get posts.'

'But I didn't pull any strings,' she protested. 'My father doesn't even know where I'm working.'

'Really?' Elliot exclaimed in surprise. 'But surely—'

'I'm sorry, Elliot,' she interrupted quickly, though in truth she wasn't one bit sorry to put a stop to a conversation she would far rather not have had. 'I have to go. Jane seems to want me.'

And she did. Calm, implacable Jane, who never flapped, was in a flap now.

'What is it—what's wrong?' Hannah asked as she joined her outside cubicle 7.

'John Keir, forty two years old, came in ten minutes ago with severe chest pains, and I'm not happy.'

Neither was Hannah after she'd examined him. John Keir's pulse was 145, his breathing was rapid, and his skin was warm and clammy to the touch.

'How long have you felt like this, Mr Keir?' she asked.

'A couple of hours,' he gasped. 'Maybe more. At first I thought it was simply indigestion. Some friends and I went out for a pub lunch, you see, but now it feels like I've got an elephant sitting on my chest.'

'Do you have pain anywhere else?' Hannah said as Jane swiftly began inserting an IV drip.

'It's down my left arm now as well,' he replied with difficulty, 'and in my jaw.'

Hannah eyes met Jane's. Mr Keir couldn't have described the classic symptoms of a heart attack better if he'd tried.

'Get me a BP and respiratory rate, Jane,' she said, pulling the ECG monitor quickly across to the trolley.

'You'll be wanting supplementary oxygen, too?' Jane said, reaching for the nasal cannula.

Hannah nodded as she began affixing the ECG machine's sticky electrodes to John Keir's arms, legs and chest. The extra oxygen should help the man's breathing and hopefully bring his blood pressure down. A nitroglycerine capsule under his tongue, and morphine given intravenously, should relieve his pain, but they needed to know what his heart was doing, and only the ECG machine could tell them that.

And it did. Myocardial infarction. The horizontal lines appearing at regular intervals on the graph paper could mean only one thing—acute myocardial infarction.

'Resps 130 over 90, breaths 24 a minute,' Jane murmured, and Hannah bit her lip. This was far too serious for her to handle on her own, and she knew it.

'Jane, go and see if you can find Elliot or Robert,' she said in an undertone, 'and I want you to page Cardiology for me, too.'

'But—'

'Just do it, Jane,' she insisted.

With a backward glance of concern the sister was gone, and Hannah smiled encouragingly down at John Keir as she inserted another IV line into his arm.

'You said you went out for a pub lunch,' she commented,

deliberately making conversation to calm him. 'Somewhere nice?'

'The Arches in Piccadilly,' he replied with a wobbly smile. 'Last time I'll be going there, believe me. One tomato risotto with avocado, followed by lamb steaks cooked in sage butter, and I end up in hospital.'

Hannah chuckled, understanding the effort it must have taken John Keir to make a joke at a time like this, then glanced up at the drip. It was open and running and hopefully it would soon dilate the arteries around John's heart, helping the blood to flow more freely and making it less likely to form clots.

Unfortunately, none of the drugs she'd given him through the IV drip could unclog any clots already present. Only tissue-plasminogen activating factor and streptokinase could do that, but even healthy people without heart problems could sometimes bleed too much when they were given those two drugs, and the thought of John Keir bleeding internally, as well as suffering from a myocardial infarction, horrified her

She needed advice, and she needed it quickly. As though on cue, Jane suddenly came through the cubicle curtains with Robert at her side.

'Drug situation?' he declared, pulling on a pair of latex gloves.

'Nitroglycerine by mouth, morphine intravenously. Nitro drip with heparin and aspirin,' Hannah replied.

'TPA and streptokinase?'

She shook her head. 'I wasn't sure about the dosages—'

'No problem,' he interrupted.

With an ease she could only envy, he swiftly made the calculations and administered the two drugs. They should work quickly, and they did.

'BP and pulse rate seem to be stabilising, Robert,' Jane announced.

'OK, page IC for me, Jane. Tell them we'll be sending Mr…Mr…'

'Keir—John Keir,' Hannah supplied for him.

'A Mr John Keir along after he's been seen by the cardiology specialist. Hannah, keep an eye on the ECG monitor for arrhythmia—abnormal heartbeats.'

She nodded. 'Do you want—?'

She didn't get a chance to say any more. The alarm on the ECG machine suddenly went off and she stared at it in horror.

Ventricular fibrillation. John Keir's heart had gone into chaotic, uncoordinated spasm. No blood was flowing from his heart into his brain, which meant that he would soon be dead unless they did something. But to Hannah's dismay she couldn't move, couldn't even think. All she could feel was panic—a terrified, mind-numbing, panic—and desperately she glanced across at Robert, willing him to do something.

He did. He leant past her and thumped John Keir hard in the centre of his chest with his fist. Hannah's eyes flew back to the ECG monitor. Nothing. Nothing was happening. The graph paper was still spewing out the same wild, haphazard strokes, then with a discordant beep the alarm suddenly clicked off, and John Keir's heart rhythm jolted back to normal.

'Sorry about that.' Robert smiled as John Keir gazed up at him in confusion. 'Hitting somebody isn't exactly the best way to win friends, but sometimes it can be very effective.' He glanced across at Jane. 'BP now?'

'One hundred over sixty.'

Normal, considering the circumstances.

'Any sign of arrhythmia, Hannah?' he asked.

'No,' she mumbled.

Robert shot her a puzzled glance, but she didn't see it. All she could think was that John Keir's blood pressure was normal. He wasn't out of the woods yet by any means, but for now, at least, he was stable again.

'Where the hell is that cardiology consultant?' Robert demanded. 'You did say you'd paged him, didn't you, Jane?'

She nodded. 'He said he was on his way.'

'Don't tell me I've missed all the excitement,' the consultant said as he swung into the cubicle.

'I sincerely hope so,' Robert replied dryly. 'I think Mr Keir's had more than enough for one afternoon.'

So had she, Hannah thought as John Keir was wheeled off to Intensive Care. She'd had more than enough to last her a lifetime.

A sob sprang to her lips and she crushed it down with difficulty. She'd failed. This had been her first big emergency, and she'd failed.

'Are you OK, Hannah?'

She glanced over her shoulder to see Robert gazing at her with concern, and shook her head. 'I don't ever want to be that frightened again as long as I live. If you hadn't been here—done what you did—'

'It comes with practice.'

'He could have died,' she continued, her eyes large brown pools of distress and defeat. 'I just stood there—useless—frozen—'

'Hannah, nobody expects a junior doctor to have the knowledge and skill of a special registrar,' he protested.

Perhaps not, but she'd bet money Laura wouldn't have frozen. In fact, Laura would probably have performed open-heart surgery with a teaspoon if she'd needed to.

'I'm useless,' she murmured wretchedly. 'Completely useless—'

'Hey, you can stop that right now!' Robert exclaimed, striding quickly across the cubicle and grasping her firmly by the shoulders. 'Who gave that guy the nitro, heparin and aspirin? *You* did! Who had the sense to get help when she needed it? *You* did!'

'Yes, but—'

'Hannah, you did everything I—or indeed anyone else—could have expected in the circumstances, so why are you being so hard on yourself?'

Because for years my father told me I'd never be good enough to be a doctor, she thought. For years I had to listen to him telling me I wasn't bright enough, or strong enough, or talented enough.

'I guess…' Her tears were still far too near to the surface for comfort, and she swallowed hard. 'I guess it's because I'm a wimp.'

He smiled. A gentle smile that seemed to curl down right into her toes. 'Oh, Hannah, you're not a wimp. You might be an idiot at times, but you're most definitely not a wimp.'

She gave a short, hiccuping laugh that wasn't quite a sob. 'Am I supposed to take that as a compliment?'

'It's meant as one.' He nodded, and she knew he wasn't lying.

But as she continued to gaze up at him she suddenly realised something else. The strange, fluttery sensation in the pit of her stomach was back again. That confusing, disturbing, awareness she'd experienced in his flat had returned, and she didn't want to feel it. She desperately didn't want to feel it.

Awkwardly she backed away from him, all too conscious that her cheeks must be red. 'I have to get back to work. Jane…Elliot…they'll be wondering where I am.'

'Hannah…' Robert took a step towards her, then stopped. 'If you ever feel the need to talk to someone, perhaps feel that things—people—are getting on top of you…'

She wished he hadn't said that. He'd been the last person to be on top of her, well, almost, and she didn't want to remember that. Didn't want to remember the way he'd kissed her, how his fingers had curled round her breasts, and how he'd pressed his long, hard length against her.

'I'll…I'll bear that in mind,' she floundered, backing away from him still further.

'Hannah—'

'Oh, I'm sorry,' Elliot said, abruptly halting as he came through the cubicle curtains. 'I didn't realise you were busy, Robert, but the night staff have just come on duty—'

'And I'm just going,' Hannah broke in quickly.

'Hannah, wait a minute—'

But she didn't wait. She simply took to her heels and ran.

Idiot. *Idiot!* she berated herself when she reached the staffroom and leant against the door, her heart pounding. Are you deliberately trying to make yourself look ridiculous? Deliberately trying to look a fool? Look at the situation. Yes, just *look*!

Robert was married to a girl who was beautiful, and talented, and smart. Even if he wanted to get involved with somebody again, it wouldn't be with somebody like you.

And even if he was interested in you, you swore you'd never ever get involved with another doctor again, remember, so get a grip on yourself. Go home, have something to eat, and then you'll be able to get this whole ridiculous situation into perspective.

And the hot meal did help. The long, hot shower she took afterwards helped even more.

You've got to start socialising, she told herself as she stepped out of the shower, slipped into her bathrobe and went through to the sitting room to collect her hairdryer. You go to work, come home, then study. No wonder you're behaving like an idiot. If you don't get yourself a social life pretty damn quick, you're going to start finding creepy Jerry Clark from Radiology attractive next.

She chuckled, switched on the dryer, then switched it off

again when she heard the sound of someone knocking on her door.

It would be Melanie Johnson from the flat above, dropping by to collect the notes she'd wanted to borrow. Melanie, who was scatty and crazy and exactly the kind of company she needed right now. With a smile she called out, 'Come in. The door's not locked.'

Which would have been exactly the right thing to say if it had been Melanie, but it wasn't. It was Robert Cunningham.

For a second she froze, all too acutely aware that she was naked beneath her bathrobe, then with a deep blush of embarrassment she dropped the hairdryer, grabbed the belt of her robe and tightened it into a firm knot.

'I thought…I thought you were Melanie,' she said, in case he thought she made a habit of asking people into her flat when she was wearing a bathrobe. 'Melanie Johnson,' she added as his eyebrows rose. 'She has the flat above me, and wanted to borrow some of my notes on blood diseases. She had flu when we had the lecture, you see, and…and…'

And she was babbling, she realised as he gazed at her silently. Babbling a lot of nonsense that he couldn't possibly be interested in.

Well, what did he expect? she thought crossly. She hadn't asked him to drop by, she hadn't wanted him to drop by, and if he wanted scintillating conversation he'd come to the wrong place.

'What can I do for you?' she asked as coolly as any girl dressed solely in a wet bathrobe, with bright red cheeks and soaking wet hair, could be expected to. 'Is there some problem at the hospital?'

'No problem, no,' he replied. 'Reception told me that a letter came for you this morning marked ''personal'', and I thought it might be important.'

In truth, he hadn't thought anything of the kind. He'd

come because he still felt guilty, because she'd seemed so depressed over John Keir, and when he'd seen the letter he'd hoped it might be from a friend who could cheer her up, but the minute he'd walked into her flat he'd known he shouldn't have come.

Did she have any idea how revealing her bathrobe was when it was wet? He knew, and wished he didn't, and with a supreme effort of will he shifted his gaze to her face and kept it there.

'Thanks for bringing it round,' she murmured, taking the letter from his outstretched hand.

She didn't looked grateful. In fact, she looked as though he'd just handed her a ticking time bomb to hold.

'Is there something wrong?' he said curiously.

'Of course not,' she replied brightly, shoving the letter into her pocket. 'It's just a letter from an old schoolfriend, that's all.'

And I'm Santa Claus, Robert thought grimly as he stared at her.

How could he have been so stupid? It was obvious now that the letter was from a boyfriend, or a lover. Probably the same lover or boyfriend who'd brought her rushing down to London to work, and, judging from her expression, a letter was the last thing she'd expected.

Well, when you fell in love you got hurt. Everybody knew that. Look at Elliot, divorced now for five years and still unable to form a lasting relationship. And as for himself...

No, he didn't want to think about himself. Didn't want to remember how loving Laura had brought heartbreak and disaster to them both. Quickly he glanced round the sitting room, looking for a way to change the subject. 'These flats are even worse than I remember.'

'You remember?' she repeated.

'My...my wife had one of these flats before...before we

got married.' So much for trying not to remember, he thought bleakly. So much for trying to forget. Nothing would ever help him to forget. Nothing.

'Would you like a cup of coffee, or tea?' she said swiftly, guessing at the thoughts which must be going through his mind. 'It would be no trouble…'

'Thank you, but I have to go.' Robert walked towards the door, then paused and turned back towards her, his face determined. 'I never…I didn't ever thank you properly for taking care of my arm and wrist.'

Hannah gazed at him in dismay. She didn't want to talk about this, not right now and preferably never. 'It was no trouble—no trouble at all,' she replied hurriedly. 'I was only too happy to be there.' Oh, she hadn't meant that— or at least she had, but not in the way he might think. 'What I mean is—'

'I know what you mean,' he interrupted, and she wondered if her cheeks were as red as his. They certainly felt like it. 'I just…well, I wanted to say thank you, and…' A small muscle in the corner of his jaw tightened. 'And to say that I hope I didn't… That is, my behaviour—'

'There's no need to say anything,' she declared, her voice slightly strangled. 'In fact, I'd far rather you didn't.'

He nodded, but he didn't move, made no attempt to open the door. Oh, please, just go, she thought. You've done what you came to do so, please, please, just go.

'I'll say goodnight, then,' he said at last, hesitantly, almost she thought reluctantly, and this time she didn't try to stop him.

Instead, she waited until she heard the sound of his footsteps growing fainter and fainter in the corridor outside, then let out her breath in a long, slow whoosh of relief.

She never wanted to have another conversation like that as long as she lived. He'd been so clearly deeply embarrassed, and she…! If he'd only left that stupid letter until morning—

The letter. Quickly she pulled it out of her pocket and stared down at it.

How had her father found out where she worked? She'd told no one, refused even to so much as give him a hint, so how had he found out? Probably by phoning every hospital in the country, looking for her, she decided bitterly. Probably by calling in every favour he was owed.

Well, she wasn't going to read it now. She didn't know if she was ever going to read it. Deliberately, she threw the envelope onto the coffee-table, switched on her hairdryer and went over to the mirror, only to stare at herself in appalled horror.

Oh, no, she could see the outline of her breasts, even her nipples, through her wet bathrobe, and if she could see them that meant Robert must have seen them, too.

So what if he did? her mind protested. Considering the man was married to a woman whose figure would have made Marilyn Monroe envious, your two poached eggs are hardly likely to have taken his breath away.

And they *were* poached eggs, she thought vexedly, turning sideways to gaze at them critically. Two small, flat, unsexy, poached eggs. If only they were bigger, fuller, higher—

'Oh, for God's sake, get a grip,' she told her reflection. 'Even if you had breasts the size of melons, Robert Cunningham wouldn't be interested in you, and that's exactly how you want it to be, you know it is.'

And as she switched on her hairdryer and began drying her hair, she tried very hard to make herself believe it.

CHAPTER FIVE

'I'M AFRAID your eye is going to be very painful for quite some time,' Hannah said as she slipped an eye patch carefully round the young man's head. 'The antibiotic eye drops I've given you should help a little, and they ought to get rid of any infection, but don't forget to give this referral note to our receptionist on your way out, and she'll make sure you get an appointment at our ophthalmology clinic.'

''Strewth, but I look like Long John Silver,' the man exclaimed with dismay as he got off the trolley and looked at himself in the mirror.

'Be grateful you'll eventually be able to see out of that eye,' Hannah replied. 'Riding a motorbike without goggles might be considered macho but, believe me, losing your eyesight isn't.'

'Yeah, right. Thanks for your time, Doc,' he replied, zipping up his leather jacket. 'And I'll remember what you said about the goggles.'

She doubted it. He'd probably be out on his motorbike in a couple of days, still not wearing his goggles, and end up back in A and E with something considerably more serious.

Cynic, her mind whispered. Too damn right I'm cynical, she thought. Cynical, and jaded, and depressed.

She was so tired, that was the trouble. Not just physically tired—that she thought she could have coped with—but mind-numbingly, brain-sappingly tired, and yet she'd only just come on duty. Only just arrived for the start of the night shift with another eight long weary hours to go.

How did Robert, and Elliot, and Jane work here day after

day, night after night? Where did they get their inner resources from, or had her father been right all the time when he'd said she didn't have the temperament to become a doctor?

She'd thought he'd been wrong. She'd been determined to prove him wrong, but now... Now, she honestly didn't know any more.

'Ah, Hannah, my dear!' Mr Mackay, the consultant in charge of A and E beamed as he breezed down the treatment room towards her, with Robert at his side. 'I need your opinion on the patient in cubicle 1. Woman in her mid-fifties, brought in by her husband because of excruciating pain in the upper left quadrant of her stomach. She was sick after dinner tonight, and brought up some blood.'

Opinion be damned, she thought wearily as she stared up at the consultant's cheery face. Mr Mackay had plainly just realised she'd been with them now for over two months and he was trying to find out whether she was up to scratch or not.

The symptoms he'd outlined indicated that his patient might be suffering from a bleeding stomach ulcer. It probably was a bleeding ulcer, but there was no way she was going to make any snap diagnosis in front of the consultant.

'Was there a lot of blood when she was sick?' she asked.

'Not a lot, no.'

'And the colour of the blood. Was it bright red, or very dark?'

'I believe the patient said she thought she'd merely brought up some coffee until she realised it was actually blood.'

Hannah nodded. Many patients with slow-bleeding ulcers said their vomit looked exactly like coffee grounds.

'I'd do a guiac test,' she said firmly. 'If she's bleeding from a stomach ulcer—which I strongly suspect she is—

her stools will look black and tarry, and that will confirm the diagnosis.'

'You'll be pleased to know that it did,' Mr Mackay said, his smile widening. 'I've got young Kelly Ross sitting with her at the moment, but if you could pop in occasionally, to check there's no change, I'd be most grateful. She's going to have a long wait for Theatre, you see—apparently they're really busy tonight.'

Well, bully for them, Hannah thought sourly as the consultant walked away. And so much for Mr Mackay wanting her opinion. As she'd suspected, he'd simply been testing her, and at midnight on a busy Friday night she could do without someone examining her medical ability.

Slowly she began to walk down the treatment room only to discover to her surprise that Robert came after her.

'You did very well just then,' he said approvingly. 'Being grilled by a consultant in the middle of the night isn't the easiest thing in the world to handle.'

'No,' she murmured.

'And you took your time over the diagnosis, didn't say the first thing that came into your head which can always be a danger when you're put on the spot,' he continued. 'I'm really proud of you.'

'Yeah, well, thanks,' Hannah said without enthusiasm.

He shot her a puzzled glance. 'Are you OK, Hannah?'

No, she wasn't OK. She hadn't been feeling 'OK' for quite some time now, but not for the world would she ever have admitted it to anyone, far less to the special registrar.

'I'm fine, thanks.'

His gaze swept over her. 'So those dark shadows under your eyes, they're some new sort of fashion statement, are they?'

If he was trying to be smart, she didn't appreciate the joke. If he was showing true concern, she didn't think she could handle it right now.

'It's the fluorescent lighting in here,' she said tightly. 'It would make even a beauty queen look rough.'

It was true, it would, but Robert knew only too well that the fluorescent lighting couldn't possibly make her look even thinner now than when she'd first arrived two months ago. It couldn't make her face seem to consist of nothing but a pair of huge, dark eyes. And it most certainly couldn't give her a face that was paper-white and strained.

'I'd say you were anything but fine,' he declared. 'In fact, I'd say you were working too hard.'

'No harder than anybody else,' she protested.

Yes, but none of us seems to be as driven as you, he wanted to reply. None of us seems to be constantly trying to prove something, and he couldn't for the life of him think why. She was a good doctor, a dedicated one, and she had nothing to prove, least of all to him.

He tried again. 'Hannah, nobody would be surprised if you were finding working in A and E very stressful—'

'Are you saying my work isn't satisfactory?'

There it was again, he thought in confusion. The stricken look he'd seen on her face many times before. The instant assumption that he was criticising her.

'Your work is perfectly satisfactory—in fact, considerably more than satisfactory,' he replied, frowning with annoyance as he noticed Elliot coming towards them. 'All I'm saying is, if you ever feel you need help—advice—ask for it.'

'I will.' She nodded. 'If I need it.'

She wouldn't, he thought as he watched her hurry away. There was something in her that seemed to consider asking for help a sign of weakness, something that made her see an offer of help as a sign of failure, and if she wasn't careful he very much feared she was going to grind herself into the ground.

'Something wrong with Hannah?' Elliot asked curiously as he joined him.

'She's doing too much,' Robert said in exasperation. 'She looks like a ghost, and she won't accept help.'

'I seem to recall Hannah's predecessor—Dr Jarvis—being exactly the same,' Elliot observed, 'and I don't remember you offering to hold his hand. In fact, I thought you said "Good riddance" when he left.'

It was true, he had, but Robert didn't much care for the knowing, amused smile on the SHO's lips. The smile which always seemed to appear on Elliot's face whenever he voiced his worries about Hannah.

'It's not the same thing,' he retorted.

'Yeah, I can see that.' Elliot grinned, and before Robert could reply the SHO had strolled away, whistling what sounded suspiciously like 'Love is a many splendoured thing' under his breath.

Robert glared after him. So what if he was concerned about Hannah? It was his business to be concerned. She was the newest member of staff, young and inexperienced, and just because he'd never taken an interest in the welfare of a twit like Graeme Jarvis...

OK, so maybe he was having difficulty forgetting the image of a wet bathrobe clinging to a pair of small erect nipples, but that was only because he was a man, not a monk, and for Elliot to imply...

It meant nothing, he told himself angrily as he went into the office to see if the blood samples he'd taken for his patient had come back yet. All it meant was that Elliot had a weird and very warped sense of humour.

Hannah could have done with some of the SHO's sense of humour when the doors of the treatment room swung open and two paramedics pushed in a trolley carrying a young man who was bloodstained and motionless.

'There's no need to rush, Doc,' one of the paramedics

declared as she and Jane ran towards him. 'There's not a lot you can do for this one. Bullet wound to his head, and with the responses we're getting on the Glasgow coma scale I'd say he's had it.'

'Any idea what happened?' Hannah asked as the paramedics wheeled their trolley into cubicle 3, and she nevertheless began to insert an endotracheal tube, while Jane set up IV lines.

'Your guess is a good as mine,' the paramedic replied. 'Where we picked him up, people don't like to get involved. "Didn't see nothing, mate", "Didn't hear nothing, mate"—you know the kind of place.'

Hannah did. So many of their patients came from exactly the same sort of area, and at a guess she'd say it was a drug deal gone wrong. Bullet wounds were nearly always a drug deal that had gone wrong.

'Any ID?' she asked.

'Sam Armstrong, according to the letters in his pocket. We'll get Reception to check out the address but, like I said, I don't think there's any hope for him.'

Hannah didn't think there was either. The top half of Sam Armstrong's head was a crumpled mass of damaged bone and tissue. The ventilator she'd attached him to would keep him breathing, and they could monitor his blood pressure and heart rate, but that was all they could do. With his brain almost certainly irreparably damaged, he was effectively dead.

'Do you want me to page Neurology?' Jane said.

Hannah nodded. The neurosurgeon would arrange a CT scan, but from the looks of things it was merely going to be a formality.

'Nice-looking young man, too,' Jane continued. 'What a waste.'

It was an even bigger waste for the kids he'd sold drugs to, Hannah thought bitterly. She'd noticed there were no puncture marks on Sam Armstrong's arms, or in his groin. He was clearly too smart to take drugs himself. He just peddled them.

There was nothing else she could do for him, and in truth there was nothing more she wanted to do. All she wanted was to go home and go to bed, and when Elliot hurried towards her to tell her of the case of child abuse waiting in another cubicle, she most definitely wanted to go home.

'Seems the poor kid just walked into the police station, took off his shirt and showed them his back,' he declared. 'The police brought him in to us for confirmation of his injuries before they press charges. Look, I'm really sorry about this, Hannah,' he continued, seeing her expression. 'I'd take the case myself, but I've got a guy bleeding like a stuck pig in 7, Robert's working on an RTA in 2, and Mr Mackay's got what looks to be a massive stroke in 5. There's only you left to deal with it.'

'Is anybody with him? The boy, I mean?'

'I've sent Jane in to sit with him. And I'd better warn you—the kid's in a bit of a mess.'

A mess was right, Hannah thought as she went into the cubicle and found Jane cradling the child in her arms. He couldn't have been any more than eight years old and yet every part of his thin, underdeveloped little body was a mass of bruises and scars. Shiny, flat, well-healed scars which must have been inflicted when he'd been about four. Dark red ones which she guessed had been caused last year, and livid, bright red ones which had probably been inflicted as recently as yesterday.

'Why didn't he go to the police before?' Hannah said through a throat so tight it hurt.

'He said he could take it,' Jane replied huskily. 'It was when his mother started beating his little brother—'

'His *mother* did this?' Hannah gasped.

Jane nodded, her lips grim. 'Makes you think, doesn't it?'

No, it didn't make her think, Hannah decided as she catalogued every bruise, scar and lesion. It made her want to inflict similar injuries on the boy's mother, to let her see how it felt to be on the receiving end of such pain.

'What happens now?' she asked after Jane had gently helped the boy back on with his clothes.

'I should imagine he and his brother will be put into a children's home until the court case, and then they'll probably be fostered.'

'I hope they lock his mother up and throw away the key,' Hannah said grimly. 'I hope—' She stopped and frowned, suddenly aware of angry raised voices coming from outside in the treatment room. 'What on earth's going on out there?'

'I don't know,' Jane replied. 'But I've never heard Mr Mackay quite so angry.'

Neither had Hannah, and it didn't take her long to find out why.

'At last!' the A and E consultant exclaimed the minute he saw her. 'I want to know what idiot gave Mrs Forsyth a glass of water!'

'Mrs Forsyth?' she repeated in confusion.

'My slow-bleeding ulcer. Some stupid idiot gave her a glass of water, and now I'm going to have to phone Theatre to cancel surgery!'

And he would have to cancel. Even something as simple and innocuous as a glass of water could cause vomiting in an anaesthetised patient, with material from the stomach aspirated into the lungs.

'You said her husband brought her in,' Hannah observed. 'Could he have given her the water, thinking it wouldn't matter?'

'He says he didn't, and I believe him,' the consultant

replied. 'Which means it must have been one of my staff, and I want to find out who!'

She could understand his anger—she would have been furious herself—but to her dismay she suddenly noticed Kelly Ross staring at the ground as though she hoped it would open up and swallow her. Oh, no. If Mr Mackay discovered the student nurse was to blame he'd come down on her like a ton of bricks.

She took a deep breath, and steeled herself for the consultant's inevitable wrath.

'I'm afraid I can't help you, sir,' she murmured. 'I've no idea how this could have happened.'

'It's your *business* to know!' he retaliated. 'I put you in charge of this patient!'

'I realise that, sir, and I take full responsibility for what has happened,' she replied, managing to meet the consultant's blazing eyes, though her stomach was churning. 'And I can only repeat that I'm sorry, and promise it won't happen again.'

'A fat lot of use that is!' he exclaimed. 'I'm the one who's going to look as though he's in charge of a bunch of bloody fools when I phone Theatre and tell them they can't operate!' He started away angrily, then swung back, and she waited, all too aware that Jane was studiously avoiding her eye and Elliot looked deeply embarrassed. 'The neurosurgeon's just pronounced the guy in 3 clinically dead. His mother's in the relatives' waiting room. See if you can do something right for a change by asking her if she'll agree to some organ donations.'

Hannah stared after him in dismay. She hated asking relatives for organ donations. Some people reacted so badly—shouting at you, demanding to know what kind of bloodthirsty ghoul you were—and it didn't matter that Sam Armstrong was a drug dealer. His mother was still going to be devastated when she told her the situation.

'But he's still alive?' Mrs Armstrong declared when Hannah had explained how seriously injured her son was. 'You're saying he's been badly hurt, but he's still alive?'

'Only because of the life-support machine,' Hannah said gently. 'Mrs Armstrong—'

'He's such a good boy, Doctor,' the woman interrupted. 'A lot of the kids round our way they're into drugs, stealing cars, vandalism, but Sammy...' Mrs Armstrong's small, plump face lit up with pride. 'He wants to make something of himself. I says to him, "Sammy, you work hard all day stacking shelves and sweeping floors at the supermarket. Why do you want to go to college at night? You're young, you should be out enjoying yourself." And he says, "Ma, I'm going to be somebody. I'm going to get a good job, then we can all live somewhere nice where they don't have spyholes in the doors, and bars on the windows."'

Tears welled in Hannah's eyes, and she desperately blinked them away. She didn't want to hear this. It had been easier when she'd thought Sam Armstrong was a drug-dealer, a low-life. She didn't want to know that he'd been a good son, an ambitious young man and a kind one. 'Mrs Armstrong—'

'His friend Joe—he told me what happened. He and Sammy, they were on their way home from the night college, you see, and they see this black boy attacking this white kid. Joe, he thinks they should just pass by, not get involved, but Sammy, he says, no, they gotta help. So he drags this black boy off the white kid, and the black boy— he pulls out a gun—'

'Your son was a very brave man, Mrs Armstrong, a very brave man,' Hannah interrupted, wishing the woman would just stop, wouldn't tell her any more. 'That's why my consultant was wondering whether you might be prepared to—'

'I don't have much money, Doctor,' the woman continued, pulling a battered purse out of her handbag, 'but I want you to take this to help make my Sammy well again.'

Hannah stared at the purse in dismay. 'Mrs Armstrong, it isn't a question of money—'

'I've been saving up to help Sammy with his college fees, you see. There's £200 here, Doctor. I know it's not a lot, but I clean offices at night and I can get more work, clean more offices—'

'Mrs Armstrong, there's nothing we can do!' Hannah said desperately, then bit her lip when the woman flinched. 'I'm sorry. So very sorry, but all the money in the world isn't going to make Sammy well again. There's nothing we can do. I wish there was. I truly, truly wish there was, but there isn't.'

For a long moment Mrs Armstrong stared at her, her eyes large, black pools of pain and distress, then slowly she put her purse back into her handbag. 'I see. I understand. Can I…can I see him, Doctor?'

Hannah nodded, and gently guided the woman along the corridor to the trauma room. Kelly was there, looking as grim as she herself felt, but she'd done a good job on Mrs Armstrong's son. There wasn't a mark on the young man's face. The only evidence of his horrific injury was the bandage she'd tied tightly round the top of his head.

'Would you like me to stay with you?' Hannah asked as Mrs Armstrong approached the trolley.

'No. Thank you, dear, but, no,' she replied with a tremulous smile. 'Sammy and me, we'd just like to be alone together for a little while, if you don't mind.'

Blindly Hannah went out of the trauma room. This was turning out to be a lousy shift, a really lousy shift, and it wasn't over yet. It was only four o'clock in the morning. She had another three hours to go. Another three hours before she could go home, and try to forget the grief on Mrs Armstrong's face.

And it wasn't going to be the only thing she'd have to try to forget, she realised with a sinking heart when she walked through the treatment-room doors and Mr Mackay bore down on her expectantly.

'Any luck with the organ donations, Hannah?'

She cleared her throat awkwardly. 'I'm sorry, sir, but I didn't ask. She was so upset, you see—'

'What did you expect?' the consultant exploded. 'That she'd be doing cartwheels, hanging out flags? Of all the—'

'Asking relatives to agree to organ donation is one of the toughest jobs there is, boss,' Robert said quietly as he joined them. 'You should have asked me to do it, and not expected Hannah—'

'Do you have any idea how long the waiting list is for transplants?' the consultant continued as though Robert hadn't spoken. 'Of the number of people who are waiting, hoping, for a phone call!'

'I know, sir,' Hannah began, 'and I'm sorry—'

'You're sorry. You're *sorry*?' The consultant turned a deeper shade of red. 'Where's Mrs Armstrong?'

'In the trauma room—'

'I'll speak to her myself. And as for you...' The A and E consultant didn't say she was a complete waste of space, but Hannah knew he was thinking it. 'Take a break, get yourself a cup of coffee, and get your act together!'

How was she supposed to do that? she wondered as she went slowly out of the treatment room. How could she make herself tougher, stronger, less feeble?

The truth was she couldn't. The even more unpalatable truth was that she wasn't a doctor, she would never make a doctor, and it was time she faced up to it.

Tears blurred her vision as she went into the staffroom, switched on the kettle and sat down limply on one of the old battered chairs, not realising she wasn't alone until a hand came gently down on her shoulder and she looked up to see Robert was there.

'He didn't mean it, Hannah,' he murmured, his voice soft, understanding. 'It's been a rough night, and he's simply tired like the rest of us.'

'It's not what Mr Mackay said,' she said miserably. 'Or at least, it's not just that he obviously now thinks he's hired an incompetent idiot. It's Sammy Armstrong. Robert, I took one look at him and thought, black kid, mid-twenties with a bullet wound—drug-dealer. And he wasn't—he *wasn't*!'

'Hannah—'

'What's happening to me?' she continued, knuckling her tears away, her lips trembling. 'I never used to make snap judgements about people, I never used to be so hard and uncaring. What kind of unfeeling bitch am I becoming?'

Robert pulled over another chair and sat down opposite her. 'You can't be a bitch if you care, and you wouldn't be crying if you didn't care. Hannah, you've just discovered you're human like the rest of us. You're tired, stressed—'

'I wish I was like you,' she blurted out. 'So confident, so sure of yourself.'

He shook his head ruefully. 'Would you believe there are times when I'm terrified witless?'

She stared at him in surprise. 'You're frightened?'

'Hannah, we *all* are. Frightened we'll make a mistake, frightened we'll miss something, and desperately, desperately frightened that one day we'll be so damned tired we'll kill somebody.'

'I thought it was only me who felt like that,' she murmured as he got to his feet, spooned some coffee into two cups and handed her one 'You, Elliot, Jane—you never seem to flap or panic. I thought it was just me who was scared all the time.'

'Why do you think Elliot jokes so much—or Jane and

Flo?' he asked. 'It's their way of dealing with the stress. We all have to find our own particular way of handling it.'

'What's yours?' she asked without thinking, only to colour as he smiled.

'You mean apart from generally behaving like a bear with a sore head? I switch off completely when I go home, and that's what you ought to do.'

'I suppose I could always join one of the hospital clubs—'

'Absolutely not,' he said firmly. 'You need to meet and socialise with people who aren't medical. Our world is so full of pain and heartache that you can find yourself developing a battlefield mentality if you're not careful, living for the day, seizing the moment as though it were your last. That's why so many relationships between hospital staff end in disaster. If you want to join a club, join one that doesn't have a doctor or a nurse on its books.'

Hannah gazed at him thoughtfully. Looking back, she could see she would never have become involved with Chris if she hadn't been so lonely and stressed, but Robert had sounded almost as though he was speaking from personal experience. Jane had said he'd been shattered when his wife had died, but had his marriage been in trouble before Laura's death? She would have dearly liked to have asked, but didn't dare.

'The other departments in the hospital call A and E "The Pit",' she murmured.

He nodded. 'It can seem that way at times, and it's not just because we're constantly on the receiving end of a stream of human misfortune. It's because we can never refuse to treat anyone no matter how drunk or nasty they might be.'

Hannah stared down at her cup of coffee. 'I said I wouldn't treat that horrible man who was so rude to Flo unless he agreed to let her dress his hand.'

'Did you mean it? I mean, could you really have sent him out, knowing he might bleed to death?'

She bit her lip and sighed. 'I guess not. Though I'd have made damn sure his hand hurt like hell by the time I'd finished with him,' she added belligerently.

Robert laughed, a surprisingly deep and infectious sound, but as she blew her nose and laughed too she suddenly realised how tired he looked, his black hair dishevelled, his chin showing dark stubble.

'I'm sorry to be such a wimp,' she began guiltily. 'You've got enough on your plate without—'

'It was Kelly who gave the woman with the bleeding ulcer the glass of water, wasn't it?' he interrupted.

Her heart sank and she tried to meet his gaze and couldn't. 'It might have been anyone—'

'But it was Kelly. Hannah, covering up for her was a very kind and loyal thing to do, but it was also stupid.'

'She's so very young—'

'And you're ancient, I suppose,' he said with a ghost of a smile. 'I'll have to tell Mr Mackay—'

'But—'

'Hannah, she should have known not to give any patient anything until she'd checked with a doctor, and now we're going to lose valuable—maybe vital—time before we can treat her.'

He was right, she knew he was, and she sighed. 'Just lately I seem to be getting everything wrong…'

'Will you get off that guilt trip?' he protested. 'You're a good doctor.'

'Not a gifted or a talented one,' she said a little wistfully, and to her surprise his grey eyes suddenly became cold.

'Is that what you want?' Robert demanded. 'You can't be happy simply being a good doctor—you've got to be some high-flying, brilliant one instead?'

In truth, she wanted only to be as good as she could be,

but she didn't want him to think she was lacking in initiative, a non-achiever, or worse.

'Would it be so very wrong if I were ambitious?' she said, taking a sip of her coffee to buy herself some time.

He hadn't used to think it was, Robert remembered. In fact, he'd applauded Laura's ambition until they'd got married and he'd discovered just how very ambitious she'd been. If Hannah felt the same—that promotion was more important than anything else—then he had all the more reason to keep his distance, to clamp down hard on his body's unsettling reaction to her.

'It depends on why you decided to become a doctor,' he replied, his eyes fixed on her. 'If your aim is to find some new treatment then I'll support you all the way, but if you see the profession as a means of gaining power and status, a giant ego trip…'

Hannah had never wanted to be as successful as her father, not ever. All she'd ever wanted had been to help people, to make them well again, but would he think her naïve, and childish, if she said that?

'I suppose so,' she muttered, and to her surprise he abruptly got to his feet.

'Ambition can be a two-edged sword, Hannah,' he said tightly. 'Handle it with care.'

His face was all dark planes and shadows under the harsh fluorescent lighting, and she didn't know what to say. All she knew was that somehow she'd said the wrong thing, and she desperately wanted to make it right.

'Robert—'

'Sorry to interrupt, Robert,' Jane said, popping her head breathlessly round the staffroom door, 'but it's bedlam out here, and if Mr Mackay doesn't get help soon I think he's going to burst a blood vessel.'

'I'm coming,' he replied, but as Hannah got to her feet

he shook his head firmly. 'Take another ten minutes, finish your coffee.'

'I've had enough—'

'Sit down and drink your coffee, Hannah,' he ordered, and as Jane disappeared again Hannah's lips twitched.

'What was that you were saying about ego trips, and some doctors loving the power?'

A smile of genuine amusement lit up his face. 'You're feeling better, I see.'

'I am, thanks to you,' she replied, then grimaced. 'I always seem to be thanking you, don't I?'

'You'll be all right, Hannah,' he declared. 'You have great compassion and dedication. Hold onto those two things, and you'll be fine.'

She nodded, but he must have seen a trace of lingering doubt in her face because he suddenly reached out and tilted her chin upwards with his fingers.

'No more self-flagellation, OK? No more agonising.'

She laughed a little shakily. 'I'll try my best.'

'You do that.' He smiled, but as he continued to gaze down at her his smile slowly disappeared, to be replaced by a look that made her heart begin to race, her breath catch in her throat.

'Hannah…'

She could hear the banging doors, the hum of conversation and clatter of trolley wheels on vinyl in the corridor outside, but all she was really aware of was that something was happening that she didn't understand.

'Robert…'

He took a step forward and she forgot to breathe as he cupped her face with his hands. He was going to kiss her again—she knew he was—and he did, but not as she had expected.

He simply tilted her head and placed a kiss on her forehead. A kiss that was as gentle and tender as it was frustratingly brief.

'You're a nice kid, Hannah, a great kid,' he murmured, his voice suddenly rough, husky. 'Try not to change.'

And with that he walked away, leaving her staring blankly after him. A nice kid? He thought she was a great *kid*?

He hadn't thought she was a child that night in his flat. He hadn't thought she was a child when he'd kissed her, and held her. And she didn't want him to think of her as a child. She wanted...

Oh, she was so damned confused she didn't know what she wanted any more, but it was certainly not for Robert to think of her as a kid!

CHAPTER SIX

'SO, YOU'RE quite happy with Hannah's work, then?' Mr Mackay asked, shuffling the papers on his desk and determinedly avoiding his special registrar's eye.

'More than happy,' Robert replied with surprise. 'Boss, if you're still concerned about that fiasco with the bleeding stomach ulcer case, and Sam Armstrong—'

'Kelly has been reprimanded for her part in the affair, and as Mrs Armstrong agreed to donate some of her son's organs after I'd spoken to her I consider the subject closed. I simply wondered...' The consultant shuffled his papers again. 'As Hannah's been with us now for two months, I merely wondered how you felt she was settling in, whether there were any problems.'

A slight frown creased Robert's forehead. 'Did you expect there to be any?'

'Good grief, no!' Mr Mackay exclaimed with what he hoped was a suitably reassuring smile, though in reality he was already beginning to wish he'd never started this conversation.

He wouldn't have either if Charles Blake hadn't rung him up yesterday completely out of the blue, clearly worried about his daughter.

Initially he hadn't blamed the man. Hell, he had two grown-up daughters himself and the last branch of medicine he'd have wanted either of them to specialise in was A and E, but what had worried him—more than worried him—was Charles Blake's apparent fear that Hannah might not be pulling her weight. It had been an odd thing for a father to say—a very odd thing—and the more the A and E consultant had thought about it, the more uneasy he'd become.

'So you have no worries about her work?' he pressed.

'None at all,' Robert declared. 'She's a good doctor, and she'll become an excellent one in time. She suffers from a severely over-developed inferiority complex, but apart from that I can find no fault with her.'

The consultant nodded. He suspected he'd have a huge inferiority complex too, if his father had undermined his confidence the way Charles Blake clearly did his daughter's. The man might have a string of qualifications and awards to his name, but he clearly merited a big fat zero on the sensitivity scale.

'Boss, this sudden concern of yours with Hannah,' Robert continued, his frown deepening. 'Is there something I should know—something you're not telling me?'

The consultant's heart sank. He'd promised Hannah he wouldn't tell anyone who her father was, appreciating her desire to be accepted for herself, but he'd also had his own reasons for wanting to keep her parentage a secret.

Robert Cunningham would blow a fuse when he found out. Born into a poor, working-class family, Robert had no time for rich, well-connected students, and the minute he found out who Hannah's father was he'd undoubtedly accuse her of pulling strings to get the job. It wouldn't make a blind bit of difference to point out that nobody in their right mind would pull strings to get a job at St Stephen's.

'Of course there's nothing you should know,' the consultant protested. 'Look, I don't have to explain my interest to you,' he continued, taking refuge in anger. 'This is my department and it's part of my job to keep my finger on the pulse!'

'Yes, but—'

'I have to go,' the consultant said abruptly, getting to his feet fast. 'I've a meeting with Admin in ten minutes, and you…I suggest you get back to work!'

And before Robert could reply his boss had made a bee-line for the door and was gone, leaving him gazing blankly after him.

What in the world had that been all about? Robert wondered as he left the consultant's office and walked down the corridor. Normally Mr Mackay was only too pleased to leave the supervision of the junior members of staff to him, and yet the consultant had looked almost guilty when he'd asked him if there was anything he should know.

In fact, if the consultant had been a younger man he'd even have started to wonder if his interest in Hannah was more than strictly professional, but his boss was a happily married man of some twenty-five years, and he…

Was becoming fixated, Robert decided as he pushed open the doors of the treatment room and felt his pulse rate rocket when he saw Hannah laughing at something Jane had just said.

Dammit, she was just a girl. A girl who possessed a pair of beautiful dark eyes and wonderfully curly hair, but she was still just a girl. He might well be attracted to her—OK, all right, he admitted it—but that didn't mean he had to give in to that attraction. He was a mature adult male, not a teenager, and it was about time he started acting like one.

The only trouble was that it was a hell of a lot easier to think about than actually do, he realised with a groan as Hannah suddenly threw back her head and laughed again and he felt his groin tighten painfully. A hell of a lot easier.

'RTA on the way, Robert!' Floella suddenly called. 'Teenage couple—the bloke sounds to be in much worse shape than the girl.'

Which was exactly what he needed, Robert told himself as he strode towards the trauma room. Work. To bury himself in work, and maybe that would also bury his intrusive and relentless libido.

And it did. At least it did until he and Elliot had stabilised the young man and sent him to Intensive Care, and he went in search of Hannah to see how she was coping with the injured female passenger.

'She's conscious, knows who and where she is, and she can move her arms and legs,' Hannah reported. 'The only thing she's complaining about is some pain in her neck.'

Robert nodded, and noticed with approval that not only had Hannah kept on the cervical collar which had been placed around the girl's neck at the scene of the accident, she'd also immobilised her on a hard board.

'Have you paged Radiology yet?' he asked.

'Jerry Clark's on his way down now.'

Oh, he was, was he? Robert thought grimly.

Ever since Hannah had told him about the X-ray technician's behaviour he'd had to keep his temper under a very tight rein whenever Jerry Clark appeared. And the rein got even tighter today when Jerry breezed into the cubicle with a smile at Hannah that made Robert's fingers itch to rearrange the technician's plump features.

'Neck and back X-rays only, please, Jerry,' he said brusquely, before turning his attention back to the young girl lying nervously on the trolley. 'Dr Blake tells me your neck's very sore. Do you feel any numbness or tingling in your hands and feet?'

'None at all,' she replied. 'How's my boyfriend? Nobody will tell me anything—'

'You just lie there and relax, and let us do the worrying,' Robert interrupted smoothly. 'Aren't those X-rays ready yet, Jerry?' he continued, frowning across at the technician.

'They are, and they're negative. No sign of any damage to the neck and back at all.'

Hannah breathed a sigh of relief. A broken neck and

subsequent paralysis was always a possibility after a bad road accident like this, but luckily the girl was fine.

'I suggest you give her a complete check-over in case she's sustained fractures anywhere else,' Robert commented. 'The cervical collar can come off now—'

'Sorry, Robert, but could you come right away?' Floella said anxiously, popping her head through the cubicle curtains. 'We've got a guy in 7 who looks to be haemorrhaging pretty badly.'

He was already walking towards the staff nurse and Hannah smiled encouragingly at the girl. 'You heard what the man said. Have you any other aches and pains I should know about?'

'My knee and arm hurt a bit,' the girl admitted.

'Jerry, can I have X-rays of the right knee and arm?'

'Your wish is my command, sweetheart,' he replied with what Hannah presumed he considered his most ingratiating smile, and she turned her back on him irritably.

How Jerry had ever got it into his head that he was irresistible to women was beyond her. Elliot was irresistible to women, and Robert...

No, she wasn't going to think about Robert, she told herself firmly. She'd been doing her level best for the past few days not to think about Robert, and she was actually succeeding. Well, some of the time she was. Occasionally she was. Now and then she was.

'Definite fractured right knee and arm,' Jerry declared. 'I'd better get going. Unless, of course, there's something else you'd like me to do for you?'

How about going and playing on the motorway in the rush hour? Hannah thought sourly as he leered across at her on his way out, but when the girl lying on the trolley uttered a small moan, she forgot all about the technician.

'What's wrong?' she asked, going quickly over to her.

'It's my neck. It's really, really sore. Do you think I could have a pillow?'

There had been no sign of any back or neck injuries on the X-rays. The girl wasn't complaining of any numbness or tingling in her arms and legs, so there was no earthly reason why she shouldn't have a pillow, and yet suddenly Hannah felt uneasy.

'Try this and see if this helps,' she suggested, folding the smallest towel she could find and slipping it under the girl's head.

You're wasting time, her mind whispered as she hovered beside the trolley. The waiting room's packed and as the girl's been thoroughly X-rayed there's no need for her to still be in the treatment room. You should be sending her along to the plastering department to have her knee and arm set. But something, a small nagging little doubt at the back of her mind, just wouldn't go away.

'Does it feel any better with the towel under your head?' she asked.

'Sort of.' The girl frowned. 'My neck doesn't hurt nearly so much but my fingers have gone all tingly.'

'Have they?' Hannah said with a calmness she was very far from feeling. Gently she slid the towel out from under the young girl's head, though all her instincts were urging her to yank it away fast. 'I won't be a minute,' she continued, walking towards the cubicle curtains. 'There's just…just something I want to check on.'

'Fine.' The girl smiled, but Hannah knew she was anything but 'fine', and the second she was out of the cubicle she began to run.

'Right, page the neurosurgeon and get Jerry Clark back immediately,' Robert ordered when Hannah explained what had happened. 'You're sure the only time you moved her was to slide the towel under her head, and then to take it away again?'

Hannah nodded.

'OK, put the cervical collar back on, and when Jerry shows up I want to be there.'

And he was, with a vengeance.

'I want more X-rays, Jerry, and this time I want them done properly,' he said curtly.

'Properly?' the technician repeated, his face going from white to red in quick succession. 'Are you calling my professional competence into question?'

Robert would have dearly liked to have accused him of a lot more, but right now he didn't have the time, not with the neurological surgeon on his way down to give a second opinion.

'Jerry, I want more X-rays,' he said again, his voice ice-cold. 'Either you take them for us or I can ask your boss to come down and do the honours. The choice is yours.'

Jerry took them.

'Well, would you look at that?' the neurosurgeon muttered when he joined them and studied the new set of X-ray plates. 'I'm not surprised it wasn't noticed before. It's so faint even I can hardly see it, and if Hannah hadn't mentioned the tingling in her fingers I would never have thought to look for it.'

The young girl had broken her second cervical vertebrae. Nerves to her entire body passed through this bone, nerves that controlled her breathing, movement, and feeling.

'How do your fingers feel now?' Robert asked, turning to the girl on the trolley.

'They're not tingling any more,' she replied, 'but my neck's sore again.'

Hannah met Robert's eyes with relief. The girl might have broken her neck and would have to wear a brace screwed into her head for the next few months, but if they hadn't got that second set of X-rays, if she'd been moved without the support of a cervical collar, she would have been paralysed for life.

'Well done,' Robert said to Hannah after the neurosurgeon had transferred the girl up to his ward. 'What made you suspect something was wrong?'

'I don't know,' she admitted. 'Call it a gut feeling—intuition, perhaps.'

'Then I suggest you immediately start cultivating both,' he said warmly. 'That sort of talent could be worth its weight in gold in A and E.'

She smiled, but when he did, too, a slight sigh escaped her.

He had such a nice smile when he cared to use it. Such a very nice smile. The trouble was that it would keep inducing that unsettling fluttering sensation deep in the pit of her stomach. It would persist in resurrecting the silly thoughts and feelings she kept having about him—thoughts and feelings which she knew perfectly well *were* silly until he smiled at her.

'I must go,' she mumbled. 'We're mobbed as usual—'

'You're looking a little better,' he interrupted. 'Have you been taking my advice—getting out more?'

'Sort of,' she replied. 'I've started going for long walks when I finish work. I used to walk a lot at home in Edinburgh—I found it cleared my head, helped me to sleep better—and it seems to be helping.'

'You walk on your own at night?' Robert said, aghast.

Just the thought of what could happen to her, doing that, was enough to make his blood run cold. Then offer to walk with her, the little voice in his mind said, and he all but laughed out loud at the suggestion. Dammit, he knew he'd like nothing better than to walk with her, to make sure she was safe, but if he couldn't control his intrusive libido in a crowded place like St Stephen's, God knew what would happen if he walked alone with her at night.

But he knew one thing for sure. He had to put an end to her nightly strolls.

'Hannah, walking alone in London at night—it's not a good idea.'

'You're not going to give me the "London isn't Edinburgh" speech again, are you?' she groaned. 'Look, I'm not an idiot. I don't walk in the parks, or down lonely streets. I stick to places where there are lots of people.'

'I don't give a damn if you walk in Piccadilly Circus!' he burst out. 'Promise me you'll stop doing it!'

'Oh, for heaven's sake…'

'Promise me, Hannah,' he insisted. 'And no crossing your fingers behind your back when you're doing it,' he added, correctly reading her mind.

A splutter of laughter came from her. 'I didn't know you were a mind-reader.'

'There's a lot of things you don't know about me,' he said, grinning.

He *grinned*? Robert Cunningham could grin like a regular, normal person?

He was right, there was a lot she didn't know about him. But you'd like to find out, wouldn't you? her mind said, and she determinedly trampled on the little voice.

'OK, I promise,' she said. 'But I still think you're being silly.'

He thought he was, too, as she walked away, but not in the way Hannah meant.

Why did he like her so much? And it was liking now, as well as lust. He liked her freshness, her total lack of guile. He admired her honesty, even if he often thought she was far too hard on herself.

In fact, if he was going to be really honest, he liked everything about her. The way she looked, the way she smiled. Her courage and dedication. Hell, he even liked the way she caught her lower lip between her teeth when she was puzzling something out. The way she blew the curls away from her face with an impatient huff when she was angry.

But it was a liking that could go nowhere. Even if she liked him—and he thought she did—there could be no future for them.

He couldn't give her what she needed. He didn't think he could give any girl that any more. Laura had managed not only to destroy his love during their marriage but also his ability to trust, and without trust there was nothing.

It was better to keep his distance from Hannah Blake, he decided as he saw her deep in conversation with a member of the local fire brigade, a slight frown on her face. Better for her, for him, for everybody.

'What's the problem?' he asked, his professional instincts instantly clicking into place as Hannah walked quickly towards him.

'What do you know about taps?' she asked, her lips twitching slightly.

'Taps?' He frowned.

'Bath taps. The fire brigade have just brought in a Mr and Mrs Fuller. The couple got married this afternoon and are booked into a hotel honeymoon suite for the weekend. Apparently Mrs Fuller decided to have a bath as they'd had such a long drive down from Shrewsbury, but the water felt a little hot after she got in, and when she was trying to turn on the cold water tap with her toes—'

'She's a contortionist, is she?'

'Of course not.' Hannah laughed. 'You don't have to be a contortionist to turn off taps with your toes. I do it all the time.'

'You do?' he said faintly.

'It's quite easy really, and Mrs Fuller would probably have been fine if she hadn't added so much bubble bath to the water and made the bath slippery.' Hannah frowned.

'Actually, it's something I'd better remember myself. I tend to be a bit heavy-handed, too, when it comes to bubble bath.'

Robert wished she hadn't said that. He *really* wished she hadn't said that. He was already having a hard enough time trying to crush down the image which had sprung into his mind of Hannah naked in a bath. Hannah pink and glowing. Hannah with little droplets of water running down between—

And now she'd gone and added bubbles to his mental picture. White, frothy bubbles that probably clung, and slid, and—

'I presume the fire brigade have cut off the tap at its base?' he said quickly.

She nodded. 'They're suggesting we try using something called a whizzer saw. Apparently it has a diamond tip and they use it for cutting through steel rings, but its main drawback is we'd have to turn off any oxygen in the vicinity.'

'I know,' Robert replied. 'I've used one before.'

'You have?' Hannah said in amazement. 'I didn't realise so many people got their big toes stuck up taps.'

'They don't. The particular case I worked on wasn't a tap, and it wasn't attached to the patient's toe, but it did require a whizzer saw to remove it.'

Something about the pinkness of his cheeks made Hannah decide she'd rather not know what he'd removed, and from where, and instead she said, 'Would you come and take a look at Mrs Fuller, and see what we can do?'

Judging by Mrs Fuller's mortified expression as he strode through the cubicle curtains, Robert thought the new bride would have been quite happy if he'd suggested amputating her toe.

'I have never been so embarrassed in all my life,' she wailed while her husband patted her hand soothingly. 'The indignity of it. Carried out of the honeymoon suite and down through the hotel lobby on a stretcher by the fire brigade—'

'It would have been all right if you hadn't sat up and told everyone you weren't ill,' her husband pointed out. 'People would have been sympathetic.'

'And they would have thought I'd had a stroke or a heart attack,' she protested. 'I couldn't let them think that. It would have been a wicked thing to do.'

'So we got all the comments instead,' he said with sigh. '"Cor!" and "That must have been some wedding night!" being the only ones I'd care to repeat in mixed company.'

Hannah bit down hard on her lip, and said a little unsteadily, 'Would it be worth applying some ice, do you think?'

Robert shook his head. 'It's the toe inside the tap that's swollen, and applying ice to the rest of the foot isn't going to help. I'm afraid it's going to have to be the whizzer saw.'

It sounded terrifying. It looked even worse when Robert switched it on. And when he brought it down on the tap and a great plume of sparks shot up into the air, Hannah could see why the fire brigade had insisted that all oxygen in the vicinity had to be switched off.

Being blown to bits clearly wasn't of the utmost concern to Mrs Fuller. She let out a scream that all but shattered Hannah's eardrums, sat bolt upright on the trolley and shrieked, 'Switch it off! I've changed my mind! I'll live with the tap—buy bigger shoes, go barefoot!'

'It's going to be all right, Mrs Fuller,' Hannah declared, holding her firmly. 'Dr Cunningham knows what he's doing.' At least she hoped he did. 'It will only take a few minutes…'

It did, but it seemed like an eternity before Robert straightened up with a pleased smile.

'One tap   slightly the worse for wear, I'm afraid—removed as promised,' he announced, holding it out to Mrs Fuller.

Mrs Fuller looked as though she didn't know whether to laugh or cry, and opted for blowing her nose instead. 'I'm so sorry, Doctor. Screaming, and bawling, and carrying on like that—'

'There's absolutely no need to apologise,' Robert interrupted. 'I doubt if anyone would have sat quietly while somebody took a saw to their foot. How does the toe feel?'

'Sore,' she admitted.

'Can you move it at all?' he asked.

She could, and luckily it didn't appear as though she had suffered any lasting damage. Her foot would be pretty painful for a few days if she tried to put any weight on it, but apart from that she'd survived unscathed from her ordeal with the tap.

'I bet she never tries to turn off a tap with her toes again,' Jane said when Mr and Mrs Fuller had gone, taking the remnants of the bath tap with them as a souvenir. 'Can't you just imagine the kind of ribbing they're going to get for the rest of their honeymoon?'

'The fire chief told me the hotel is actually going to charge them for damage to the honeymoon suite,' Hannah said in disbelief. 'OK, so maybe she's wrecked the bath, but most honeymooners don't spend their wedding night in the bath, do they?'

Robert didn't suppose they did, but it certainly opened up a whole array of interesting thoughts. Thoughts he'd far rather not have, he decided as he felt a tide of dark colour creeping up the back of his neck.

'Something I can do for you, Kelly?' he asked, noticing the student nurse hovering nearby, clearly trying to attract his attention.

'It's the patient in cubicle 7, Dr Cunningham,' she began as Jane walked away, still laughing about Mrs Fuller's predicament. 'Dr Mathieson says he's just suffering from minor cuts and bruises—the man was mugged, you see—but…'

'But?' Robert pressed, confused as Kelly's voice trailed away into silence.

'The thing is…' The student nurse gazed unhappily up at him. 'The thing is, he's got Aids, Dr Cunningham, and Dr Mathieson has asked me to clean his cuts, and—'

'And if you put on a pair of latex gloves while you're treating him, the chances of you catching it are nil unless you feel there's a danger you might suddenly be seized by an overwhelming desire to make love to him!' Robert said tartly.

Scarlet colour swept over Kelly's face and bright tears shimmered in her eyes. 'I know that, Doctor, but, you see, my brother—he died last year of Aids. It's one of the reasons I decided to become a nurse, and the patient—Mr Seller—seeing him, it reminds me—'

'Why didn't you say so in the first place?' Robert asked quickly, compassion and sympathy plain on his face. 'I'll look after him for you—'

'I'll do it, Robert,' Hannah broke in. 'You're just going off duty.'

'So are you,' he pointed out, glancing up at the treatment-room clock.

'Yes, but it will only take me half an hour—'

'Fifteen minutes if we share,' he interrupted. 'And I bet I've got more experience of Aids patients than you do,' he added as a clincher.

No amount of experience was going to help Colin Seller, Hannah thought as she gazed sadly down at the young man's ravaged body. In fact, she doubted if anything could. He had all the classic outward symptoms of advanced Aids, and it wasn't a pretty sight. Small, fluid-filled blisters—herpes simplex covered his face, and Kaposi's sarcoma—

tumours consisting of blue-red nodules—had already begun to appear on his feet, legs and arms.

'I understand you've been mugged, Mr Seller?' she said, gently beginning to clean the cuts on his face and arms.

He nodded. 'Crazy, isn't it? You'd think it would have been obvious to anyone that I don't have any money.'

It should have been. Colin Seller's clothes might be clean and neat but they were obviously old and his shoes had holes in them.

'Your Aids,' she continued as Robert began removing the dirt from the cuts in Colin Seller's legs. 'What sort of medication are you taking to keep it under control?'

The man shrugged. 'No point in controlling it. It's going to kill me eventually so why postpone the inevitable?'

'But if you don't take any medication—'

'The tumours will affect my gastrointestinal and respiratory tracts, causing severe internal bleeding, and lymphoma of the brain. And if I'm real lucky I might get toxoplasmosis which can lead to lung and heart damage and severe encephalitis.' Colin Seller smiled as Hannah stared at him, open-mouthed. 'I've got Aids, Doctor. That doesn't mean I'm brainless. At least not yet.'

'Then why don't you take the drugs we can give you?' she protested. 'OK, so they may not be able to cure you, but at least we might be able to keep you alive until we can find a cure.'

'Doctor, I've lost my lover to Aids, my family have disowned me, and I've no job, no home, no nothing. Sometimes…sometimes living just gets too painful, and you'd prefer not do it any more.'

She put down the piece of gauze she'd been using and clasped the young man's hand in her own. 'I'm sorry. I know that's a really dumb and inadequate thing to say, but I'm truly, truly sorry.'

Colin Seller clearly didn't think it was dumb, and neither did Robert as he stared across at her.

She meant it, he realised. She wasn't just mouthing the stock set of comforting phrases they all learnt at med school. Hannah truly meant it.

Laura hadn't possessed one tenth of the compassion of this girl. She might have been the most brilliant junior doctor he'd ever met, but personal success had meant everything to her, and the emotional needs of her patients had come a very poor second.

And not just her patients' emotional needs, he remembered with a twist of pain. The night she'd died he'd accused her of wanting the acclaim and fame that medicine could bring more than she wanted him, and she'd told him that even if he was content to work for the rest of his life in a run-down dump like St Stephen's, she wasn't. And it had been then that he'd told her he wanted a divorce. Then that he'd known their marriage was over, and that it should never have occurred in the first place.

'I think it's time you went home, Hannah,' he said with an effort, hearing the babble of voices outside that heralded the arrival of the night staff. 'It will only take me a couple of minutes to finish up in here.'

'But—'

'Home, Hannah,' he insisted, leading her purposefully towards the cubicle curtains. 'It's late, and you've done enough.'

'But—'

'You do what the man says, Doctor.' Colin Seller grinned, his cruelly disfigured face lighting up with amusement. 'Seems to me like you need someone to take care of you.'

It seemed that way to Robert, too, but he couldn't be that man, and he knew he couldn't.

'I just wish there was something more we could do for

him,' Hannah sighed as Robert propelled her through the curtains.

'I think you already have,' he murmured.

'I know it's his choice not to take any medication,' she continued as though Robert hadn't spoken, 'but if there was only something else we could do. Something that would make him a little more comfortable.'

'Perhaps there is. Now, off you go,' he concluded, giving her a gentle nudge. 'And no more taking long walks on your own, remember?'

'Aye-aye, sir,' she replied, standing smartly to attention, and chuckled as she heard the clear sound of his laughter following her out of the treatment room.

It had been an odd day, she decided as she collected her coat and bag from the staffroom. That young girl earlier in the afternoon who could so easily have been paralysed, the honeymoon couple...

Her lips curved as she walked out through the waiting room. The poor girl had been so mortified, and her husband had been terrific. It must be wonderful to have someone care that much for you. To have someone love you so much that only your welfare mattered.

Colin Seller didn't have anyone who cared for him, she thought sadly as she walked out of the hospital, shivering slightly at the contrast in temperatures. She so wished they could have done something for him, something to help him, but she couldn't think what.

You're a doctor, Hannah, not a social worker, she told herself firmly as she turned up her coat collar against the falling sleet. You can only do what you can do. But as she paused at the kerb she suddenly noticed that Robert was crossing the street ahead of her, and a slight frown creased her forehead.

He was walking oddly, skirting the icy puddles, carefully avoiding the potholes in the road, and as she continued to watch him she suddenly saw why. He wasn't wearing any shoes.

He'd given them to Colin Seller. She knew without a shadow of a doubt that he'd given them to the young man, and a hard lump formed in her throat as she stared after him, watching his painful progress, his head bent low against the biting wind. There *had* been something they could do for Colin Seller, and Robert had done it. Not given him a long lecture on the importance of taking his drugs, or a reprimand for failing to do so, but given him something which showed that somebody cared about his welfare.

And it was in that split second that she suddenly realised something else. Something she should have known before—perhaps *had* known before—and hadn't wanted to admit.

She'd fallen in love with Robert Cunningham. Somehow, some way, she'd managed to fall in love with this difficult, prickly, oh, so nice man, but the trouble was, she didn't know what she was going to do about it.

CHAPTER SEVEN

'MR MAITLAND was brought in by his wife about ten minutes ago,' Robert explained as Hannah accompanied him down the treatment room. 'He has a high fever, stiff neck and also seems to be slightly confused and disorientated. His wife is terrified he has meningitis.'

Hannah nodded. Even the word was enough to strike terror into most people's hearts, but it didn't need to. If the condition was diagnosed early, the prognosis for a full recovery was usually excellent.

'Nobody is really certain what causes meningitis, are they?' she observed. 'All we know for certain is that an infection must have entered the cerebrospinal fluid which surrounds and protects the brain and spinal cord.'

'That's right.'

'And you're going to do a spinal tap to see if Mr Maitland's cerebrospinal fluid is infected?'

Robert smiled as he led the way into cubicle 5. 'No, I'm not. You are.'

She stumbled in dismay as she followed him. She'd thought he was going to show her how the procedure was done, not that she was going to do it herself. She was sure that's what he'd said. 'Robert, I really don't think—'

'Any change in Mr Maitland's condition, Flo?' he asked, completely ignoring Hannah's panic-stricken appeal.

'No deterioration that I can see,' the staff nurse replied.

'Good, good.' He nodded. 'OK, Hannah, we've anaesthetised the skin overlying the lumbar vertebrae so what I want you to do first is to press your thumb into the middle of Mr Maitland's back, then gradually move your thumb down the bony prominences.'

Robert quite clearly wasn't going to take no for an answer—not when he was already holding the box of latex gloves out to her—and reluctantly she took a pair, and even more reluctantly pulled them on.

'What am I looking for when I'm moving my thumb down Mr Maitland's back?' she asked.

'The undulations of the spinal column as you get nearer to his buttocks.'

'The undulations?' Hannah repeated.

'Each one is a single vertebra, and we're looking for the third and fourth, which are just above the base of the spine. Look, let me help you,' he continued, moving behind her and placing his hand over hers as she gazed uncertainly up at him. 'The secret is not to be too tentative. You can't possibly hurt bone simply by pressing it.'

She knew that, but she also knew it would have been considerably easier for her to concentrate if it hadn't been Robert showing her the technique. If it hadn't been his hand guiding hers, and his subtle aftershave she could smell, and his chest resting against her back.

How had she fallen in love with this man? Why had she fallen in love with him? She didn't know him—not really— but she knew with absolute certainty that it wasn't simply a physical attraction she felt for him any more. She cared about him. She worried about him. And she wanted to see him smiling and happy, instead of sad and strained all the time.

'I—I can feel the vertebrae,' she stammered, deliberately not looking up at him. 'What do I do now?'

A hollow, very fine needle appeared before her eyes.

'Insert this between the third and fourth vertebrae to pierce the meninges that covers the spinal cord, and extract some fluid for analysis.'

This time she did look up at him, but in total panic. What if she put the needle in the wrong place? What if she paralysed Mr Maitland?

'You can't do any damage, Hannah,' Robert continued gently, correctly interpreting her expression. 'The spinal cord only goes as far as the lower portion of the middle of the back, and as you'll be inserting the needle into an area well below that, you can't possibly do Mr Maitland any harm.'

That was easy for him to say, she thought as she gingerly inserted the needle. He'd probably done hundreds—OK, maybe nearer dozens—of spinal taps. This was her first.

'I've got it!' she said in amazement as the cerebrospinal fluid shot up into the needle without any effort at all. 'I've actually done it!'

'I said it was easy, didn't I?' he replied, but as she turned and beamed up at him, his heart twisted inside him.

It was his own fault, of course. Offering to help her, using that as a feeble excuse to stand close to her, to hold her lightly, if only for a few seconds. It was the kind of sick ploy someone like Jerry Clark would have used, and if he now felt like hell it was his own just deserts.

Not if you're falling in love with her, his mind whispered, and unconsciously he shook his head.

He wasn't falling in love with her. OK, so he liked her. OK, so he seemed to spend an inordinate amount of his time thinking about her, but that was just physical attraction. Love was for teenagers. Love was just desire and sex wrapped up in a romantic name. He'd been down that road once, and he didn't want to go down it again—ever.

'So, what do we do now?' Hannah asked.

God alone knows, Robert thought, only to realise from her expectant expression that she was referring to something entirely different.

'Flo will send the sample off to the lab,' he said quickly.

'They'll check it out for bacteria and white blood cells, then get back to us.'

'I presume if it *is* meningitis, it's going to be meningococcal?' Hannah remarked as she followed him out of the cubicle. 'At thirty-eight, Mr Maitland's not likely to have contracted pneumococcal meningitis, although I understand—'

She didn't get the chance to say what she understood because the doors of the treatment room suddenly slammed open and a young man appeared, wide-eyed, sweating and dishevelled.

'Can somebody help me, please?' he yelled. 'My wife— she's out in the van, and she's in labour!'

Hannah was halfway through the waiting room, clutching the obs kit, before she realised Robert was with her.

'I thought maybe two heads might be better than one,' he said with a grin. 'I mean, childbirth isn't exactly our speciality, is it?'

It wasn't, and when Hannah clambered into the back of the van and saw the young man's wife, her legs wide apart and the top of a little dark head protruding from her vagina, she was more than relieved to have Robert with her.

'Just as well I told Jane to page the labour ward,' Robert observed, pulling off his sweater and rolling up his sleeves. 'It looks as though mum's cut it a bit fine.'

A bit fine was right. With a sharp cry the woman suddenly bore down heavily, and Robert only just got his hands up in time to catch the tiny scrap of humanity as it shot out of its mother.

'My baby?' the woman gasped, trying to lever herself upright. 'Is my baby all right?'

'She's fine,' Robert replied, wrapping the baby in his sweater after Hannah had clamped and cut the cord. 'You have a beautiful baby daughter.'

And she was beautiful, Hannah thought, staring down

into a pair of enormous blue eyes. Wet and bloody, but bright-eyed and alert, and quite, quite beautiful.

'I think you've got a fan there,' she commented, seeing the baby snuggle into Robert's chest as members of the labour ward arrived and whisked the mother away to the delivery room to deliver the placenta.

He shook his head wryly. 'I'm afraid she's labouring under a grave misapprehension. My sole contribution to her arrival in the world was to catch her as she shot past.'

'Yes, but, boy, what a catch.' Hannah laughed, then glanced around with a slight frown. 'What happened to the father?'

'He keeled over the moment you dashed out of the treatment room. Kelly's probably reviving him with tea and sympathy even as we speak.'

She chuckled. 'Poor man. I bet he'll never forget his daughter's arrival.' She tickled the little girl under her chin. 'She is lovely, isn't she?'

'Yes. Yes, she is.'

Robert's voice was soft, husky, but when she glanced up at him he wasn't looking at the baby at all, but at her.

Did he mean he found her attractive, desirable? Did he mean what she hoped—oh, how she hoped—he meant? Her breath seemed to be wedged somewhere in the centre of her chest but she managed an uncertain smile. 'They say… People say…all babies are beautiful.'

'Do they?' he murmured, his eyes catching and holding hers. 'Then I guess…if everyone says that…'

She couldn't have looked away if she'd tried She couldn't have moved if she'd wanted to. Something in his eyes—something that sent a quiver of sensation running through her body—held her rooted to the spot, and when he cleared his throat huskily, she held her breath expectantly.

'Hannah—'

'Dr Cunningham, this is *most* unprofessional!' Sister
Strachan from the special care baby unit declared, appearing in front of them without warning. 'It's well below freez-
ing out here and this…' She fingered Robert's sweater with
clear distaste. 'This is hardly adequate clothing for a new-
born.'

'You're perfectly right,' he replied as she held out her
arms and reluctantly he handed the baby to her. 'I'm sorry,
Sister.'

'Name?'

He gazed at her in confusion. 'Dr Robert Cunningham.
Special registrar, A and E—'

'The *baby's* name, Doctor,' Sister Strachan interrupted
in exasperation. 'All kinds of complications can arise in
SCBU if we don't know this little mite's surname.'

Robert looked even more shamefaced. 'I don't think we
actually got the baby's surname, did we, Dr Blake?'

Sister Strachan's eyes rolled heavenwards when Hannah
shook her head, and with a look that spoke volumes she
clutched the baby to her ample bosom and strode away,
muttering darkly.

'Bang goes my credibility in SCBU for the foreseeable
future,' Robert sighed as he led the way back into A and
E.

'Maybe she might forgive us if we send up little Miss
No Name's father once he's recovered from the shock?'
Hannah suggested.

He shook his head and laughed. 'Not a hope, I'm afraid.
We're dead ducks as far as Sister Strachan is concerned.'

Hannah laughed, too, but as she followed him back into
the treatment room her main emotion was frustration.
Somehow she sensed that he'd been about to say something
momentous just before Sister Strachan had interrupted him,
and now the moment had been lost. And not just lost. She
had the depressing feeling it would never come again.

'Mr Maitland's results are back from the lab,' Jane said the minute she saw Robert, 'and you'll be pleased to know it's negative on the meningitis. Looks like he's simply got a very bad case of the flu, but do you want me to arrange for him to go up to the medical ward for observation?'

Robert nodded.

'A successful birth, and a good result for Mr Maitland,' Hannah declared. 'Hey, maybe this is going to be one of our better days.'

'Never, *ever* say that, Hannah,' Jane protested in dismay. 'The minute anyone says that in A and E, you can be sure the floodgates will open.'

And they did. Within half an hour the waiting room was packed, and Robert and Hannah were desperately attempting to extract information from a very drowsy and equally belligerent overdose patient.

'Why don't you just go away and leave me alone?' the woman flared as Robert tried to find out what pills she'd taken. 'I don't want you to help me! I just want to die!'

'Won't you at least tell us when you took the pills?' Hannah said coaxingly. 'Was it an hour ago—two hours—longer?'

'Sod off, why don't you?' the woman retorted. 'Just sod off, and leave me alone!'

'Alcohol as well as pills, from the smell of her breath,' Robert observed. 'Can't whoever brought her in give us any information?'

Jane shook her head. 'All her boyfriend knows is that they had a huge row last night and when he went round to their flat to collect his clothes he found her in the bathroom, clutching an empty pill bottle.'

'Which he didn't think to bring in with him.' Robert sighed. 'OK, Jane, get me a sample for a blood alcohol level, a toxic screen to identify what she's taken and a CBC and ECG. If she's taken any of the tricyclic antidepressants they can play havoc with the heart rhythm.'

'Are you going to try to make her vomit?' Hannah asked, knowing that they couldn't wait for the results of any of the tests Robert had ordered but had to immediately attempt to prevent the digestion and absorption of any pills the woman had taken.

Robert shook his head. 'God only knows when she took her overdose, and if she took it more than two hours ago any pills will already be in her intestines and making her vomit won't help at all.'

Which meant they would have to use the tube. It was an unpleasant and uncomfortable enough procedure on a patient who wanted to be helped, but on someone who decided to fight them it proved to be a nightmare.

'Leave me alone!' she shrieked, lashing out with her hands and feet as Jane tried to insert the tube into her mouth. 'I don't want you to help me. I want to die. Do you hear me? I *want* to die!'

'I know you do, but I'm afraid we're not going to let you,' Robert said grimly, clasping hold of her arms. 'Keep going, Jane, Hannah.'

It was easier said than done, Hannah thought wryly as she and Jane tried to ease the tube into the woman's mouth, down through her oesophagus and into her stomach. It was like dealing with a writhing eel, a writhing eel with lethal flailing feet as she soon discovered when one caught her in the stomach and sent her flying back against the cubicle wall to land in an undignified heap on the floor.

'Are you OK, Hannah?' Robert demanded with concern.

Gingerly she got to her feet and rubbed her bottom. 'A case of hurt dignity, that's all.'

'You're sure?' he insisted, but when she nodded he turned to the woman on the trolley, his face grim 'Now listen to me, and listen good. We're going to get those pills out of you whether you like it or not. If you choose to do something stupid like this again after you're discharged, that's your prerogative, but at the moment you are in our care and we are damned well going to help you, whether you want it or not!'

Whether his outburst had stunned her or whether the woman had just grown tired of fighting them was unclear, but she didn't say another word as Jane and Hannah slipped the tube down into her stomach and began the unpleasant task of sucking up any pill fragments.

And it was unpleasant. Not only did they have to suction the remnants of the pills away, they then had to clean out the woman's stomach by pouring water down the tube followed by a slush of charcoal to absorb any remaining medication.

'What will happen to her now?' Hannah asked when the results from the lab confirmed that, though their patient had taken Valium mixed with alcohol, her CBC was fine.

'We'll send her up to IC to ensure she doesn't slip into respiratory or cardiac failure,' Robert replied, stripping off his latex gloves and binning them. 'Once they're happy with her she'll be referred to a psychiatric ward for evaluation.'

Hannah sighed as she watched the woman being wheeled out of the treatment room. 'It must be truly awful to feel your life isn't worth living.'

'Yes.'

She glanced round at him quickly. His answer had been low, scarcely audible, and his face was dark, shadowed. Did he feel that way, too? Had he loved his wife so much that he felt his own life wasn't worth living?

'Robert—'

He was already walking away from her, and as she stared after him she couldn't help a wistful sigh escaping from her—a sigh she speedily smothered when she heard Elliot's deep chuckle behind her.

'Really smitten, aren't you, love?'

Hot colour flooded her cheeks. 'I don't know what you're talking about.'

'Yeah, and my other leg's got bells on it!' he exclaimed. 'Does he know how you feel?'

For a second she considered lying, but Elliot was a friend, a good friend, and whatever else he was he most certainly wasn't a gossip. 'I don't think he even knows I exist.' She sighed.

'You really think that?' he said in surprise.

She nodded sadly. 'I'm the kid. Little Miss Muffet.'

'Little Miss Muffet?' Elliot repeated, bewildered.

'It's a long story, Elliot. Let's just say I know what I'm talking about.'

'Hannah, I don't think you do. In fact—'

'RTA on the way, folks!' Mary on Reception called urgently from the office door. 'Mother and three kids. The kids look to be in the worse shape!'

They were, and once Mr Mackay and Robert had stabilised them sufficiently to be moved, they were immediately sent off by ambulance to the Royal Sick Children's where they would receive more specialist care.

'Mrs Ogilvie seems to have got off amazingly lightly— just cuts and bruises,' Hannah observed when Robert joined her outside cubicle 8. 'I've got her on an IV line to counteract the possible effects of shock, and Jane's linked her to the ECG machine as a precaution.'

'Good work.' He nodded approvingly. 'Any sign of chest damage from the steering-wheel?'

'None at all. Like I said, when you consider her car skidded straight into a wall, she's had a miraculous escape. How are her children? She keeps asking about them, and I've been fobbing her off.'

'Keep on fobbing her off. The last I heard they were all stable, but things can change very fast, and the less stress she has to bear at the moment the better.'

Hannah nodded. 'Apparently she was driving her children over to her mother's for the afternoon. Has anyone telephoned Mrs Ludlow yet? According to Gwen Ogilvie, Grandma gets panicky if they're even ten minutes late—'

'Hannah—Robert!' Jane suddenly yelled from inside the cubicle. 'I've got no pulse!'

No pulse? Hannah's eyes flew to Robert's. But that meant…that meant…

Without a word they dashed through the cubicle curtains. Jane had already started CPR and swiftly Hannah and Robert inserted an endotracheal tube. They had to get Gwen's heart beating again, but first they had to make sure that sufficient oxygen was reaching her brain.

'Ventilator linked—still no BP or pulse!' Jane announced, her face grim.

'Epi. push intravenously,' Robert demanded, and the moment the epinephrine was added to the IV line he picked up the defibrillator paddles. 'OK, everyone stand clear!'

Obediently Jane and Hannah stepped back from the trolley and quickly Robert placed the paddles on Gwen Ogilvie's chest. Her body arched and convulsed as the electricity surged through her body, but the ECG monitor remained resolutely flat.

'Lidocaine!' he called.

The drug was swiftly added to the IV line, then they all stepped away from the trolley again as Robert upped the voltage on the defibrillator to 360.

It didn't do any good. Nothing did any good. They gave Gwen Ogilvie every drug at their disposal to try to kick-start her heart, but still nothing happened, and eventually Robert switched off the defibrillator and threw down the paddles.

'OK, that's it, folks,' he muttered. 'We gave it our best shot, but…' He glanced across at Hannah who was staring down at Gwen Ogilvie's inert body. 'Are you OK, Hannah?'

'Yes…yes, of course I am,' she replied.

She wasn't. Robert could see very well she wasn't. There was a dazed, disbelieving look about her eyes, the look all junior doctors wore when they encountered their first failure, and his heart went out to her.

'Hannah, listen…' He paused and frowned. All too clearly he could hear the sound of their receptionist outside in the treatment room, pleading, cajoling, and the sound of a man's raised voice angrily, arguing back. 'What the hell's going on out there?'

Hannah neither knew nor cared, but she obediently followed him out of the cubicle, to find their receptionist desperately attempting to restrain a young man in his mid-thirties.

'Robert, I'm sorry, but I couldn't stop him,' the receptionist said, her cheeks red, her eyes apologetic. 'It's Eric Ogilvie—Gwen Ogilvie's husband.'

Robert nodded. 'Perhaps you'd like to come with me to one of our waiting rooms, Mr Ogilvie—'

'But the police said you have my wife here,' Eric Ogilvie interrupted, throwing off Robert's hand as he tried to steer him towards the door. 'Where is she? I want to see her!'

'Of course you do,' Robert said quietly, gently but firmly clasping Mr Ogilvie's arm again and motioning to Hannah that she should accompany them. 'I just need to talk to you first.'

And he did. With an understanding and sympathy that brought a hard lump to Hannah's throat, he explained what had happened.

'But you said she wasn't hurt in the crash. He did say

that, didn't he?' Eric said, his eyes swivelling round to Hannah in mute appeal.

'We don't know why she suffered a heart attack,' she said softly. There would be time enough later to tell him there'd have to be a post-mortem. 'Perhaps there was a weakness, and the shock of the accident—'

'But she was always so fit,' Eric protested. 'Never a day's illness. Are you sure you've got the right Gwen Ogilvie? She's small, blonde, with a tiny scar on her left cheek. She fell off a garden swing, you see, when she was six, and it's very distinctive—'

'It *is* your wife, Mr Ogilvie,' Robert said gently. 'Look, is there anyone we can call for you—a relative who could come—?'

'I was supposed to drive the kids over to their grandma this afternoon, but I've got this really lousy cold, and Gwen…' Eric shook his head as though to clear it 'We had a bit of a row before she left—she was worried in case she'd be late for her appointment with the obstetrician.'

'The obstetrician?' Hannah repeated, her heart sinking.

'She's pregnant, three months pregnant. We're hoping it's going to be a girl this time. I suppose I ought to phone—cancel the appointment. Doctors don't like to be kept hanging about, do they? And—'

'Mr Ogilvie—'

'You're sure it's her?' Eric interrupted. 'She's small, you know, with blonde hair and a little scar down the left hand side of her cheek. There must be hundreds of Gwen Ogilvies in the world. It would be so easy to make a mistake…to…to get the wrong girl…'

He was crying now, low strangled sobs that were convulsing his whole frame, and Hannah went to him quickly. She'd never heard a man cry before, never seen one cry, and the worst of it was that there was nothing she could do but hold his shaking body and wish, like Eric Ogilvie, that it had all been a terrible mistake.

She got through the rest of the afternoon on autopilot. I'm fine, she kept telling herself as she sounded people's chests, listened to their symptoms and patched them up as best she could. I'm a doctor, I can cope with this, she kept repeating like a mantra, and wished that somehow she could make herself believe it, and that the hard, cold lump around her heart would go away.

Never had a shift seemed so endless. Never had her nerves felt quite so strained to breaking point, and when she noticed Jerry Clark walking down the corridor towards her as she came out of A and E's small dispensary, she strode on past him without a word.

'Hey, cat got your tongue, beautiful?' he called after her, but when she didn't even pause he hurried after her. 'I hear you had a bit of an accident earlier this afternoon. Fell on your cute little butt, so I hear.'

'I'm busy—'

'We all are, sweetheart, but I just wanted you to know that if you need someone to kiss it better, I'll be only too happy to oblige.'

He was smiling at her with that smile which always made her want to scrub herself down with disinfectant, smirking like some sniggering schoolboy poring over a dirty magazine, and suddenly something snapped inside her.

'Quite frankly, I wouldn't let you kiss the floor I walked on!' she exclaimed, her face white with anger. 'In fact, I'd prefer not to even breathe the same air as you do in future!'

His jaw dropped. 'Hey, it was a joke, Hannah—'

'My name is *Dr Blake*,' she interrupted, unaware that her voice was rising in pitch. 'And let me tell you this. If you don't stop your crass attempts at flirtation, which are as unwelcome as they are revolting, I'm going straight to the head of Human Resources to file an official complaint against you!'

Jerry's eyes narrowed into small slits. 'Now, hold on there a minute Miss High-and-Mighty Blake. There's such a thing as slander—'

'And there's such a thing as sexual harassment, Jerry,' Robert said icily, appearing without warning at the end of the corridor, his face tight. 'I suggest you think about that—think long and hard. Hannah, I need to talk to you in the staffroom if you can spare the time.'

'Talk to me?' she murmured, gazing up at him, bemused and bewildered. 'But I have patients to see. You have patients—'

'And Elliot can manage for a few minutes without us,' he declared, propelling her inexorably towards the staffroom, but by the time they'd reached it she'd already guessed what he wanted to say.

'Robert, you don't need to tell me that I shouldn't have lost my temper—that I should have gone through official channels—'

'Official channels be damned.' He smiled. 'I'd have happily held your coat for you if you'd wanted to sock him.'

'But—'

'Hannah, he had it coming, and if it's any help I'll make damn sure that Radiology sends us a different technician in future.'

'You can do that?' she said faintly.

'You bet your life I can,' he replied. 'In fact, I can personally rearrange Jerry's not so charming features for you if you want, and take the greatest pleasure in doing it.'

She chuckled a little shakily. 'I don't think that's a good idea. In fact, I know it's not, but I appreciate the offer.'

He stared at her thoughtfully for a second, then sat down. 'You could have had this out with Jerry weeks ago. Why now? Why lose your temper now?'

She picked up one of the dog-eared magazines on the coffee-table, then put it down again. 'I guess…I guess he just caught me on the raw. It's been one of those days, you know? I was really worried about doing Mr Maitland's spinal tap, then that lovely baby arrived, and…'

'Gwen Ogilvie,' he finished for her gently.

She didn't want to talk about Gwen Ogilvie. She'd spent the whole afternoon determinedly not thinking about Gwen Ogilvie, but suddenly the words started tumbling jerkily out of her.

'I was talking to her before you arrived. She was telling me all about her children, the schools they went to, how Duncan—that's her eldest boy—was becoming really cheeky and she was getting worried about him. We were talking just like two ordinary, normal people, and then…and then…'

'Hannah—'

'Why, Robert? *Why?*' She hiccuped as the hard lump around her heart cracked, and tears began to spill down her cheeks despite her best efforts to prevent them. 'She wasn't much older than me. She had so much to live for—her husband, her children, the new baby coming. Why did she have to die when other people—horrible, dreadful people—survive?'

'I don't know.'

The admission sounded as though it had been dragged from somewhere deep inside him and her eyes flew to his face with horror. His wife. How could she have forgotten that his wife had died in St Stephen's after a road accident? That he'd been on duty when they'd brought her in?

'Oh, God, I'm sorry—so sorry!' she gasped, dragging a hand roughly across her wet cheeks. 'And I accused Jerry of crassness—of insensitivity. Your wife—Laura…'

'It's all right, Hannah.'

'No, it's not!' she protested. 'It isn't all right. I should have thought. Every time an RTA comes in, you must remember, it must bring it all back.'

It did, but not in the way Hannah meant. Oh, he remembered the impotence he'd felt as he'd watched Laura slipping away from him despite all his skill. The rage he'd felt at her dying. But most of all he remembered the guilt. The unbearable guilt of knowing she would still have been alive if it hadn't been for him. She would still have been alive if he hadn't married her and discovered it had been a huge mistake, then demanded a divorce.

'I'm so sorry, Robert,' Hannah said again, and he saw the sympathy in her large brown eyes and couldn't bear it.

He didn't want her sympathy, he deserved none. It was his fault Laura was dead. His fault she was lying in that cold grave.

But as he continued to stare at Hannah he realised something else. It wasn't simply sympathy he saw in her eyes. There was love there, too. Love and need. A love and need he knew he felt as well, despite all his attempts to deny it, and his heart contracted with pain.

He didn't want to fall in love again. He didn't want this lovely, vulnerable girl to be in love with him. He'd hurt her as he'd hurt Laura—he knew he would—and because he knew that, he determinedly forced a careless, dismissive smile to his face.

'Far worse things have happened to other people. I'll survive.'

'But you must miss her dreadfully,' she murmured, her eyes still shimmering with unshed tears.

'Good heavens, no,' he replied with a casual negligence that tore at his heart. 'It happened over a year ago, and there's no sense or point in wallowing in grief.'

The sympathy that had been in her eyes was instantly replaced by shock and disapproval. Which was exactly

what he'd wanted, he told himself as she blew her nose
and hastily made her excuses.

Only a fool wouldn't have learned from bitter experience. Only a fool would let his heart rule his head. And if
he felt something wither and die inside him as she disappeared out of the staffroom without a backward glance, it
was for the best. Better for her to be hurt now than later.
Far, far better.

CHAPTER EIGHT

'I SHOULDN'T laugh—I really, really shouldn't,' Hannah said, 'but—'

'You can't think of anyone who looks less like Superman?' Floella suggested, her lips twitching, as they watched their portly patient being wheeled out of the treatment room, the remnants of his Superman costume lying in pieces at his feet.

Hannah nodded unsteadily. 'The poor man. He was trying so hard to be romantic for his wife's birthday, and now he's going to be in traction for weeks with that slipped disc.'

'His wife didn't think it was particularly romantic,' Jane observed, her grey eyes dancing. 'Not when he got stuck halfway between the roof of their garden shed and bedroom with that box of chocolates in his mouth.'

'And the fire brigade didn't think it was very romantic either when they had to rescue him,' Floella gurgled. 'In fact, they said it was the best laugh they'd had in years. The poor man's never going to live it down. He'll probably have to move house, leave town—'

'And if you three have got nothing better to do than stand around gossiping all evening, perhaps Mr Mackay and I should take a long hard look at our staffing requirements!' Robert snapped as he strode past them.

Hannah bit her lip, Jane flushed crimson and Floella spluttered with indignation as Robert disappeared into the office.

'I've had it!' she exclaimed. 'I really have had it! I know he's always expected high standards from us—and quite right, too—and I know he has a quick temper, but these last two weeks have been impossible. You only have to smile and you get your head bitten off!'

'And I was beginning to think he didn't look quite so stressed,' Jane sighed. 'That he was starting to ease up on his workload, but…'

'Someone is going to have to talk to him,' Floella said firmly. 'Working in A and E is hard enough, without having to tiptoe around your special reg, especially when you haven't got the faintest idea why you're tiptoeing around him in the first place!'

Hannah nodded absently, only to suddenly realise that two pairs of eyes were fixed expectantly on her. 'Oh, no—no way—not me! I'm just the junior doctor, the new kid on the block.'

'Yes, but he likes you,' Jane urged. 'In fact, you're the only person he hasn't been appallingly rude to recently.'

'Give him time,' Hannah said ruefully. 'Look, if you're so worried about him, why don't you speak to Mr Mackay, the department consultant? He's the boss—'

'And about as much use for something like this as a wet flannel,' Floella said. 'You'd be so much better, Hannah. He likes you, as Jane said, and—'

'No,' Hannah interrupted firmly. 'I'm sorry, but there's no way I'm going to talk to him—no way!'

And she couldn't, she thought as she walked quickly down the treatment room. How could she speak to a man who was doing his level best to avoid her? How could she possibly have any kind of conversation with someone who spent the whole time fidgeting with his watch, examining his tie and looking everywhere but at her?

And it had been like that ever since Gwen Ogilvie's death. Since he'd told her, quite callously and dismissively, that he never thought about his wife.

She didn't believe him. Oh, she'd been shocked and horrified at the time, but the more she'd thought about it, the more she'd become convinced that he'd deliberately set out to make her think the worst of him.

And yet why in the world would anyone want to do that? It didn't make any sense. In fact, nothing about Robert Cunningham made sense at the moment, she thought in confusion, turning in answer to Jane's urgent call.

'RTA on the way, Hannah! ETA, five minutes, and it looks like a bad one!'

It was. In fact, it was by far the worst road accident Hannah had ever seen.

'How on earth did that happen?' she said with horror as the paramedics carefully transferred their casualty onto the examination trolley and she saw the two-foot steel bar imbedded in his chest.

'Mr Ingram was on his way to collect his kid from a Hallowe'en party when he hit some ice on the motorway and collided with the crash barriers,' one of the paramedics replied. 'His seat belt snapped, he went straight through the windscreen—'

'And part of the crash barrier ended up imbedded in his chest,' Robert finished grimly as he, Floella and Jane joined them. 'What's his GCS?'

'Two-two-five.'

A score of 8 or lower on the Glasgow coma scale meant you had very serious injuries indeed and, at 9, Trevor Ingram was much too close for comfort. There was no way they could remove the metal bar—that was a job for the operating-theatre staff—but if they didn't stabilise him quickly, the young man wouldn't even reach the theatre.

'Intubation?' Hannah declared, immediately reaching for an endotracheal tube to replace the ambu-bag the paramedics had been using, but Robert shook his head.

'Not with those facial injuries. I doubt if you'd be able to see clearly enough into his mouth to be sure of getting the tube down his throat and into his trachea. I'll have to do a crike.'

A cricothyrotomy. A delicate and precise procedure which involved making a vertical incision into the throat, followed by a horizontal cut into the cricothyroid membrane. A breathing tube was then inserted into the hole and attached to the ventilator, but in inexperienced hands a lot could go wrong. You could put the tube in the wrong place, even sever one of the big arteries in the oesophagus, and if you did that then your patient was in mega-trouble.

'BP dropping,' Floella warned after Robert had performed the cricothyrotomy, making the whole procedure look like child's play. 'Sixty over forty.'

'And he doesn't seem to have any breath sounds on the right side,' Hannah advised, listening carefully to Trevor Ingram's chest through her stethoscope.

Air was seeping into the young man's chest with every breath he took but it wasn't going out again, and a large bubble of air was compressing the collapsed lung on his right side. Unless they relieved the tension pneumothorax, Trevor Ingram's heart, and the great blood vessels surrounding it, would eventually become so compressed that no pumping action would be possible, and no blood would reach his brain.

'ECG status, Jane?' Robert demanded.

'Jumping around a bit, but not worryingly so.'

He nodded and quickly stabbed a needle into the young man's chest. The trapped air was released almost immediately, but though Trevor's trachea started to shift back to the middle of his neck, a chest tube would have to be inserted to help re-expand his lung.

'O-negative up and running, Robert,' Floella called.

'OK, get me a CBC, urine sample and guiac test. I'll want chest, neck and pelvis X-rays as well. Hannah—chest tube, please.'

Did he mean she was to insert it? It certainly looked that way, and carefully she made a small incision into Trevor Ingram's chest down into the lining around his lung. With equal care she then inserted the tube, which would suck out the blood and air and eventually reinflate the young man's lung.

'BP rising,' Jane announced, 'but we can't get the IVs in, Robert. His veins won't take them.'

Robert swore under his breath. Without IV lines to provide the fluids needed to temporarily replace the blood Trevor Ingram was losing, there was no way they could support his blood pressure while they attempted to bring his bleeding under control.

'I'm going to have to go for a central line directly into the internal subclavian veins in his neck,' Robert declared.

It required great skill to do that without hitting a major artery, but with an ease Hannah could only admire Robert soon had the central line inserted.

God, he was good, she thought enviously. Nothing threw him, nothing disturbed him. OK, so perhaps he'd been a little—all right, then, very—difficult to work with lately, but he was still the best special registrar in the business. And the kindest, she added mentally as Craig Larkin arrived to take the X-rays they needed.

Robert had been as good as his word about contacting Radiology to tell them Jerry Clark was no longer welcome in A and E. Craig Larkin had taken his place the very next day—calm, efficient and utterly professional—and he was now an accepted member of the team. What Jerry thought of the change was anybody's guess, and Hannah neither knew nor cared.

But she did care about the man standing opposite her, oblivious to everything apart from the patient in his charge. Cared deeply and desperately, but from the distant way he'd been treating her since Gwen Ogilvie's death she'd been forced to come to the depressing conclusion that her feelings weren't reciprocated.

'No blood in the urine or guiac test, Robert,' Jane declared, 'and the CBC results suggest we're winning.'

They were when Floella finally announced Trevor Ingram's BP was 95 over 60.

It wasn't a wonderful blood pressure, but at least it meant they'd stabilised him sufficiently to be sent to the operating theatre where the difficult task of removing the metal bar from his chest could begin.

'Well done, everybody,' Robert said, pulling off his latex gloves and running his fingers through his damp hair. 'That was good work.'

It was. Good, united teamwork. The kind of work Hannah had always dreamt, hoped, she'd be a part of and, though she felt completely drained, she felt elated, too.

'Do you think he'll make it, Robert?' she asked as Trevor Ingram was wheeled out of the treatment room, the IV bags swinging above him.

'It all depends upon what they find when they remove the steel bar,' he said, rubbing the back of his neck wearily. 'I hope he makes it. After what he's been through, he certainly deserves to.'

'If I'd been through what he has, I'd want to keep a part of that crash barrier as a souvenir,' she observed.

'If it were me I'd have it mounted permanently on my dashboard as a reminder to slow down the next time there's icy weather,' he replied.

She chuckled, and for a second—an infinitesimal second—saw the beginnings of an answering smile curve his lips. Then it was gone.

'Right— Yes, well, this certainly isn't getting on with the work,' he declared brusquely, and before she could say a word he walked away, leaving her gazing unhappily after him.

Was this how it was going to be from now on? Conversations limited to a simple 'yes' or a 'no' unless it was something to do with work? Shared smiles out of the question because they suggested a familiarity and friendship that didn't exist?

It had all been so different two weeks ago when little Miss No Name had been born. Then she'd felt a closeness to him, a bond she'd believed he felt as well, and yet now…

Now she would infinitely have preferred Robert to have been as sharp with her as he was with everyone else in the department. At least it would have been better than this cool distancing. At least it would have shown he recognised she was alive, that she was there.

'I take it things aren't going well in the romance stakes?' Elliot murmured softly as he joined her.

'You could say that,' she replied through a throat so tight it hurt.

The SHO sighed. 'Well, all I can say is the guy needs his head examined.'

'I think maybe I'm the one who should be having that done, don't you?' she replied sadly.

'You're far too good for him—he doesn't deserve you,' Elliot declared stoutly. 'In fact, I never could understand what you saw in him in the first place, especially when there was someone like me around.'

She blew her nose and managed a watery smile. 'So you're on offer, are you?'

'I could be if I thought you'd be even remotely interested.' He smiled, and if his smile didn't quite reach his eyes she never noticed. 'Robert *is* in love with you, you know. He may not realise yet—or perhaps want to admit it…'

'So you've got the second sight now, have you?' She couldn't help but chuckle.

'Absolutely,' he replied, his mouth turning up at the corners. 'Not to mention also being modest, shy, retiring—'

'And soon to be made redundant if you don't get back to work!' Robert exclaimed as he strode past them and into cubicle 6.

For a moment Elliot said nothing, then he turned to Hannah, his face rueful. 'All I can say is if he doesn't face up to the fact that he's besotted with you soon, he won't have a member of staff left who's still speaking to him.'

She bit her lip. 'Elliot, it isn't me. I wish it was, but it's not. I don't know what's wrong with him, but his bad temper's got nothing to do with me.'

'If you say so, love,' he said. 'But in the meantime I'm afraid it's back to the grindstone, and roll on eleven o'clock.'

Hannah heartily wished it was eleven o'clock, too, by the time she'd finished examining her next patient—a tiny, frail-looking eighty-five-year-old—who despite her apparent fragility had managed in the space of fifteen minutes to comment adversely on her hairstyle, clothes and medical abilities.

'Boy, but is she a real charmer,' Floella muttered as she collected the blood samples Hannah had asked for.

'To be fair, she has very bad arthritis in her hands and feet, which probably doesn't do a lot for her temper,' Hannah murmured back, determined to be charitable, then frowned. 'Reception said she had a suspected fractured leg, didn't they?'

Floella nodded. 'According to her son, she fell in the house just before dinner, and he's worried she might have broken her leg.'

There hadn't been a single bruise on the old woman's leg, neither had she complained of any pain when Hannah had examined her. She'd complained about everything else, but not about pain in her leg.

'Flo, could you go out to the waiting room and check with her son again? Maybe he's given Reception the wrong information. It's very easily done when someone's upset.'

Floella was back within seconds, her face furious. 'We've been had, Hannah. It's a granny drop!'

'A what?' Hannah said in confusion.

'The classic answer of what to do with Grandma or Grandad when you decide to take a holiday,' the sister replied bitterly. 'If you're too mean to spend money on a home help or a hotel, you simply drive to the nearest A and E and drop the problem off.'

'I don't believe it!' Hannah gasped.

'Neither will Robert when he finds out we've been conned,' Floella groaned. 'He'll have to phone Geriatrics to see if they can find her a bed, and by the time they've finished giving him merry hell he'll want our guts for garters.'

He did. Or, more precisely, he wanted Hannah's.

'How could you have been so stupid?' he demanded, angrily stabbing his hands through his black hair. 'Falling for a scam like that. It's one of the oldest tricks in the book!'

'In which case you should have warned me and I'd have been prepared,' she protested.

'Do you have to be told everything?' he snapped. 'Can't you use whatever little brain and common sense you've got and figure some things out for yourself?'

Well, she'd wanted him to be rude to her, she remembered, but that didn't mean she had to like it, and she discovered she didn't—not at all.

'And just how—exactly—am I supposed to predict which sons are going to dump their mothers on us?' she retorted.

'Perhaps if you weren't so damned naïve—'

'I'd rather be naïve than a complete cynic like you!' she

threw back at him. 'Look, I made a mistake, OK? I'm sorry, OK? What do you want from me—blood?'

What he wanted, he realised, looking down at her flushed cheeks and furious eyes, was to kiss her senseless. What he really wanted was to take her to bed and make love to her.

Why couldn't he just fall out of love with her? He'd fallen out of love with Laura, so why couldn't he do the same with Hannah? Hell, he'd tried hard enough. Keeping out of her way, exchanging the barest minimum of conversation with her—but it hadn't worked.

All he felt was lousier than before. Lousy, and frustrated, and angry. Angry with her for making him feel this way. Angry with himself for being stupid enough to have fallen in love again. And angry with everybody else because...because... Well, he didn't know why he was angry with everybody else. He just knew that he was.

'What I want, Dr Blake, is for you to shape up your ideas,' he said tightly. And to stop wearing that damn perfume you always wear. The one that smells of bluebells and daffodils. To stop looking at me with those big brown eyes of yours, all hurt, and baffled, and confused. 'What I want is you to start behaving in a professional manner!'

'A professional manner?' she repeated. 'You have the nerve—the *gall*—to suggest that because I was conned by that old lady's son I'm not *professional*?'

Of course he hadn't meant that, but there was no way he was going to explain to her what he really meant. And to his relief he didn't have to. As he cleared his throat to reply, the doors of the treatment room suddenly clattered open and a wild-eyed, panic-stricken girl appeared, with a baby in her arms.

'Please—please, will somebody help me? My son... My baby's not breathing properly!'

The tiny mite was almost blue, his chest was caving in

with the effort to breathe, and together Robert and Hannah rushed towards him, their argument immediately forgotten.

'How old is he?' Hannah asked, taking the child from his mother's arms and quickly carrying him into one of the cubicles.

'Two weeks old. He was born two weeks ago.'

A premature baby for sure, Hannah decided, placing her stethoscope swiftly onto its little chest. A full-term baby wouldn't have been nearly so small and fragile, and though the poor little mite had obviously been crying, he wasn't crying now. All of his tiny energies were concentrated on simply trying to breathe.

'How long has your son been like this?' Robert asked, quickly setting up a tiny drip and linking the baby to the ECG monitor.

'Two—maybe three days.'

Robert's eyes met Hannah's. Three *days*? What kind of mother allowed her child to suffer like this for three days? Judging by his temperature, the baby probably had a massive infection of some kind, and leaving him without medical treatment for even three hours was far too long.

They could stabilise his condition—in fact, the drip Robert had inserted was already improving the baby's colour and breathing—but the special care baby unit was the best place for him, and that was where he would go after they'd extracted as much information out of the mother as they could.

'Was it a normal birth?' Hannah asked as she took the baby's blood pressure.

'I think so,' the girl replied uncertainly. 'I mean, I've never had a baby before, so I can't really say whether it was any different to anyone else's labour.'

'What Dr Blake meant was did the midwife notice anything unusual when your son was born?' Robert asked.

'Jaundice perhaps, or breathing problems, anything like that?'

The girl frowned. 'Not that I recall, though they did say they'd found amphetamines in his body when he was born.'

And how do you suppose the amphetamines got there, you stupid girl? Hannah fumed. You put them in him. You must have been pill-popping when you were pregnant, and now your son is suffering because of it.

But she didn't say that. Never judge, she'd been taught at med school, never criticise. You're a doctor whose primary function is to heal, but to her dismay it soon became apparent that Robert had already judged and he was going to announce his verdict whether the young girl wanted to hear it or not.

'I presume you went to antenatal classes?' he demanded.

'I went once or twice,' the girl said, 'but it was such a hassle getting there—'

'Then you presumably missed the talk about how everything you put in your mouth would go straight into your baby's body!' he said caustically. 'Your son has breathing difficulties because he was born a drug addict. Your son has a fever because he's suffering from withdrawal symptoms.'

'Dr Cunningham, I really don't think this is perhaps the best time—'

'Your baby is going to have to do cold turkey because of your irresponsibility,' Robert continued as though Hannah hadn't spoken, his eyes fixed icily on the baby's mother. 'His little body is going to be racked with pain and agony because of you, and I hope when you sit by his incubator and hear his tiny screams that you remember that!'

And before Hannah could stop him he had swung out of the cubicle, leaving her staring after him in stunned horror. Never had she seen Robert come so close to completely losing his temper before. OK, so what he'd told the baby's mother was true. And, OK, the girl was obviously clueless, but a cubicle in the middle of A and E was hardly the proper place or the right time to tell her so.

'I'm…I'm so very sorry,' she said awkwardly as the girl began to cry. 'Dr Cunningham…he's been under a lot of strain recently, and I can only apologise for his…his brusqueness.'

And get you and your baby up to SCBU as fast as I can, she added mentally, quickly poking her head round the cubicle curtains to find Elliot, Jane and Floella standing outside, their faces concerned and worried.

'Oh, Hannah, this really can't go on, you know,' Jane said, lowering her voice as the members of the night shift began to arrive. 'It's one thing to be snippy with us, but—'

'We're here to treat, not to judge,' Elliot finished for her. 'Hannah, he was completely out of order.'

'I know that, but—'

'Won't you at least try to talk to him?' Jane continued as Hannah gazed at her unhappily. 'You could do it tonight. You could go round to his flat, speak to him privately…'

'But, Jane—'

'What if he does something worse tomorrow?' the sister declared. 'Hannah, he's the best special registrar I've ever worked with, and…well, I know he's got his faults, but I'm worried sick about him.'

Hannah was too, which was why she found herself standing on the doorstep of Robert's flat some time later, pale and nervous but utterly determined.

'So little Miss Muffet is doing house calls now, is she?' he commented coldly when he opened the door and saw her. 'Well, I'm sorry to disappoint you, but I don't believe I need your medical services tonight.'

And to her dismay he actually began to shut the door on her.

'OK, we can have this conversation on the doorstep for all your neighbours to hear,' she said grimly, quickly putting her foot in the doorway and keeping it there. 'Or you can invite me in to listen to what I have to say like a civilised human being.'

For a second she thought he really was going to make her say it on the doorstep but then, without a word, he turned on his heel and strode down the hall, leaving her to follow him.

And she did, into what had to be the most cheerless sitting room she'd ever seen. Oh, it was nicely furnished if your taste ran to the basic, and spotlessly neat, but it wasn't a home. Homes had clutter. Homes had ornaments and photographs, and books and magazines lying where people had left them. This room had all the charm of one of those huge corporate hotels. Anonymous, functional and completely soulless.

'Oh, for God's sake, will you stop hovering over me like some student nurse checking out her first patient?' he exclaimed irritably as he sat down. 'Take a seat, say what you've got to say, then I'd be obliged if you'd leave and allow me to enjoy what remains of my evening in peace.'

Now was the moment to tell him that it was scathing comments like that which were putting everybody's backs up, but the words wouldn't come, and it wasn't because she'd suddenly got a bad attack of cold feet. It was because he looked so lost somehow, sitting in this soulless, cheerless flat, with nothing but his memories for company.

'Robert…I'm here because everyone's so worried about you—'

'What you mean is everyone's had enough of my bad temper, and you were unlucky enough to draw the short straw to tell me so,' he flared.

She coloured slightly. 'In a way I guess that's so, but we *are* worried about you. That girl and her baby…'

'I went too far—I admit it,' he exclaimed. 'I'll go up to SCBU tomorrow and apologise to her. Happy now?'

No, she wasn't, not by a long shot. 'Robert, we all know you're unhappy, and we want to help you. We know how much you loved your wife—'

'Do you remember me telling you once that we should trade secrets?' he interrupted. 'That I would tell you why I intended to get blind drunk on the anniversary of my wife's death if you would tell me why you took a job in London instead of Edinburgh?'

She shifted uneasily in her seat. Now wasn't the right time to tell him about her father. She didn't know when that would be, but it certainly wasn't now. 'Robert—'

'Well, I'll tell you for free,' he continued, his face bleak, empty. 'I wanted to get drunk that night because I killed her. I killed Laura.'

Her eyes flew to his face in confusion. 'But she was hit by a car outside the hospital—'

'And she wouldn't have been if she hadn't left St Stephen's so angry that the last thing she was thinking about was road safety,' he said bitterly. 'We'd had a row— a huge one—and I…I told her I wanted a divorce. If she hadn't been angry with me that night, she would still be alive. I killed her, Hannah. I might not have been driving the car, but I still killed her.'

She didn't know what to say, but she knew she had to say something. 'You said you had a row…?'

'The last of far too many,' he murmured, leaning back in his seat and closing his eyes. 'Laura…Laura was by far the most gifted doctor I've ever met, and it never occurred to me to look beyond that. To see that the only thing she really cared for wasn't me, or her patients, but her work and the success it could bring.'

'But surely she must have loved you if she married you?' Hannah protested.

'I think…I think she loved me as much as she was capable of loving anyone, but I wanted more, you see. I wanted to be the most important thing in her life, and she couldn't give me that. Maybe I was selfish, unrealistic. Maybe I wanted too much, but…' His lips twisted. 'Oh, Hannah, you can have no idea what it's like to live with someone—to love them deeply, desperately—and yet to know that you only ever occupy a tiny, unimportant part of their heart.'

But she did know, she thought as the memories came flooding back.

Memories of herself as a child, sitting up well past her bedtime waiting for her father to come home from the hospital. Longing to see him, to talk to him, to have him cuddle and hold her. And of her father coming home and absently patting her on the head before he disappeared into his study to plan his next big operation.

'Robert—'

'Would you tell the others I appreciate their concern for my career, and apologise to them for my recent behaviour?' he interrupted quickly. 'Tell them…' He managed a smile. 'Tell them I'll try to do better in future.'

There was nothing left to say. She'd done what she'd been asked to do, and slowly she got to her feet, and even more slowly walked over to the sitting-room door, but when she reached it she turned to face him.

'It wasn't your career we were concerned about, you know. We care a great deal for you. Jane, and Flo, and Elliot, and…me.'

'Hannah—'

'In fact…' She took a deep breath and threw all caution to the wind. 'I more than care, Robert. I—'

'Don't!' he interrupted, springing to his feet. 'Don't— please, don't say it.'

'Why not?' she asked, her heart beginning to beat very fast. 'Why don't you want me to say it?'

'Because you and I... Hannah, I've thought and thought about this, and I do want you—I won't deny it—but it would never work.'

'Wouldn't it?' she whispered.

He shook his head. 'I was no good for Laura—I'm no use for any woman—and I couldn't...I just couldn't bear it if I made you unhappy.'

'I don't think you'd make me unhappy, Robert,' she said huskily. 'In fact, I know you wouldn't, and I'm going to say the words whether you want me to or not. I love you, Robert Cunningham.'

He didn't answer, and it was she who took a step towards him, hesitantly, uncertainly, and for a second she thought he was going to back away, then suddenly his face cracked.

'Oh, hell! Oh, hell, Hannah!'

And suddenly she was in his arms, and he was covering her face with tiny, searing kisses and brokenly saying her name over and over again. Tears slid from the corner of her eyes as his lips claimed hers, his mouth hungry, desperate, and she kissed him back just as fervently, giving him all that she was, knowing only that this was right. This was meant to be.

'You're beautiful...so beautiful,' he murmured into her throat, his breathing shallow and unsteady as he carried her into the bedroom, then gently removed her clothes, leaving her dressed only in her bra and briefs.

'I'm not,' she mumbled, suddenly awkward and embarrassed as his gaze travelled over her. 'I'm too skinny.'

Gently he reached out and cupped her lace-covered breasts in his hands. Even more gently he caressed each one through the fabric with his thumb until her already tingling nipples hardened with a pleasure that was almost pain. 'Hannah, you're so beautiful I want to throw you on that bed and make love to you until dawn, but…'

'But?' she gasped, her eyes large and luminous, her breathing now as unsteady as his.

'Are you absolutely sure you want to do this?' His hands slid down her sides and came to rest on the waistband of her briefs. 'Please…please, be sure, because this time…this time even if St Stephen's itself burst into flames, I wouldn't be able to stop.'

'I don't want you to stop,' she said, putting her hands over his and gently pushing downwards so her briefs slipped to the floor. 'And believe me,' she added, unclipping her bra so her breasts sprang free. 'Believe me, I have never been more sure of anything in my life.'

And she *was* sure as he gathered her to him. Was never more certain as he paid tender homage to every inch of her throbbing body with his mouth and hands and tongue. And when he finally joined with her, and took her to heights she'd never even dreamt of, far less imagined, she knew that this was the man she'd been born for.

CHAPTER NINE

'YOU'RE not actually going to eat all of that, are you?' Elliot exclaimed, cradling a cup of black coffee in his hands and gazing with a barely concealed shudder at Hannah's canteen dinner of chicken pie, chips and beans.

'You bet I am,' she said with a grin, forking a piece of pie into her mouth to prove it. 'In fact, I have it on the very highest authority that nobody should start a shift in A and E without a decent meal inside them.'

'Uh-huh. And this highest authority...' Elliot took a sip of coffee and cocked his head at her thoughtfully. 'He wouldn't happen to be a tall, dark-haired individual who goes by the name of Robert Edward Cunningham, would he?'

Hannah's lips quirked. 'Maybe.'

'Uh-*huh*. And as I appear to be on a winning roll here, would I also be right in surmising that this particular Robert Edward Cunningham and a certain Dr Hannah Blake have finally got it together?'

'Elliot—'

'Because if they haven't,' he continued doggedly as a rosy glow crept across her cheeks, 'I want to know why Robert's been going around A and E for the last three weeks with a silly grin on his face, and you have the look of a girl who has been very soundly loved.'

Hannah blushed scarlet, but with over sixty members of staff eating and talking in the canteen this evening she reckoned she could probably have shrieked 'Stop, thief!' and no one would have heard her. 'OK, all right. We're sort of together—'

'About damn time.'

'But we don't want anybody to know about it yet,' she insisted. 'It's too soon, you see.'

He drew a finger across his throat. 'Not a word will pass my lips, love. All I want to know is whether you're happy.'

She was. Blissfully, unbelievably happy. And no more so than when she was bidding a decorous goodnight to Robert in the staffroom—a goodnight he always echoed just as solemnly—and knew that within half an hour she'd be in his flat, in his bed, and they would be making glorious, unending love until the sun rose.

'You're the best thing that's ever come into my life,' Robert had murmured into her hair one morning as he'd held her close. 'But Laura and I... We didn't really know one another before we got married, and this time I don't want any secrets between us—no dark corners—so neither of us will ever have any regrets.'

Regrets—how could she possibly have any regrets? she wondered. She loved him, and knew he loved her. OK, so maybe he hadn't actually said that he did, but Laura had hurt him badly and it would take time for him to trust her. Time for him to realise she truly did love him, and they had all the time in the world for him to learn that.

'Have you told him who your father is yet?' Elliot asked abruptly.

Well, perhaps not all the time, she realised, putting down her knife and fork, her appetite suddenly gone.

'Almost.'

'Hannah, you can't ''almost'' tell someone something like that,' Elliot protested. 'Either you have, or you haven't!'

She bit her lip. 'Look, I'll get round to it, OK? It's been a bit difficult, finding the right moment—'

'Good grief, woman, how can there possibly be a wrong

moment? All you have to do is open your mouth and say, ''Charles Blake is my father.'''

'Yes, but—'

'Sweetheart, you *have* to tell him. Believe me, the longer you wait, the harder it will get, and if Robert finds out himself…' He rolled his eyes heavenwards. 'Hannah, I don't have half the hang-ups that Robert Cunningham does, but if I was in love with you, and you kept something like this a secret from me, even I'd start to wonder what else you had to hide. Love, you've *got* to tell him—and tell him soon.'

'I will—I promise I will,' she insisted. 'When…when the time is right.'

And as Elliot shook his head and swore under his breath, neither of them noticed that Jerry Clark was sitting two tables from them, a thoughtful, malicious smile spreading across his face.

'Ten years ago A and E would have been packed to the rafters on November 5th with burns cases like this,' Robert murmured as he and Hannah carefully began covering the burns on Harry Ryan's hands and arms with sterile, non-stick, moist dressings. 'This poor little chap's our first casualty, and hopefully he's going to be our last.'

'That advertising campaign the government did a few years back certainly made a huge difference,' Hannah observed, as the whooshes and bangs in the distance indicated that somewhere in the city yet another bonfire-night display was getting under way. 'When the public saw the kinds of horrific injuries both adults and children could get from exploding fireworks, most people decided to take their kids to organised events instead of having parties in their back gardens.'

'It's a pity Harry's parents didn't do that.' Robert sighed. 'Imagine anyone being stupid enough to allow a six-year-old to hold a box of fireworks. You wonder where some people's brains are.' He glanced across at Jane. 'How's his BP and pulse rate now?'

'Stabilising nicely now the IVs are up and running,' she replied.

Robert nodded. The biggest danger in a case like this—apart from the severity of the burns—was that the victim would go into hypovolaemic shock when the body attempted to repair itself by withdrawing fluids from the uninjured areas of the body. Replacing those lost fluids as quickly as possible was imperative before liver and kidney damage could occur.

'What should we do about the minor blisters on the side of his neck?' Hannah asked, smiling encouragingly down at the little boy who was lying, white-faced and tearstained, on the trolley, a nasal cannula plugged into his nose to give him added oxygen. 'Should we dress them as well, or—?'

'Leave them alone,' Robert said, staring at the blisters critically. 'The burns unit won't thank us for sending him up looking like a mummy, and they have their own procedures for dealing with minor injuries.'

'Then I think that's all we can do,' Hannah said, putting the last of the dressings in place and straightening up. 'Like you said, the rest is really up to the burns unit.'

And they'd have their work cut out with this one, she thought sadly as Harry Ryan was wheeled out of the treatment room. He'd sustained third-degree burns to his hands and arms and it was going to take years of painful skin grafts to repair the damage. And even then there would be no guarantee that he'd ever fully regain the use of his hands and arms.

'Our burns unit is one of the best in London, Hannah,' Robert murmured, clearly reading her mind.

'I know,' she replied. 'It's just . . He's so very little, Robert, and I keep thinking if he were mine . . .'

'If he was yours, I'm sure you'd have taken much better care of him so he didn't end up here in the first place,' Robert declared firmly.

She was tempted to tell him that hundreds of children with good and caring parents ended up in hospital every day. That she'd met some children in the short time she'd worked in A and E who seemed to have been born with a suicide mission in life, but she didn't.

She was too busy suddenly wondering what it would be like to have a child of her own. She'd never thought of herself as a mother, never even imagined herself as one, but now... To feel a child growing inside her, to watch its first tottering steps. And she didn't want just anybody's child, she realised. She wanted Robert Cunningham's.

'Maybe...maybe one day, Hannah?' he said softly, glancing down at her with a knowing smile.

'I'd like that,' she replied, her own lips creasing in response. 'I'd like that very much indeed.'

'And I'm sure whatever it is you'd both like is really interesting, but we do have patients waiting,' Mr Mackay observed tersely as he strode past them.

Robert stared after the A and E consultant, openmouthed, then grinned. 'That is the first time in my life I've actually been accused of wasting time. What are you doing to me, Hannah Blake?'

'Making you a little more human, I hope.' She chuckled, but as he walked away she noticed Jane looking at her from across the treatment room, a puzzled, quizzical look on her face.

It had been a look she'd seen before over the last three weeks. A look that made her wonder how much longer she and Robert would be able to keep their relationship a secret. Frankly, she was amazed they'd managed it this long. Sometimes she thought it must be obvious to everyone. And sometimes, when Robert smiled at her—that very spe-

cial smile she knew he reserved solely for her—she was
certain the whole world must know.

'I take my hat off to you, Hannah.'

'You do?' she replied, whirling round guiltily to see
Floella behind her. 'Why—what have I done?'

'Only single-handedly managed to turn our special registrar from the grouch of the millennium into a big, cuddly
pussy cat.' The staff nurse beamed. 'I don't know what you
said to him a couple of weeks ago but he's been a different
man ever since. In fact, I actually heard him *whistling* when
he came on duty tonight.'

He whistled in the bath every morning, too. Well, he
hadn't this morning, but that could have had something to
do with the fact that she'd joined him, and he'd had other
things on his mind at the time.

'You OK, Hannah?' Floella continued with a slight
frown. 'You look a bit flushed. Liz in Admin was telling
me there's a flu bug going round the hospital—'

'I'm not surprised, considering they keep the temperature
in here on a level with Barbados while outside it's freez-
ing,' Hannah declared quickly. 'It's enough to make anybody sick. And talking about sick, who's next?'

'Ben Ryder—three years old—sounds like asthma.'

It wasn't. In fact, by the time she'd finished examining
the little boy she was completely stumped.

'You said your son only started wheezing recently, Mrs
Ryder?' she queried as she put down her stethoscope.

The small, dark-haired woman nodded. 'He was as right
as rain at teatime, Doctor, or I'd never have taken him to
the fireworks display, but when we got home he started to
sound like this.'

'Has he ever shown any signs of bronchitis—asthma?'
she asked, clutching at straws.

'No, never. In fact, he had his check-up at the clinic only
last week, and they said he was as fit as a fiddle.'

Hannah's frown deepened. Ben Ryder's temperature, pulse and blood pressure were normal. There were no signs of blueness about his lips or tongue, and he was alert, if a little tearful.

In fact, if he hadn't got this wheeze—a wheeze that seemed to be getting worse—she would have said there was nothing wrong with the child. Perhaps she should page Paediatrics, get their consultant to come down and have a look. Ben could have a lung or a heart problem that hadn't been detected yet. Or maybe he was suffering from a severe allergic reaction to something, and his wheezing was the precursor to him going into full anaphylactic shock.

And, then again, perhaps not. An idea suddenly flashed into her mind.

'Jane, would you tilt Ben's head for me?'

Quickly the sister did as she asked.

'Can you see anything? Mrs Ryder whispered as Hannah squinted up into the little boy's nose.

A donkey, Hannah thought with a smile, remembering Robert's words. It was a donkey, not a zebra.

'Your son's got a stone up his nose, Mrs Ryder,' she announced as she straightened up. 'While you were watching the fireworks he must have got a bit bored, picked one up and stuck it up his nose.'

'Why, the little…' Mrs Ryder was torn between laughter, exasperation and tears. 'Can you get it out?'

'Jane, could you get me the smallest forceps you can find, please?' Hannah asked.

Within seconds the stone was out, and Mrs Ryder was carrying a thoroughly chastened Ben out of the treatment room.

'Take a tip from me, Doctor,' Mrs Ryder said wryly. 'Don't ever have children. Not only do they give you grey hairs, the only way a woman can survive is to grow eyes in the back of her head!'

Hannah laughed, but her face became slightly pensive when the mother and son had gone. Grey hairs and eyes in the back of her head seemed a small price to pay to have a miniaturised version of Robert. A tiny, black-haired, grey-eyed bundle of mischief who would stick stones up his nose and get into all kinds of scrapes. Or perhaps even a daughter who would have Robert's black hair and smile, and...

For goodness' sake, get a grip! her mind shrieked. The man hasn't even told you he loves you yet, and you're already thinking children, a future, a lifetime together.

Because this is right, her heart answered back. Because even when I was engaged to Chris, I never thought of myself with children of my own, never really thought beyond the wedding day, but with Robert...

With Robert she could picture the two of them growing old together, worrying about their children together, and still loving and caring for one another.

'You wouldn't credit the things children can get up to when you take your eyes off them for a second, would you?' Jane chuckled.

Hannah shook her head and smiled. 'Have you ever thought about having children, Jane?' she asked before she could stop herself.

'Have I ever...?' The sister looked at her in surprise. 'What on earth put that question into your head?'

'I don't know,' Hannah replied, all too annoyingly aware that she was blushing. 'Maybe I'm getting broody or something.'

'I'd watch it, then,' Jane chuckled again. 'Quite normal, rational women have been known to get themselves into all sorts of trouble when they start to get broody.'

'I'll remember that,' Hannah said, fighting down her mounting colour without success. 'But, seriously, Jane, *have* you *ever* thought about having children?'

The sister sighed, her grey eyes suddenly a little rueful,

almost a little sad. 'Of course I have, but some things…some things just aren't meant to be. You can love someone until you're blue in the face, and if they don't even know you're around…'

Jane wasn't looking at her as she spoke but at something else across the room, and as Hannah followed her gaze she suddenly realised with a shock that it wasn't a something the sister was gazing at so wistfully, but a someone.

Elliot Mathieson.

Sensible, level-headed Sister Halden was in love with Elliot Mathieson. She would never have guessed it—not in a million years.

'Jane—'

'Did I tell you that bloke with the steel bar in his chest is doing really well in Intensive Care?' her colleague interrupted. 'The newspapers are calling him the miracle man, and I'm not surprised. Just the thought of having a steel bar imbedded in my chest is enough to give me nightmares.'

It wasn't a very subtle way of changing the subject—in fact, it wasn't subtle at all—but what could Hannah say? That she was sure everything would turn out right for Jane in the end? They both knew it wouldn't. They both knew only too well that Elliot was never going to settle down with anyone.

'Jane, I'm sorry—'

'Lord, but standing here talking about children isn't getting on with the work.' The girl smiled with an effort. 'I've a stack of forms to fill in and if I don't get them in before Friday Admin will hang me out to dry and I won't be a sister any more, far less a mother!'

Hannah chuckled but her laughter died when Jane bustled off purposefully down the treatment room.

To love someone, and know they scarcely noticed you… She'd experienced a little of that with Robert, and it had been miserable, wretched. She was so lucky, she thought as she checked the white board, then walked quickly towards cubicle 1. Lucky that the man she'd fallen in love with loved her. Lucky that for once in her life everything seemed to be going right.

In fact, she felt so happy today that she didn't even feel angry when the patient asked for a second opinion. All she felt was irritated.

'It sounds to me from his symptoms that he's got a classic case of heartburn,' Robert declared when she explained her problem. 'To be fair to your patient, it can be very easy to think you're having a heart attack if the pain is really severe, but if you were having a heart attack the pain wouldn't be worse at night when you lie down, then get better when you sit up.'

'*I* know that—and *you* know that,' she said, 'but I just can't convince *him*. I've shown him his ECG reading—even let him see his BP—but the trouble is that his father died at forty-two from a cardiac arrest and he's convinced the same thing's going to happen to him.'

'Cubicle 1, you said?' Robert queried. 'OK. Leave him to me.'

And to her amazement, within fifteen minutes Robert was escorting a clearly very relieved patient towards the exit.

'How did you do that—what did you say?' she demanded.

'Trade secret.' He grinned.

'You're not getting away with that,' she protested. 'Come on—confession time.'

He laughed. 'OK. I simply gave him some hospital-strength indigestion-busting solution which eased his heartburn, and when the pain disappeared he had to accept he wasn't dying after all.'

'Robert Cunningham, you're wonderful!' Hannah beamed.

He glanced over his shoulder, then back at her, and his voice when he spoke was husky. 'And have I told you recently that I think you're pretty wonderful, too?'

A smile curved her lips. 'Oh, maybe once or twice.'

'Once or twice?' he protested.

'OK, make that three or four times.' She laughed, her eyes sparkling.

He stared at her for a moment, indignation and amusement warring with each other on his face, then growled, 'Woman, will you stop looking at me like that?'

'Like what?' she protested, truly bewildered.

'All flushed, and glowing, and completely and utterly desirable.' Robert shook his head ruefully. 'Hannah, you're playing hell with my concentration. All I can think when I look at you is roll on half past eleven.'

'Something special happening at half past eleven, is there?' she asked, schooling her features into a picture of bland innocence.

'I'm hoping so,' he replied, his eyes suddenly gleaming. 'I'm hoping that by the time I get back to Wellington Place a very special girl might be waiting in my bed for me.'

'Well, I suppose you can always hope,' she replied, deciding to tease him just a little, and saw a smile tug at the corners of his mouth.

'And if this very special, very particular girl *should* happen to be in my bed,' he continued, his eyes fixed on her, dark with promise, 'and *should* happen to be willing…'

'Willing to do what?' she said a little breathlessly.

'Turn up at half past eleven, and you'll find out.' He winked.

A splutter of laughter came from her as he disappeared into his office, laughter that became acute consternation when she noticed Floella and Jane tucking into a huge box of chocolates.

'Oh, heck, it's not somebody's birthday today, is it, and I've forgotten?' she asked as she joined them.

'Uh-uh,' Floella mumbled through a mouthful of chocolate. 'Do you remember Sheila Vernon?'

Hannah frowned. 'Can't say the name rings a bell.'

'Of course it does,' the staff nurse protested. 'Ruptured ovarian cyst. The gynae consultant came down to confirm it, and he wasn't best pleased at the time because he'd been having coffee with Gussie Granton up in Paediatrics. That's all off, by the way,' Floella continued, helping herself to another chocolate. 'Gorgeous Gussie's on the loose again, and rumour has it that as Elliot and Robert are the only male members of staff she hasn't dated—'

'You were talking about Sheila Vernon, Flo?' Hannah said pointedly.

'Were we?' The staff nurse frowned. 'Oh—yes, so we were. Well, apparently she was discharged from Women's Surgical last week, and in grateful thanks for the care she got at St Stephen's she sent a box of chocs to Women's Surgical and one to us.'

'How very kind of her,' Hannah exclaimed, popping a chocolate into her mouth.

'Unusual, too,' Jane observed. 'Most people remember to thank the staff on the wards after they've come in as an emergency, but precious few remember the poor Cinderellas down in The Pit who first diagnosed what was wrong with them. In fact, I can remember one time when—'

'Hannah, could I have a word with you?' Robert interrupted, appearing beside them without warning.

'Would you like a chocolate?' She smiled, holding the box out to him. 'Sheila Vernon—'

'No, I don't want a chocolate. What I want is a word with you—*now*!'

Slowly she put the box of chocolates down. Something was wrong—very badly wrong. His face was white and taut, and mentally she reviewed all the casualties she'd seen that night. There'd been nothing particularly serious—actually, it had been a relatively quiet evening for them, apart from the constant sounds of rockets and bangers going off outside the hospital.

'Robert—'

'In my office!'

He whirled round on his heel before she could say another word, and quickly she followed him, all too aware that Floella and Jane were staring after her with concern. His office. Not the staffroom for a cup of coffee and a cosy chat. His office meant he didn't want anyone to hear their conversation. His office meant trouble—big trouble.

'What is it—what's wrong?' she asked, the moment he'd shut the door.

'This!' he exclaimed, picking up a sheet of paper from his desk and waving it under her nose. 'I want to know if what it says in this is true!'

'If you'd keep the damn thing still long enough for me to be able to read it, I might be able to answer you,' Hannah said, bewildered. 'What is it?'

'I came in to collect some files I needed and found this anonymous note on my desk.'

'Bin it,' she declared firmly. 'Anybody who hasn't got the guts to sign their name—'

'Is Charles Blake your father?'

The colour drained from her face instantly. Never in all her wildest dreams would she have imagined that he might want to speak to her about that. 'Robert—'

'Is—it—true?' he said, each word cold and clipped.

She stared at him unhappily for a second, then nodded. 'Yes—yes, it's true, but, Robert, I can explain...'

Furiously he threw the sheet of paper down on his desk, and distractedly she noticed it was typed. She supposed people who wrote anonymous letters always typed their poison, and seeing Robert's face—his eyes a mixture of anger, hurt and disillusionment—she knew that if she ever found out who'd sent it, she'd pummel them senseless.

'Robert...' She put her hand out to him and felt utter dismay when he backed away. 'Robert, does it matter who my father is?'

'Yes, yes, it matters,' he said, his lips compressed into a tight white line. 'It matters because you didn't tell me. It matters because I had to find out from...from this...' He picked up the sheet of paper again and crushed it between his fingers. 'And it matters because you *lied* to me.'

'I didn't lie! I just...' She flushed scarlet. 'I just didn't tell you.'

'And why not, Hannah? Why didn't you tell me?'

'I didn't think it was important,' she faltered. 'Elliot said I should—'

'You told Elliot?' he thundered, and she flinched. 'Who else at St Stephen's knows? The porters, the cleaners, the guy who sells newspapers in the canteen?'

'Only our consultant,' she said quickly, 'and he only knows because it's on my CV, but I didn't tell Elliot—he found out himself.'

'And that's supposed to make me feel better, is it?' He strode over to his waste-paper bin and threw in the letter. 'That's supposed to make everything all right?'

She took a hesitant step towards him. 'Robert, when I came to St Stephen's I didn't want anyone to know who my father is because I didn't want anybody to have any preconceptions about me. I wanted to be judged on my own merits—'

'Yeah, right.'

'I did!' she insisted as his lip curled. 'My father didn't even know where I was working—I wouldn't tell him—'

'Because you knew he'd think you were slumming it with the peasants in St Stephen's?'

She stiffened. 'I don't know who you're insulting most by saying that—me, or everyone else who works here.'

He had the grace to flush slightly, but he wasn't finished, not by a long shot.

'I'm surprised *Daddy* didn't offer to get you a post in some nice, comfortable, civilised, private hospital.'

'I didn't want a job like that.' Oh, hell, that hadn't come out at all the way she'd intended, she realised, seeing his eyebrows snap down. 'I mean—I meant—I wanted to get a post on my own without his help. I didn't tell him I'd got a job here—I don't know how he found out—'

'That letter I brought round to your flat,' Robert interrupted with dawning comprehension. 'It was from him, wasn't it?'

She nodded. 'And if you think back, you might remember I wasn't exactly over the moon to receive it. Robert...Robert, surely all that really matters here is you and me, not who my father is?'

For a second she felt she'd almost convinced him, then he shook his head.

'If your father had been a teacher or a dustman, it wouldn't have mattered a brass farthing to me, but your father is Charles Blake, Hannah, one of the foremost consultants in the country.'

'Yes, but—'

'And the only reason I can come up with to explain your reluctance to say anything is that you're ashamed of your association with me. You thought I might want to meet him, and you didn't want to introduce somebody ordinary and run-of-the-mill like me to your precious father.'

Of course she wasn't ashamed of him—she'd never be ashamed of him—but he was right, she suddenly realised with dismay. She hadn't wanted him to meet her father.

Time and time again she'd put it off, convincing herself that now wasn't the right moment, that tomorrow would be better, but the bottom line was that she hadn't told him because she'd been afraid. Afraid that once Robert knew, he might become like Chris. Afraid he might become so obsessed with what her father could do for him that she'd be sidelined, marginalised into a small corner of his life.

It was an ignoble thought—an unworthy one. She knew Robert was nothing like Chris, would never be anything like Chris, but the tiny seed of doubt had been there. The tiny gnawing seed of doubt had kept her silent.

And Robert saw the shame in her face and misinterpreted it completely.

'So, I was right!' he exclaimed, a tide of dark, livid colour appearing on his cheekbones. 'You *are* ashamed of me. I'm just some bit of rough you've picked up for convenient sex until Daddy selects someone more suitable for you to settle down with and raise 2.2 children!'

'No—*No!*' she gasped in horror. 'Robert, I *love* you!'

'Love means trust, Hannah,' he said tightly. 'Love means honesty. If I learned nothing else when I was married to Laura, I learned that.'

He was already walking to his office door, and she hurried after him.

'OK...OK, you want honesty from me—I'll give you honesty,' she said. 'I didn't tell you who my father was because...because I was frightened.'

He turned to face her, his eyes cold, impassive. 'Frightened of what?'

'Robert, all my life I've known—been told—how brilliant my father is, how talented. All my life I've known that as soon as I've said I'm his daughter, all anybody wanted to talk about was him.'

'Go on.'

Never had he looked so grim, so unapproachable, but she'd started and she knew she couldn't stop now.

'I fell in love two years ago—or rather I thought I did. His name was Chris, and we were going to be married until I found out he only wanted to marry me because he hoped my father would help his career.'

'And you thought I might be the same?' he exclaimed, anger and hurt plain in his eyes. 'You thought I was a scumbag like that?'

'No—*no*!' Oh, she was saying this all wrong. Her words were coming out all tangled and twisted and wrong. 'No, I didn't think that—I know I didn't—but I think that perhaps…perhaps…'

'You're saying you didn't trust me. That's what you're saying, isn't it?' he demanded.

She gazed pleadingly up at him, willing him to understand. 'I wanted to trust you. I was sure that I did, but… Robert, you can have no idea what it's like to grow up knowing no one's interested in you, only your father. To stand in your own home when your father gives a dinner party and pray—*pray*—that somebody might talk to you because you're you, and not because you're Charles Blake's daughter.'

He stared at her for a long moment, then his lip curled. 'You're right, Hannah, I don't understand. You see, my family were too dirt poor to give any kind of party, far less a dinner party.'

'Robert—'

'We have patients waiting, Dr Blake. They require our medical skills, and I suggest we get back to them.'

'But, Robert, we haven't finished—'

'Oh, but we have,' he said, his face a cold mask. 'We have most certainly, definitely finished.'

And before she could utter a word he'd gone, leaving her standing in the centre of the empty office, knowing that it wasn't just their conversation that was finished. They were, too.

CHAPTER TEN

'THANK God you've made it in this morning, Hannah!' Jane exclaimed with relief, when she came through the treatment-room doors. 'Honestly, I don't know if I'm on my head or my heels today. What with half the hospital staff down with flu, and the other half marooned at home because of this snow...'

'And Maintenance say it's getting worse,' Kelly Ross chipped in as she joined them. 'Apparently there's almost six inches of snow on the pavements now, and there's no sign of it stopping.'

'Oh, terrific,' Jane groaned. 'The next thing you know we'll be—'

'Jane, could you make sure Admin gets those requisition forms today?' Robert interrupted. 'They've been on the phone, saying they should have received them yesterday, and I've promised you'll fill them in and send them along.'

'Then you'll just have to phone them back and *un*promise,' the sister protested. 'Robert, you've seen what the waiting room's like. I'll be lucky if I get a chance to go to the loo, far less put pen to paper today.'

Irritation was plain on his face but he didn't say a word, and as he walked away a deep frown creased Jane's forehead.

'You know, this is going to sound really dumb and downright contrary of me,' she murmured, 'but I think I preferred it when he got angry. Oh, I don't mean I want him snippy and impatient all the time again, but...'

'It's like standing next to a rumbling volcano.' Kelly nodded. 'You don't know when it's going to explode, only that it's going to, and the suspense is killing you. Hannah—'

'Sorry, but I have to go,' she said hurriedly. 'I think Flo wants me.'

And she did, judging by the staff nurse's wave, but Hannah would have grasped at any excuse to get away from what looked like developing into an in-depth discussion of what could possibly be wrong with Robert.

She didn't need a discussion. She knew what was wrong. He was angry with her. Angry, and hurt, and disappointed, but instead of exploding—getting his anger out into the open—he was turning it inwards, allowing it to simmer and fester, and as Kelly had said, one day it was going to blow.

'There wasn't any need for you to rush,' Floella remarked with a smile. 'It's no big emergency, just a tourist from the States who suffers from high blood pressure and has lost his medication. He's not registered in this country with a GP, so—'

'He's hoping we can provide a prescription for the drugs he needs,' Hannah finished for her. 'OK, I'll have a word with him. What's his name?'

Floella's lips twitched. 'Would you believe Rock Cadwallader?'

He didn't look like a Cadwallader in his denim jeans, cowboy boots and a jacket that wouldn't have looked out of place in the Rocky Mountains. But as the American got to his feet, and Hannah stared up at what must have been six feet five inches of solid muscle, she decided he most definitely looked like a rock.

'It's the most vexatious thing, ma'am,' he declared in answer to her query. 'I always keep the dang pills with me, never pack them in my luggage, but when I checked into the hotel, the little critters had disappeared. I reckon I must have pulled them out of my pocket when I was consulting my little old *London A-Z* street atlas.'

Good grief. He only had to add 'Aw shucks' and 'heavens to Betsy', and she'd be wondering where he'd parked his horse, Hannah thought, suppressing a smile as she took his blood pressure.

'Gone right through the roof, has it?' he asked when she straightened up with a slight frown.

'It's certainly higher than it should be,' she admitted, 'but I shouldn't think the worry over losing your medication has done it a lot of good. Can you remember what your doctor prescribed for you?'

'Not the brand names, I'm afraid, but I can give you my doc's address and telephone number, and he'll be able to tell you. All I know is that I'm on beta blockers, ACE inhibitors and a vasodilator.'

'You must rattle,' Hannah said with a smile, and a broad grin lit up Mr Cadwallader's deeply tanned face.

'Sure do. In fact, my secretary reckons she can hear me three blocks away.'

Hannah laughed. 'Do you have your doctor's telephone number with you? Oh, terrific. I'll get our receptionist to telephone him, then you can be on your way.'

'Much obliged to you, ma'am,' he replied. 'I wouldn't want to be without my drugs for any length of time in this cold weather, and it's cold enough out there today to freeze the hide right off a skunk.'

Hannah didn't know if it would, but Reception had told her that they'd already been inundated by patients suffering from breathing problems because of the sub-zero temperature, not to mention the fractured limbs caused by people slipping on the snow-covered pavements and a rash of car accidents due to by the treacherous roads.

'Is that guy for real?' Elliot gasped, when Mr Cadwallader had gone, after kissing Hannah soundly on both cheeks and waving her a cheery farewell.

'You'd better believe it.' She chuckled. 'In fact, he's very big in ladies underwear in the States—'

'I'm surprised he can find anything to fit him—'

'And... *And*,' she continued with a reproving glance at Elliot, though her eyes sparkled, 'he's also promised to send me some extremely expensive briefs and bras when he gets home as a thank you for all my help.'

'Carried out a personal fitting, did he?' the SHO asked, his eyebrows waggling.

'Certainly not.' She laughed. 'I'll have you know that Mr Rock Cadwallader is a perfect gentleman.'

'Or a fool, like somebody else I could mention,' Elliot sighed as Robert strode past them with the barest of nods. 'How much longer is he going to keep this up, Hannah?'

'Permanently, I'm afraid,' she replied with a brave attempt at a smile that didn't fool Elliot for a second. 'You warned me this would happen so I really only have myself to blame.'

'Yes, but it's been over a month now,' the SHO protested. 'Have you tried talking to him again, explaining...'

'He thinks I was using him, Elliot,' she interrupted, a dull tide of colour spreading across her too-pale cheeks. 'It's not simply that I didn't tell him who my father was. He thinks I was only amusing myself with him until someone better came along.'

He stared at her in disbelief. 'But it's obvious you're in love with him. Good heavens, you light up like a neon sign whenever he's near.'

'If I do, then he either doesn't see it or doesn't choose to, which is why...why I've got myself another job. I had to, Elliot,' she continued as his jaw dropped. 'The atmosphere in A and E's impossible. Kelly said it was like working next to a rumbling volcano, and she's right, and it's all my fault. There's so much anger inside Robert, so much hurt and bitterness, and every time he sees me, it simply fuels those feelings.'

'But, Hannah—'

'Elliot, I've admitted I was wrong, I've told him I'm sorry, but I won't beg.' Her bottom lip trembled and she brought it back rigidly under control. 'Call it pride, call it whatever you like, but if he can't accept my apology—can't understand why I did what I did—then maybe…maybe I'm better off without him.'

'Oh, love…'

'Aren't you going to ask me about my new job?' she said, forcing a smile to her lips, unable to bear the sympathy in Elliot's eyes. 'For all you know I could have got myself a post with some mega-rich oil sheikh who's going to shower me with diamonds, and give me the kind of life you only ever see in the movies.'

'If he's in the market for a male doctor, can I have a job, too?' Elliot grinned, knowing full well what she was doing, and why. 'What is this new job, then—where is it?'

'Botswana. I've been accepted by Médicins Sans Frontières,' she continued as his eyebrows rose. 'I saw an advertisement in the paper, asking for applications from doctors and nurses, and I contacted them, and they've accepted me.'

'So when do you leave?'

'In a month. I really should give six weeks' notice but when I handed in my resignation this morning to Mr Mackay he said he'd sort it out with Admin.'

'But that means you'll be leaving right after Christmas,' Elliot protested. 'Some of the staff won't be back from their holidays and they'll miss your farewell do.'

'I'd much rather you didn't organise anything,' Hannah said quickly. 'I haven't been here any length of time.'

'Since when did a minor detail like that ever stand in the

way of a good night out?' Elliot laughed. 'And we can't possibly let you go without a party.'

But I don't want a party, Hannah thought miserably as the SHO completely ignored all her protestations and began rattling off possible venues and whether a buffet would be preferable to a sit-down meal. All I want is to slip quietly and unobtrusively away, and never see Robert Cunningham again.

No, she didn't really want that. She might be angry with him, and hurt at the way he'd effectively shut her out of his life for the past month, but she still loved him.

If only he'd talk to her. If they could just talk she was sure she could make him see that she really did love him, that her fears had been born out of insecurity, not a lack of trust.

But he wouldn't talk to her. Oh, he was polite and courteous enough when they were treating patients together, but the minute she tried to instigate any kind of conversation other than a medical one he became as remote and distant as a sphinx.

Which was why she was leaving. Leaving before she embarrassed both herself and him by making a pointless and stupid scene. Leaving because she knew that as far as Robert was concerned their relationship was irrevocably over, and to stay on here, feeling as she did, would be impossible.

'I wish you weren't going,' Elliot said sadly. 'We're going to miss you. *I'm* going to miss you.'

'Rubbish!' Hannah smiled. 'If my replacement turns out to be a twenty-four-year-old blonde with a 40DD bust, one glance at her and I guarantee you won't even remember my name!'

He laughed, too, but as she walked away the smile rapidly faded from his lips. It was a shame, a damn shame. Hannah was clearly deeply unhappy, and Robert... Robert was watching Hannah as she walked over to the white board and it was obvious he was also miserable. Well, it was time for some straight talking, Elliot decided grimly, and this morning he was just the man to do it.

'Something I can do for you?' Robert said as the SHO strode purposefully towards him.

'More like the other way round, actually,' he answered. 'I want to know what the hell you think you're doing?'

'Right now, listening to my SHO not making a whole lot of sense,' Robert replied smoothly.

'It's Hannah.'

'There's a problem with her work?'

'Of course there isn't a problem with her work,' Elliot protested, thrusting his hands through his blond hair with exasperation. 'Robert, you're in love with her, she's in love with you—'

'And I don't think my private life—or Dr Blake's for that matter—is any of your concern.'

'Dr Blake—*Dr Blake*. Dammit, Robert, this is Hannah we're talking about!' Elliot flared. 'She's the best thing that ever walked into your life, and she's going to walk right out again if you don't do something soon. Laura—'

'You can stop right there!' Robert interrupted, his face ice-cold.

'No, I damn well won't!' the SHO retorted. 'I never thought you and Laura were right for each other—'

'And since when did you become an expert on women?' Robert exclaimed, equally angry now. 'Married to Donna for three years, divorced for five, and all you've got to show for your thirty-two years is a string of girlfriends, none of whom has lasted longer than a month!'

'Which is why when someone special like Hannah comes along a man should grab hold of her with both hands,' Elliot insisted. 'Robert, you love her. Don't drive her away because of a misplaced sense of pride. Hold onto her!'

Robert stared at him coldly, only the jerking of a muscle at the side of his jaw betraying just how very angry he was. 'Have you finished?'

'Robert, listen to me—'

'Butt out of my life, Elliot. Butt out, and if you've got any sense, keep out!'

The nerve of the man—the sheer, unmitigated gall—Robert thought furiously as he strode down the treatment room. Kelly took one look at his face and scuttled quickly out of his path.

Just who did Elliot think he was? Handing out advice like some third-rate, half-baked agony aunt. He didn't need any advice. He knew the score. Hannah hadn't trusted him, and she'd used him. That was it. End of story.

And do you truly believe she was using you? his mind demanded. Do you honestly think she's nothing more than a pampered rich kid who decided that some sex with a bit of rough would make her life at St Stephen's more bearable?

He groaned aloud as he forced himself to remember the nights he'd spent with her. Hannah didn't possess the experience or the guile to use anybody. Emotionally she'd still been a virgin when he'd first made love to her, and it had been a wonder and a joy for him to watch her blossom in his arms, to see her grow in confidence, to...

And he didn't want to remember any of this, he realised, clenching his hands into hard, tight fists. It didn't alter anything, it didn't change anything. OK, so maybe she hadn't been using him and, OK, so she had a huge inferiority complex because of her father and what had happened with this Chris—damn him for all eternity—but nothing could excuse or alter the fact that she'd lied to him, deceived him. Dammit, he'd asked her for honesty, and if she couldn't even be honest about who her father was, there was no future for them.

'That man's going to burst a blood vessel if he doesn't get rid of what's eating him soon,' Floella observed as she watched Robert disappear into cubicle 8.

'We have patients to attend to, Flo,' Hannah said brusquely. 'And I'm sure Dr Cunningham is both big enough and old enough to sort out his own problems.'

'Yeah, right.' The staff nurse nodded, but as they walked together towards cubicle 2 Hannah couldn't help noticing that Flo was shooting her a very puzzled, thoughtful glance.

And to her dismay it was a glance Jane began to mirror as the rest of their shift sped by in an exhausting round of even more broken limbs, angina attacks and minor road accidents. Jane and Flo had clearly found time to put their heads together, and this time they'd come up with the correct answer.

Oh, how she wished it was already the end of December, she sighed wearily when her shift finally ended and she went along to the staffroom to collect her coat and handbag. Actually, make that January 1st, she amended with a sinking heart as she opened the staffroom door and found Robert waiting for her, his face a mixture of anger and bewilderment.

'Mr Mackay's just told me you've handed in your resignation, that you've taken a post with Médicins Sans Frontières?' he announced without preamble.

'That's right,' Hannah replied, amazed at how calm her voice sounded when she felt anything but.

'Are you out of your mind?' he protested. 'Hannah, doctors who work for Médicins Sans Frontières go into war zones, famine and flood areas!'

'There'd hardly be any point in setting up an organisation to help the victims of such catastrophes if the doctors they employed never travelled any further than Watford Gap, would there?' she pointed out, opening the door of her locker only to see him bang it shut.

'Hannah, you could get killed—you could catch any number of life-threatening diseases!'

'They're going to give me shots for typhus and cholera—'

'I don't give a damn if they inoculate you against every communicable disease known to mankind, you can't possibly do it!'

'You mean you don't think a pampered rich kid like me will be able to hack it?' she said tightly, opening her locker again and taking out her coat.

'I never said you were a pampered rich kid.'

'No, but you thought it, didn't you?' she retorted, and saw a betraying flush of colour darken his cheeks. 'And you're right—I was pampered as a child. So pampered that my father gave over the whole top of our house to me and my nanny when I was born, with a separate entrance and exit so that he wouldn't be disturbed by my presence. So pampered that I was able to keep a special calendar of the days when I actually saw him, when he remembered to talk to me.'

He stared at her, horrified. 'Hannah—'

'And I became even more pampered when I grew up,' she continued bitterly. 'He didn't send me away to boarding school as he could have done. Oh, no. He kept me home so that whenever I was lucky enough to see him he could ask how I'd got on at school, dissect my exam results and tell me how he'd always wanted a brilliant, talented son to follow in his footsteps and how disappointed he was to have fathered a dumb-cluck daughter instead.'

Robert was appalled. Appalled and furious, fit to kill. How could anyone treat another human being—let alone their own flesh and blood—like that? How could anyone be so self-absorbed that the feelings of their own child meant nothing to them?

'Hannah, I'm so sorry—'

'It's in the past now,' she said dismissively. 'I haven't seen my father in over two years, and I don't intend to. I have my own life to live, and that's what I mean to do.'

He stared down at his hands, then up at her. 'Hannah, this job you've accepted... Are you sure it's what you want?'

'It will be challenging, and I think that's what I need right now,' she replied slipping on her coat.

'Working at St Stephen's is a challenge,' he pointed out. 'Dealing with the constant stream of people who come through our doors is a challenge. Hannah, you're an excellent doctor, you fit in well with the team, you're a natural for A and E—'

'And with a glowing testimonial like that I could get a job in any A and E department in the country,' she interrupted. 'So why should I stay at St Stephen's?'

His gaze locked with hers for a second, then fled. 'Hannah... Hannah, you must know how I feel about you.'

'Must I?' she said, her heart suddenly beginning to race.

'Dammit, you should!' he flared. 'We were lovers in case you've forgotten. You're important to me, and I...I care about what happens to you.'

She was important to him. He cared about what happened to her. Perhaps a month ago that would have been enough. Perhaps a month ago she would have fallen happily into his arms again, and into his bed, but it wasn't enough any more. She wanted more. She wanted him to tell her he loved her.

'How much do you care, Robert?' she said through a throat so tight it hurt.

Say it, damn you, she thought as he stared down at her, his face unreadable. If you'd only say those three little words I'd phone the headquarters of Médicins Sans Frontières right now and ask them if I could possibly withdraw my acceptance.

But he didn't say them. He merely muttered, 'I have no right to try to run your life for you, Hannah, and if this is what you truly want…'

I want you, you big, stubborn idiot, she longed to yell back at him, but she didn't. Instead she quickly walked towards the staffroom door. 'I'll see you tomorrow, Robert.'

She half thought he would try to stop her. She definitely thought he might come after her, but he did neither, and tears welled in her eyes as she walked along to the waiting room.

Look, does it really matter if he doesn't say the words? her mind whispered. You know deep down that he really loves you. But it does matter, her heart answered back. If Robert can't say 'I love you' then maybe she'd been right when she'd told Elliot she'd be better off without him.

'I'm afraid it seems to be getting worse out there, Hannah,' one of the secretaries on Reception called as she passed. 'Would you like me to call you a taxi?'

'I'll be fine.' She managed to smile back. 'It's not as though I have very far to go.'

At least not yet, she thought when she stood outside the hospital and quickly unfurled her umbrella, but in a month's time…

In a month's time all this would be a distant memory. St Stephen's, the A and E department, all the staff who worked in it. And Robert. Would he become a distant memory, too?

No, he would never be that, she realised. She would always love him, always want him, and because her eyes were blurred with a mixture of tears and snow as she began crossing the road, and because her head was bent against the icy wind, she didn't see the car coming round the corner until it was too late. Didn't hear the screech of its brakes until it hit her, and then all she felt was a searing, agonising pain in her leg as she was dragged along the road.

Faintly she heard the sound of a car door opening, then a man hoarsely repeating that it hadn't been his fault, that she'd simply stepped out in front of him, but when she tried to raise her head, to tell the frightened voice that she was perfectly all right, hands began to lift her. Hands that belonged to worried faces. Hands that were making the pain in her leg worse, much worse, and when she fainted for the first time in her life, her last thought was that at least it didn't hurt any more. Nothing hurt any more.

So she didn't see Elliot's shocked face as they carried her into A and E. Didn't feel Jane's hand gently lifting her wrist to take her pulse, her expression horrified, and didn't hear the deep, guttural cry Robert gave when he realised who it was.

'I think I should handle this one, don't you?' Elliot said, striding towards him to bar his way.

'Like hell you will,' Robert exclaimed. 'I'm the special registrar—'

'And this is personal for you. She's our colleague, our friend, but to you—'

'Elliot, if you don't get out of my way, I swear I'll knock you from here into the waiting room!' Robert exploded. 'Jane, I want an ECG, CBC, guiac and urine tests.'

'Chest, pelvis and leg X-rays?' the sister queried, quickly inserting an IV line into Hannah's arm, then linking her to the heart monitor.

'Everything. I want X-rays of everything.'

Jane glanced across at Elliot, her eyebrows raised, and he nodded. 'You heard what the man said. He wants X-rays of everything.'

'BP 130 over 90, pulse 80 beats a minute,' Floella announced.

'Pretty good for someone who's just been dragged along

the road by a car,' Elliot murmured, listening to Hannah's chest through his stethoscope. 'In fact, I think it looks a lot worse than it actually is.'

Robert hoped that it was. He prayed that it was.

She looked so fragile and white lying on the trolley, her only vestige of colour the trickle of blood running down onto her cheek from the graze on her temple. If he should lose her... Oh, God, if he should lose her the same way he'd lost Laura, he knew he wouldn't want to go on living.

'What idiot demanded X-rays of everything?' Craig Larkin protested as he came through the cubicle curtains. 'Radiology isn't some branch of your local photographer's, you know.'

'Craig...' Jane caught him by the arm, and nodded her head in the direction of the trolley.

He looked across, gasped out loud, then muttered tightly, 'Fine. Right. X-rays of everything.'

'Guiac and urine tests normal, Robert,' Floella declared. 'ECG a little fast but not worryingly so, CBC perfect.'

Which only left the X-rays, he thought, unclenching his fingers slightly. 'Jane, could you—?'

'Well, hello there, sleepyhead,' the sister said with a smile as Hannah's eyes suddenly fluttered open. 'Honestly, the things people will do to get a few weeks off work!'

'Robert...?' she said faintly, and he was at her side in an instant. 'The car driver. It wasn't his fault—'

'Never mind about that now,' he interrupted. 'How do you feel?'

She tried to move and decided that was a very bad idea. 'Like a herd of elephants have trampled over me, then returned for a repeat performance.'

'That bad, eh?' he said softly, smoothing her hair gently back from her forehead.

She nodded. 'And worse.'

'One fractured left leg, and absolutely no other damage

that I can see,' Craig declared, beaming at her. 'Hannah Blake, I want you to know you've just taken ten years off my life.'

'Sorry,' she murmured, then winced.

'What is it—what's wrong?' Robert demanded. 'Have you a pain in your chest, difficulty in breathing?'

'No, I haven't got a pain in my chest, or difficulty in breathing,' she replied crossly, 'though I have to say it's a miracle that I don't, considering some idiot's got me wired up like a prize turkey!'

'I think we can safely say that Hannah's feeling better.' Elliot grinned, relief plain in his face.

She wasn't feeling better. Her leg hurt, her side hurt, and she felt a quite overwhelming desire to burst into tears, but she managed a wobbly smile. 'Please, won't somebody take all this paraphernalia off me? You heard what Craig said. I've just broken my leg.'

Elliot glanced enquiringly across at Robert and he nodded reluctantly, but when Jane and Floella had removed the ECG stickers, and Jane grasped the end of the trolley, ready to wheel Hannah to the plastering department, Elliot suddenly motioned to Robert to follow him.

'What's wrong?' Robert said as soon as they were standing outside the cubicle. 'Do you think we might have missed something?'

'No, of course I don't think we've missed something,' the SHO replied. 'I want to know when you're going to tell her.'

'Tell her what?' Robert said in confusion.

'That the local supermarket is doing a special this week on Christmas puddings!' Elliot exclaimed in exasperation. 'That you love her, of course, you idiot!'

'Elliot—'

'Robert, she could have been killed tonight, and then you'd never have had the chance. All you have to say is,

''I love you, Hannah.'' Why is that so very hard for you to say?'

'Elliot—'

'All that crap you gave Hannah about her not being honest with you. Have you been honest with her? *Have you?*'

He hadn't, Robert thought as the SHO hustled Floella and Jane out of the cubicle, muttering something garbled about needing to discuss something in private with them, then throwing him a meaningful look. He'd condemned Hannah for her failure to be honest with him, but he'd been anything but honest with her. All that rubbish about caring for her, about her being important to him. Damn it, he *loved* her, so why couldn't he just say it?

Because I'm afraid, he suddenly realised. I'm like Hannah, afraid to trust my own feelings. Afraid that, having made one mistake, I might be wrong again.

But he wasn't wrong this time, he knew he wasn't. He loved her, he always would, but after doubting her honesty, hurting her so badly, would she believe him?

There was only one way to find out.

'Where's everybody gone?' Hannah protested when he stepped back through the cubicle curtains. 'I was beginning to think I really did have something seriously wrong with me, and no one was willing to tell me.'

'You're fine, but I'm not,' he murmured, sitting down on the edge of the trolley and gently taking her hand in his. 'I've just found out I have an incurable affliction that only you can heal.'

'An incurable—'

'Hannah, when Laura died I swore I'd never fall in love again,' he continued as she gazed up at him in confusion. 'And then you came into my life. Little Miss Muffet, so eager and keen. Little Miss Muffet, with her big brown eyes and determination to put the world to rights.'

'Robert, I'm not Laura,' she began hesitantly. 'By all

accounts I don't have the figure, the height or the brains to be Laura even if I wanted to.'

'And I'm not Chris,' he said softly. 'I have neither the personal ambition nor the capacity to toady to anyone even if I wanted to.'

She stared down at the sheet covering her. 'I really do trust you, you know. I can see that it didn't look that way—'

'Hannah, I love you.'

'Y-you what?' she stammered.

'I love you, and I want to marry you.'

She gazed up at him in disbelief, then shook her head. 'I know what you're doing. You feel sorry for me because of this accident—'

'Hannah, I'm an A and E doctor,' he protested. 'If I proposed to every female accident victim I'd ever seen, I'd be a serial bigamist by now.'

'Yes, but—'

'Hannah, I *love* you. Do you want me to buy a megaphone—stand outside the hospital and shout it to all of London? I'll do it if it will convince you. I love you, Hannah Blake, and I want to marry you, if you'll have me.'

'You mean it?' she whispered, her eyes fixed tremulously on his face. 'You're not simply saying it because I've been hurt? Robert—Robert, where are you going?' she added quickly as he got off the trolley and began to stride towards the cubicle curtains.

'To find a shop that sells megaphones! Hannah, I want you more than I've ever wanted anything in my life,' he declared as she began to laugh. 'So, will you marry me, have my children, grow old with me?'

She opened her mouth to tell him she'd like nothing better, only to gasp as she suddenly remembered something. 'Robert, I'm supposed to be leaving for Botswana at the end of the month. I know I can't go now until my leg heals, but my contract's for two years. Once I leave Britain, I won't see you again for two years.'

'You will if Médicins Sans Frontières would be interested in employing a husband-and-wife team,' he said. 'One enthusiastic junior doctor married to a somewhat old and battered special registrar.'

'You'd do that for me?' she said huskily. 'Give up your career here at St Stephen's for me?'

He cupped her face gently in his hands. 'Hannah, don't you realise even now that you're more important to me than anything else in the world? I admit it will be a wrench to leave here. Elliot, Jane, Flo and myself, we've made a good team—but you and I could help so many people, working with Médicins Sans Frontières. People who desperately need us and our skills.'

'And we could come back,' she said thoughtfully. 'Once we'd fulfilled our contract, we could come back again and work here at St Stephen's, couldn't we?'

He nodded. 'So there really only appears to be one thing left that we haven't settled yet,' he murmured softly, placing tiny, feather-light kisses gently across her forehead. 'For the *fourth* time, Hannah Blake, will you marry me?'

She gazed up at him, saw all the love and trust she had ever wanted to see in his face, and smiled. 'Oh, yes, Robert. Oh, *yes!*'

And as his lips came down on hers, she thought she heard Elliot's delighted exclamation of 'About bloody time, too!' coming from outside the cubicle, but all she really knew as Robert tenderly gathered her into his arms was that at last she had come home.

DR MATHIESON'S DAUGHTER

BY
MAGGIE KINGSLEY

CHAPTER ONE

ELLIOT MATHIESON gazed blankly at the solicitor for a second, then shook his head. 'I'm sorry, but there has to have been some mistake. I have no daughter.'

The solicitor sifted through the papers on his desk and selected one. 'We have a birth certificate with your name on it, Dr Mathieson—'

'I don't care if you have a hundred birth certificates with my name on them. I have no daughter. No children at all, come to that!'

'Your wife—'

'My *ex*-wife—'

'Was quite adamant in her will that Nicole is yours,' the solicitor declared calmly. 'I can, if you wish, instigate court proceedings to dispute paternity, but…'

It would be a waste of time, Elliot finished for him silently. Whatever else Donna might have been, she hadn't been a fool. She would have known Nicole's paternity could be easily established by means of a simple blood test.

Which meant he had a child. A six-year-old daughter he'd known nothing about until he'd stepped into the solicitor's office this morning, but how?

He and Donna had been divorced for five years. They hadn't even spoken to one another since that disastrous attempt at a reconciliation in Paris almost seven years ago. A reconciliation which had ended in heated words and angry exchanges.

But not at first, he suddenly remembered, his blue eyes darkening with dismay. There'd been no angry words on

5

that first night when they'd gone out to dinner, she'd invited him back to her flat for coffee and somehow they'd
ended up in her big double bed.

Oh, hell, but it must have happened then. Nicole must
have been conceived then.

'I realise this has come as something of a shock to you,
Dr Mathieson,' the solicitor continued, gazing at him not
without sympathy, 'but I'm afraid there really wasn't any
easy way of breaking the news. If you wish to dispute
paternity—'

'Of course I don't,' he interrupted brusquely. 'I accept
the child is mine.'

The solicitor smiled with relief. 'Then Nicole will be
arriving from Paris tomorrow—'

'Arriving?' Elliot's jaw dropped. 'What do you mean,
she'll be arriving?'

'She can hardly remain in France now her mother is
dead, Dr Mathieson.'

'What about my wife's sister? Surely she—'

'I'm afraid we haven't even been able to inform Mrs
Bouvier of her sister's death. She and her husband are on
an archaeological dig in Iran where communications are
very poor. And you are the child's father, Dr Mathieson.'

'Yes, but I can't possibly look after a child,' Elliot protested. 'I've recently been promoted to special registrar in
St Stephen's A and E department. I work long hours—
never know when I'm going to be home—'

'You could employ a nanny or a housekeeper,' the solicitor suggested. 'Or what about boarding school? Many
professional people send their children to boarding
schools.'

They did, but he'd have to be the biggest louse of all
time to send a six-year-old kid who had just lost her
mother to a boarding school. A nanny or a housekeeper

might be the answer, but where on earth did you get people like that in twenty-four hours?

'Look, it's not that I don't want Nicole living with me,' he declared, raking his hands through his blond hair in desperation. Like hell it wasn't. 'But I don't know anything about raising a child.'

'Nobody does initially,' the solicitor said bracingly.

Which was all very well for him to say, Elliot thought when he left the solicitor's office some time later, but where did that leave him?

He hadn't even got used to being special registrar at St Stephen's yet, far less the two new members of staff who'd replaced Robert Cunningham and Hannah Blake when they'd got married and left to work for Médecins Sans Frontières. The last thing he needed was a child on top of all his other responsibilities.

Oh, cut the flannel, Elliot, his mind whispered as he strode down the busy London street, heedless of the falling sleet and biting March wind. You wouldn't want this child no matter what the circumstances. You wouldn't want *any* child who reminded you of your marriage to Donna.

'Hey, watch where you're going, mate!' a plump, middle-aged man protested as Elliot collided with him on his way to the entrance to the St Stephen's Accident and Emergency unit.

Watch where he was going? A couple of hours ago Elliot Mathieson had known exactly where he was going, but now...

Now he had a daughter arriving from France tomorrow. Now he was being forced to remember a time in his life he'd tried for the last five years to forget, and he didn't like it. He didn't like it at all.

'I thought Elliot was only going to be away an hour?' Floella Lazear protested, her round face looking distinctly harassed as she crossed the treatment room. 'What on earth can be keeping him?'

Jane Halden tucked a wayward strand of thick black hair back under her sister's cap and wished she knew. Elliot had told them of his ex-wife's death in a car crash in France, and her London solicitors' urgent request to see him, and she'd assumed—they all had—that he must be a beneficiary in Donna's will, but two hours was an awfully long time for the solicitor to tell him so.

'Maybe his ex-wife's left him a fortune,' Charlie Gordon observed, joining them at the whiteboard. 'She was a successful fashion designer, wasn't she? Maybe she's left him so much money he's handing in his resignation even as we speak.'

'I wish somebody would leave me a fortune,' Floella sighed. 'I'd be off to the travel agent's before you could say enema.'

Charlie laughed. 'What would you do if somebody left you a lot of money, Jane?'

Check into a health farm and lose twelve kilos, she thought. Treat myself to every beautifying facial known to womankind, then throw out all my chain-store clothes and buy designer labels.

'I haven't the faintest idea,' she replied.

'Got everything you want, huh?' The SHO grinned.

'Something like that.' She nodded. And she did. Well, almost everything. She had a job as senior sister in A and E, which she loved, a flat that might be a shoebox but at least it was hers, and if there was no man in her life, well, two out of three wasn't bad. 'How about you, Charlie?' she asked. 'What would you do with a windfall?'

'Send a bottle of champagne and a huge box of chocolates to my girlfriend in Shrewsbury every day to make sure she doesn't forget me.'

'And in six months she'd be a twenty-stone alcoholic, you idiot!' Floella laughed.

A deep blush of embarrassed colour spread across the SHO's face and Jane quickly came to his rescue. 'I think it's a *lovely* idea, Charlie, and your girlfriend's a very lucky girl.'

And she was, too, Jane thought as the SHO hurried away, the colour on his cheeks even darker. They were lucky to have him. Big, bluff, and hearty, Charlie had settled in well into Elliot's old SHO job. It was just a pity the same couldn't be said for their new junior doctor, she thought with a groan as she noticed the man in question bearing down on her. Richard Connery might be bright and enthusiastic, but he was also abrasive and far too self-confident for his own good.

'My patient in 6 has a fractured right arm, Sister Halden,' he declared without preamble. 'Please, arrange for him to go to X-Ray.'

Like he couldn't arrange it himself? she thought as he strode away again before she could reply. No, of course he couldn't. It was obviously too far beneath his dignity to speak to anyone as lowly as a porter so he expected her to drop everything and do it for him.

'And what—pray tell—did his last servant die of?' Floella exclaimed angrily. 'Honestly, Jane—'

'I know, I know,' she interrupted, 'but just leave it right now, Flo, OK?'

'But he has no right to talk to you like that,' the staff nurse protested. 'You're the senior sister in A and E. You've at least six years more medical experience than he has—'

'And if you say I'm old enough to be his mother I'll hit you!' Jane declared, her grey eyes dancing, and a reluctant smile curved Floella's lips.

'Yeah, right. Like you're old Ma Moses. But you know what I mean. It's just not on.'

It wasn't, but working in A and E was difficult enough at the moment, what with Elliot still finding his feet as special registrar and Charlie Gordon learning the ropes as SHO, and the last thing they needed was a full-scale row.

'Try to be patient with him, Flo. I know he can be difficult,' she continued as the staff nurse shook her head, 'but he's only been with us a month, and I'm sure a lot of his abrasiveness is due to him finding the work a lot harder than he imagined.'

'Rubbish!' Floella retorted. 'He just enjoys treating nurses like dirt!'

She didn't need this, not right now, Jane thought as the staff nurse stalked off. Teamwork was important in every department in the hospital, but in A and E it was vital. Without teamwork they couldn't function, but it was going to take time to create a new team, and time, as Floella had just so forcefully revealed, was the one thing they didn't have.

With a sigh she went into cubicle 6 where Richard's patient was still waiting.

'My arm is definitely broken, then?' the elderly man queried, wincing slightly as she helped him into a wheelchair. 'The young lad who saw me earlier said he thought it was, but I wasn't sure whether he was fully qualified to make the diagnosis or not.'

Jane hid a smile. 'Dr Connery's pretty sure your arm's fractured, but to make one hundred per cent sure we're going to send you along to X-Ray. Hey, look on the bright side,' she added encouragingly as his face fell, 'you'll get lots of sympathy from your female admirers.'

'I hope not or my wife will break my other arm,' he observed, his faded brown eyes twinkling. 'Oh, well, I suppose it could have been worse, and at least it's given me the opportunity to meet a very pretty and charming young lady.'

Jane chuckled. She knew very well that she wasn't pretty, and she supposed that at twenty-eight she wasn't exactly young any more, but that didn't mean it wasn't nice to hear a compliment.

Right now, she could have done with hearing a lot more. It might have cheered her up. In fact, ever since Hannah had married Robert—and it had been a lovely wedding despite the bride's leg being in plaster—she'd been feeling oddly down.

Probably because it's the fourth wedding you've been to in as many months, her mind pointed out, whereas you…

No, she wasn't going to think about her love life. Actually, her completely non-existent love life.

And whose fault is that? Her little voice asked. OK, so Frank was a rat, and you wasted two years of your life believing his protestations of undying love, but what happened after he dumped you? You promptly fell in love with Elliot Mathieson. A man who's had more girlfriends since he got divorced than most other men have had hot dinners. A man who could hurt you a hundred times more than Frank ever did if he found out how you really feel about him.

'Jane, we've got trouble!'

With an effort she turned to see their student nurse gazing at her in dismay. 'What's up, Kelly?'

'We've got that man back in again—the one who thinks his brain's been taken over by aliens. I've phoned Social Services but—'

'They said it's our pigeon,' she finished for her wryly. Social Services always said psychiatric cases were their pigeon unless someone was so bad they had to be sectioned. And Harry's delusions weren't nearly frequent enough yet to have him compulsorily detained in a psychiatric ward. 'Has Charlie seen him?'

'He's given him a tranquilliser, and he seems pretty quiet at the moment, but you know what happened last time.'

Jane did. Before the tranquilliser could take effect Harry had practically wrecked one of their ECG machines, thinking it was an alien life form. 'OK. I'll sit with him—'

'RTA on the way, Jane!' Floella suddenly called from the end of the treatment room. 'Three casualties, and two look really serious!'

Jane bit her lip. Damn, this would have to happen right now with Mr Mackay, the consultant in charge of A and E, off on his annual break and Elliot not back from the solicitors yet.

'Kelly—'

'Yeah, I know.' The student nurse sighed. 'Make the alien a nice cup of tea, and do my best.'

'Good girl.' Jane nodded, but as she hurried down the treatment room a sigh of relief came from her when Elliot suddenly appeared.

'Now, that's what I call perfect timing,' she said with a smile.

'Perfect timing?'

'We've an RTA on the way,' she explained, 'and I was just wondering how on earth we were going to cope with the casualties.'

'Oh—Right. I see.'

She glanced up at him, her grey eyes concerned. 'Everything OK, Elliot?'

'Great. Fine,' he replied, but he was anything but fine she decided as he walked quickly across to Charlie Gordon.

He looked… Not worried. Elliot never looked worried no matter how dire the situation, but he most definitely looked preoccupied. Preoccupied and tense, and still quite the handsomest man she'd ever laid eyes on.

In fact, there ought to have been a law against any man being quite so handsome, she thought ruefully. His thick blond hair, deep blue eyes and devastating smile would have been quite potent enough, but when you added a six-foot muscular frame, a pair of shoulders which looked as though they'd been purpose-built for a girl to lean her head against...

It was an unbeatable combination. The kind of combination which turned even the most sensible women into slack-jawed idiots whenever he was around. Herself included, as Jane knew only too well, but she'd always had sense enough not to show it.

Not that it would have made any difference if she had, of course, she realised. Elliot's taste ran to tall, leggy women. Women like Gussie Granton from Paediatrics whose figure would have made a pin-up girl gnash her teeth.

Nobody would ever gnash their teeth over her figure, she thought wistfully, unless it was in complete despair. She was too short, and too fat, and a pair of ordinary grey eyes and stubbornly straight shoulder-length black hair were never going to make up for those deficiencies.

'You have a wonderful sense of humour, Jane,' her mother had told her encouragingly when she was growing up. 'Men like that.'

Yeah, right, Mother. And Frank's admiration for my sense of humour lasted only until a red-haired bimbo with the IQ of a gerbil drifted into his sights, and then he was off.

What on earth was wrong with her today? she wondered crossly as she heard the sound of an ambulance arriving, its siren blaring. All this maudlin self-pity. All right, so she was in love with Elliot Mathieson, and had been ever since he'd come to St Stephen's two years ago, but he was never going to fall in love with her. She was simply good old Janey and it was high time she accepted that. Time she realised it was only in the movies that the plain, ordinary heroine got the handsome hero, and this wasn't the movies—this was real life.

'OK, what have you got for us?' Elliot asked as the doors of the treatment room banged open and the paramedics appeared with their casualties.

'One adult, plus a seventeen-year-old boy and fifteen-year-old girl. The youngsters suffered the worst damage. They were in the back seat and neither was wearing seat belts.'

Elliot swore under his breath. 'Are they related in any way?'

'The adult's the father. He has a fractured wrist, ankle and minor lacerations.'

'Richard, Kelly—you take the adult—'

'But what about my alien?' the student nurse exclaimed.

'Oh, Lord, he's not back in again, is he?' Elliot groaned. 'Has anyone given him any tranquillisers?'

'I have,' Charlie Gordon said, nodding.

'Then get one of the porters to take him up to Social Services.'

'Elliot, they'll throw a blue fit if we dump him on them!' Jane protested.

'Let them,' he replied grimly. 'It'll give them a chance to see that care in the community means more than simply leaving psychiatric cases to fend for themselves. Charlie, you and Flo take the boy. Jane, I'll need your help with the girl.'

He was going to need his skill a whole lot more, she thought when she helped the paramedic wheel the girl into cubicle 2.

The teenager was a mess. Countless lacerations to her

face and arms, compound fractures to the right and left tibia and fibula which would require the services of both orthopaedics and plastics, but it was her laboured, rasping breathing that was the most worrying. If she wasn't helped—and quickly—not enough oxygen would reach her brain and she'd be in big trouble.

'ET, Jane,' Elliot demanded, though in fact there had been no need for him to ask. She was already holding the correct size of endotracheal tube out to him, and gently he eased it past the girl's vocal cords and down into her trachea. 'IV lines and BP?'

'IV's open and running,' she replied, checking the drip bags containing the saline solution which was providing a temporary substitute for the blood the teenager was losing. 'BP 60 over 40.'

Elliot frowned. Too low, much too low, and the girl's heartbeat was showing an increasingly uneven rhythm.

Quickly he placed his stethoscope on the injured girl's chest. There were no breath sounds on the left side. She must have been thrown against one of the front seats in the crash and her left lung had collapsed, sending blood and air seeping into her chest cavity.

'Chest drain and scalpel?' Jane murmured.

He nodded and swiftly made an incision into the upper right-hand side of the teenager's chest, then carefully inserted a plastic tube directly into her chest cavity. 'BP now?'

'Eighty over sixty,' Jane answered.

Better. Not great, but definitely better. The chest drain had suctioned the excess air and blood out of the girl's chest. She was starting to stabilise at last.

'You'll be wanting six units of O-negative blood, chest, arm and leg X-rays?' Jane asked.

Elliot's eyebrows lifted and he grinned. 'This is getting seriously worrying.'

'Worrying?' she repeated in confusion.

'Your apparent ability to read my mind.'

Just so long as you can't read mine, she thought, and smiled. 'It comes with working with you for two years.'

He was surprised. 'Has it really been that long?'

'Uh-huh.'

He supposed it must have been, but Jane… Well, Jane just always seemed to have been there. Skilled, intuitive, able to instinctively predict whatever he needed whenever he needed it.

But even she couldn't get him out of his current predicament, he thought, watching her as she inserted another IV line to take the O-negative blood they would use until they'd made a cross-match. Nobody could.

If his mother hadn't just left for Canada to stay with his sister Annie for the next three months to help her through what was proving to be a particularly difficult first pregnancy, she would have taken Nicole like a shot—he knew she would. Or if the agencies he'd phoned could have provided him with a nanny or a housekeeper immediately, but none of them could supply anybody until the beginning of April, and that was a month away.

Which meant that not only was he up the creek without a paddle, he was sitting in a leaking boat as well.

How could Donna have done this to him? She'd known the hours he worked, that everything could alter in an instant if a bad accident like this came in. What had she expected him to do with Nicole, then? And what about after school, at weekends?

It probably hadn't even occurred to her, he decided bitterly. Live for today—that had always been Donna's motto. Live for today, and don't think about tomorrow.

Which was what attracted you to her in the first place, his mind pointed out. Her vitality, her lust for life, not to mention a husky French accent and a face and figure that had done irreparable damage to his libido.

But it hadn't lasted. Within three short years the marriage had been over, leaving him bitter and disillusioned. And now Donna was dead, killed in a car crash. And he had a daughter arriving tomorrow and no earthly idea of how he was going to cope.

'Elliot, are you quite sure you're OK?' Jane said, her gaze fixed on him with concern when the teenager was wheeled out of the treatment room towards the theatre after Radiology had confirmed that the patient did, indeed, have compound fractures, but no other major damage. 'You seem a bit, well, a bit preoccupied this afternoon.'

'Perils of being a new and very inexperienced special reg,' he replied, managing to dredge up a smile. 'Too much to think about.'

She didn't press the point, though he knew she wasn't convinced, and with relief he strode quickly down the treatment room to check on the other casualties. He didn't want to talk about his problem—didn't even want to think about it. All he wanted to do right now was to bury himself in work and forget all about his daughter, and he managed to do just that until late in the afternoon when the sound of children crying caught his attention.

'What on earth's going on in cubicle 8, Flo?' he asked curiously. 'It sounds like somebody's being murdered in there.'

She sighed. 'It's a case of child neglect. Two girls and a boy, aged between one and four. The police brought them in ten minutes ago for a medical assessment before they contact Social Services. Apparently their dad's in jail, their mother is God knows where and a neighbour phoned the police because she hadn't seen them out and about for a week.'

'Medical condition?' Elliot demanded, his professional instincts immediately alert.

'Excellent, considering they've been living in an unheated flat for the past week, and the oldest child told the police they haven't had anything to eat for two days.' She sighed and shook her head. 'Honestly, some people should never have children.'

People like him, Elliot decided, but it was too late to think about that now, too late to regret that night in the hotel in Paris. 'Who's with them?'

'Jane. Charlie's checked them over, and there's nothing we can do for them except clean them up and give them some food, but...' She shrugged. 'It's better than nothing, isn't it?'

He supposed it was as he strode into the cubicle to find Jane sitting on the trolley, holding the youngest of the three children in her arms while the other two clung to her, wide-eyed and clearly terrified.

'Need any help?' he asked.

She shook her head and smiled, apparently completely oblivious to the overpowering smell of dried urine and faeces emanating from the trio. 'No, thanks. I've sent down to the kitchens for some food, and Kelly's organising a bath for them all.'

'What about clean clothes?' he suggested.

'Flo's phoned her husband and he's bringing some of their twins' old things over.'

There was nothing for him to do here, then, Elliot realised, but still he lingered, watching in admiration as Jane managed to eventually coax some smiles from the children.

She was good with kids. Actually, she was quite amazing with kids. He'd seen her get a response from even the most traumatised of children simply by sitting with them, holding them, murmuring all kinds of nonsense.

And suddenly it hit him. He had the answer to all his problems sitting right in front of him. Jane. Jane would be perfect for Nicole, just perfect.

But would she do it? Would she be prepared to move into his flat to help him out until he could get a nanny or a housekeeper in a month's time?

Of course she would. Jane helped everybody, and it wasn't as though he was asking a lot. Not much, he observed sourly. Just for her to take over your responsibilities, that's all. Nonsense, he wasn't asking her to do that. He wasn't even thinking about himself at all. He was simply thinking about Nicole.

And Jane clearly thought he was, too, when he whisked her into his office and explained what had happened after the police had collected the three abandoned children and taken them off to Social Services.

'Oh, the poor little girl!' she exclaimed, her eyes full of compassion. 'Why on earth didn't Donna tell you about her before?'

He'd wondered about that, too, but all he could think was that she must have been so angry with him when they'd parted that this had been her way of punishing him.

'You're going to have to go very carefully with her,' Jane continued, her forehead creased in thought. 'Not only has she lost her mother, but coming to a strange country, to a man she doesn't know... She's going to need lots of love and attention.'

'But that's the trouble,' he declared. 'How can I give her lots of love and attention when I'm hardly ever going to be there? Janey, you know what our hours are like—'

'We'll all help out,' she said quickly. 'It's a nuisance Mr Mackay being away, but when he gets back I'm sure he'll agree to letting you work days for a while. In the meantime, we could ask Charlie if he'd mind doing most of your night shifts—'

'I don't want Charlie to do my night shifts!' he snapped, then flushed as Jane's eyebrows rose. 'Janey, I've got to be honest with you...'

He paused. How to explain? How to say that it wasn't just a question of the day-to-day complications of taking care of a child that was worrying him, but that he didn't want this girl because she would remind him of a time in his life he preferred to forget. Jane would ask why. She'd ask questions. Questions he didn't want to answer.

Better by far for her to think he was selfish, he decided. Better for her to believe he was the biggest heel of all time than for him to have to reveal the sorry details of his failed marriage.

He took a deep breath. 'Janey, the thing is, kids...they're not really me. I never wanted any—never planned on having any. I'm a loner at heart, you see, always have been.'

Oh, he was something all right, she decided as she stared up at him in utter disbelief. How could he be so unfeeling about a child? And not simply any child. *His* child. *His* daughter.

'So you're getting your mother to look after her, I presume?' she said tightly.

'I can't. She flew out to Canada last Saturday to stay with my sister for the next three months. Annie's been having a really rotten time with her first pregnancy—'

'Then you're hiring a nanny?' Jane asked, her heart going out to his poor little motherless, unwanted child. 'Or are you too damn mean to fork out the money?'

'It's not a question of money!' he exclaimed, his cheeks reddening. 'None of the agencies I contacted could get me anybody until next month, which is why...' He quickly fixed what he hoped was his most appealing smile to his lips. 'Janey, I need you to do me a huge favour. I want you to come and live with me, to help me look after Nicole.'

'You want me to...' Her mouth fell open, then she shook her head. 'I'm sorry, but I think there must be something wrong with my hearing. I could have sworn you just said you wanted me to come and live with you to look after your daughter.'

'I did—I do. Janey, listen, it makes perfect sense,' he continued as she stared at him, stunned. 'You're a woman—'

'I also like pasta but that doesn't make me Italian,' she protested. 'If you're so desperate for help, why don't you ask Gussie Granton? She's your current girlfriend, according to the hospital grapevine, and as a paediatric sister she's bound to know more about children than I do.' He had the grace at least to look uncomfortable and her grey eyes narrowed. 'You've already asked her, haven't you, and she said no.'

Gussie had. Oh, she'd been wonderfully understanding, her luscious lips curving into an expression of deepest sympathy, but, as she'd pointed out, the demands of her job simply didn't give her the time to take care of a child.

'Janey—'

'So you decided that as your mother couldn't do it, and Gussie wouldn't, muggins here might fit the bill,' she interrupted, her voice harder and colder than he'd ever heard it. 'Well, you can forget it, Elliot. Forget it!'

'But you've *got* to help me,' he cried, coming after her as she made for his office door. 'Surely you can see that I can't do this on my own?'

'You're thirty-two years old, Elliot,' she snapped. 'Get off your butt and try!'

'But you're so good with kids—the very best,' he said, his blue eyes fixed pleadingly on her. 'And I'm not asking you to do it for ever—just for a month. Until I can get a nanny or a housekeeper. *Please*, Janey.'

She'd heard that wheedling tone in his voice before. It was the one he used on women when he wanted a favour, and it usually worked on her, too, but not today.

'No, Elliot.'

'Look, I'm not asking you to go into purdah for the next month,' he said quickly. 'I have a three-bedroom flat—you can have your friends round whenever you want, go out whenever you want. All I'm asking is for us to dovetail our shifts and personal commitments so at least one of us will be there when Nicole comes home from school.'

'*No*, Elliot.'

'Janey, please. I'm begging you. If you won't do it for me, won't you at least do it for Nicole?'

Blackmail. It was blackmail of the worst possible kind, and anyone who agreed to move in with him under those circumstances needed their head examined. Anyone who had secretly been in love with him for the last two years and agreed to do it needed that head certified.

Tell him it's his problem, not yours, her mind insisted. Tell him to go fly a kite, preferably on the edge of a very high cliff in the middle of a howling gale. OK, so his little girl must be grief-stricken to have lost her mother, but it's *not* your problem.

And she cleared her throat to tell him just that when an image suddenly came into her mind. An image of a little girl with big, frightened eyes. A little girl lost, and alone, and deeply unhappy.

'Just for a month, you said?' she murmured uncertainly.

He nodded, hope, desperation, plain in his eyes.

'You'll have to do your fair share, Elliot,' she declared. 'Nicole is your responsibility, not mine.'

'Oh, absolutely— definitely,' he replied, nodding vigorously.

Only an idiot would agree to this, she thought as she stared up into his handsome face. Only a fool would ever say yes. And yet, before she could stop herself, the words 'All right, then, I'll do it' were out of her mouth.

And as a broad smile lit up his face, and her heart turned over in response, she knew that she wasn't simply an idiot. She was completely and utterly out of her mind.

CHAPTER TWO

'She's arriving this evening, then, on the nine o'clock plane from Paris?' Floella declared as she helped Jane carry a fresh supply of medical dressings out of their small dispensary into the treatment room. 'Poor little soul. Losing her mother like that. My heart goes out to her, it really does.'

And I don't know why MI5 doesn't simply throw in the towel and hand over all its surveillance work to St Stephen's in future, Jane thought ruefully.

How *did* they do it? She'd told nobody about Nicole, and she was pretty sure Elliot hadn't told anybody either, and yet it had taken the staff less than twenty-four hours to discover not only that he had a daughter but what time her plane was arriving as well.

'I bet Gussie's spitting nails about you moving into Elliot's place.' Floella chuckled. 'I hear she's been itching to become his live-in girlfriend.'

'I'm not exactly moving in with him, Flo,' Jane said quickly. 'Simply helping out until he can employ a house-keeper.'

'Oh, I know *that*,' the staff nurse said dismissively. 'We all do.'

Which was another thing that was beginning to seriously annoy her, Jane thought, putting down the boxes of Steri-Strips she was carrying with a bang. The way everyone had instantly assumed there wasn't anything personal about the arrangement.

OK, so there wasn't, but that didn't mean she had to like the idea that nobody thought there might be. She wasn't *that* plain, and was it really so unlikely that she and Elliot could have become an item? Apparently it was.

'Elliot, we were just talking about your little girl.' Floella beamed as he strode down the treatment room towards them. 'You must be really excited at the prospect of meeting her.'

Jane didn't think he looked even remotely excited, but to his credit he managed to mumble something suitably enthusiastic in reply.

'You must bring her into the hospital one day, so we can all meet her,' the staff nurse continued. 'And, don't forget, if you ever need a babysitter, I'll be only too happy to oblige.'

Elliot smiled and nodded but as Floella bustled away he shook his head wryly. 'You know, this has got to be the worst-kept secret in the hospital.'

'Do you mind everybody knowing about Nicole?' Jane asked.

He shrugged. 'She's a fact of life. Whether I mind or not is immaterial.'

Which sounded very much as though he did mind. As though he'd far rather she didn't exist.

She'd thought—hoped—that since last night he might have had time to see what a great gift he'd been given, how lucky he was, but nothing, it seemed, had changed. He still saw his daughter as a nuisance, an unwelcome intrusion into his life.

'I'd better get back to work,' she said abruptly, but before she could move he suddenly clasped her hands in his.

'Jane, what you're doing for Nicole—for me—I just want to thank you again. It's really good of you to help me out like this, and I do appreciate it.'

Like hell you do, Elliot, she thought sourly, trying very hard not to notice the way her skin was traitorously reacting to the touch of his fingers. You just think you've got it made. You just think you've managed to offload your responsibilities onto someone else. Well, you're going to find out very quickly that I'm not a complete pushover. You're going to do your full share of taking care of your daughter, or my name isn't Jane Halden.

Determinedly she extricated her hands from his. 'I'd better go—'

'Did you remember to arrange with one of the night staff to start a little earlier tonight so you can come out to the airport with me?' he interrupted.

She nodded, though she still thought Nicole would probably have preferred him to meet her alone.

'I thought we'd take her out to dinner,' he continued. 'A sort of welcome-to-London treat. I know this fabulous restaurant in town which not only does the most amazing lobsters but also the best prawns this side of the Channel.'

He had to be joking. One look at his face told her he wasn't.

'Don't you think fish fingers and chips at home would be a much better idea?' she said quickly.

'Jane, she's French—'

'And she's six years old, Elliot. Look, I wouldn't be at all surprised if she's exhausted and a bit weepy when she arrives,' she continued as he opened his mouth, clearly intending to argue with her, 'so I really do think fish fingers and chips in your flat would suit her much better than dinner out at a fancy restaurant.'

He frowned uncertainly. 'If you say so. I don't think I've got any fish fingers in my freezer but I could easily buy some.'

Frankly she'd have been amazed if he'd had fish fingers in his freezer. *Pâté de foie gras*, quail and partridge eggs for sure, but not fish fingers and chips.

In fact, when she'd dropped off her clothes at his flat this morning her heart had quite sunk when she'd seen where he lived. Oh, his home was beautiful—all gleaming modern furniture and immaculate white walls—but not by any stretch of the imagination could it have been described as child-friendly. Indeed, its pristine elegance had intimidated her, so who knew what it would do to Nicole?

Flowers might soften the look, she thought suddenly, make it seem more homely, and she'd just opened her mouth to suggest it when two paramedics appeared, their faces taut, grim.

'Twenty-three-year-old mum with bad burns to her face, arms and upper torso. Apparently she was frying some chips for her kids' tea when the pan caught fire. She threw some water on it—'

'And the whole thing went up like a torch,' Elliot groaned as the paramedics wheeled the mother into cubicle 1. 'Didn't she know that oil and water don't mix?'

'Do you want me to page the burns unit?' Jane asked, beckoning to Floella to assist him.

'Please. You'd better alert IC as well. And, Jane…' She turned, her eyebrows raised questioningly. 'Make it fast, eh?'

She nodded. Shock was always the biggest hazard in cases like this. Shock and the danger of infection, and the sooner they could get the young mother stabilised and transferred to specialist care, the better.

And the sooner Richard Connery lost his high-and-mighty attitude the happier she'd be, too, she decided when she put down the phone to see the junior doctor snapping his fingers imperiously at her.

No wonder Floella's temper was close to breaking point, she thought as she walked towards him. Her own was getting pretty wafer-thin as well, and it was getting harder and harder for her to continue believing that Richard's high-handed manner was due to him finding the work in A and E a lot more stressful than he'd expected.

'How can I help you, Doctor?' she asked, determinedly bright as she joined him in cubicle 8.

'Being here considerably earlier would have been a start,' he declared irritably. 'I've been waiting ten minutes for nursing assistance.'

'We're very busy this afternoon, Dr Connery—'

'And I don't have time to listen to excuses,' he interrupted. 'My patient is suffering from acute appendicitis and I need liver, pancreatic and guiac tests to confirm it before I send him up to Theatre.'

It wasn't the only thing he needed, she thought grimly, but she managed to keep her tongue between her teeth and quickly took the samples he wanted.

'Well, is it a ruptured appendix, as I said?' he declared when she returned later with the results.

She cleared her throat awkwardly. 'Could I have a word with you in private Dr Connery?'

'I don't have time for a chat, Sister,' he retorted. 'All I want is a simple answer to a simple question. Is it a ruptured appendix or not?'

Well, he'd asked for it, she thought, and as he'd asked for it he was going to get it. 'I'm afraid it isn't, Dr Connery. Your patient has gallstones.'

'Gallstones?' Richard's normally pale face turned an interesting shade of pink, and he snatched the sheet of papers from her fingers. 'Let me see those results!'

'It can be very easy to confuse the two,' she murmured for the benefit of the young man who was lying on the trolley, glancing from her to Richard with clear concern. 'The symptoms—pain, nausea and sickness—'

'Are you presuming to give me lessons in diagnosis, Sister Halden?' Richard interrupted, his face now almost puce.

Of course I'm not, you big ninny, she thought. I'm simply trying to get you out of a jam. You should never have told your patient what was wrong with him until you were a hundred per cent sure, and making a diagnosis without having the results of your tests was just plain stupid.

But she didn't say any of that. Instead, she said as calmly as she could, 'Would you like me to make arrangements for your patient to be taken up to Men's Surgical, Dr Connery?'

From his expression Richard looked as though he'd far rather have thrown her under the nearest bus, but he managed to nod.

But he wasn't finished. The minute the young man on the trolley was wheeled out of the treatment room, he rounded on her furiously.

'I do not appreciate being made to look a fool, Sister Halden! That man was *my* patient—in *my* care—and you deliberately undermined his confidence in me!'

'I did no such thing,' she protested. 'I didn't want to give you those results. I asked if I could discuss them with you in private, but you insisted on having them.'

He had, and he knew it. He was also plainly acutely and deeply mortified, and despite her anger she couldn't help feeling a certain sympathy for him.

'Dr Connery…Richard… Look, it's no big deal,' she said gently. 'OK, so your initial diagnosis wasn't correct, but you were sensible enough to order all the necessary tests—'

'I am not a child so stop humouring me!' he interrupted. 'I am the doctor here, Sister Halden, and I suggest you don't forget it!'

He stormed away before she could answer him, but to her dismay her troubles weren't over. As she turned to go back into the cubicle to remove the paper sheet from the examination trolley and replace it with a fresh one, Elliot suddenly appeared and it was clear from his grim face that he'd heard every word.

'Does he always talk to you like that?' he demanded. 'He does—doesn't he?' he continued, seeing the betraying flush of colour on her cheeks. 'Right. It's obviously high time I had a chat with that young man.'

'Oh, Elliot, don't,' she said quickly, dreading the inevitable friction that such a course of action would create. 'He knows he was wrong, but he's very young, still finding his feet—'

'And using them to walk all over you by the sound of it,' he snapped. 'Jane, it's not on. There's such a thing as staff courtesy, not to mention the fact that even a first-year medical student would know never to make a diagnosis before they'd done every test.'

'I know that, but, please, won't you leave it for now?' she begged. 'I'm sure when he's had time to think about it he'll realise he shouldn't have behaved as he did.'

'And if he doesn't?' he demanded. 'If he continues to treat you like this?'

'He won't—I'm sure he won't,' she insisted, and for a second he frowned, then sighed and shook his head.

'You know something, Janey, you're far too soft-hearted for your own good.'

Too damn right I am, she thought, or I'd never have agreed to help you with Nicole, and she would have told him so, too, if she hadn't suddenly noticed he was smiling at her. Smiling the smile that made grown women grow weak at the knees, and her own were none too steady at the moment.

Why in the world had she ever agreed to move in with this man? Her brain must have been out to lunch. Her common sense must have gone with it, too, she realised, feeling an answering smile being irresistibly drawn from her. To live with him. To see him at breakfast. Last thing at night...

Then remember why you agreed to do it, she told herself

sharply. Remember that he's simply using you until he can employ a housekeeper, and that he doesn't give a damn for his daughter.

And if that doesn't bring you down to earth, she thought grimly when the doors of the treatment room swung open and Gussie Granton suddenly appeared, Elliot's current girlfriend certainly should.

'Hello, Gussie,' Elliot said in clear surprise. 'We don't often see you down in A and E. Something I can do for you?'

Gussie wrapped one curl of her long blonde hair round her finger and threw him a provocative glance from under her impossibly thick eyelashes. 'Not in public unfortunately, darling.'

Oh, barf. Barf, barf, and triple barf, Jane thought, deliberately beginning to edge away, but she didn't get far. Gussie placed a beautifully manicured hand on her arm, and subjected her to a smile. A smile which had quite a struggle to make her eyes.

'Don't run off, Jane. At least not until I tell you how very sweet I think you're being to help us out like this. I would have taken care of Nicole in a minute if I could, but being a senior sister in Paediatrics...' She sighed heavily. 'I just don't have any time to myself.'

And I do? Jane thought waspishly. Like being a senior sister in A and E is a dawdle? Like I simply turn up every day, do my eight-hour shift, then go home and put my feet up?

For two pins she'd have liked to tell Gussie where to stick her thanks. Forget the two pins, she decided. She'd do it for free. And right now. 'Gussie—'

'Elliot, darling, it's just occurred to me that you might like some company when you go out to the airport to meet your daughter,' Gussie continued, completely ignoring her.

'I could easily get one of my staff to swop shifts with me—'

'There's no need,' Elliot interrupted. 'Jane's already agreed to come with me.'

'Has she?' Gussie's large brown eyes narrowed slightly, then she smiled again at Jane. And this time her smile most definitely didn't reach her eyes. 'My word, but you are proving to be a little godsend, aren't you?'

Elliot thought she was. In fact, after a sleepless night spent tossing and turning, he was all too aware of how very kind Jane was being, but he wished Gussie hadn't said it—at least not in that particular way. There'd been a very definite edge to her voice. An edge which had made him feel uncomfortable, and if he'd felt like that he was sure Jane did as well.

'Gussie, I'm afraid, can be a bit overbearing at times,' he said the minute the paediatric sister had gone.

'That's one way of putting it,' Jane replied tersely.

He coloured. 'She does mean well, though, even if it doesn't always sound like it.'

Oh, Gussie had made her meaning perfectly clear, Jane thought tightly, walking over to the thirteen-year-old boy and his mother who had come through from the waiting room into cubicle 8.

Hands off—he's mine. That was what she'd said, and there'd been no need. Gussie was welcome to Elliot. In fact, right now the paediatric sister could have had him gift-wrapped with a bow round his neck.

'Your son's had this pain at the top of his chest for the last three days, you said?' Elliot said, once Jane had got the boy and his mother settled.

'At first I thought David had simply pulled a muscle, playing basketball,' the boy's mother replied, twisting her hands together convulsively, 'but when the pain didn't go away—'

'Keen on sport, are you, David?' Elliot asked as Jane helped the boy off with his shirt.

'Only basketball,' he replied. 'The other boys at my school prefer soccer, but basketball... Basketball's the best.'

Gently Elliot pressed on the boy's chest. 'Does it hurt when I do this?'

The boy shook his head. Not musculoskeletal pain, then, Elliot decided, or the pain would have increased under pressure.

'Do you have any other aches and pains anywhere?' he asked, taking his stethoscope out of his pocket and smiling encouragingly at the teenager.

'I don't think so.' David frowned. 'Sometimes I get an odd feeling in my back, but that's all.'

Elliot's ears pricked up. 'Odd in what way?'

'It's hard to explain. It's...it's a sort of ripping feeling. I'm sorry but I can't really describe it.'

He didn't need to. The minute Elliot placed his stethoscope on the boy's chest he heard a distinctive whooshing sound. A sound similar to that he'd heard in much older patients with leaky heart valves. But surely a boy of thirteen was far too young for that?

'Jane, could you get me an ECG reading, please?' he murmured casually.

She nodded.

'So, you play a lot of basketball, do you, David?' he said as Jane deftly applied the sticky electrodes to each of the boy's arms and legs, then across his chest.

'His school thinks he could play professionally when he's older,' his mother replied, clearly torn between maternal pride and concern.

'My height helps a lot,' her son said quickly, shooting his mother the speaking glance all boys used when they were deeply embarrassed. 'You don't have to jump up so far to reach the basket when you're as tall as me.'

And he was tall—almost as tall as I am, Elliot thought pensively. Rangy, too, with extremely long fingers, and suddenly somewhere in the back of his mind a memory stirred. A memory of something he'd read in a medical journal a long time ago, and he hoped to heaven he was wrong.

'ECG reading normal,' Jane murmured.

'Chest X-ray, please, Sister Halden,' he said, then turned to the boy's mother. 'Has your son always been tall for his age?'

'Not when he was a toddler, but when he hit seven...' She shook her head ruefully. 'It costs me a fortune every time he needs new clothes and shoes. Nothing in any of the ordinary kids' shops fits him, you see.'

Because he wasn't an ordinary boy, Elliot thought sadly, when Radiology had processed David's chest X-rays.

He had Marfan's syndrome, a rare, inherited condition which caused the aorta—the major blood vessel leading from the heart—to become abnormally enlarged, and one of the first indications of the condition was that sufferers were always extremely tall as children with unusually long fingers.

'Historians think Abraham Lincoln might have had Marfan's, don't they?' Jane commented after the boy and his mother had been transferred up to the medical ward where further tests could be performed.

Elliot nodded. 'Thank goodness his mother brought him in when she did. With that enlarged aorta, he could have had a heart attack at any time, but at least now we can give him beta-blockers to control his heart problems, and got him fitted with an orthopaedic corset before his spine starts to become deformed due to the weight of his bones.'

'No more basketball for him, though, I guess,' Jane sighed.

'No. No more basketball,' he answered, and wondered why he should find that thought so deeply depressing.

Oh, he'd always cared about the patients who passed through his hands, had fought tooth and nail to save many of them, but this young boy...

Perhaps it was because he seemed so very young, scarcely more than a child, despite his height. Perhaps it was because all of his dreams to become a world-class basketball player were now lying in the dust.

No, it wasn't that, he realised. It had been the look of total devastation on his mother's face when he'd taken her into one of their private waiting rooms to explain what was wrong.

David's mother would willingly have given everything she possessed to spare her son pain. Would even have given her own life if he could have been cured. That was love. Real love. And he felt none of that for his daughter.

You don't know her yet—haven't even met her—his mind pointed out, and unconsciously he shook his head. It wasn't as simple as that. Even if he'd wanted to be a father—and at the moment he certainly didn't—he didn't know how to be one.

He could do Lover. Oh, he could do a great Lover, provided there was no talk of long-term commitment. He could even do Friend. A sympathetic, willing shoulder for any woman to lean her head on if she needed it, but Father?

There was no way he could do Father—no way—and a wave of panic washed over him.

Panic that didn't get any less when a case of accidental poisoning came in a mere forty minutes before he and Jane were due to leave for the airport.

'We're really cutting it fine,' Jane murmured, seeing his

eye drift to the treatment-room clock while they waited for the results of the blood count and chemistry tests. 'Thank goodness we brought a change of clothes into the hospital just in case.'

He nodded, but he'd hoped to have time to shower, to wash the smell of the hospital off him before he met his daughter, but now it looked as though he'd be phoning the airport to tell them to look after her until they could get there. It was a great start. A really great start.

'Look, why don't the pair of you just go?' Charlie Gordon said. 'It's not like we need either of you here. Flo and I can look after your patient.'

Elliot shook his head. 'It's asking too much—'

'Elliot, I'd bet money that your blood pressure is higher right now than your patient's,' the SHO said with a grin.

'Probably, but—'

'Charlie's right, boss,' Floella chipped in. 'We don't need you here, and it would be awful if your little girl arrived with nobody to meet her.'

She was right, it would. But still he looked across at Jane uncertainly. 'What do you think?'

'Who am I to disagree with the others?' She smiled. 'Come on. Let's go.'

They made the airport with five minutes to spare.

'Relax, Elliot,' Jane said, seeing him scanning the Arrivals board anxiously for information about the 21.00 plane from Paris. 'The plane might land at nine o'clock, but she'll have to collect her luggage first, remember, so try to relax.'

Relax? How could he possibly relax when all his instincts were urging him to run, to leave town, to give no forwarding address? He glanced at his watch, then straightened his tie. 'Do I look all right? I mean, this suit...?'

'You look fine.' Actually, she wished he'd brought a

pair of casual trousers and a sweatshirt to change into at the hospital instead of a suit and tie, but now was hardly the time to tell him so.

'Should I get her some flowers, do you think?' he continued, seeing a man emerging from the florist opposite with an enormous bouquet. 'Girls always like flowers, don't they?'

'Daffodils would be nice…'

'Not roses, then?' he queried. 'You think roses would be too much?'

For sure they would be too much. Roses were for an adult, not a little girl, and she would have told him that if she hadn't suddenly caught a glimpse of his face.

He looked tense. Tense, and taut, and grim.

Surely he couldn't possibly be nervous at the prospect of meeting his daughter? Of course he wasn't. The very idea was ridiculous. He was resentful, yes. Probably even a little bit angry at his ex-wife for doing this to him, but super-confident Elliot nervous about meeting a child? No way. Never. And yet…

Gently she put her hand on his arm. 'Elliot, all she needs is to feel loved and wanted.'

'Loved and wanted.' He nodded, for all the world as though he were ticking off a mental check list of dos and don'ts.

'Just be her father,' she continued, 'and she'll adore you.'

Be her father? He couldn't do it—he knew he couldn't—but a voice over the loudspeaker had announced the arrival of Flight 303 from Paris, and Jane was pushing her way through the crowded concourse, leaving him with no choice but to follow her.

'Do you have a photograph so we'll know what she looks like?' she asked, breaking into his thoughts.

It had never occurred to him to ask if the solicitor had

one! Relax, he told himself, feeling a trickle of sweat run down his back. How many six-year-old kids can be travelling on the plane from Paris? Even if there are dozens she'll have somebody from Donna's French solicitors with her.

She didn't. She was on her own. OK, so one of the air stewardesses was holding her hand, but she was still on her own, and somebody had pinned a label onto her coat for all the world as though she were a parcel to be collected, not a child, not a person.

A surge of quite unexpected anger flooded through him. Anger that was just as quickly replaced by an altogether different emotion as the stewardess led his daughter towards him.

She looked exactly like Donna. The same long auburn hair, the same large dark eyes, the same elfin features. The face that stared uncertainly up at him was the one which had loved and then taunted and mocked him during his marriage, and despite all his best efforts to prevent it he felt himself beginning to withdraw. Knew it was wrong, that she was only a child, but he couldn't stop himself.

And Nicole sensed his withdrawal. He could see it in the clouding of her eyes, and though he managed to swiftly dredge up his brightest smile he knew the damage had been done.

'Elliot….'

Jane's hand was at his back, urging him forward, and he cleared his throat awkwardly.

'Hello, Nicole. I'm…I'm your father.' She gazed up at him without expression and a fresh wave of panic assailed him. What if she didn't speak any English? Donna had been French. She might never have seen any need for her daughter—his daughter, he reminded himself—to learn English.

'Nicole…I'm… *Moi…Je…Je…*' He bit his lip. Oh,

God, but he'd never been any good at languages. 'Nicole… *Moi…votre père?*'

'I know.'

The reply had been barely a whisper.

'And this…' He caught Jane's hand in desperation. 'This is my friend, Jane Halden. We…we're…'

'Flatmates,' Jane said quickly, coming to his rescue. 'Your father and I are flatmates.'

What now? Elliot wondered as the air stewardess disappeared, the loudspeaker announced the arrival of the 21.15 from Berlin and his daughter stared at the floor. What did he do and say now?

Jane had no such doubts. She simply got down on her knees, gave the little girl a hug and began talking about the flight from Paris.

Which is what he should have done, he realised bleakly as he retrieved Nicole's luggage. But it was too late to think about that now. Too late for a lot of things.

All he could do was drive them back to his flat and listen to Jane and Nicole chattering away quite happily while he sat in silence, feeling as much use as a lamb chop in a vegetarian restaurant.

Dinner was no better. Nicole ate little, and said less. Jane—bless her—kept up a steady stream of conversation while Nicole valiantly attacked her fish fingers, but it was a relief when his daughter finally pushed her plate away and asked if she could go to bed.

Jane didn't linger long afterwards. There was plenty she wanted to say. Things like 'What happened to the famous Mathieson charm?' And 'Couldn't you at least have *tried* to make some conversation?' But it would keep.

A lot of things would keep, she decided as she took her pyjamas out of her suitcase and smiled ruefully as she looked at them.

Passion-killers. That's what Frank had called the men's

red-and-white-striped pyjamas she liked to wear, and she supposed they were, but she liked them, always had. They were cosy on wintry nights, cool on hot summer evenings, and if they were as sexy as a pair of flannelette knickers then so much the better while she was staying with Elliot.

Not that she had anything to fear on that score, she thought wistfully as she changed into them. She was just Jane. Just good old dependable Jane.

And you should thank your lucky stars you are, her mind declared while she brushed her teeth. How long do Elliot's girlfriends usually last—a month, six weeks? Gussie was doing well at two months. Actually, Gussie was doing incredibly well to have lasted two months.

Sleep, she told herself firmly. Get into bed and get some sleep. And she tried. She really did try, but two o'clock saw her no sleepier than before, and she'd just decided to get up and make herself a cup of tea when she heard it.

The unmistakable sound of a child's muffled sobs in the silence.

She was out of bed in a second, tiptoeing quickly down the corridor so as not to wake Elliot, but her stealth was unnecessary. He was already awake, already heading in the same direction, and he came to a halt with clear relief when he saw her. She stopped too, but it wasn't relief she felt. It was an altogether different emotion.

He only wore boxer shorts to bed. Nothing on top at all. Nothing to disguise the fact that his chest was even broader and more muscular than she'd ever imagined. And the boxer shorts… She swallowed convulsively, and resolutely shifted her gaze to his face and kept it there.

'Nicole's crying,' he said unnecessarily.

'She'll be missing her mother,' she managed to reply. 'Feeling a bit lost.'

'I guess so.'

'I'll leave you to it, then,' she continued, half turning to go.

'Leave me?' he gasped. 'But you can't. I mean, I don't know what to do!'

'Elliot, all she needs is for you to hold her, cuddle her!' she exclaimed, unable to hide her exasperation. 'How hard can that be?'

'Can't you do it?' he begged.

'Elliot—'

'Janey, I told you I wasn't any good with kids. I'll only muck it up if I go in there, say the wrong thing.'

'But—'

'And I have to get some sleep,' he continued in desperation, seeing the shock and disapproval in her face. 'I've got a meeting with Admin tomorrow about next year's budget, and I must have my wits about me.'

For a second she stared at him speechlessly, then she drew herself up to her full five feet one, her grey eyes blazing.

'Go, then!' she snarled. 'Go and get your precious sleep, and I hope you have nightmares. You deserve to, because you sure as hell don't deserve a lovely little girl like Nicole!'

And he didn't, she thought furiously when she went into Nicole's bedroom and gathered the little girl into her arms. He didn't deserve anybody's love.

To think that at the airport she'd been stupid enough to wonder if his apparent callousness might be an act. An act he'd adopted because he was terrified that he wouldn't be able to cope. But it wasn't an act. He was just selfish to the core.

And as she cradled Nicole to her, holding the little girl tightly until she finally fell asleep, she didn't know that Elliot remained outside the bedroom door, listening. Didn't know that as he stood there, his hands clenched against his sides, his forehead leaning against the door, that he felt not only like the biggest heel of all time but also the world's biggest failure.

CHAPTER THREE

'Hey, Elliot, I know everyone says fatherhood's tough, but don't you think trying to cut your own throat is a bit drastic?' Charlie Gordon grinned.

'Oh, ha, ha, very funny,' Elliot replied, gingerly rubbing his lacerated chin. 'Jane's been using my razor to shave her legs again, and it was blunt as a stone this morning.'

'Don't you just hate it when girls do that?' Charlie laughed. 'I mean, it's bad enough when they hang their wet tights and underwear all over the shower rail—'

'Not to mention all those creams and potions they stack along the bath.' Elliot sighed ruefully. 'Two weeks ago I had a bathroom to call my own, and now—'

'It's become a branch of your local chemist,' Charlie finished for him. 'Still, all that clutter's nice in an odd sort of way. Makes a man's flat seem more homely somehow.'

It did, Elliot acknowledged. Just as he also knew that he could never have got through this last fortnight without Jane, in spite of all her clutter. She was the oil that kept everything running. The cement without which everything would have fallen apart. Without her, Nicole's arrival would have been even more of a nightmare than it actually was.

And it *had* been a nightmare, despite the fact that he'd tried really hard to involve himself in Nicole's life. He'd had to, and it wasn't just because he knew Jane's watchful eyes were constantly on him. It was because he'd felt so guilty about the way he'd reacted when he'd first seen Nicole, the way he'd chickened out of comforting her on that first night, but nothing he'd done had worked.

With Jane his daughter was completely at ease, laughing and smiling, but the minute he tried to engage her in conversation all her animation disappeared. Oh, she was polite enough, answering all of his questions, dutifully telling him about her new school, but it had been a duty. A duty she'd got over as quickly as she could.

'Nicole settling in OK at her new school?' Charlie continued as they walked together towards the treatment room.

'Very well, thanks.' Elliot nodded.

And that had been because of Jane, too. He didn't know how she'd managed to do it but somehow she'd contrived to make friends with the mother of one of the girls in Nicole's class, and now invitations were starting to arrive for Nicole to come to tea.

'You must find Jane a great help,' Charlie said as though he'd read his mind.

'Couldn't do without her,' Elliot admitted frankly.

'Nice girl, Jane,' the SHO continued, seeing her coming out of one of the cubicles. 'Lovely smile, too. Sort of lights up her face, if you know what I mean.'

Elliot didn't. To him, Jane was… Well, Jane was just Jane but, judging by Charlie Gordon's admiring gaze, he clearly didn't think so.

Actually, now he came to think of it, the SHO had no business to be thinking *anything* about Jane, Elliot decided irritably. Dammit, the man had a girlfriend in Wales or Norfolk, or some such outlandish place, and if he was planning on fooling around with Jane, breaking her heart…

'Charlie—'

'Good grief, what in the world have you done to your face, Elliot?' Jane asked, smothering a chuckle as she joined them.

'Somebody—*somebody*—has been using my razor to shave their legs again,' he observed.

'Sorry,' she said guiltily. 'I'll try to get to a chemist some time today before I go home.'

'Better buy some plasters while you're about it,' Charlie declared as he headed off towards Reception. 'Those bits of toilet paper he's currently got stuck to his chin aren't exactly going to inspire much confidence in our patients.'

Elliot whipped the forgotten pieces of toilet paper off quickly, but not fast enough. Jane let out a peal of laughter, and as he stared down at her he realised that Charlie was right.

She did have a nice smile. Wide, and full, and generous. She had nice hair, too. Thick and black, it shone like silk when she took it down from its topknot back at his flat after work and brushed it out. And she didn't do anything special with it. Simply washed, then blow-dried it. He knew that because he'd watched her doing it last night when she'd been helping Nicole with her homework.

'S-sorry?' he stammered, suddenly realising from her expectant expression that she must have asked him something. 'What did you just say?'

'I asked—I *asked*—if you remembered that Nicole's going round to her new friend Stephanie's house for tea tonight,' she said tightly. 'But as usual, when it comes to talking about your daughter, you weren't listening!'

He groaned inwardly as Jane whirled angrily round on her heel and strode away. Damn Charlie Gordon. If the SHO hadn't been wittering on about how nice Jane was, and what a terrific smile she had, he would have been paying attention to what she was saying, and not simply gazing at her.

It had taken him three days after the fiasco of Nicole's arrival to get Jane to say anything to him beyond an abrupt 'Yes' or 'No' to any of his questions, and the last thing he wanted was to go through that again.

Swiftly he hurried after her, catching up with her beside

the whiteboard. 'Jane, I'm sorry. I wasn't being uncaring but I was thinking about something else. I was wondering...' Think of something fast, Elliot, he told himself, and make it good. 'I...I was trying to figure out if I could afford another bathroom.'

'Yeah, right,' she said tartly.

'It's true,' he protested, crossing his fingers behind his back. 'One bathroom isn't really sufficient for the three of us, and I was wondering whether the cupboard in the hall could become an extra toilet.'

She gazed at him suspiciously. 'Why do I get the feeling you're spinning me a line?'

'Do I look like the kind of man who would?' he exclaimed, opening his blue eyes very wide.

'Absolutely one hundred per cent,' she replied. 'Elliot, I've known you for two years, seen how you operate, so cut the flannel. Were you *really* thinking about a bathroom?'

He stared at her for a second, then his mouth turned up at the corners. 'Actually, I was thinking what a very nice smile you had.'

Her jaw dropped, then she began to laugh. 'You're impossible, you know that, don't you? Expecting me to swallow a load of old baloney like that—'

'It's true—Scout's honour.'

'Elliot, you were never a Scout,' she protested. 'The kind of man every mother warns her daughter about, but never a Scout. Honestly, sometimes I don't know why I put up with you!'

''Cos you like me?' he suggested, his blue eyes sparkling.

Oh, I do, she thought, laughing and shaking her head. I do, but I just wish you would use some of that charm of yours on your daughter for a change.

To be fair to him, he'd certainly been making more of

an effort, talking to Nicole about her new school, the things she was learning, but he was so stiff with her, so formal. It was obvious that all the little girl wanted was to be loved, and yet Elliot either couldn't, or wouldn't, see it.

'Elliot…'

The rest of what she'd been about to say died in her throat as the treatment-room doors opened, and a young woman stood there, dishevelled, wild-eyed and panic-stricken.

'Please! Please, can somebody help me? My boyfriend. He's out in the car. He has an allergy to almonds, and I think he's dying!'

Elliot reached for an Ambu-bag and was off at a run, with Jane and the young woman not far behind.

'What's his name?' he demanded when they reached the car and he threw open the front passenger door.

'Keith. Keith Fuller,' the young woman sobbed, her face chalk-white with fear. 'We were just leaving to go to work, and—'

'Keith—Keith, can you hear me—do you know where you are?' Elliot asked, lifting the young man's head back from the dashboard.

A slurred, incoherent mumble was his only reply.

With a muttered oath Elliot peeled the sterile cover off the Ambu-bag, took out the long polystyrene tube and skilfully worked it down the young man's throat and into his trachea. Then, just as deftly, he attached the Ambu-bag to the end of the tube and began squeezing it, sending air rushing into Keith's chest.

'Wheelchair?' Jane queried.

Not ideal, but Keith couldn't walk. Giving the Ambu-bag to Jane, Elliot levered the young man into the wheelchair with as much care as was possible under the circumstances, and at a run they set off back to the treatment room.

'OK, IV line with adrenaline and corticosteroid,' Elliot ordered the moment the young man had been transferred onto the examination trolley in cubicle 7. 'It looks to me like a full-blown anaphylactic shock.'

It looked that way to Jane, too, as Floella led the weeping girlfriend away. Keith's chest was covered in a mass of deep red welts, his face was red and puffy and his eyes were swollen shut. Somehow he must have eaten almonds without realising it, but the 'how' could wait until later. Right now, they had to concentrate on counteracting the massive amounts of histamine that the young man's body was producing.

'BP?' Elliot demanded, raising the young man's legs to try to improve the flow of blood to his heart and brain.

'Eighty and dropping,' Jane answered, and heard Elliot swear.

The adrenaline and corticosteroid should have acted almost immediately but the young man was still fighting for breath and his circulation was collapsing. He was slowly but surely suffocating.

'Come on, *come on*!' Elliot exclaimed, checking the young man's pulse again. 'You are not going to die on me. I am *not* going to allow you to die on me!'

'BP 85,' Jane announced.

It was up a little, but not enough. Keith's heart was thundering like a train, and if the adrenaline and corticosteroid didn't work soon he'd have a lot more than anaphylactic shock to worry about.

'I want more fluids,' Elliot ordered. 'Up the adrenaline, too, Jane, and get ready in case we have to perform CPR.'

She nodded. If he had a heart attack on top of everything else...

She didn't want to think about the consequences and

determinedly she concentrated on inserting another IV line while keeping her eyes on the BP gauge.

90…95…100. They'd got him!

'That was a close one,' she murmured.

'Too damn close if you ask me.' Elliot grinned. 'Well done.'

'Well done, you, too.' She smiled back, then noticed that Keith had opened his eyes and was staring up at them in confusion. 'How do you feel, Mr Fuller?'

'Terrible,' he croaked, licking his lips gingerly. 'Where am I?'

'St Stephen's Accident and Emergency unit,' Elliot replied, relieved to see that the puffiness around the young man's face was finally beginning to lessen, the welts on his body fading. 'Giving Sister Halden and myself the fright of our lives.'

'Was it almonds again?' the young man asked.

Elliot nodded. 'Any idea how you managed to eat some?'

Keith Fuller hadn't, but his girlfriend supplied the answer. She'd had muesli for breakfast and a tiny fragment of almond must have become lodged in her teeth. When they'd kissed he'd been exposed to the almond and, hey presto, full anaphylactic shock.

'Almost quite literally the kiss of death, in fact,' Elliot observed after the young man had been transferred to IC for observation.

Jane nodded and laughed, but as she did so Elliot suddenly realised that Charlie Gordon had been right about something else, too. Her face *did* light up when she smiled.

Funny how he'd never noticed it before. Neither had he noticed that she had a small dusting of golden freckles on her nose and cheeks. She was quite small, too. Five feet one, he reckoned, and built on generous lines, with wide, curvaceous hips and full, high breasts.

And he knew something that Charlie didn't. She wore plain white cotton bras and briefs. He knew it because he'd seen them draped over the shower rail in the bathroom alongside Nicole's little tights and underwear.

Gussie wore skimpy, transparent bras and briefs. The kind guaranteed to have any red-blooded male wanting nothing more than to tear them straight off her. Jane's underwear was sensible. Sensible, plain white briefs, sensible, plain white bras.

Actually, no. Now he came to think of it, the bras weren't plain. They had tiny little flowers embroidered on them, and some lace on the bits which would cover her breasts. The breasts that were high, and full, and...

And it was obviously time he made a date with Gussie, he decided, feeling a slow crawl of heat edging up the back of his neck. Jane... Well, good grief, she was a very nice girl and everything, but if he was starting to think about her breasts, he definitely needed to make a date with Gussie.

'Something troubling you, Elliot?' Jane asked, her face concerned.

Too damn right there was, he thought, tugging at his collar, but to his relief he was saved from answering.

'I think Richard wants your help,' he said, noticing the junior doctor waving to them from outside cubicle 7. But as she turned to go he put out his hand to stay her for a second. 'Has he come to his senses yet—manners-wise, I mean?'

'Oh, he's been much better lately,' she replied brightly. Actually, he'd taken to virtually totally ignoring her ever since the incident with the gallstones, but frankly she much preferred it to his previous behaviour. 'I think he's finally beginning to settle in at last.'

Elliot hoped he was. Staff friction was bad for morale, and love affairs between members of staff were even worse, he thought with a deep frown, seeing Charlie beaming at Jane as she passed him.

It's none of your business if Charlie is interested in Jane, he thought after he'd reassured the woman with a stiff neck and fever in cubicle 3 that she didn't have meningitis as she'd feared, but simply a bad cold and a strained shoulder muscle.

The guy's not married, and Jane's single, so it's none of your business. And it wasn't, but that didn't mean he wasn't going to keep his eye on the situation, he decided as he heard the high-pitched wail of an approaching ambulance. Both eyes if necessary, he told himself as the doors of the treatment room opened and the paramedics appeared.

'His name's Vic Imrie, and he's fifty-two,' one of the paramedics announced as he and his colleague wheeled their casualty in. 'His son found him collapsed on the floor by the side of his bed. There were two empty pill bottles and a half-full bottle of whisky beside him, and the son thinks he's taken an overdose.'

'Any idea what he's taken?' Elliot asked, beckoning to Jane and Kelly as the paramedics transferred Mr Imrie from his stretcher onto the trolley.

'Tetrabenazine and Valium. He's being treated by his GP for Huntington's chorea. Unfortunately the son doesn't know how many pills he took, or when. It could be a couple of hours, maybe more.'

In which case none of the drugs would still be in Mr Imrie's stomach. They would already be on their way to the intestines.

'You said his son telephoned you,' Elliot said. 'Is he a widower, then?'

The paramedic shook his head. 'Apparently, his wife went to the opening of a new art gallery in town. The police are trying to contact her, but...'

The condemnation in the paramedic's voice was clear. Any wife who went off to the opening of a new art gallery, leaving a clearly very ill man at home, wasn't up to much.

'Huntington's is an inherited disease, isn't it?' Kelly asked when the paramedics had gone and she was helping Jane to insert a cannula into Vic Imrie's nose to aid his breathing. 'Causing a gradual degeneration of the brain?'

Jane nodded grimly. It was, and the disease was one of the most devastating imaginable. Not only did it cause random, jerky, involuntary movements and grimaces, there were also personality changes as the disease progressed, changes that led to memory loss, and eventually dementia.

And if that wasn't catastrophic enough, symptoms of the disease didn't usually appear until a sufferer was between the ages of 35 and 50, by which time they'd probably already had children. Children who each had a fifty per cent chance of inheriting the disease.

'Mr Imrie—Mr Imrie, can you tell me where you are, and what day of the week it is?' Elliot demanded, putting his head down close to the man's lips, but nothing the man said was even remotely coherent, and he turned to Jane quickly. 'OK, I want a blood sample for a blood-alcohol level, and a toxic screen to find out exactly what he's taken. Just because we've got two empty pill bottles doesn't mean that's all—or even what—he's ingested.'

'An ECG and chest X-ray, too?' she queried as she began removing Vic Imrie's clothing.

'Absolutely.' He nodded.

But they all knew that they couldn't wait for the results of any of these tests. The most important thing at the moment was to prevent the digestion and absorption of as much of the drugs that Mr Imrie had taken as possible, and as most of the pills were probably in the intestine, that meant a stomach pump.

'BP, Jane?'

'One-thirty over ninety.'

A bit high, but normal in the circumstances.

'OK, let's get his stomach emptied,' Elliot said.

It was easier said than done. Mr Imrie might be frail because of his Huntington's chorea, and almost comatose, but he still fought Jane all the way as she pushed the tube up into his nose, then down through his oesophagus and into his stomach.

'Is it in?' Elliot asked when she finally straightened up.

'You bet it is,' she replied.

'ECG?'

She glanced across at the monitor. 'Still normal.'

With the tube in place it was a simple matter to flush Mr Imrie's stomach out with clear water, before passing a slush of charcoal and a cathartic down the tube which would hopefully absorb any remaining medication. A simple job, but a messy and an unpleasant one.

'The results are back from the lab, Elliot,' Kelly announced. 'Tetrabenazine, Valium and whisky.'

He nodded. 'We'll just have to hope we've got most of it out. Jane—'

'He's arrested,' she yelled as the alarm on the ECG monitor suddenly went off. 'V-fib!'

Ventricular fibrillation. Vic Imrie's heart had gone into total chaotic activity, with no co-ordinated pumping action.

Without a word having been said, Jane and Kelly were already beginning to perform cardiopulmonary resuscitation, and swiftly Elliot whacked Vic Imrie in the centre of his chest, hoping to provoke a electrical current across his chest to the heart to induce his heart rhythm back to normal.

It didn't work.

'Defibrillator, Jane!' he demanded.

Quickly she handed the two paddles to him. He set the machine at 200, rubbed the paddles together with electrical conducting gel to prevent the patient's skin from burning, then called, 'Everybody stand clear!'

Obediently Jane and Kelly stepped back from the trolley, and Elliot placed the paddles on Vic Imrie's chest. A surge of electricity coursed through his body. He convulsed briefly, then lay still.

'Nothing,' Jane reported, glancing at the monitor.

'OK, stand clear again, everybody,' Elliot announced, only to pause with a frown as he heard the sound of angry, raised voices coming from outside the cubicle curtains. 'What the hell's going on out there?'

'Kelly, go and find out,' Jane ordered.

The student nurse nodded but suddenly the curtains round the cubicle were pulled open and a middle-aged woman appeared.

'Don't—oh, please, don't do that!' the woman insisted, tears streaming down her face as Elliot placed the paddles on Vic Imrie's chest and he convulsed again. 'Hasn't he gone through enough already? Hasn't he suffered enough already? Why can't you just leave him alone?'

'Get her out of here,' Elliot ordered as two security guards piled into the cubicle behind the woman.

'But I'm his wife,' she protested as the guards took her firmly by the arms. 'And I don't want you to do that. He wouldn't want you to do that!'

Did Mrs Imrie know what she was saying, what she was suggesting? Elliot wondered, and decided she did. Sufferers of Huntingdon's chorea could live for as long as thirty years after the disease was first diagnosed. Thirty years of physical and mental degeneration. Would *he* want anyone he loved to go through that?

He wouldn't, but it wasn't his decision to make. He was a doctor, trained to do everything in his power to save life, not to end it, and determinedly he motioned to the security guards.

'Take her out.'

Sobbing bitterly, Mrs Imrie allowed the security guards to lead her away, and Elliot upped the charge on the defibrillator to 300. Still there was no change, but when he increased the power to 360 the ECG machine suddenly blipped into life.

'OK, now we're rolling,' he declared. 'Pulse, Jane?'

'Very weak and slow.'

'Right. Give him atropine in the IV line. With luck it should make his heart beat faster.'

It did.

'BP now, Jane?'

'One hundred over sixty.'

That meant they'd stabilised him enough to go up to IC, and normally such a result would have brought beaming smiles of relief from everybody, but not this time.

This time no one said a word as Elliot mechanically replaced the Ambu-bag the paramedics had inserted with an endotracheal tube, and quickly checked Vic Imrie's BP and pulse rate again.

'You did a good job, Elliot,' Jane said as he stood watching the staff from Intensive Care wheeling Vic Imrie away.

'Maybe,' he replied, his voice tired, defeated, 'but the real question is, was it the right one?'

What could she say to him? she wondered, remembering how devastated Mrs Imrie had looked, how much her husband had struggled against the stomach pump. Nothing but the truth.

'I don't know. I honestly don't know. All you can do— all any of us can do—is the job we've been trained for.'

'Even if it's not what the patient wants?' he asked, his eyes bleak. 'Jane, did you get a look at the size of the lids on those pill bottles?'

'The size of the lids?' she echoed in confusion.

'They're tiny, awkward, and the top of a bottle of whisky isn't much bigger. And Vic Imrie has Huntington's chorea.'

Her eyes widened. 'Elliot, do you know what you're suggesting?'

He nodded. 'That he couldn't have opened them himself, not with those tremors in his hands. I think his wife gave them to him with his consent.'

Elliot was saying he thought it was a case of assisted euthanasia. That Vic Imrie had decided he didn't want to go on living any more, and had asked his wife to help him die.

'What are you going to do?' she asked, and he shrugged wearily.

'Nothing. We both know euthanasia's illegal in this country, but do we really want that couple taken to court?'

She didn't. It wouldn't achieve anything. It wouldn't miraculously cure Vic Imrie. OK, so if Mrs Imrie was sent to prison she wouldn't be able to help him to kill himself, but that didn't mean he wouldn't try again. And the next time it could be something infinitely more messy and painful than an overdose.

And Elliot wondered, too. Wondered at the strength of Mrs Imrie's love. A love which had been so great she'd been prepared to help her husband to die even if it meant she was left devastated and guilt-ridden for the rest of her life.

He'd thought he'd loved Donna that much once, he remembered as Jane hurried away to speak to one of their receptionists who had appeared at the treatment-room door, her face grim. In fact, it had been he who had insisted on the church wedding, the white dress, the morning suits, because he'd been so sure it would last for ever.

But it hadn't lasted. Within a year, he and Donna had been arguing, and within two years...

Never again, he'd told himself when the divorce papers had come through. Never again would he ever fall in love, and he'd kept that vow—intended to go on keeping it. To feel the kind of pain Mrs Imrie must have been going through, was still going through... No, he didn't want that. He didn't think he could handle that.

'What is it—what's wrong?' Elliot asked as Jane came running back to him.

'We've got a three-month-old baby girl on the way. She's not breathing and she has no pulse. Sounds like a SIDS.'

Elliot groaned inwardly. He didn't need this. A case of sudden infant death syndrome was bad enough at the best of times, but he really didn't need this right now.

They tried their best. They always did try their best, but Elliot knew the moment he saw the baby that it was hopeless. She was mottled, cool and lifeless, and after forty-five minutes he gave the order to stop trying to resuscitate.

"It's every parent's worst nightmare,' Floella sighed, her eyes full of pity, as Jane gently wrapped the baby in a shawl. 'And it's always the same story. The baby was fine when I put her into her cot. No, she wasn't ill, apart from a slight cold.'

'I just hope somebody finds out what causes it soon,' Jane murmured. 'There have been so many suggestions. Like it's caused by putting a baby to sleep face down, or it's because of prematurity, or cold weather, or the parents smoking in the same room. And yet we still don't know anything for sure other than it's slightly more common in boys than in girls, and more deaths occur in the winter.'

'Look, I'll take the baby down to Pathology,' Floella said quickly, seeing Jane gently stroke the wisps of golden hair on the little girl's head. 'You get off home. Your shift's over—'

'I'll wait for Elliot,' Jane interrupted. 'I've a feeling he might need some company.'

And he did. Never had she seen him look so defeated as when he came out of their private waiting room, having spoken to the baby's parents. Oh, she'd seen him upset when they'd lost a patient they'd fought hard to save, but never had she seen him look so drained, so haggard.

'Want to talk about it?' she asked as they walked together out of the hospital.

For a moment she didn't think he was going to answer, and when he spoke his voice was ragged.

'It's the irony of it, Jane. We saved Vic Imrie, though both he and his wife wanted him to die, but we couldn't save that baby and she had everything to live for. It's the irony—*the irony*!'

What could she say to him? What could anybody say? Nothing that would really help, and gently she linked her arm in his and said through a throat so tight it hurt, 'Let's go home, Elliot.'

And they did, both of them lost in their own private worlds. Both of them hurting, but both equally reluctant for their own private reasons to reach out to one another for comfort.

And there was little comfort for Elliot when they did get home and Nicole returned from her friend's house.

'I don't know what to do with her, Jane,' he sighed the minute his daughter had gone to her room, pleading she wanted an early night. 'No matter what I say, I just don't seem to be getting through to her.'

'It's only been two weeks, Elliot—'

'I try to make conversation with her—I really do try,' he insisted, 'but all I ever get is "Is it OK for me to do this?" and "Is it OK for me to do that?" It's as though she's a guest in my home.'

'Which is probably how she feels right now,' Jane said

gently, as he got to his feet and refilled his wineglass. 'She needs time to feel at home—'

'But she gets on so well with you,' he said, trying and failing to keep the envy out of his voice. 'I've heard the two of you laughing, but with me… Somehow, I just never seem to hit the right note with her. I listen to myself talking to her sometimes, and I sound so false. So pompous, aloof—'

'Could it be because you're trying too hard?' Jane suggested. 'Maybe if you concentrate on simply being her father, on being there when she needs you, you might find it easier.'

He gazed at her silently for a moment, then bit his lip. 'The trouble is, I don't think I can. This afternoon with Vic Imrie—when he went into cardiac arrest—that's what I'm good at, Jane. Medicine. Mending broken limbs, damaged hearts. That's what I can do.'

She put down her glass, bewildered. 'What are you trying to say?'

How much was he prepared to tell her? he wondered, seeing the confusion in her eyes. Was he prepared to tell her the truth about his marriage to Donna? No, he couldn't tell her that, he thought bitterly, could never tell anyone that. He could tell her of his doubts and fears about being able to be a father, but that was all he could tell her.

'But every father feels that way,' she insisted when he'd explained how he felt. 'Nobody is born one. It's something you have to learn, something that comes with practice.'

'Jane…Jane, you don't understand!' he exclaimed, desperately thrusting his hands through his blond hair. 'I'm a wash-out with *all* relationships. The only thing I can handle is a brief love affair with no hard feelings when it ends, but I can't do that with Nicole. I can't flirt with her, or hand her a line. She wants—needs—commitment, and I don't think I can do it.'

'Of course you can,' she protested. 'I've seen you with the kids in A and E—'

'That's medicine again, Jane. I'm treating their injuries, their pain. I'm not living with them, having to relate to them.'

He hadn't used the word 'love', she noticed, but she let that pass. Just as she didn't ask the one question that had been niggling at her ever since Nicole had arrived. Why he'd looked so strange at the airport when he'd first seen his daughter. There was much more to this than a simple fear of not being able to cut it as a father, but for now she didn't ask.

'Look, you're off duty tomorrow afternoon. Why don't you take her somewhere?' she suggested instead. 'The park—the zoo—somewhere like that. I'm sure her teachers would understand if you wanted to pick her up from school early.'

'What good would that do?' he demanded.

She didn't know, but she did know he had to do something. 'I simply wondered if perhaps you both got out of the house into neutral territory, did something different together…'

'I might find it easier.' He nodded, clearly warming to the idea. 'We could make a whole afternoon of it. Go to a café for tea—'

'We?' she interrupted in dismay. That wasn't what she'd intended at all. She'd wanted him to be alone with Nicole, to be forced into talking to her—*really* talking to her. 'Elliot, the whole point of the exercise is to give you and Nicole a chance to get to know one another better.'

'But you'd have to come with me,' he said. 'I couldn't possibly do it on my own.'

'Elliot—'

'Please,' he insisted, his eyes fixed on her. 'Jane, I need your help.'

How often had she heard that? For years, it seemed. Ever since she was small people had always turned to her for help, for her to get them out of a jam, and she was so tired of doing it, so tired of being taken for granted.

But as his deep blue eyes stayed pleadingly on her, she knew she couldn't refuse. It would be good old Jane to the rescue again, and with a deep sigh she said, 'All right, then. I'll come.'

CHAPTER FOUR

'WELL, you could have knocked me down with a feather when Gussie let slip in the canteen that she hadn't been out with Elliot for two weeks.' Floella chuckled, her large brown eyes sparkling as she and Jane stripped the paper sheet off the examination trolley in cubicle 5 and replaced it with a fresh one. 'I mean, *Elliot*? I know he seems to be really keen on being a father to Nicole, but he's the last guy in the world I'd ever have believed would turn celibate!'

'Flo—'

'I wish you'd heard her, Jane,' Floella prattled on. 'To hear Gussie talk, anyone would think you were keeping Elliot chained up in his flat or something!'

'Me?' Jane protested. 'How has him not dating her got anything to do with me?'

'Oh, *I* know it hasn't, and *you* know it hasn't, but you know what Gussie's like. According to her, nobody does anything in this life unless it's for sex or money, so naturally she thinks you've been using your presence in Elliot's flat to roll your eyes at him, and give him that come-hither look.'

Much good it would have done her if she'd tried, Jane thought ruefully. If she'd done any rolling of her eyes at Elliot he would simply have rushed her off to the hospital ophthalmology department to have her eyes tested.

'So it's working out OK, then—you helping Elliot to look after his daughter?' Floella continued as she followed Jane out of the cubicle.

'I think so,' Jane replied. 'We have our ups and downs,

of course.' That was putting it mildly. Last night they'd had a humdinger of a row over Charlie Gordon of all people. Elliot had declared he didn't think the SHO was reliable when it came to personal relationships, she'd told him he was talking through his hat, and… 'Nicole's still having nightmares, but we're hoping they'll lessen once she starts to feel more secure.'

'They should do,' Floella said, 'but these things take time and a lot of patience.'

'I thought it might help if we got her out a bit more,' Jane continued, 'so we're taking her to the zoo this afternoon after work.'

'The zoo?'

'Nicole's never been to one and I thought she might enjoy it.'

'You're going to the zoo with Elliot and Nicole?'

'Yes, I'm going to the zoo with Elliot and Nicole,' Jane declared, beginning to laugh. 'Honestly, Flo, are you taking in anything I'm saying?'

'Oh, I'm taking it in all right,' Floella said dryly. 'I'm just wondering if you are.'

'What on earth does that mean?' Jane asked, bewildered.

'Jane…' Floella bit her lip. 'Jane, has it ever occurred to you that you might be getting rather too fond of Elliot's daughter?'

'Of course I'm fond of her,' Jane protested. 'She's a lovely little girl—'

'And she's not yours. Look, I guess what I'm trying to say is be careful,' Floella continued, her large dark eyes concerned. 'You're only going to be taking care of her for a month. Don't get too involved.'

'I'm not getting involved, I'm just helping.'

'Yeah, right, but just be careful, OK?'

Careful about what? Jane thought angrily as the staff nurse walked away, and she saw Elliot beckoning to her from cubicle 2. She was only doing what any other half-decent person would have done in the circumstances. It didn't mean she'd forgotten that taking care of Nicole was only a temporary arrangement. It *didn't*.

'Problems, Elliot?' she asked, forcing a smile to her lips as she joined him.

'Not a problem as such,' he replied, his lips quirking. 'What do you know about handcuffs?'

'Handcuffs?' she echoed. 'Not a thing, apart from the fact that the chaps in blue will snap them on you if you get into trouble. Why?'

'I've got one very embarrassed lady in 2. Apparently she and her boyfriend were making mad, passionate love—'

'At eleven o'clock in the morning?'

'Yeah, I know. Some people have all the luck, don't they?' He grinned. 'Anyway, like I said, they were making love, but to add spice to the occasion she was all trussed up in handcuffs, and now she can't get them off.'

'Did she try rubbing butter over her hands and wrists?'

'Is that the voice of experience talking, Sister Halden?' he asked, his blue eyes dancing. 'Because if it is—'

'No, of course it's not,' she protested, blushing furiously to her annoyance. 'I just wondered if perhaps something oily—'

'She's tried butter, Vaseline, hand cream and face cream, but nothing has worked. All that's happened is she's now got pretty deep abrasions to her wrists, abrasions I can't treat until we get the cuffs off her.'

'Looks like a job for the police department, then,' she said, then frowned. 'I wonder if one key fits every pair of handcuffs, or if each set has its own particular key?'

'If they do we could be in for a very long morning,' he said with a sigh. 'OK. Could you phone the local police station for me?'

'Will do.'

'Oh, and, Jane,' he called after her, laughter plain in his voice, 'just remember the next time someone wants to make mad passionate love to you, tell them the handcuffs are out.'

Yeah, right, she thought with a sigh. Considering she had nobody in her life right now to make any kind of love to her, she would have been more than happy to wear handcuffs if a bit of loving had been on offer.

In fact, now she came to think about it, nobody had ever made mad, passionate love to her, with or without handcuffs. Frank's idea of passion had been two minutes of foreplay, followed by a few hefty thrusts which had left her staring up at the ceiling wondering if this was all there was to it.

She'd bet money that the women Elliot made love to didn't think afterwards that they'd have had a lot more fun and considerably more satisfaction if they'd simply eaten an entire carton of ice cream. She'd bet...

No, she wasn't going to bet anything, she told herself firmly after she'd phoned the police station and endured their hoots of laughter and ribald comments. Thinking about sex and Elliot Mathieson at the same time was a bad idea. Thinking about sex *with* Elliot Mathieson was an even worse one, especially as he'd behaved like a perfect gentleman since she'd moved into his flat.

Actually, it was even more demoralising than that, she thought as the doors of the treatment room opened and two paramedics appeared. She didn't think Elliot even realised she was a woman. To him she was simply Jane. Helpful, sexless, good old Jane.

'Gang fight, Sister!' one of the paramedics called. 'Twenty-three years old, no ID, multiple stab wounds to his face, arms and upper and lower torso!'

And losing more and more blood by the second, Jane thought as she raced towards them, and Elliot did, too.

'Boy, but somebody obviously meant business with this guy!' Elliot exclaimed, grimacing as he stared down at the young man's bloodstained face and body. 'OK, we'll need six units of O-negative for starters, an ECG reading and an IV to replace the blood he's lost. Charlie— Where the hell's Charlie?'

'Here, boss,' the SHO replied, arriving in time to help them to push the trolley into one of the cubicles.

'Stick around until we find out what we've got, OK?'

Charlie nodded, but it didn't take them long to discover that what they had was a mess. The knife slashes on the young man's arms and upper torso would heal, but two of the stab wounds had pierced his stomach, and if he managed to survive them he was still going to be left with a face his own mother wouldn't recognise.

'Do you want to retain the cervical collar?' Charlie asked as Jane swiftly cut off the young man's clothes, then attached him to the ECG machine to monitor his heart rhythm.

Elliot shook his head. 'I can't see any sign of any spinal injury, but we need to tube him for sure and it will be easier with the collar off.'

'BP 160 over 95, pulse 140,' Jane declared. 'Heart rate very erratic but no sign of any arrhythmia. Guiac test to check for blood in his stools and a urine analysis?'

'Please,' Elliot replied.

'You should become a doctor, Jane,' Charlie remarked admiringly as Elliot checked the young man's airways to ensure there was nothing in his mouth then deftly inserted an endotracheal tube into his throat. 'Talk about being on the ball. She's terrific, isn't she, Elliot?'

She was, but that didn't mean Elliot had to like Charlie Gordon saying it, or the way Jane's cheeks became pink from the compliment. The SHO was getting too damn familiar, he decided. In fact, it seemed to him that every time he turned round lately Charlie was talking to Jane, making her laugh.

He'd warned her about him already, but all he'd got back for his pains had been a flea in his ear. A very strident flea in his ear, he remembered ruefully, but that didn't mean he was going to give up. Somebody had to make her see she was much too nice for her own good, too ready to always believe the best in people.

And you'd better get a grip, he told himself as he placed his stethoscope on the young man's chest to ensure the endotracheal tube was in the right place. Anyone would think you were getting interested in Jane yourself, the amount of time you seem to spend speculating on her private life.

Of course he wasn't getting interested, he thought with irritation. All he was trying to do was ensure that a nice girl like her didn't end up being hurt. OK, he admitted that he liked her, admired her, respected her— And what about her breasts? his mind whispered. You noticed her breasts, remember.

Yes, but only because I'm suffering from a massive attack of sexual deprivation right now, he argued back, trying very hard not to notice the breasts in question as Jane leant over to attach another IV line.

'Blood in both urine and stools, Elliot,' she announced. 'Looks like both kidney and liver damage.'

'This guy needs Theatre and fast,' he replied. 'Charlie, could you page them, let them know we've got an urgent one on the way if we can stabilise him?'

'Sure thing,' the SHO replied.

'What do you want to do about his face?' Jane asked as Charlie sped away. 'Will we suture, or leave that to Plastics?'

Elliot glanced critically down at the cut that ran the full length of the young man's cheek from his eye down to his mouth. 'It's a job for Plastics, though not even they will be able to give him back the face he once had.'

'I understand some gangs see scars as a badge of honour,' Jane observed.

'I wouldn't be at all surprised,' Elliot sighed. 'How's his BP doing?'

'BP 120 over 80.' It was still too high, but now that they were pumping in the O-negative blood at least it was coming down and the ECG monitor was showing no worrying irregularities. 'Elliot—'

She didn't get the opportunity to say anything else. The curtains round the cubicle were suddenly thrown open, and to her horror a young man appeared, a knife in his hand, murder plain on his face.

'I'm sorry, sir, but you really shouldn't be in here,' Elliot declared with a calmness that was amazing. 'If you'd like to go through to Reception, fill in one of our forms—'

'I ain't here to fill in any bloody forms,' the young man interrupted. 'I'm here to finish what me and my mates started.'

And he meant it, Jane thought. Without a shadow of a doubt, he meant it. Somehow she had to buy them some time. Time so that either she or Elliot could hit the panic button on the wall behind them to summon the security guards.

'I don't think there's any need for you to finish him off,' she observed, noticing out of the corner of her eye that Elliot was edging slowly round the trolley towards her. 'He's dying as it is.'

'Is that right?' the young man sneered. 'Well, maybe I should just hurry him along and save you a lot of hassle.'

He took a step forward and Jane did, too. 'I'd wear

surgical gloves if you intend going anywhere near him,' she said quickly. 'He's got Aids.'

The young man whitened and stepped back. 'Aids?'

She nodded. Elliot was almost there. Almost close enough to reach the panic button. 'Advanced Aids, according to our special registrar.'

For a second the young man stared at her uncertainly, then his lip curled. 'He ain't got Aids. Me mates and I would have known about it weeks ago if he had.'

'Not necessarily,' she said desperately. 'Do you think he'd want it known—would you, if it were you?'

A mixture of conflicting emotions flashed across the man's face, then he shook his head. 'You're lying to me, you bitch, trying to save that no-good, low-down—'

He let out a strangled, high-pitched cry as a security guard suddenly came from nowhere and grabbed him round the neck, but he wasn't finished yet. Furiously he lashed out with his fist, sending Jane spinning back against the cubicle wall, and with a cry of rage Elliot lunged forward and twisted the young man's arm behind his back. The knife in his hand clattered to the floor, and when a second security guard arrived Elliot all but threw the young man into his arms.

'Jane, Jane, are you all right?' he exclaimed hoarsely, as the young man was dragged away.

'Fine,' she replied, already back in position by their patient. 'His BP's 110 over 80 now. I know it's still a bit high, but could we risk sending him to Theatre with that?'

'Jane—'

'I don't like his colour. I think if we wait too long we could be looking at renal failure here.'

She was right, they could, and quickly he pulled himself together.

'OK, Theatre it is,' he replied, but the minute Floella and Charlie had wheeled their patient out of the treatment room he snapped off his latex gloves, caught Jane by the shoulders and turned her round to face him, his blue eyes worried and concerned. 'Are you really OK? I mean, really and truly OK?'

'Of course I am,' she protested. 'I'm a bit shaky round the knees…' Actually, now that the man had gone, and she'd no patient to focus on, she felt very shaky, but there was no way she was going to admit it. 'My elbows got a bit of a bang, but apart from that I'm fine.'

He stared at her silently for a moment, then shook his head, and his voice when he spoke was husky, uneven. 'You know, you're quite something, Jane Halden.'

To her dismay her throat constricted and she knew that if he said just one more word she was going to disgrace herself, and embarrass him, by throwing herself onto his chest and bursting into tears. Quickly she forced a smile to her lips.

'Yeah, right, Elliot, and whatever new favour you're wanting, the answer is no.'

A brief answering smile sprang to his lips, and then it was gone.

'You could have been killed!' he exclaimed, his relief giving way to anger. 'Never do that again, do you hear me? *Never*!'

'Do what?' she protested. 'I was simply unlucky enough to get in the way of his fist.'

'Talking to him like that,' he continued as though she hadn't spoken. 'Trying to distract him—'

'It worked, didn't it?' she interrupted.

'That's not the point—'

'Elliot, I don't see why you're making such a fuss,' she said, stripping the blood-soaked paper sheet off the examination trolley and binning it. 'I've been in far greater danger in A and E before, and you never got all macho and protective over me then.'

It was true, he hadn't. Oh, he'd always been worried when one of them had been threatened by a member of the public, feared that it was only a matter of time before somebody got seriously hurt, but he'd reluctantly accepted—as they all had—that it was one of the hazards of the job. And yet now…

Never had he felt such rage before, never had he felt such fear.

Of course you were angry and afraid, he told himself as he watched Jane binning the soiled dressings they had used and saw from the reddening on her elbows that she would be black and blue tomorrow. Dammit, it was Jane who'd been in danger, Jane who'd been slammed into the wall. She's your colleague, your friend, so it's only natural you should feel this way.

And would you have felt the same if it had been Gussie or Floella or Kelly?

Of course he would, he thought firmly, only to suddenly realise it wasn't true. Oh, he would have been concerned about them, angry with the perpetrator, but he wouldn't have felt the overwhelming fear and anger he felt now, and he couldn't understand it. He couldn't understand it at all.

All he knew for certain as he noticed that a policeman had arrived to release the woman in 2 from her handcuffs—handcuffs Elliot hoped he'd use on the young thug who'd attacked Jane—was that he was glad their shift was nearly over. Glad that he'd persuaded Jane to go with Nicole and him to the zoo. After this morning's incident, if she hadn't agreed to come with them he'd have spent the whole afternoon wondering what kind of trouble she was getting into.

At least at the zoo he'd be able to keep an eye on her. At least there he'd be able to relax and enjoy himself.

* * *

He didn't.

Oh, it was a beautiful afternoon, the blue sky shot with the high clouds of early spring, the daffodils starting to die back but the tulips just beginning to open, and everything should have been perfect—but it wasn't.

They took Nicole to see the elephants and the giraffes, and the little girl managed to look dutifully enthusiastic. They took her to watch the penguins and the monkeys being fed, and she laughed at all the right places, but by the middle of the afternoon when Nicole had answered all of Elliot's questions in monosyllables or not at all he was gazing over his daughter's head at Jane in despair.

'Look, why don't you get us all a hot dog from that stand over there?' she suggested. 'I'd love one, and I'm sure Nicole would, too.'

Nicole didn't look as though she cared much one way or another but Elliot made his escape with relief and Jane walked with Nicole towards one of the benches beside the duck pond and sat down.

'It's nice here, isn't it?' she commented.

Nicole nodded noncommittally.

'I'm surprised you've never been to a zoo before,' Jane persisted, extracting a bag of dried bread from her handbag so the girl could feed the ducks. 'I understand there's a very big one in Paris.'

'There is. Mama said she would take me there one day, but…'

The little girl shrugged, and Jane cleared her throat. How was she going to say what she wanted to say tactfully, without it sounding as though she was either begging on Elliot's behalf or trying to blackmail his daughter?

Just say it, a little mental voice insisted, and she did.

'Nicole, I know that sometimes…sometimes your father might appear a bit cool and aloof, but he cares a great deal for you.'

'No, he doesn't,' the little girl replied. 'In fact, he doesn't like me at all.'

'Oh, but he does!' Jane protested, aghast. 'In fact—'

'I like you,' Nicole interrupted, throwing a piece of her bread towards the expectant ducks. 'I think you're nice.'

'Well, thank you,' Jane declared, considerably flustered. 'Nicole, your father—'

'My papa and you—you are lovers?'

'No, of course not!' Jane exclaimed, blushing furiously. 'We're simply friends, that's all. We work together, share a flat…' At least they were sharing one for a month, but she saw no need to tell the child that the arrangement was temporary. 'Nicole, your father loves you—'

'He doesn't. I saw his face when I arrive. He does not want me living with him. I am…' She frowned. 'My friend Stephanie, she uses a word… A pest. That's it. I am a pest to my papa.'

'Nicole—'

'I should have stayed in Paris. I had lots of uncles there. I should have stayed in Paris with one of them.'

Uncles? Elliot had told her his ex-wife had had a sister, a Michelle Bouvier who was an archaeologist, but he'd never mentioned any brothers. 'Nicole, these uncles of yours—'

'They weren't my *real* uncles, of course,' the little girl continued, as though that should have been self-evident. 'They were my mama's boyfriends, but she said it would make things easier if I called them uncle.'

'Did she?' Jane said faintly.

Nicole nodded. 'Some were nice. Some were not so nice, but Mama seemed to like them all.'

All? Good grief, how many had there been?

'Nicole—'

'Two hot dogs, as requested,' Elliot announced brightly, and Jane didn't know whether to feel relieved or sorry that he'd arrived when he had, and decided that she wished he'd come earlier.

If he'd arrived earlier he would have heard what Nicole had said, and then she wouldn't have to do anything about it. And she didn't want to do anything about it. She wished the girl hadn't told her, wished she'd never suggested coming to the zoo in the first place. If they hadn't come, and Nicole hadn't casually dropped her bombshell, she wouldn't have that knowledge lying on her chest like a lead weight.

And Elliot didn't look any happier than she felt when his daughter took her hot dog and the bag of stale bread over to the duck pond.

'Well, I don't think we can say that this outing is turning out to be any kind of success, do you?' Elliot said ruefully.

'I think Nicole liked the bush-babies—'

'Yes, but we're not exactly talking, are we?' he interrupted. 'I mean, she's over there eating her hot dog, and I'm over here with you.'

She sighed. 'I'm sorry. I thought it was a good idea—'

'I'm not blaming you,' he said quickly. 'I would never blame you.'

You would, if you knew what I know, she thought, staring down at her uneaten hot dog, which suddenly had all the appeal of yesterday's leftovers. If I hadn't said anything to Nicole, I would never have known, and I wish to heaven I didn't.

'Jane.'

'Mmm?'

'You'd feel a lot better if you simply said whatever you've got on your mind, instead of chewing your poor lips to ribbons.'

He'd swung round on the bench to face her, his blue eyes dancing, and she flushed guiltily. 'It's nothing '

'In a pig's eye is it nothing,' he protested. 'Come on. Spit it out. What have I done wrong now?'

'Nothing. You've done nothing wrong. It's just…'

'Jane, unless you're trying to work up the courage to tell me I have a personal problem my friends are too embarrassed to mention, I think I can handle whatever you want to say,' he declared, a smile tugging at the corners of his mouth. 'Come on, spit it out.'

She didn't want to tell him what Nicole had said. She'd have given anything in the world not to tell him what his daughter had revealed, but he was waiting, and she knew he wouldn't take no for an answer.

'Nicole…when you were getting the hot dogs…she was talking about her mother. She said— Now, Elliot, she could have got this all wrong, completely misunderstood the situation,' she added quickly, seeing the amusement in his face turning to bewilderment, 'but she told me…she said she had lots of uncles in Paris. Uncles who used to come and stay with her mother.'

'She said *what*?'

'Elliot, she's only six,' Jane continued, thankful that Nicole was too happily engaged in jumping off and on the decorative stones that edged the gravel path round the duck pond to hear him. 'She probably didn't understand what she was saying, how we might interpret it—'

'Oh, she knew, all right!' Elliot declared, his voice grim. 'Donna was a tramp when we were married, and she clearly continued being one after we got divorced. I could kill her for exposing Nicole to this. If she were alive, I *would* kill her!'

She gazed at him in complete shock. She'd always assumed that he and Donna had got divorced because, like so many other couples, they'd simply grown apart, but now…

'Do…do you want to talk about it?' she offered, not

knowing whether she really wanted to hear or not but feeling she had to say something.

She didn't think he was going to answer—part of her hoped that he wouldn't—then he leant back against the bench and clenched his hands tightly in his lap. 'I thought Donna was the most incredible, beautiful girl in the world when I met her. I fell madly in love with her, begged her—badgered her—to marry me, and eventually she said yes, and for a year we were happy.'

'And then?' she said softly.

'She got bored. Her job took her all over Europe, from one fashion shoot to the next, and she met a lot of interesting, vibrant people who were a lot more exciting than the husband she'd left at home, slaving away at his boring old hospital. So she slept with a few—just to relieve the boredom, of course, you understand?' he continued, his lip curling. 'Then she slept with a few more, and I found out.'

'Oh, Elliot—'

'Please... Please, don't say you're sorry,' he interrupted, his mouth curving into a sad travesty of a smile. 'Say anything you like but, please, don't say you feel sorry for me.'

So she didn't say it, though she desperately wanted to, and as she gazed at him compassionately a thought came into her mind. A thought that might explain so much. 'Elliot, Nicole... Is she very much like her mother?'

A betraying muscle tightened in his cheek. 'Yes.'

'And does...' She cleared her throat. 'Does that bother you?'

The tendons on his knuckles showed white against the rest of his skin. 'Yes, it bothers me,' he said tightly. 'In fact, if you want the honest truth, it bothers the hell out of me.'

'Because you think if you allow yourself to love Nicole as you loved her mother, she might hurt you, too?'

He kicked one of the pebbles on the gravel path in front of them and sent it ricocheting off the fence opposite. 'Jane, every time I look at her I see Donna. I keep telling myself that she's a child, that I'm not being fair, but… It's sick—*I'm* sick!'

'I'd say you were pretty normal myself,' she said gently. 'Look, how do you think widows or divorced mothers feel if their sons look like a husband they either loved or hated?' she continued as he shook his head. 'It's not easy for them, but they get beyond it, grow to love their sons for themselves.'

'I guess so,' he murmured.

'I *know* so,' she insisted, and his mouth twitched into not quite a smile.

'Bloody-minded, aren't you?'

'Of course I am,' she declared, relieved to see that some of the shadows were lifting from his eyes. 'I'm from Yorkshire, and everyone from Yorkshire's bloody-minded, unlike you soft southerners.'

This time he did laugh. 'Jane, how come a girl like you isn't married or something? I'd have thought some lucky bloke would have snapped you up years ago.'

Her own smile didn't slip for an instant. 'Too choosy, I guess.'

'Stay that way,' he declared, thinking of Charlie. 'Get the very best—you deserve it.'

Maybe she did, but the trouble was that she didn't want the very best, she thought wistfully. She wanted the man sitting next to her. A man who could be thoughtless and stupid and downright blind at times, but still she wanted him.

'And because you're the nicest, kindest person I know,' he continued, 'I want to ask you a huge favour. I want you to stay with me and Nicole until my mother comes back from Canada at the beginning of June.'

Her smile vanished. 'Oh, Elliot—'

'Janey, it's been working really well—the three of us living together. Nicole adores you, and I can go to work, secure in the knowledge that you're there when I can't be.'

'But, Elliot—'

'Janey, I *know* my mother, and I *know* you. The agency could send me anybody, and Nicole's had so much upheaval in her life already, I don't want to put her through more unless I have to.'

Say no, her heart urged as he gazed at her hopefully. Floella was right. You *are* getting too involved. It's bad enough that you're in love with him, but what if you start loving his daughter, too? Get out now before you're in way over your head.

'Elliot, I really don't think this is a good idea—'

'Give me one good reason why not,' he demanded.

She couldn't. At least not one she was prepared to tell him.

'Good, that's settled, then.' He beamed, taking her silence for agreement. 'Now, there's just one other thing I was wondering—'

She never did find out what it was because a sudden sharp cry of pain had her whirling round on the bench to see Nicole lying spread-eagled on the gravel. Jane was on her feet in an instant and running towards her before she realised Elliot was, too, and with difficulty she slowed her pace. Nicole was already sitting up, tears trickling down her cheeks, clearly more frightened than hurt by her fall, and Jane held back deliberately, wondering what he would do.

And at first, to her dismay, he didn't do anything. Oh, he bent over and said something to his daughter, but he didn't *do* anything.

'Pick her up,' she muttered under her breath. 'Elliot,

pick her up, hold her, whisper any nonsense you like, but *pick her up!*'

He couldn't have heard her—there was no way he could have heard her at that distance—but suddenly he did just that, and as he wrapped his arms around his daughter and Nicole clung to him and sobbed into his chest, Jane felt a hard lump in her throat.

It was a step. All right, so perhaps it wasn't a very big one, but at least it was a step.

And as she continued to watch them, her lips curving into a tender smile, she suddenly realised something else. Something that caused the smile on her lips to disappear in an instant.

She'd been wrong when she'd told herself that she should get out now before she grew to love Nicole. It was already too late. She already loved the little girl, and all she could see ahead for herself was heartbreak.

CHAPTER FIVE

'I THINK you're out of your mind.'

'I know, Flo, so you've said,' Jane sighed as they came out of the staffroom and made their way back to A and E. 'Every day since last week.'

'I mean, agreeing to do it for one month was bad enough, but agreeing to do it for three! I think you're crazy.'

'Flo, could you just drop it, please?' Jane pleaded. 'OK, I'm out of my mind. OK, I'm crazy, but it's my life.'

Floella opened her mouth, then closed it again and shook her head. 'Just don't turn round in two months' time and say that I didn't warn you.'

'I won't.'

'And don't expect any sympathy from me when you're sobbing into your coffee because Elliot's whisked his daughter off to live with his mother in Hampshire.'

'Definitely not.' Jane nodded, and a rueful smile appeared on the staff nurse's face as she pushed open the doors of the treatment room and they walked through them together.

'You're too damn soft for your own good, you know.'

Everyone seemed to be telling her that recently, Jane realised as Floella hurried off to speak to Kelly. And everyone was right. But what else could she have done? If she'd walked away, and later discovered that Nicole was desperately unhappy with the housekeeper Elliot had hired, she knew she could never have lived with herself.

And what about you? her little voice demanded. If you can't leave now, how in the world are you going to be able to cope when Elliot takes Nicole to live with his mother, and you only get to see her occasionally, or maybe not at all?

I'll deal with it, she told herself. Somehow, some way, I'll deal with it.

'Could you give me some help, Sister Halden?'

She turned to see Richard Connery gazing enquiringly at her, and managed to smile. 'What can I do for you?'

'I've a Mr Lawrence in 6 who appears to have fractured his right arm. He's obviously in a great deal of pain, but he's also very frightened, and I thought it might help if he had a nurse standing by while I examined him.'

She nodded, and wished with all her heart that Floella could have heard him. The staff nurse still believed that the only help the junior doctor required was the sharp imprint of her shoe on his backside as she booted him from A and E, but even a week ago it would never have occurred to Richard to consider the mental state of a patient. He was learning, she thought with relief. At long last, he was learning.

And he was certainly right about his patient. The young man in cubicle 2 was obviously terrified. His hands were shaking, there were beads of sweat on his forehead and Jane thought that if he hadn't been sitting down he would have fainted.

'I hear you've been in the wars, Mr Lawrence?' she said with her most encouraging smile.

The young man nodded convulsively. 'I was painting my sitting-room ceiling and fell off the stepladder. Stupid—really stupid.'

And not true, she thought with a slight frown.

Oh, his right forearm was definitely fractured. Not only was it very swollen and tender, it was also hanging at an odd angle, but it was equally obvious that he couldn't possibly have done it when he'd been painting a ceiling.

82	DR MATHIESON'S DAUGHTER

For a start, his clothes were all wrong. Nobody painted
a ceiling while wearing a pair of smart grey trousers and
a pale beige sweater, and there wasn't a trace of paint on
his clothes or on his hands. Either he was a remarkably
neat painter, or he'd washed and changed before coming
into A and E, and how anyone could have done that with
a fractured arm was beyond her.

'So he didn't do it painting,' Richard said dismissively
when she voiced her doubts after he'd given the young
man some painkillers and sent him off to X-Ray. 'What
difference does it make? His arm's clearly fractured, and
surely our job is to treat that, not to question how he did
it?'

He was right. It was none of their business how the
young man had fractured his arm, but as she walked over
to the whiteboard to put an asterisk by Mr Lawrence's
name to indicate he hadn't yet been discharged she
couldn't deny she would dearly liked to have known.

'You're looking very pensive, Jane,' Charlie remarked,
almost bumping into her as he came out of cubicle 6.
'Something bothering you?'

'Curiosity, that's all.' She smiled. 'I'm simply eaten up
with curiosity.'

'Well, you know what they say,' he replied. 'Curiosity
killed the cat.'

'Yes, but satisfaction brought it back,' she pointed out,
her grey eyes sparkling. 'Unfortunately, in this particular
case, I don't think I'm going to be satisfied.' Her gaze
swept over his blue suit, crisp white shirt and crimson tie.
'You're looking very smart today, Charlie. Going somewhere after work?'

'I'm picking up my girlfriend from the railway station.
She's got a whole fortnight off work and she's going to
spend it in London with me.'

'Oh, I am pleased for you,' she said, and meant it. The

SHO had been looking a bit down recently, and she knew it was because he was missing his girlfriend.

'Actually, there was something I'd like to ask you,' Charlie continued. 'I don't know London very well yet, and I wondered if you could recommend a nice restaurant I could take her to.'

She frowned. 'Have you a price limit?'

He shook his head and grinned. 'For Barbara, the sky's the limit.'

'Lucky girl.' She laughed. 'In that case, take her to Brambles.'

He took a piece of paper out of his pocket and wrote it down. 'Is it a nice place—I mean *really* nice? You see…' a deep flush of colour appeared on his cheeks '…if all goes well, I'm planning on asking Barbara to marry me.'

'Charlie, I'd marry you myself if you took me to Brambles!'

He roared with laughter, and she did, too, and neither of them noticed Elliot watching them from across the treatment room, his face like thunder.

Charlie Gordon had a nerve. Stringing along some poor girl back in his home town and trying to chat up another. And the annoying thing was that Jane seemed to be responding to him.

Dammit, look at the way she was smiling up at him. He couldn't ever remember a time when she'd smiled at him like that. Oh, she smiled, of course, but now that he came to think of it there always seemed to be an odd mixture of scepticism and wariness in her amusement.

Well, she should have reserved some of that wariness for Charlie Gordon, he thought angrily. She should have kept *all* of it for the SHO, and he was going to tell her so whether she gave him another flea in his ear or not.

But not right now, he realised with frustration as one of

their receptionists escorted a woman and a young boy in a wheelchair into the treatment room.

'The kid's eight years old, and his mother reckons he's drunk,' the receptionist told him under her breath.

'I don't know where he got it from, Doctor,' the child's mother declared, clearly torn between fury and concern. 'We don't have any alcohol in the house. Both my husband and I aren't drinkers, except on rare occasions—birthdays, Christmas, times like that—but as soon as I saw him I knew he was drunk—'

'Your son isn't drunk, Mrs Fraser,' Elliot interrupted. 'Now, if you'd like to go through to one of our private waiting rooms with Staff Nurse Lazear—'

'But I want to stay with him,' Mrs Fraser protested. 'If he's not drunk, what's wrong with him?'

'You'll know as soon as we do,' he said soothingly.

'Yes, but—'

'Mrs Fraser, your son is in the very best of hands,' Jane said reassuringly as Floella began to lead the woman away, 'and there's really nothing you can do here.'

Reluctantly the mother allowed Floella to usher her away, and Jane raised her eyebrows at Elliot questioningly. 'Drugs?'

He shook his head. 'Solvent abuse. Look at the sores around his lips, how flushed he is, and don't you smell something familiar?'

Jane leant down, sniffed, then drew back. .'Cleaning fluid. He's been sniffing cleaning fluid?'

Elliot nodded grimly. 'OK, get me an ECG reading and BP. Solvents can sensitise the heart to the effects of adrenaline and the last thing we want is for him to have a heart attack. Keep him lying on his side, too,' he continued. 'If he's sick, as I suspect he probably shortly will be, he might suffocate on his own vomit.'

The boy's ECG and BP were as normal as they could

be under the circumstances, and there was nothing more they could do for him. What he needed now was constant monitoring, and Intensive Care was the best place for that, but as the boy was wheeled away Jane noticed Elliot's eyes following him.

'Something worrying you?' she asked. 'Something you think we might have missed?'

He sighed and shook his head. 'I was just thinking that they're getting younger and younger, aren't they?'

'I'm afraid so,' she replied.

'I was also thinking that it could be Nicole in a couple of years' time.'

'It won't be,' she said reassuringly. 'She'll have more sense. You'll make sure she has more sense.'

'Maybe,' he murmured with a slightly crooked smile, 'but it's such a dangerous world for kids out there now, Jane. When you and I were young, the biggest thing our parents had to worry about was us being knocked down by a car, but now…'

'You'll take care of her—you're already doing it,' she said firmly.

And he was. OK, so things weren't exactly perfect yet by any means. Nicole was still far too withdrawn, too nervous in his presence, and he still had trouble relaxing with her, but it would come, she knew it would.

'I couldn't have done it without you,' he declared. 'You've been a real godsend, Jane.'

It was what Gussie had said, only considerably more sarcastically, she remembered, and she shook her head as she binned her latex gloves. 'I only did what anyone else would have done in the circumstances.'

'No, you did more,' Elliot insisted, putting out his hand to stop her as she turned to go. 'If you hadn't been there, willing to prop me up, to put up with me and all my hang-ups and insecurities, I don't know what I would have done.'

There was warmth in his eyes, warmth that made her heart skip a beat, but she managed to reply lightly, 'It's what friends are for, Elliot.'

He smiled, but as he continued to stare down at her the smile slowly disappeared. Disappeared, to be replaced by a look of confusion and puzzlement. Until he was gazing at her as though he'd never actually seen her before, and every alarm bell known to mankind went off in her head.

'I'd better get on,' she said, taking a step back from him. 'We're mobbed as usual out in the waiting room, and it isn't going to get any emptier if we stand around here talking.'

'No, it won't, but, Jane—'

'I think Flo's wanting me,' she lied, and before he could say anything else she wheeled swiftly round on her heel and walked away.

What in the world are you doing? she thought as she strode down the treatment room, all too aware that his eyes were following her. You're in love with the guy. You've been in love with him for the last two years, and now that he seems to be actually realising you're a woman and not simply sexless Jane, you've just run a mile. Have you got rocks in your head, or something? I thought this was what you wanted.

And it was, but it wasn't, she realised. Oh, she wanted him to fall in love with her, of course she did. She wanted him to clasp her in his arms and declare his everlasting love for her. But that was just the problem. Elliot didn't do everlasting. Elliot's idea of everlasting was a couple of months. And was that what she wanted—two months of being loved, followed by a lifetime of loss?

Deliberately she shook her head. She didn't want that.

She couldn't handle that. It was better to keep him at arms' length than to go through that.

And it should be easy for her to do, she told herself as the doors of the treatment room opened and a woman in her early thirties appeared, chalk-white and walking gingerly. She'd spent two years successfully keeping her feelings hidden from him. She could keep on doing it. She had to.

'Elliot, Charlie—I need one of you now!' she called as the woman suddenly crumpled to the floor, clutching her stomach in obvious agony.

It was Elliot who came. Elliot who helped her carry the woman into a cubicle and get her on to the examination trolley.

'I'm sorry...so sorry,' the woman gasped, 'but I think...I think I'm going to be sick!'

Jane got the bowl under her chin in time.

'Better now?' she asked gently, when the woman finally slumped back onto the trolley, ashen and exhausted.

'No, I'm not better,' the woman exclaimed, tears slowly beginning to trickle down her cheeks. 'I'm pregnant—ten weeks pregnant—and I think I'm losing my baby.'

'What's your name?' Elliot asked as Jane swiftly began to strip off the woman's tights and skirt.

'Sally. Sally Thomson. My husband and I have been trying for six years to have a baby, and I can't lose it—*I just can't!*'

'Let's not jump the gun,' Elliot said soothingly. 'Can you tell me where the pain is?'

'Here,' Sally Thompson sobbed, pointing to the lower left side of her stomach. 'I've had a bit of diarrhoea, too, and...and I'm bleeding. It's a miscarriage, isn't it? I'm having a miscarriage.'

'Did you feel the pain before you started to bleed, or

after?' Elliot asked as Jane took the woman's blood pressure.

'I'm sorry?' Sally said, wiping a hand across her tear-stained face.

'The pain you felt. Was it there before you started to bleed or did it begin afterwards?' Elliot repeated.

Sally Thompson frowned in concentration. 'It was painful first.'

Elliot's eyes met Jane's. Not a miscarriage, then. In a miscarriage pain always followed the bleeding. What Sally Thompson was suffering from was infinitely sadder than a miscarriage. She had an ectopic pregnancy. Instead of the fertilised egg implanting itself in her uterus, it was growing in one of her Fallopian tubes, and if it wasn't removed immediately the consequences could be disastrous.

'I'll page Gynae,' Elliot murmured, and was gone in a second.

'Am I losing the baby, Nurse?' Mrs Thompson asked, gripping Jane's hand convulsively.

'I'm afraid so,' she said gently.

There was no point in telling the woman any more. She was devastated enough already, without having to find out the very real possibility that the damage to her Fallopian tube might mean it would be even more difficult for her to conceive again in the future.

'Don't you just wish some days that you'd stayed in bed?' Floella said ruefully when the clock on the treatment-room wall finally showed the end of what had proved to be a very long and weary shift. 'In fact, some days I wish I'd listened to my mother and become a secretary.'

'Yeah, right.' Jane smiled. 'And you'd have been bored out of your skull in three months.'

Floella laughed. 'Probably. It's just...sometimes... Well, you know what I mean.'

Jane did. She loved her job. Could never imagine doing

anything else even when the days were rough, and heart-breaking, but today... Today she would be glad to go home and put her feet up.

But not right away, she realised when she went into the staffroom to collect her coat and bag and found Richard sitting there, looking downright miserable.

Don't ask, she told herself. Just take your bag and go. But she knew that she wouldn't, and with a deep sigh she went over to him and sat down.

'Want to talk about it?'

'It's not your problem.'

Why did people always say that when in reality they desperately wanted somebody to listen? she wondered rue-fully, and with an effort she fixed what she hoped was her most encouraging and sympathetic smile to her lips. 'Don't you think I should be the best judge of that? Come on. Tell me.'

'It's Mr Lawrence.'

'Lawrence?' she echoed. 'I'm sorry, do I know him?'

'He's the guy who told us he'd been painting and fallen off his stepladder.'

'I remember now.' She nodded. 'Was there a problem with his arm—wasn't it fractured after all?'

'Oh, it was fractured all right,' Richard exclaimed bitterly, 'but the trouble is that the fracture was at least a year old. Well healed but at an angle.'

Jane's heart sank. She knew what was coming, she just knew she did, but she had to ask. 'And Mr Lawrence?'

'Gone. Did a runner as soon as the X-rays were taken. He was a drug addict, wasn't he? I was conned by a drug addict.'

She nodded. 'I'm afraid so.'

'Oh, God, I feel so stupid!' the junior doctor exclaimed. 'Why don't you just tell me I'm an idiot, a prat? I de-serve it!'

She shook her head and smiled. 'Richard, everyone's been outsmarted by a drug addict at least once in their career. Hannah Blake—the junior doctor we had before you—was conned by one as well, so don't think you're the first and you most certainly won't be the last. Druggies are clever. They have to be to get what they want, and I have to say, passing off an old fracture as a new one in order to get some painkillers is pretty smart.'

'Jane...' His cheeks darkened. 'You don't mind if I call you Jane, do you?'

Her smile deepened. 'I've been hoping you would for ages. Every time you called for Sister Halden, it took me a couple of seconds to realise you meant me.'

He didn't smile. Instead, he bit his lip. 'I don't know how you can be so kind. I've been so awful to you—to all the nurses. I never intended to be like that. I don't know why I was—'

'Forget it. It's all water under the bridge now.' He didn't look convinced. He also didn't look any happier, and though she knew it would mean a rush to get home for Nicole on time, she forced herself to say, 'Is there something else bothering you, Richard?'

He stared down at his hands, then up at her again. 'I don't think I've got what it takes to be a doctor.'

'Of course you have,' she protested. 'Look, that drug addict you treated—'

'It's not just him,' he interrupted. 'It's... Jane, I've always wanted to be a doctor. Even when I was at school I wanted to be a doctor, and when I went to med school I decided that A and E was going to be my speciality, but I'm so scared all the time. Scared I'm going to do the wrong thing, scared I'm going to miss something.'

'Richard, everyone feels like that—truly they do,' she said gently, 'and I think you're being way too hard on yourself. How long have you been with us now?'

'Almost two months.'

'Exactly.' She nodded. 'Graduating from med school doesn't mean you're a doctor. It means you've just started out on the long road to becoming one and, believe me, you'll never stop learning.'

'I guess.'

He looked so miserable, and suddenly so very young, that she quickly did a mental review of the contents of Elliot's fridge and made up her mind.

'Look, why don't you come round to the flat tonight for dinner? Sometimes it helps to talk about your fears and worries, rather than letting them fester away inside you. Or perhaps you'd prefer to talk to Elliot about it,' she added hurriedly as he stared at her, open-mouthed.

'Oh, God, no!' he blurted out. 'I'd much rather talk to you. Dr Mathieson… He's…well, he's a bit overpowering, don't you think?'

'Is he?' Jane said in surprise. 'I can't say I've ever found that, but, then, I've known Elliot for more than two years so I guess I've got used to him. So, would you like to drop by tonight? I can offer you chicken curry and a sympathetic ear, if that's any use to you.'

'Are you sure?' Richard said uncertainly. 'I mean, won't Dr Mathieson mind me coming round?'

'Why should he?' she protested. 'Look, I won't tell him why you've come if that's what's bothering you. I'll just say I invited you for dinner.'

'But won't that make it worse?' the junior doctor asked, looking decidedly uncomfortable. 'I mean, won't it be a bit awkward for you, what with…' The colour on his cheeks grew even deeper. He took a deep breath, and got it out in a rush. 'I mean, won't he object, what with you and him living together and everything?'

Jane smiled. 'How long did you say you've been working at St Stephen's now, Richard?'

'Two months.'

'And you still haven't learned that Elliot favours long-legged girls with perfect figures?' She shook her head. 'I think it's time you spent less time worrying about your medical capabilities and more time listening to the hospital grapevine. Elliot and I might be living in the same flat, but we're certainly not living together. I'm there to help look after his little girl.'

'Really?' Richard didn't look convinced.

'Really,' Jane insisted, getting to her feet and reaching for her coat. 'Come round about eight. Nicole will be in bed by then and I can assure you Elliot won't mind a bit.'

But he did. The minute she told him his blond eyebrows snapped together. 'What do you mean, you've asked Richard Connery round for dinner?'

'I thought it would be a kind thing to do,' she replied, closing the oven door and putting on the timer. 'He's new in London, this is his first post and I think he feels a bit lonely.'

'Then let him join one of the hospital clubs,' he retorted, striding into the sitting room and throwing his jacket over the back of one of the chairs. 'He'll be able to meet plenty of people there.'

'That's not very sociable,' she said as she followed him. 'Elliot, I like him—'

'Oh, do you?'

'Yes, I do,' she retorted, beginning to get seriously irritated as he all but glowered at her, 'and when I agreed to move in here with you, one of the conditions was that I could have friends round whenever I wanted to.'

'So Richard's a friend now, is he?' Elliot said tightly. 'He gets invited round to dinner, does he? Jane, much as I don't want to interfere in your private life—'

'My private life?'

'I'd like to point out that Richard's years younger than you are.'

He thought it was a date, she realised. He thought she'd invited Richard round because they'd made a date, and it was on the tip of her tongue to tell him he'd got it all wrong when she suddenly wondered why she should.

Elliot had no right to be standing there, looking all disapproving and suggesting she was cradle-snatching. If she *had* wanted to date Richard Connery it was none of his damn business, and he was just about to find that out.

'Elliot, I'm twenty-eight years old, and Richard is twenty-three,' she declared icily. 'That hardly makes him my toy boy, and as you appear to have acquired such a downer on him, I'll make things easy for you. I'll entertain him in my room. You won't even have to see him.'

'Your room?'

'Yes, my room,' she snapped. 'The one at the end of the corridor, the one with my clothes and books in it.'

'Jane—'

'Unless you have any objections, of course?'

He did. The biggest one being that he knew of only one form of entertainment which took place in a bedroom, and he most certainly didn't like the idea of Richard and Jane indulging in it.

'You can use the sitting room if you like and I'll stay in my study,' he said grudgingly, but Jane wasn't buying any of it.

'Thanks, but, no, thanks,' she said, her voice cold, clipped. 'I wouldn't want to put you to any trouble. My bedroom will do fine.'

And she was as good as her word. The minute the junior doctor arrived she whisked him straight into her room, without even allowing Elliot to say hello, and firmly shut the door, leaving him fuming and frustrated in the hall.

It's all your own fault, he thought. She has a perfect

right to entertain anyone she likes, and you had no right to object.

Yes, but that was before I knew she was going to invite Richard Connery round, a kid who's scarcely out of nappies. Dammit, it would have been bad enough if it had been Charlie, but at least the SHO could string more than two words together.

Stringing words together didn't appear to be a problem for Richard tonight, he realised as he hovered in the hallway, trying without success to hear what all the talking and occasional burst of laughter was about.

Look, at least they *are* still talking, he thought, and not making love. Nobody could continue to talk like that if they were making love. They wouldn't have the breath, for a start.

If he could only find out what they were saying. In the movies people always put a glass against a wall to listen. Quickly he went into the kitchen, picked one up off the draining-board, then put it down again with a bang. This was ridiculous. Jane was entitled to her privacy. He had no right to spy on her. And the glass trick probably wouldn't work anyway.

The sound of a door opening along the corridor had him shooting across to the kitchen window and gazing out into the back garden with apparently rapt interest.

'Oh, I didn't realise you were in here,' Jane said, coming to a stop as she saw him.

Dammit, she looked all flustered and flushed, but at least she was still fully clothed. Clothed in a loose T-shirt and a pair of jeans. Tight jeans. Figure-hugging jeans. Jeans which clung and outlined her full, round bottom, and a top that was just loose enough for a man to slip his hands under if he felt so inclined.

He swallowed hard. 'I was just about to make myself something to eat.'

'I've made a curry for Richard, but there's more than enough for three if you want some,' she offered, taking a bottle of wine out of the fridge.

'Jane, about you and Richard—'

'Oh, I'm sorry,' the junior doctor said, a warm tinge of colour coming to his cheeks as he appeared at the kitchen door. 'I didn't realise you were in here, sir.'

It's my home, Elliot wanted to snap back, and don't call me 'sir'. It makes me sound ancient and decrepit, and I'm neither.

'Do you need any help with the food, Jane?' Richard asked, turning to her before Elliot could say anything.

'I'm fine, thanks. Though if you could take the wine and the glasses through, that would be a big help. Elliot, do you want a plate of this or not?' Jane continued, opening the oven door as Richard disappeared with the wine and the glasses. 'It's chicken curry.'

His favourite, and he was so hungry he could almost taste it.

'I'm not very hungry, thank you,' he said stiffly. 'In fact, I think I might have an early night.'

Jane glanced up at the clock on the wall in surprise. 'At nine o'clock?'

'I really don't think when I choose to go to bed is any of your business,' he retorted, knowing quite well that he was sounding unbelievably petty and childish but completely unable to stop himself.

She shrugged. 'Suit yourself.'

He hovered for an instant, hoping she might try to dissuade him, but to his chagrin she didn't.

'I'll say goodnight, then,' he said coldly. 'And I'd be obliged if you and your *friend* don't make too much noise and wake Nicole.'

And before she could answer he strode out of the

kitchen, down the hall into his bedroom, and only just restrained himself from slamming the door shut.

Elliot didn't restrain himself, however, from pulling off his shoes and throwing them one by one at the bedroom wall.

Damn Richard Connery. He hoped he choked on his chicken curry. He hoped the wine tasted like vinegar, and the junior doctor had an attack of diarrhoea which kept him off work for the rest of the week.

You're jealous!

OK, all right, he was jealous, he admitted it.

And the reason you're jealous is because you're attracted to Jane yourself.

Of course he wasn't, he retorted, only to realise to his dismay that it was true. He didn't know how it had happened, or when, but he did know one thing. It was an attraction that was going to go nowhere. An attraction he firmly intended making sure went nowhere.

When he and Donna had divorced he'd pledged two things. Never to date anyone who worked in his department—it always led to unpleasantness when the relationship ended—and always to date women who knew the score. Women who would shrug their shoulders when he walked away, as he always did.

And Jane was disqualified on both counts.

She didn't know the score. She was too nice, too kind and too gentle to play the kind of games he normally played, and he'd hurt her, he knew he would, and he didn't want to do that.

Which was why he was going to make a date with Gussie for tomorrow night. Gussie knew the score. Gussie could probably have written the rule book. In fact, now he came to think about it, he probably wouldn't be having these disturbing thoughts about Jane in the first place if he hadn't had to put his social life on hold because he'd been reluctant to ask Gussie round to the flat with Nicole there.

You could have gone round to Gussie's place, his mind pointed out.

OK, so he could, but somehow it hadn't seemed fair to ask Jane to look after Nicole so that he could enjoy Gussie's ample charms.

Well, now he didn't care whether it was fair or not. He was going out with Gussie tomorrow night, or he'd go crazy.

CHAPTER SIX

'NICOLE, Stephanie's mother will be here in five minutes to pick you up and drive you to school, and if you're not ready both you and Stephanie will be late!'

'I know, Jane,' came the shouted reply from the bathroom, 'but I can't find my history book, or my white T-shirt for games!'

'Try the floor behind the sofa in the sitting room for your history book, and your bedroom for your T-shirt!'

For a second there was silence, then the resounding clatter of running feet, followed by the bang of a bedroom door, and Jane winced as she sat down at the kitchen table.

'Overindulged a little on the vino with Richard last night, did we?' Elliot observed, lowering his newspaper to gaze over the top of it at her speculatively, his blue eyes cool.

Actually, she had the mother and father of all headaches this morning, which had a lot more to do with the fact that she hadn't been able to get rid of Richard until two o'clock, but she had absolutely no intention of telling Elliot that.

'Lack of sleep, actually,' she couldn't resist replying, and was gratified to see a flash of anger appear in his blue eyes before he disappeared behind his newspaper again with a furious rustle.

Well, so what if her reply had suggested she'd spent a night of unbridled passion with Richard Connery? she thought waspishly. After Elliot's performance last night—implying she was cradle-snatching, going off to bed in a huff—she was damned if she was going to tell him the truth. That the only passion which had occurred in her bedroom had been Richard's enthusiastic recounting of his family history dating back to when his great-great-grandfather had been a doctor in Leeds.

'Nicole said she'd like chicken for her dinner tonight,' she observed, quickly slipping a paracetamol into her mouth and swallowing it down with some coffee. 'Would that suit you? If it doesn't I could pick up something else on my way home—'

'Actually, I won't be home for dinner,' Elliot interrupted, lowering his newspaper again, but this time he looked awkward, uncomfortable.

'I thought you had tonight off?' She frowned, then groaned. 'It's not one of those admin meetings again, is it? Honestly, the amount of time they spend discussing budgets—'

'It's not a meeting,' Elliot interrupted. 'I...I've got a date. With Gussie.'

There, it was out. He'd said it, and he waited, half expecting Jane to round on him, to tell him he'd got a nerve, expecting her to look after his daughter while he swanned off with Gussie Granton, but she didn't.

'Oh... Right... I see,' was all she said.

'The thing is, Gussie and I haven't been out for a while,' he said hurriedly as Jane began collecting the dirty breakfast dishes and carrying them over to the sink.

'Elliot, you don't have to explain,' she interrupted, her voice carefully neutral. 'You're going out with Gussie. Fine. End of story.'

And it should have been, he told himself. Dammit, they'd agreed that neither of them would give up their social lives, that as long as one of them was here to look after Nicole they could each go out, but...

'Look, I'll speak to Gussie, tell her something's come

up,' he declared, annoyingly aware that his cheeks were slightly flushed. 'We can go out another time.'

'Don't be silly,' Jane protested, running some water into the sink. 'There's absolutely no need for you to cancel. I hadn't planned on going out tonight anyway.' Chance would have been a fine thing, she added mentally, considering nobody's asked me. 'So it's no problem for me to look after Nicole.'

'And you really don't mind?'

Oh, she minded all right. She minded like hell. 'Of course I don't,' she said brightly, pulling on her washing-up gloves with a snap. 'In fact, I hope you and Gussie have a very pleasant evening.'

Which was exactly what he should have wanted to hear, he realised, but perversely he discovered that he didn't. Was he really such boring company that she couldn't wait to get him out of the house?

Perhaps he was, he thought with dismay, suddenly remembering how Jane always seemed to shoot off to her room the minute Nicole went to bed, saying she had things to do. Gussie didn't seem to find him boring. Anything but. Gussie thought he was witty, and attractive—

'Who's Gussie?'

It was true, Elliot thought as he and Jane turned in unison to see Nicole standing in the kitchen doorway, a frown creasing her forehead. Little pitchers did have big ears.

'She's a friend of mine,' he replied quickly. 'Now, have you got everything you need for school? Your packed lunch, your homework—'

'And you are going out with her, Papa?' Nicole continued, her large, dark eyes on him, her frown deepening. 'On a date?'

Two pairs of eyes were fixed on him now, he noticed. One set accusing, the other apparently indifferent, and to

his annoyance it was the indifferent grey eyes which bothered him the most.

'Well, it's a sort of a date,' he said awkwardly. 'I mean,
I'll be having dinner with her.' At Gussie's flat, actually,
but there was no way he was going to tell his daughter
that. 'Jane will be here to look after you—'

'I think if you are going out to dinner with someone, it
should be with Jane,' Nicole interrupted. 'I *like* Jane.'

'And *I* think that sounds like Mrs Massey arriving to
pick you up for school,' Elliot declared, clear relief appearing on his face as a car horn sounded in the street
outside, but his daughter was having none of it.

'My Aunt Michelle—Mama's sister—gave me a book
when I was small called *Gussie's Birthday Party*. Gussie
was a big fat elephant. Is she fat, too, this Gussie of
yours?'

'No, she is not,' Elliot replied, the colour on his cheeks
darkening by the second as he desperately tried to catch
Jane's eye, only to discover she seemed to be finding the
whole thing highly amusing. 'In fact, she's actually very
slim, with blonde hair and...' And this conversation was
getting out of hand, he decided. 'I think it's time you went
to school, young lady.'

'Yes, but if you want to take someone out to dinner,
why don't you take Jane?' Nicole continued. 'She's never
been anywhere since I arrived. Why don't you go out with
Jane instead of this Gussie person?'

'School, Nicole!'

'Yes, but—'

'School!'

And Nicole went, but it didn't stop her muttering darkly
under her breath about fat elephants.

'Honestly, the things kids say!' Floella laughed. 'I remember being in the supermarket once when my twins were

small and this huge woman walks by, and I mean really huge—at least 135 kilos—and my daughter pipes up, "Mummy, is that lady going to have a baby?"'

Jane laughed, too, and if her laughter wasn't quite as hearty as Floella's, thankfully the staff nurse didn't seem to notice.

I'm an idiot, she thought as she watched Elliot crossing the treatment room. I *do* have rocks in my head. To think that only yesterday I was getting myself all in a tizz, thinking he might actually be starting to realise I'm a woman, and what happens? He blithely turns round this morning and tells me he's going out with Gussie.

The plain and simple truth was that Elliot liked women—*all* women. Flirting was as natural to him as breathing, so she'd been right when she'd vowed to keep him at arm's length. She'd been right, so why didn't that knowledge make her feel any better?

'Jane, I wonder if you could give me some help in here, please?' Richard asked, popping his head round the curtains of cubicle 3.

'Jane?' Floella murmured, her eyebrows shooting up to her hairline. '*Jane?* And did mine ears deceive me, or was that also a "please" I just heard?'

'It's a long story, Flo.' Jane couldn't help but chuckle. 'I'll tell you about it some time.'

'You'd better.' The staff nurse grinned, and Jane shook her head and laughed as she walked across to Richard.

'What have you got?' she asked.

'Forty-five-year-old man,' he murmured, deliberately keeping his voice low. 'His wife brought him in because he's been having blinding headaches for the past week. No history of migraine, nor has he had a fall or been involved in a car accident recently. It could just be stress, but...'

Jane nodded. Richard was right to be cautious. A painful headache could be caused by something as simple as a bad day at the office, but it could also be a warning symptom of a life-threatening ruptured aneurysm in the brain.

'Is there a problem here?' Elliot demanded, joining them without warning, his eyes flicking coldly from Jane to Richard.

Quickly Richard gave him all the information he had, but Elliot knew he was only half listening to him. Try as he might, he couldn't prevent his eyes from drifting back to Jane. She looked so pale this morning, pale and tired and a little depressed. And there were dark shadows under her grey eyes, too, shadows he was positive hadn't been there yesterday or he was sure he would have noticed them.

Richard didn't look at all tired, he thought grimly. He looked bright and alert, as though somebody had recently given his confidence quite a boost. Quite how, Elliot preferred not to contemplate.

'Do you mind if I sit in with you for this patient?' he asked, bringing Richard's explanation to a sudden halt. 'No reflection on your capabilities, of course,' he added smoothly as the junior doctor stared at him in clear dismay, 'but it's part of my job. Checking everything's running smoothly.'

And it was, he told himself as Richard nodded and led the way into the cubicle, looking slightly less confident than he had before, and Jane shot him a puzzled glance. Special registrars were supposed to make sure that the junior doctors on their team were up to scratch, and if his interest was slightly more personal than it should have been, it was nobody's business but his own.

To his chagrin, however, it didn't take him long to discover that not only was Richard Connery quite a personable young man, he was also very good at his job.

He could neither fault the thoroughness of his examination nor the way he asked his questions. He would have liked to, but he couldn't.

'Would you care to take a look yourself, Dr Mathieson?' Richard asked, turning to him as though he'd read his mind.

Elliot doubted that there was any need, but he took Richard's seat in front of the patient and quickly shone a light into the man's eyes to check whether both of his pupils were equally round and reacted to the light.

'You told Dr Connery you haven't experienced any stiffness in your neck,' he murmured. 'Have you felt any weakness in your arms or legs, or feelings of feverishness, like you're coming down with the flu?'

The man shook his head, only to quite clearly wish he hadn't, and Jane smiled at him sympathetically. The paracetamol she'd taken this morning didn't seem to have helped her headache at all, but at least she knew why she had one. Getting a full eight hours sleep tonight would solve one of the reasons. Doing something about the way she felt about Elliot… Now, that was an entirely different matter altogether.

'Ophthalmoscope, Jane,' Elliot said, interrupting her thoughts, and swiftly she handed him one, only to colour slightly as he shot her a puzzled glance.

And it was no wonder he looked puzzled, she thought, completely mortified. Never had he needed to ask her for anything before. She'd always been able to anticipate his every request, but not this morning. This morning she'd let her mind wander, and it had wandered because she'd been feeling sorry for herself, and it wasn't on. It definitely wasn't on.

Elliot didn't think it was either as he stared through the ophthalmoscope into the back of the middle-aged man's eyes, searching for any signs of increased intracranial pressure which would indicate bleeding or tumour inside the head.

Efficient, on-the-ball Jane daydreaming? Richard had obviously made a big impression last night, and he couldn't for the life of him see why. He was a pleasant enough young man, but he was just a boy, whereas Jane was a woman. A woman with luscious, generous curves. A woman with a shining fall of straight black hair and a sprinkling of golden freckles on her nose. A woman...

Who hadn't even blinked an eye when he'd said he was going out with Gussie tonight, he suddenly remembered. In fact, she'd actually said she hoped he'd have a pleasant evening.

She should have been angry. She should have torn him off a strip. She should...

Have been jealous? Is that what's really bugging you? The realisation that, though you're beginning to find yourself attracted to her, she doesn't even seem to know you're around?

It was, he realised ruefully. God knows, he'd never thought himself a vain man, but to discover that a woman might actually prefer somebody like Richard Connery to him... It was a novel experience, and one he discovered he didn't like at all.

Determinedly he got to his feet, led the way out of the cubicle, then turned to Richard. 'OK, so what do you think we've got?'

The junior doctor took a deep breath. 'I couldn't see any sign of facial drooping, which would indicate he'd had a minor stroke, nor was there any sign of tenderness in his ears, or round his face and head, to suggest an infection.'

'Meningitis?' Elliot suggested, though he knew perfectly well that it wasn't that, but it was worth a try to see if he could catch Richard out. He didn't.

'Definitely not. I suppose it could be a very bad sinus

infection—they can cause severe headaches—but he said he hadn't had a cold recently.'

'Brain tumour?'

Richard frowned. 'I don't *think* it's a tumour, but frankly I've got to admit I don't know what it is, so I'd like to send him for a CAT scan.'

Which would have been exactly what Elliot would have done if the man had been his patient. At a guess he thought it might be temporal arteritis—an inflammation of the large head arteries which, if left untreated, could cause blindness—but, like Richard, his first line of investigation now would be a CAT scan.

'Well, did he pass the test?' Jane asked as she accompanied Elliot down the treatment room, leaving Richard to make the arrangements for his patient.

'The test?' he echoed.

'I presume that's what you were doing,' she observed. 'Seeing if he was up to scratch.'

'He seems a pretty competent doctor,' he declared grudgingly, and to his annoyance Jane laughed.

'Oh, come on, Elliot, you know perfectly well that he's good. OK, so maybe he was a bit high-handed when he first arrived, but he's learned a lot since then. I think he could be a real asset to the department. He's keen, willing to learn, to listen…'

And presumably downright incredible in bed, he wanted to finish for her, but didn't. 'And would that be a personal assessment, or a professional one?' he said tightly instead.

She stared at him, puzzled. 'I don't know what you mean.'

'I *mean* that I hope your friendship with Richard isn't clouding your judgement.'

'Clouding my…' Her dark eyebrows suddenly snapped down, and she looked angrier than he'd ever seen her. 'How long have you and I worked together, Elliot? Oh, I forgot,' she added as he cleared his throat. 'You don't remember, do you? Well, it's been two years.'

'Jane—'

'Would you say we were friends?'

'I'd like to think so—'

'And do you think I would ignore any situation where I thought you might be making a mistake?'

'No, but—'

'Exactly, so in future stop talking through your hat!'

And before he could reply she was gone, leaving him staring after her, open-mouthed.

'I think you asked for that, Elliot.'

He turned to see Floella gazing up at him, her dark eyes sparkling, and a rueful smile curved his lips. 'You heard?'

'Not everything, but enough. What in the world possessed you to tell Jane she might be behaving unprofessionally?'

For a second he hesitated, then made up his mind. 'Flo, this friendship she has with Richard... Do you think that he and she... I mean, do you think that they...?'

Floella stared at him in total confusion for a second, then burst out laughing. 'Jane and *Richard*? Never in a million years! What in the world put a crazy idea like that into your head?'

The fact that Richard spent hours in her bedroom last night, he thought, but he had no intention of telling Flo that.

'I don't know,' he murmured. 'I just thought... She seems to like him—'

'Elliot, Jane likes *everyone*,' Floella interrupted. 'It's the kind of girl she is. One of the nice ones, if you know what I mean.'

He did know. Just as he also knew that a nice girl would expect faithfulness, commitment. A nice girl would be very badly hurt if someone let her down, and a nice girl would probably be a lot safer with Richard than she'd ever be with him.

'Flo—'

'RTA for you, Doc!' a paramedic called, as he and his colleague pushed a trolley through the swing doors. 'Fractured tib for sure, slight facial lacerations, and he's drunk.'

'Wonderful,' Elliot sighed, walking quickly towards them. 'Any ID?'

'His name's Jonathan Worrell, and he's a solicitor. The police found his car upside down on its roof and they reckon he skidded and simply lost control. No other vehicles involved, you see.'

'Head, leg and chest X-rays?' Jane asked as she joined them.

Elliot nodded. 'Mr Worrell, can you tell me what your first name is, please—where you work—your address?' A few mumbled, incoherent words was the only reply, and Elliot frowned. 'Was he like this when you picked him up?'

'Not quite so garbled,' one of the paramedics admitted, helping Jane to transfer Mr Worrell onto the examination trolley. 'I expect it's the booze working its way through his system.'

'He doesn't look drunk,' Jane observed when the paramedics had gone and she'd stripped off Mr Worrell's clothing.

'No. No, he doesn't,' Elliot murmured.

'Could it be a stroke?' she suggested, swiftly setting up an IV line and strapping the blood-pressure cuff round the solicitor's arm. 'Or what about drugs?'

'Maybe—maybe not. What have we got on BP and pulse?'

'BP 120 over 80,' she answered as Elliot shone his ophthalmoscope into the solicitor's eyes. 'Pulse rapid and weak.'

Elliot's frown deepened. 'I wonder if it's an extradural haemorrhage. He could have hit his head on the windscreen, fractured his skull and ruptured an artery.'

And if he had, he would be bleeding inside or around his brain, and if it wasn't treated in time Mr Worrell could die.

'Will I page Neurology?' she asked.

'We should, but...'

'But?' Jane prompted.

'It doesn't feel right, Jane. I don't know why, but it doesn't.'

She didn't disagree with him as he pulled his stethoscope out of his pocket and leant over Mr Worrell. She'd seen him have these hunches before, and they had always been right.

'What is it?' she asked, when he suddenly straightened up with a muttered oath, then ran his fingers over the solicitor's face and eyes. 'What's wrong?'

'Stupid, that's what I am!' he exclaimed. 'Stupid, stupid, *stupid*!'

'Elliot—'

'Smell his breath, Jane.'

'You mean, he *is* drunk?'

'No, he's not drunk. Smell his breath!'

She did. 'Oh, Lord, it's sweet, fruity. He's got—'

'Diabetic ketoacidosis. Dry skin and lips, soft eyeballs, slurred speech, looks drunk. He's got diabetic ketoacidosis, and I almost missed it!'

'Soluble insulin and a saline solution through an IV to prevent dehydration?' she said, quickly snapping open the sterilised bags.

'Repeated doses, little and often,' he said, nodding, 'and watch his BP in case he goes into shock.'

He didn't. Slowly but surely the colour began to return

to Mr Worrell's cheeks and gradually his eyes fluttered open.

'You gave us quite a fright there for a minute, sir,' Jane said, smiling down at him.

'W-where am I? W-what happened?' he stammered. 'I was on my way home, and I just seemed to black out.'

'You're in hospital, and you're a very lucky man,' Elliot replied. 'Did you know you were a diabetic?'

'My GP diagnosed it last month—'

'And you're not carrying a medical alert card or any extra insulin.' Elliot shook his head and sighed. 'That's a very dangerous way to live, Mr Worrell.'

It was, but the solicitor had been lucky this time. Lucky it had been Elliot who had been treating him.

'Your hunch was right, then, Elliot,' Jane commented when Mr Worrell was transferred to Theatre to have his fractured tibia set.

'I shouldn't have needed a hunch.' He frowned. 'I should have known.'

'Yeah, right.' Jane laughed. 'Like when someone's brought in to us, having trashed his car, suffered lacerations to his forehead, a compound fractured tibia and a possible fractured skull, your first thought should be diabetic?'

An answering smile was drawn from his lips. 'I guess not.'

'I *know* not, you idiot!' She laughed, and he did, too, but his laughter faded as he watched her walking down the treatment room.

It would be all too easy to fall in love with this woman. All too easy, and all too dangerous. He didn't want to fall in love again. Falling in love brought heartbreak and pain. Oh, it might start out with joy and laughter, but it always ended in disillusionment and bitterness.

Then you should be pleased Jane's not even remotely

interested in you, his mind whispered. You should be relieved it's Richard Connery she wants.

And he *was* relieved, he told himself. OK, so maybe he
wasn't pleased that she could prefer a jerk like Richard to
him, but it was better that way. Simpler. Safer.

And thank God he was going round to Gussie's flat
tonight, because at least for a few hours the one person he
wouldn't be able to think about was Jane Halden.

'Darling, I hate to point this out, but do you realise you've
done nothing but talk about Jane and Nicole ever since
you got here?' Gussie protested, as she handed him a cup
of coffee, then sat down beside him on the sofa.

'Have I?' Elliot frowned. 'I'm sorry, Gussie, and I apologise. That dinner was quite superb. In fact, I couldn't tell
you the last time I had smoked salmon. The only kind of
fish Nicole will eat is fish fingers.'

'Really. Elliot—'

'Actually, she calls them fish thumbs.' He chuckled.
'It's because they're so thick, you see,' he added as Gussie
stared at him blankly. 'Thumbs instead of fingers?'

'Oh. Right. Elliot—'

'Jane's trying to get her to eat more vegetables—cutting
them into weird and wonderful shapes—but persuading
kids to eat vegetables—'

'Must be hell,' Gussie finished for him, sliding along
the couch so her breasts brushed against his arm. 'Just as
I'm also sure that we could find a whole lot more fun
things to do than talk about them.'

He laughed. 'I'm sorry. I'm turning into a right bore
when it comes to my daughter, aren't I? It's just that never
having had a daughter before... I wish I was as good with
her as Jane is. I'm getting better, but Jane always seems
to know the right things to say and do.'

'She's quite wonderful, a perfect treasure.' Gussie nodded, running her fingers lightly up his arm and bringing them to rest on his shoulder.

'I really don't know how I'm going to manage when she leaves,' Elliot murmured, a slight frown darkening his eyes. 'I know she can't stay with me for ever…'

'God forbid.' Gussie chuckled throatily. 'For one thing, a *ménage à trois* has never appealed to me.'

His blond eyebrows snapped down. 'There's nothing like that between Jane and me. Jane…she's a very nice girl.'

'A perfect saint, in fact,' Gussie agreed, 'but us sinners do tend to have a lot more fun.'

'Gussie—'

'I thought Nicole was going to stay with your mother when she comes back from Canada?' Gussie continued, nibbling his ear gently with her teeth. 'You did say that, didn't you?'

'I did, but the trouble is I'm going to really miss her when she goes,' he replied, absently rubbing at his ear. 'And she's getting so fond of Jane.'

Gussie forced her lips into a semblance of a smile. 'Darling, if you're so worried about Nicole, would you like me to move in with you when Jane leaves? I'm sure I can organise things at work—' She came to a halt, her brown eyes flashing, as he threw back his head and laughed. 'What's so funny about that?'

Just about everything, Elliot thought. Oh, if he'd wanted someone to take to the special registrar's ball, Gussie would have been perfect, but never could he imagine her pink-cheeked and flushed, her hair scraped back from her face in a ponytail, playing an enthusiastic game of hide-and-seek with Nicole.

'Gussie, you're absolutely wonderful, and I adore you like mad,' he said with a smile, 'but a surrogate mother you're not. Jane—'

'Elliot, if you're going to spend the whole night telling me how marvellous Jane Halden is, I think perhaps you'd better leave!' Gussie snapped, then bit her lip as his eyebrows rose. 'Darling, I'm sorry,' she continued, winding her arms around his neck and pressing her body close to his, 'but a woman has her pride, and she really doesn't want to hear another woman being praised all the time.'

He supposed not. Just as he wished Gussie's perfume wasn't quite so heavy, and that she didn't wear quite so much make-up. Jane didn't wear any make-up. He'd seen her often enough first thing in the morning, her eyes cloudy with sleep, her hair tousled, and then later again at work to know that. Jane...

Abruptly he got to his feet. 'Gussie, I'm sorry, but I have to go.'

'Go?' she gasped. 'But, Elliot, you haven't had your brandy yet, or...' She ran her tongue lightly along her lips. 'Or anything.'

He didn't want the 'anything'. He knew as he left Gussie's flat, mumbling a completely garbled apology which left her staring after him in stunned disbelief, that he didn't want the 'anything' now, or at any time in the future.

'Elliot?'

Well, that made two women he'd managed to stun in the space of an hour, Elliot thought ruefully as he walked into the sitting room, and neither of them appeared to have enjoyed the experience.

'I didn't expect you back so early,' Jane continued. Actually, she hadn't expected him back at all, at least not tonight. 'How's Gussie?'

'Fine. No, don't put that off on my account,' he said quickly as she reached for the television remote control.

'I wasn't really watching it anyway. It's just another of

those mindless American soaps that never seem to get anywhere.'

'Has Nicole gone to bed?' he asked, throwing his car keys onto the coffee-table.

'About an hour ago,' she said. Ask him, she told herself. Go on, ask him. You want to know. You know you do. 'Did you have a nice evening?'

'It was OK,' he replied, offhand, dismissive. 'Gussie and I… We don't seem to have a lot in common any more.'

Privately she wondered when they ever had but, then, she'd always supposed they didn't spend much time talking on their dates.

'Did *you* have a good evening?' he asked.

'Oh, quiet, you know. I helped Nicole with her homework, we played some snakes-and-ladders. She won.'

He smiled. 'I think she cheats.'

She laughed. 'So do I.'

'Have you had supper?'

'About half an hour ago, after my bath. I was just about to go to bed.'

'So I see.'

And he did see as his eyes took in her red and white men's pyjamas, and he found himself wondering why on earth he'd ever thought Gussie's sheer nightdresses sexy.

Jane's pyjamas were sexy. Sexy in the way they revealed nothing. Sexy because they hinted at the curves that lay beneath them. Hinted, and tantalised, and simply cried out for a man to investigate them. For him to investigate them.

'Jane, what Nicole said at breakfast about you and I going out together,' he said quickly. 'I was thinking it's actually a very good idea. We could get a babysitter in— Flo's always saying she'd love to—and go out to dinner somewhere.'

'You and me?' she said in obvious surprise.

'Well, I wasn't planning on asking Stephanie's mother.'
He smiled. 'I thought we could try out that new restaurant
in town—the one that's just opened in Flynn Street—'

'Why?'

'Why?' he echoed. The girls he asked out didn't normally ask why. They were usually too busy falling over
themselves to say yes. 'Well, because…because I thought
you might enjoy it.'

Which wasn't exactly the most romantic way to ask a
girl for a date, he thought ruefully, and Jane clearly agreed,
because she shook her head. 'I don't think so, Elliot.'

'But I really would like to take you out to dinner,' he
said desperately. 'You could look on it as a sort of thank
you for all the work you've done with Nicole.'

It had been the wrong thing to say and he knew it immediately. Knew it from the stiffening of her shoulders,
the way her eyes suddenly grew cold.

'I don't consider what I've done with Nicole work,
Elliot,' she said tightly, 'and I certainly don't require dinner as a payment.'

'And I didn't mean it to sound as though it were!' he
exclaimed, cursing himself under his breath. 'What I meant
to say was…'

Hell, he didn't know what he'd meant to say. She was
sitting there in those damn pyjamas of hers, looking so
appealing, so desirable that all he really wanted was to
take her in his arms.

'Look, Jane, you haven't had an evening out since you
moved in.' Oh, that's wonderful, Elliot, he groaned mentally, seeing her bristle even more. Now you've implied
you feel sorry for her. That she's got no social life. What
on earth's wrong with you? You don't usually make such
a mess of asking a girl out, but you sure as heck are making a mess of this. 'I simply thought when Nicole suggested it—'

'That as poor old Jane doesn't get out much maybe she could do with a little treat?' she interrupted acidly. 'That perhaps a little pat on the head might keep her sweet if you need to ask her another favour?'

'No—No!'

'Then why, Elliot? *Why*?'

Because I like you, he thought as she glared at him, her face chalk-white, her eyes glittering with fury. Because I'm growing more and more attracted to you every day, and what I want right now more than anything in the world is to make love to you.

She'd slap his face for sure if he said that. Instead, he forced what he hoped was his most appealing smile to his face. 'Has anyone ever told you you're gorgeous when you're angry?'

She stared at him silently for a full ten seconds, then her lip curled. 'You have, Elliot, most generally when you think your charm and your looks will get you out of a mess. Well, not this time they won't. I won't be patronised—do you hear me? Not now, not ever!'

'Jane—'

'I'm going to bed.'

'But, Jane—'

He was talking to empty air. She'd already swung out of the room, her back ramrod stiff, her head high, and as he heard the sound of her bedroom door slamming shut, he closed his eyes tightly and groaned.

CHAPTER SEVEN

'ELLIOT says there's a two-hour waiting time in Reception now, and X-Ray are warning of at least a one-hour delay in the processing of non-urgent plates,' Kelly reported.

Jane groaned as she leafed through the stack of patient notes the student nurse had brought through from Reception. It was always the same. The minute the schools closed for their Easter break the number of accidents quadrupled. If it wasn't children throwing themselves off walls, or under cars, it was their parents attempting to electrocute themselves with their DIY equipment or driving like maniacs to beat the queues at the tourist attractions.

Thank goodness, Stephanie's mother had agreed to look after Nicole during the day. She wouldn't have been able to relax for a minute otherwise. As it was, if it was up to her, all school holidays would be cancelled. Neither she nor A and E could take the strain.

'Jane, we seem to be running really low on dressings.' Richard frowned, swiftly erasing the name of the last patient he'd seen from the whiteboard. 'Any chance of you nipping along to the dispensary to pick some up?'

'I'll try to arrange—'

'Jane, if you're going to the dispensary, could you pop into Haematology on your way back and see if you can hurry up the results for my patient in 6?' Charlie chipped in.

'Did you just say you're going to Haematology, Jane?' Elliot said as he passed. 'Because if you are, I've got some samples—'

'What am I—the local collection and delivery boy?'

117

Jane snapped before she could stop herself. 'Kelly, go and pick up some dressings, but I want you back a.s.a.p. Charlie, if you're so concerned about your results, lift the telephone. And, Elliot...' Oh, she knew exactly where she'd like to tell him to go, but she was too much of a lady to say it. 'Get a porter to take your samples!'

And before any of them could reply, she strode quickly away, all too aware that the three men were staring in stunned amazement after her.

Well, let them stare, she thought belligerently. Right now she could cheerfully have seen the three of them, and St Stephen's, at the bottom of the Thames.

No, not St Stephen's, she conceded. And not the three of them. Just him. Just Elliot Mathieson.

The nerve of the man. The sheer, unmitigated gall of him. Asking her out like that. Like he was doing her a favour. Like she ought to be grateful. Well, he could stuff his dinner invitation. In fact, she was sorely tempted to go back to the flat tonight, pack her suitcases and leave him and his daughter to get on with it.

No, she wouldn't do that, she realised as she gazed unseeingly, at the clock on the treatment-room wall. No matter how angry she might be with Elliot, she could never do that to Nicole.

She jumped as a white sheet of paper stuck to the end of a ruler suddenly fluttered in front of her nose, and turned to the bearer of it with a frown. 'What's this?'

'A substitute white flag.' Elliot grinned sheepishly. 'Jane, I'm sorry. Charlie and Richard—they're sorry, too,' he added, nodding to where the SHO and junior doctor were standing by the whiteboard, looking decidedly shamefaced. 'We didn't mean to make you feel like an errand boy.'

Yeah, right, she thought sourly. And last night I suppose

you didn't mean to make me feel like a charity case either, but you still did.

'And while we're on the subject of apologising,' he continued quickly as though he'd read her mind, 'you shot out of the house so fast this morning that you didn't give me the chance to set the record straight about last night.'

'Elliot, I think the less said about last night, the better,' she declared.

'Well, I don't!' he snapped, then bit his lip as he noticed that Floella was watching them curiously from the bottom of the treatment room. 'Jane, I really do want to go out with you. Not as a payment, not as a thank you. On a date.'

Boy, but he and Gussie must have had a real humdinger of a row if he was asking her out, she thought waspishly. Well, she had no intention of accepting. She might be a mug and a patsy in many things, but not on this.

'And as I told you last night, Elliot, thanks but, no, thanks,' she said tersely.

She was turning him down? he thought in amazement. She was actually saying no, and meaning it? She couldn't. He wouldn't let her.

Then tell her the truth, his mind urged. Tell her how you feel, why you really want to go out with her.

'Jane…Janey, look, this probably isn't the best time or place for this conversation,' he began awkwardly, 'but I meant what I said. I like you. I like you a lot. I've no idea why I didn't realise it before…'

Probably because you were too busy dating Gussie, she thought bitterly, and before her it had been Marie from Obs and Gynae and Sue from Radiology. Actually, now that she came to think of it, it would have been an awful lot easier to name the girls at St Stephen's that Elliot *hadn't* dated.

'But now I'm asking *you* out, Janey,' he continued. 'Not

because you've been such a great help with Nicole, not because I want to say thank you, but because I truly and honestly do like you very much indeed.'

And she might well have believed him if she hadn't heard him use exactly the same coaxing tone on dozens of women before. Might have been convinced by his earnest expression, the way his lips had curved into one of his lopsided, nerve-tingling smiles, if it hadn't been all too familiar. It had always worked on the women he'd tried it with, and—if she was honest with herself—it was almost working on her, too. Almost, but not quite.

'That's very nice to hear, Elliot,' she declared, 'and I like you as well, but the answer's still no. And now, if you'll excuse me, I have work to do.'

And before he could stop her she'd walked away, leaving him staring helplessly after her.

Where had he gone wrong? It had never failed in the past. A particular smile, a few soft words, and most women had come running. But it hadn't worked this time, and he couldn't for the life of him think why.

'What are you playing at, Elliot?'

He turned quickly to see Floella staring up at him, her normally cheerful face grim, her eyes accusatory.

'I don't know what you mean.'

'Oh, yes, you do,' she said. 'I told Jane to be careful when she agreed to move in with you. Told her she was storing up a whole heap of trouble for herself, but I thought that was because she might get too fond of Nicole.'

'Flo—'

'Elliot, don't mess her around. She's my friend, and if you hurt her—'

'I'd never hurt her, Flo, believe me,' he interrupted indignantly.

'And you don't think persuading her to go out with you, getting her into your bed, and then dumping her will hurt?'

'Flo—'

'And that's what you'll do, Elliot,' she continued. 'It's what you always do, so leave her alone. If you're not serious about her, leave her alone.'

Which was telling him good and proper, he thought ruefully, and Floella was right.

He didn't do commitment. He didn't do fidelity. OK, so maybe he felt an overwhelming attraction for Jane, but the last thing she needed was a man like him in her life, a man who was only comfortable with brief affairs. He'd hurt her, he knew he would, and she didn't need that, didn't deserve it.

He had to start distancing himself from her, and fast. He had to go back to seeing her as good old Janey. For his own sake, as well as for hers. And if that meant standing by and watching her becoming involved with someone like Richard Connery, he decided as he saw the junior doctor say something to her that had made her laugh, so be it.

'Kate Anderson, Doc!' a paramedic exclaimed as he rushed into the treatment room, a heavily pregnant woman on his trolley, and a white-faced man at her side. 'Twenty-two, in labour, and I don't reckon we're going to make the delivery room!'

Elliot didn't reckon she would either when the paramedics had got the woman onto the examination trolley. Her cervix was well dilated, already ten centimetres.

'Jane! Good, you're here,' he said with relief, wincing slightly as Mrs Anderson suddenly grabbed hold of his hand and squeezed hard on it. 'How are you with imminent mums-to-be?'

'Not exactly my speciality, I'm afraid,' she replied ruefully.

'Nor mine,' he replied. 'Has anyone paged the labour ward?'

'Flo was doing it when—'

'Should she be suffering so much?' Mr Anderson interrupted convulsively as his wife let out a scream. 'It doesn't seem right that she should be suffering so much. Can't you give her something—some painkiller?'

'There isn't any point, Mr Anderson,' Elliot said gently. 'By the time it took effect the baby would be here.'

'It's that close?' the young man gulped, and Elliot nodded.

'It's that close.'

'Oh, cripes, oh, God!' Kate Anderson gasped, doubling up as another contraction hit her. 'Nobody ever told me it would hurt this much. John, if you ever come near me again, if you ever even attempt to lay a finger on me—!'

'I can see the baby's head!' her husband exclaimed excitedly. 'I can see the top of its head!'

'I don't care if you can see its head, its shoulders, its entire body!' she yelled. 'I've changed my mind. I don't want to do this any more!'

'I'm afraid it's a bit late for that.' Elliot grinned. 'Breathe, Kate. Huff and pant and breathe like you were taught at the antenatal clinic.'

'But it's not working!' she wailed. 'Those stupid lessons—they're not working!'

'They are—believe me, they are,' Elliot insisted.

Believe me, he'd said, Jane thought as she quickly mopped Kate Anderson's forehead. The young woman believed him, but she couldn't.

He liked her, he'd said, but what did that actually mean? Two or three dates, a few nights of love and then goodbye, Jane, when he got bored or began to feel pressurised?

Could she be happy with that? Right now she could, she realised as she watched him urging the young woman on, smiling at her as only Elliot knew how. Right now she would happily have settled for one night in his arms, but that was only her hormones reacting. Her head was wiser, her head knew different, and it was her head she was going to listen to.

'It's coming, Kate, it's coming!' he encouraged. 'One more push. Just for me, give one big, huge push!'

And she did, with a cry that was halfway towards a scream, and suddenly the baby was there.

'Is it all right—is my baby all right?' she cried, trying to lever herself upright.

'Perfect, just perfect,' Elliot replied, swiftly cutting the umbilical cord as Jane wiped the mucus from the baby's eyes and mouth and it let out a protesting cry.

'Is it a boy or a girl?' Kate asked, turning eagerly to her husband.

'Yes,' he said, then flushed as he realised what he'd just said. 'It's a… What is it, Nurse?'

'A girl.' Jane laughed. 'You have a lovely baby girl, Mr Anderson.'

And she was beautiful, she thought as she handed her reluctantly to her mother. Perfect in every detail, right down to her tiny toes and fingernails.

And I'm getting broody, she thought as the labour staff arrived to transfer Kate to Theatre to deliver the placenta and repair the small tear she'd sustained during the delivery. I'm twenty-eight years old, soon to be twenty-nine, with no man in my life, and I'm getting broody.

'Wasn't she absolutely gorgeous?' Floella exclaimed, as the baby was whisked away by Sister Strachan of the special care baby unit for monitoring and assessment. 'I told my husband after the twins were born that there'd be no more, but when you see a little scrap like that…'

'You start getting broody.' Charlie Gordon laughed. 'Honestly, you women. Put you within ten yards of a baby—'

'Yeah, right,' Floella interrupted, her dark eyes dancing.

'Like you didn't go a bit misty-eyed yourself. I saw you, so don't try to pretend otherwise. And you weren't any better, Elliot,' she continued as he joined them, 'so don't try to tell me that you were.'

He didn't. He was too busy wishing he'd been present at Nicole's birth. OK, so he and Donna hadn't been on speaking terms, and she would probably have preferred him to be rotting in hell, but he'd seen the look of wonderment on John Anderson's face, the joy, the pride. He'd missed that, hadn't had the chance to experience that.

Maybe the next time, he found himself thinking, only to realise to his horror that his eyes had automatically drifted to Jane, and quickly he wrenched them away.

No, he wasn't going to think that, he must never ever think that. OK, so he expected that Nicole would like a little brother or a sister, but to have one would mean him making a commitment to someone—a long-term commitment—and that was the last thing on his mind.

'Well, if we've all finished admiring little baby Anderson, I suggest we get back to work,' he declared more brusquely than he'd intended. 'There are patients waiting to be seen out in Reception, and their wait isn't going to get any less if we stand around here talking about babies!'

'What in the world's got into him?' Floella demanded as Elliot strode away. 'Good grief, we see enough misery in A and E that it's nice to have a happy ending for once.'

Jane couldn't have agreed with her more as she stared after Elliot with a puzzled frown, but something had obviously got under his skin, and she couldn't for the life of her think what.

'Jane, before you go, I'd like to ask you something,' Charlie said as Floella hurried away, still muttering under her breath.

'Fire away,' she replied, forcing a smile to her lips.

'Barbara and I would like very much to invite you out to dinner with us tonight.'

'To dinner?' she repeated. 'Well, that's very nice of you both, Charlie, and I've certainly never been one to look a gift dinner in the mouth...' Unless it's being offered by Elliot, of course, she amended, but, then, his invitation hadn't been a gift, it had been a payment. 'But why?'

'She said yes, Jane,' he replied, a broad smile lighting up his face. 'I asked her to marry me when we were at Brambles, and she said yes.'

'Oh, congratulations!' she exclaimed. 'I'm so happy for you. Have you told anyone else yet? We must have a party—'

'I'd rather not if you don't mind,' he interrupted. 'Barbara wants to tell her folks first.'

'I understand.' Jane nodded. 'I'm so pleased for you, Charlie, I really am, but what has that got to do with you inviting me to dinner?'

'Well, you suggested the venue—'

'That hardly makes me a matchmaker,' she protested with a chuckle.

'And you've been a very good friend to me since I came to St Stephen's, which is why Barbara and I would like you to come out to dinner with us tonight, just to say thank you.'

He meant it, she could see that he did, and it would certainly get her out of the flat. And tonight she didn't want to be in the flat. Tonight she didn't want to be anywhere near Elliot Mathieson.

'Then I accept the invitation with pleasure, Charlie.' She smiled. 'And thank you very much for asking.'

'Thank *you*.' He smiled back. 'We'll pick you up at eight.'

'You'd better just sound your horn and I'll come out,' she advised. 'It's murder finding anywhere to park, and if you keep your engine running, I'll just run down and jump in.'

He nodded, then frowned. 'You don't have to square it with Elliot first? I know you have this arrangement whereby there's always one of you home to look after Nicole.'

'No, I don't have to talk to Elliot,' she said firmly. 'He won't mind at all.'

And he'd better not, she thought, or she would want to know the reason why.

Elliot didn't object but his jaw did drop when she came into the sitting room later that evening, one high heel on, the other still in her hand as she scanned the room, clearly looking for something.

'You're going out?' he said faintly.

'Yes, I'm going out,' she replied, homing in on the mantelpiece and retrieving her hairbrush. 'I hope you didn't have anything planned. The invitation was a bit of a last-minute affair—'

'You're going out like that?' he interrupted.

'Like what?' she said, slipping on her other shoe and turning towards him with a slight frown.

He swallowed convulsively. He'd never seen her dressed before. Not dressed to go out. Not wearing a black velvet dress with a fitted waistline and a bodice that sloped off her creamy shoulders, revealing more than a hint of the deep cleft between her breasts.

'Who?' His voice had come out in a slightly strangled squeak and he cleared his throat. 'Who are you going out with?'

'Charlie and—'

'Charlie Gordon?' he exclaimed, sitting bolt upright in his seat. 'You're going out on a date with Charlie Gordon?'

She could have explained—she supposed she ought to
have done—but suddenly she was blowed if she would.

It was the stunned expression on his face that riled her.
The look that suggested he couldn't quite believe that anybody would actually have asked her out.

'Yes, I'm going out on a date with Charlie Gordon,' she
said bluntly. 'What about it?'

'But you can't go out with him!'

Her eyebrows rose as she slipped her hairbrush into her
bag. 'Oh, but I can, Elliot. Now, I shouldn't be too late,
probably not much after ten—'

'But I've rented a video for tonight,' he protested.

'Then I hope you enjoy it,' she said calmly. 'Like I said,
I shouldn't be late. And now I really have to go,' she added
as she heard the sound of a car horn tooting in the street
outside.

'Jane, you can't do this—you shouldn't,' Elliot exclaimed, coming after her and catching her by the arm.
'Charlie... He's got a girlfriend in Wales or Lancashire—'

'Shrewsbury,' she interrupted without thinking, but he
didn't pick her up on that, he was far too worried.

'Exactly.' He nodded. 'He's got a girlfriend, but he's
asking you out, too. Don't be a fool, Jane. A man like that
will hurt you for sure.'

And you wouldn't? she thought as she stared up at him.
Elliot, you would hurt me a hundred times more—you already have—and yet you can't see it.

'I really don't see who I go out with is any of your
damn business!' she retorted, pulling free of his arm.

'Janey—'

'And that's another thing,' she interrupted. 'I really, really hate it when you call me that. You always call me
that when you're wanting a favour, when you're trying to
get something out of me, and I don't like it!'

'I didn't realise, I didn't know—'

'Why should you?' she said. 'Why should you know anything at all about me, Elliot?'

And without allowing him to reply, she walked out of the flat and down to the car where Charlie and his fiancée were waiting.

'Everything OK, Jane?' he asked. 'No problems about getting away tonight?'

'Why should there be?' she replied with a brittle smile as she slipped into the back seat. 'I'm so glad you asked me. I'm really, *really* looking forward to this.'

And to her amazement she did enjoy herself. Barbara put her at her ease in a second, the food at the restaurant was superb and if occasionally she found herself thinking about Elliot she quickly trampled on the thought.

'I wish you both every happiness in the world,' she told the couple when the waiter had cleared away their pudding plates and she insisted he bring them a bottle of champagne with their coffees. 'I don't know very much about you, Barbara,' she continued, smiling across at the small red-headed girl, 'but if Charlie loves you then you must be a very nice girl, because he's certainly a very nice man.'

'Hey, any more of that kind of talk and you'll have me blushing,' he protested, then lifted his glass of champagne. 'I'd like to propose a toast.' Obediently Barbara and Jane lifted their glasses, but to Jane's surprise Charlie put his hand over hers. ''You can't drink to yourself, love.'

'Me?' she said in surprise.

'You.' He nodded. 'I want to toast the best A and E sister I know, and also the kindest. May she have long life and happiness.'

'Long life and happiness,' Barbara echoed, and Jane blinked back the tears she could feel welling in her eyes.

The long life she might be lucky enough to achieve, but the happiness Somehow she doubted it.

'Thanks for a lovely evening,' Jane said when Charlie

had driven her home after he'd first dropped his fiancée off at his flat. 'I still don't think I deserved it, but thank you anyway.'

'I meant what I said, you know,' he said with a smile as she opened the car door. 'I do wish you every happiness.'

'And I think your Barbara's a very lucky woman.' She chuckled, kissing him lightly on the cheek.

'Looks like someone's still up,' he commented, seeing a dim glow through one of the curtains. 'Elliot checking you in, do you reckon?'

'Elliot tackling some paperwork, more like,' she said ruefully.

And most definitely not wanting to be disturbed, she decided as she let herself into the house.

Quickly she slipped off her heels and began tiptoeing along the corridor, but she couldn't have been quiet enough because she'd just passed his study when the door was suddenly thrown open and he stood there, his eyes furious, his face grim.

'Where the hell have you been?'

Her jaw dropped. 'Out to dinner with Charlie, of course.'

'Until this hour?'

She very nearly laughed. He sounded for all the world like an irate father berating his teenage daughter, but he wasn't her father and she most certainly wasn't his daughter.

Deliberately she looked down at her watch then up at him. 'Good grief, is it eleven o'clock already? I really have been painting the town red, haven't I?'

He coloured but his face didn't relax at all. 'You said you'd be back by ten.'

'I thought I would be, but I was having such a very nice time—'

'And you couldn't have phoned to say you'd be late? It never occurred to you that I—we might have been worried, or that Nicole could have been taken ill?'

'What's happened?' she demanded, worry surging through her. 'Nicole—'

'Is perfectly all right, but that's not the point.'

'Then what is?' Jane demanded, her confusion giving way to anger. 'Elliot, this is the first time I've been out in the evening since I moved in with you. Nicole wasn't left on her own—you were here with her—and you have no right to make me feel guilty. Good grief, if I'd wanted to stay out all night I could.'

'And did you?'

'Did I what?' she asked, bewildered.

'Want to stay out all night?'

His eyes were fixed on her, cold, hard, and she felt herself reddening. 'That's none of your business.'

'It is when I have Nicole's moral welfare to consider.'

'When you have her...' Jane took a deep breath and struggled to keep her temper. 'Elliot, I have been out for one evening. I have returned at what—in anybody's book—is a perfectly reasonable hour. I do not see how that in any shape or form makes me some kind of moral degenerate.'

'I didn't say it did,' he replied, his cheeks almost as red as hers now.

'You didn't have to, Elliot, and now—if you'll excuse me—I am going to bed!'

'No, please!' he exclaimed as she whirled round on her heel. 'Jane...Jane, I'm sorry. You have every right to go out whenever and with whoever you choose. I...I have no claim on you, no right to dictate anything. I just... It's just...I can't help worrying about you.'

'Elliot, I'm all grown up in case you hadn't noticed,' she protested.

'I've noticed.'

He was teasing her, of course—she knew he was. But as she looked up at him, fully expecting to see the tell-tale twinkle in his eye, the give-away quirk of his lips, she saw to her amazement that there was none.

And then she saw something else in his eyes. Something that made her breath catch and shudder in her throat.

'Elliot...'

'Jane...'

His voice was low and dark and husky. Slowly, as though in a dream, she saw his hand lift and come towards her, felt it cup her cheek, and she couldn't move. Felt rooted to the spot.

He was going to kiss her. She knew he was, and she stared up at him, wide-eyed, all too aware that her instincts were urging her to run, but she didn't want to run.

Slowly his head came down towards hers. Too slowly, much too slowly, and her hands half rose from her sides to bring him closer, only to fall back instantly as she heard a small voice whisper behind her, 'Papa?'

'N-Nicole!' Elliot stammered. 'What are you doing out of bed? It's late—'

'I heard voices, people shouting...'

'It was the radio,' Jane declared quickly. 'Your father was listening to a play on the radio.'

'I thought it was you, Papa,' Nicole murmured, tears shining in her eyes. 'I thought you were arguing, fighting with Jane—'

'Oh, no, sweetheart, never,' he declared hoarsely, going to her immediately, and lifting her into his arms. 'Jane and I... We're the best of friends, you know that.'

'But I thought—'

'You were dreaming, Nicole,' he insisted, and she buried her face in his shoulder and shook her head.

'I don't like it when people fight. Mama... She used to

fight sometimes with her boyfriends, throwing vases, dishes—'

'Come on, let's get you back into bed,' Jane interrupted, reaching for the little girl, only to see her cling even more tenaciously to her father.

'I want Papa to take me to bed,' she declared. 'Papa, I want you to do it.'

Elliot mouthed an apologetic 'Sorry' over his daughter's head, but Jane shook her head in reply.

It was how it should be. How she'd always hoped it would be. That Elliot and Nicole would finally become father and daughter, and if her throat felt tight, constricted, and she wanted to burst into tears, that was understandable, too.

Elliot turned to carry his daughter back to her bedroom, then paused. 'You'll wait until I get her settled?'

It would have been so easy to say yes. To wait for him, to let what she knew would happen if she did wait simply happen. And if Nicole hadn't arrived when she had she would have gone with him willingly, let him make love to her willingly, but the moment was broken, and the cold light of sanity had returned.

'I don't think that would be a very good idea, do you?' she replied with a crooked smile that tore at his heart.

'Jane—'

'I'm very tired, Elliot. I really would rather just go to bed.'

And he knew, too, that the moment was gone, and didn't argue with her.

It took almost half an hour to get Nicole settled again, and when he came out of her bedroom Jane's room was in darkness.

Wearily he went into the sitting room, poured himself a drink, put a CD on the stereo and sat down and closed his eyes, only to open them again when he realised what music he'd put on.

Three years ago his sister Annie had given him *The World's Best Love Songs* for his birthday and he'd burst out laughing when he'd unwrapped it. He'd stuffed it at the back of his collection, meaning to give it away to the first bring-and-buy sale that came along, and had promptly forgotten about it. And now he'd accidentally put it on.

But as he listened to the male singer telling of his lost love, of the missed opportunities, and heartbreak, a bitter smile curved his lips. The guy knew what he was talking about, and he did, too, but it wasn't Donna he was thinking of. Donna, whom he'd loved with all the intensity of a bush fire, a bush fire that perhaps inevitably had been bound to burn out, leaving desolation in its wake.

It was Jane. Jane, who had somehow managed to creep her way into his heart without him even realising she was doing it. Jane, whom he knew that he'd fallen in love with, just as surely as he knew that she didn't return his love.

CHAPTER EIGHT

'OK, WHAT have we got in cubicle 4, Flo?'

'Mrs Steel. In London from America on her honeymoon, and she's experiencing excruciating pain when she urinates. Sounds like a bad case of honeymoon cystitis to me, but I'm not a doctor.'

Oh, terrific, Elliot thought wearily. That was all he needed today. After tossing and turning all night, trying desperately hard not to think about sex, what had he been landed with? A case of honeymoon cystitis.

'Is Kelly with her?'

Floella shook her head. 'Jane.'

Even better, he groaned. A case of honeymoon cystitis, and Jane for company. The gods must really have decided to have some fun at his expense this morning.

'I understand you're experiencing pain when you're passing urine, Mrs Steel?' he said as he walked into the cubicle and the tall blonde girl lying on the trolley cautiously levered herself upright.

'And it's not just that it hurts like hell when I go,' the girl replied. 'I'm running backwards and forwards to the john practically every half-hour as well.'

'Any other symptoms?' he asked, quickly taking her pulse. 'Pain in your back or stomach?'

'And how.' She grimaced. 'It feels like someone's sticking red-hot pokers into me.'

'BP, Sister Halden?' he asked, turning to Jane.

'Normal,' she murmured, but she didn't look at him when she said it.

She'd been doing her level best not to look at him all

134

morning. OK, so at breakfast she could have argued that she was too harassed, trying to get Nicole ready to go off for the day with Stephanie and her mother to indulge in any kind of small talk, but that still didn't explain why she'd left for the hospital before he'd even realised she was gone, or why she'd been avoiding him since they'd started their shift.

He'd made her uncomfortable, he thought sadly. Last night he'd made her angry, and then he'd gone and made her feel uncomfortable, and it had been the last thing he'd wanted. He'd wanted—hoped—she might possibly have fallen in love with him, as he had with her, but she hadn't, and now she was going to be tiptoeing around him, awkward, embarrassed, and it was going to be hell.

'Do you think it's something serious?' Mrs Steel asked, her pale face worried.

Oh, it was serious, all right, Elliot thought, gazing at Jane's carefully lowered head. Falling in love was always serious, and it was devastating if the person you loved didn't love you back.

'I don't think so, Mrs Steel,' he replied, dredging up a smile. 'Could you take a urine sample, Sister Halden, while I take Mrs Steel's temperature?'

'I always think those things aren't nearly so impressive as the good old-fashioned thermometers,' the girl observed as Elliot carefully inserted an electronic probe into her ear canal. 'I love it when in the old black and white movies the doctor shakes his thermometer and puts it in his patient's mouth. It looks real neat.'

'I know what you mean,' Elliot said, smiling, 'but the trouble with the glass thermometers was that sometimes a patient could have drunk something hot or cold before we saw them, which meant the result wasn't very reliable. And if you had a patient with breathing problems it was pretty

unrealistic to expect them to keep their mouths shut while
we got an accurate reading.'

'Or you'd end up with a dead patient, huh?' Mrs Steel
grinned. 'OK, fair enough, but I still don't think it looks
as impressive as the old thermometer.'

It didn't, but it certainly confirmed that Mrs Steel's temperature was higher than it should have been, and the sample Jane had taken also revealed she had a very bad urinary
infection.

'Women's urethras are much shorter than men's, which
makes it much easier for bacteria to enter,' Elliot explained
after he'd told Mrs Steel she had cystitis. 'As you're on
your honeymoon, I imagine you're making love more than
normal—'

'Sure am.' The girl chuckled.

Lucky you, Elliot thought dryly. He couldn't remember
the last time he'd made love, and the trouble was there
was only one woman he wanted to make love to, and she
wasn't interested. Not interested at all.

'And as you're making love more than usual, and your
urethra is close to your vagina, the frequency can lead to
bruising,' he continued doggedly, 'and that in turn leads
to infection.'

'Hey, that doesn't mean I'm going to have to tell my
husband I've gone celibate, does it?' Mrs Steel exclaimed
in dismay, and Elliot laughed.

'Of course not. I'll give you some antibiotics to take,
and if you can drink as much water as possible to dilute
your urine, the pain should ease considerably then disappear.'

'He's *gorgeous*, isn't he?' Mrs Steel commented when
Jane escorted her out of the treatment room. 'I mean, if I
wasn't married, I could really fall for that guy.'

I've already fallen, Jane thought wistfully as she waved

the girl goodbye. Hook, line and sinker, and much good it's going to do me.

Last night she'd seen desire in his eyes, and if Nicole hadn't arrived when she had…

Part of her wished the little girl hadn't heard them arguing. Part of her—the weak, wimpy part—wished Nicole had simply stayed in her bed.

And then what? her mind whispered. Do you think you would have been happy to have enjoyed just a few short weeks with him, then watched him walk away?

No, she wouldn't have been happy, but Elliot's mother wouldn't be back from Canada for another six weeks. She was going to have to live with him for another six weeks. Six weeks of wanting him. Six weeks of knowing that, though he might want her too, it was only in the way a child would want a new toy. A toy that would be discarded when the novelty wore off.

Forget about the next six weeks, she told herself. What about tonight? Stephanie's mother had taken Nicole with her daughter to visit the Tower of London and Madame Tussaud's, and then they were going to have tea in a café before going on to the cinema.

She and Elliot would be alone together in his flat. Oh, they'd been alone every night once Nicole had gone to bed but she'd always managed to ensure she didn't linger long afterwards, but tonight…

Tonight Nicole wouldn't be home until after ten and she could hardly disappear into her room as soon as they'd had dinner. It would have looked weird. It would have looked as though she was afraid to be alone with him.

And she was.

'A splinter!' Floella exclaimed savagely as she came out of cubicle 8. 'The guy Richard and I have just treated came in because he had a *splinter* in his finger! This is an A and E unit, for God's sake!'

'Flo—'

'And yesterday it was a woman who'd strained a calf muscle while walking her dog. Well, pardon me if I don't consider that to be a life-threatening condition. Haven't these people heard of GPs?'

'I know, but, Flo—'

'No wonder people are having to wait hours in Reception. No wonder—'

'Flo, would you like to go with me to the cinema to-night?' Jane interrupted desperately.

'The cinema?'

'I know it's a bit short notice,' Jane continued as Floella gazed at her in surprise. 'But I haven't been to a movie since I don't know when, and everyone's raving about the new Mel Gibson one—'

'Oh, Jane, I'm sorry, but I can't. It's my husband's birth-day today and I thought I'd take him out to dinner as a special treat. What about Friday night? We could go then if you like.'

'Fine…great.' Jane smiled with an effort but the staff nurse wasn't fooled for a second.

'Jane, what's wrong?'

'There's nothing wrong.'

'Don't give me that!' Floella exclaimed. 'Jane, I've known you for six years, and I *know* when something's really worrying you. It's Elliot, isn't it?'

'Of course it's not,' she protested, feeling her cheeks beginning to redden under Floella's steady gaze. 'I don't know what put that idea—'

'Is he hassling you? Coming on to you? Jane, if he is, tell him where to get off. We both know what he's like. Oh, he's a terrific guy—wonderful to work with, and a great friend—but when it comes to women—'

'Flo, I'm not getting involved with Elliot!' Jane ex-claimed. 'He's not interested in me. Never has been.'

'He's interested now,' the staff nurse said shrewdly, 'and you're running scared if you're desperately trying to come up with some excuse to get out of his flat for the evening.'

'I'm not—'

'No?' Floella shook her head and sighed. 'Jane, the sooner you leave the better.'

Which was all very well for her to say, Jane thought as the rest of her shift dragged by, but she couldn't just pack her bags and go. What about Nicole? Who would look after her when Elliot worked nights or weekends?

It's not your problem, a little voice at the back of her mind pointed out, and she knew it wasn't, and yet…

All she could hope when the clock on the treatment room wall finally showed her shift was over was that Elliot would soon decide there were plenty more fish in the sea, and start looking for one.

All she could hope even more fervently was that tonight wouldn't turn out to be as big a nightmare as she feared.

But it did.

He watched her all through dinner. Oh, not obviously, not blatantly. The moment she looked up his eyes would skitter away, but they'd been there, she'd felt them, just as she was equally devastatingly conscious of him. Conscious of his hands as he reached for the cruet. Conscious of the taut muscle in his arms as he lifted the casserole from the table and replaced it with their pudding, so that by the time they'd finished their meal her nerves were in shreds.

'I wonder if there's anything interesting on TV tonight?' she said, desperately picking up the TV guide as they walked through to the sitting room.

A football match, a documentary about life in an NHS

A and E department and two American soaps. The soaps were out, as was the documentary. She knew everything that she ever wanted to know about working in an A and E department, but football? Men liked football. Everybody said they did. Everybody said men became so engrossed when they were watching it that they didn't notice anything else.

Everybody was wrong.

'Isn't it a very good match?' she said tentatively, seeing him shift uncomfortably in his seat for what must have been the tenth time in as many minutes.

A rueful smile curved his lips. 'Actually, I'm afraid I don't really like football.'

'You should have said—'

'I thought *you* liked it—'

He began to laugh and she did, too, but then their eyes met. Met, and held, and as she felt her breath catch in her throat she stood up hurriedly.

'W-would you like a cup of coffee—tea?'

'No, thank you.' He'd also got to his feet, and involuntarily she took a step back, only to see his mouth twist into not quite a smile. 'There's no need to be frightened of me, Jane.'

'I'm not frightened,' she managed to reply.

'So I see,' Elliot murmured, his gaze fixed on the tell-tale leaping of the pulse at her throat. 'Jane, you have nothing to fear from me. Not now, not ever. I...I can't deny that I find you very attractive—more than attractive—but I know you don't feel the same way about me and I would never pressurise you.'

'You find me attractive?' she said faintly.

'Jane...' He stabbed his fingers through his hair. 'Jane, I think you're the most beautiful, desirable woman, I've ever met.'

He didn't mean it. She was sure that he didn't mean it,

and she didn't want him to tease her, couldn't bear for him to tease her like this.

'Please, Elliot—'

'Oh, I know you don't want to hear this, and I never intended telling you—promised myself that I wouldn't— but the way I feel about you… Donna—what I felt for her was a kind of madness, a wild insanity, but for you…'

She tried to swallow, and found that she couldn't. 'Elliot…Elliot, are you saying that you love me?'

For an answer, his hand came up and cupped her cheek, and she stopped breathing.

She could have moved away. Part of her brain was telling her to do just that, but she didn't, couldn't, not when his thumb was gently caressing her skin, sending shock waves of pleasure running through her.

'Elliot…'

It was a last feeble plea, and he ignored it as she'd known he would, putting his arm round her waist, drawing her to him until they were only inches apart. Now is the time to run, the rational part of her brain insisted. Now is the moment to run as fast and as far away from this man as you can.

But she didn't want to listen to the rational part of her brain. She wanted him to kiss her. She wanted to know how it would feel, how he would taste, and it was she who closed those last few precious inches between them, so that they were standing chest to chest, hip to hip.

And Elliot? He'd never felt this way before. Never wanted not simply to make love to a woman but to cherish her, to protect her, to keep her safe. Jane was trembling, but he was trembling as well, not wanting to rush, not wanting to frighten her, but wanting her, wanting her so much.

'Jane…'

She saw the uncertainty that she knew must be in her eyes mirrored in his, and it was that which moved her more than anything he might have said. That unexpected vulnerability which made her throw all caution to the wind and gave her the courage to slide her arms up his shoulders and lock them round his neck.

'I love you, Elliot Mathieson,' she whispered.

She heard his sharp intake of breath, saw the uncertainty in his eyes disappear, to be replaced by one of joy, then he bent his head and kissed her, achingly light, achingly slow.

His body was shaking, trembling under her hands, and she arched up against him, parted her lips, felt the hot touch of his tongue and welcomed it, revelled in it. He shifted against her, drawing her even closer, caressing her back with his hands, and a groan escaped her.

'Jane…' His voice was ragged, hoarse against her hair. 'Jane, I want… You know what I want.'

She did, just as she knew that there was no way in the world she could step back now, and when he took her hand and led her to his bedroom she went with him willingly.

'God, you're so lovely,' he said unsteadily as he gently stripped away her clothes, then his. 'So very, very lovely.'

'Ten-thirty tomorrow morning,' she gasped as his fingers cupped one breast and his mouth closed over its aching, straining peak.

'Ten-thirty…?'

'The ophthalmology department. You need your eyes tested. Maybe glasses—'

'Glasses be damned.' He laughed huskily, turning his attention to her other breast. 'I know beauty when I see it, and you're beautiful.'

And she felt beautiful as he laid her on his bed and caressed her body until she was crying out with need. She felt beautiful and desirable and everything a woman should be.

'Elliot, please!' she begged, parting her legs beneath him, arching her hips under him, and with a ragged groan he gave up all pretence of control and surged into her, sending her into a glorious freefall.

She heard his cry, deep and harsh and guttural, as he stiffened against her, and then his arms were round her, holding her close as he rolled over onto his back, cradling her against him as though he never wanted to let go.

'Jane...Jane, are you crying?' he said with concern, feeling the wetness of her cheeks against his chest. 'Oh, my love, what's wrong?'

His love. He'd called her *his* love, and she lifted her head to gaze tremulously at him. 'Nothing. I'm just happy, that's all.'

He chuckled, and she felt the vibrations run the length of her body. 'Good, because so am I. In fact, I don't think I've ever been this happy.'

She knew she hadn't, and at this wonderful moment she didn't care what the future might bring. For now this was enough. For now she was in his arms, he was holding her, and it was enough.

So she only sighed slightly when the phone began to ring.

'If it's an emergency at the hospital, I'm going to tell them to get on with it,' Elliot grumbled, reluctantly easing himself out from under her.

'Oh, yeah, right.' She laughed. 'And that I believe, I don't think.'

But her laughter disappeared when she watched him answering the call, saw his face turn suddenly ashen and his knuckles whiten as he clenched the phone.

'What is it, what's wrong?' she demanded when he

banged down the phone and began scrabbling for his clothes.

'There's been an accident. They were crossing the road outside Stephanie's house and Nicole ran ahead and a car hit her.'

'Oh, God, no—is she badly hurt?' Jane cried, reaching for her own clothes.

'Charlie didn't say.'

'Charlie?'

'They've taken her to St Stephen's.'

The journey across London took an eternity. The evening traffic was heavy, every traffic light seemed to be against them and when they finally reached the hospital Elliot simply abandoned his car in the 'No Parking' zone, heedless of the protesting cry of the traffic warden.

'She'll be all right, Elliot, I'm sure she will,' Jane said, running to keep up with him as he strode through the reception area, his face taut, tense. 'We have one of the best A and E units in the city, and if anyone can help her it's Charlie and the rest of the gang.'

He didn't answer her—she doubted whether he'd even really heard her. He had only one goal and as he banged through the treatment room doors, just as Charlie Gordon emerged from a cubicle, the SHO took one look at his face and came hurriedly towards him.

'OK, what's the situation?' Elliot demanded.

'It's really too early to say—'

'Don't hand me that crap, Charlie!' Elliot exclaimed. 'I'm a doctor, remember. Just give me the facts.'

The SHO bit his lip, then nodded. 'OK. It looks like she's sustained compound fractures of both tibias. She has two, possibly three fractured ribs—'

'Lung damage?'

'Her left lung collapsed shortly after she arrived. We

think one of her fractured ribs may have punctured it, and we've tubed her.'

'Glasgow coma scale?'

'Elliot, I really don't see how you knowing it is going to help,' Charlie protested. 'Look, why don't you wait in one of our private waiting rooms—?'

'Scale of consciousness on the Glasgow coma scale, Charlie?' Elliot reiterated, his face grim.

The SHO obviously didn't want to answer. He quite clearly didn't want to answer, but eventually he muttered, 'Two, two, three.'

Jane drew in a shuddering breath. Anything less than eight meant you had very serious injuries indeed. She reached for Elliot's hand and clasped it tightly.

'Does…does she have any head injuries?' she asked, her voice choked.

'I don't know yet,' Charlie replied. 'We've taken X-rays—'

'Where is she—which cubicle?'

'Elliot, I don't think—'

'No, don't,' he retorted. 'Which cubicle is she in?'

Charlie glanced at Jane and she nodded. 'Five. She's in cubicle five, Elliot.'

Elliot brushed quickly past him, but as the SHO made to follow Jane caught hold of his arm. 'Charlie, how…how bad is it?'

'Pretty bad,' he admitted grimly. 'She's lost a hell of a lot of blood, Jane. We're pumping in O-negative while we're waiting for a cross-match, but as fast as we're pumping it in she seems to be losing it.'

'Can I see her?'

'Do you think you should?' Charlie asked, concern plain on his face. 'Jane, she looks pretty bad. I'd rather Elliot hadn't gone in either, but short of knocking him down I didn't think there was any way I could have kept him out.'

'Charlie, I'm a nurse. I see cases like this every day.'

'Maybe you do, but this is different, Jane. This is personal. This is Nicole.'

'I'd still like to see her,' she said firmly, and he shrugged in defeat.

He'd been right. Nicole did look awful. Awful, and tiny, and desperately white, but what really tore at Jane's heart was the way Elliot was standing by the trolley, holding his daughter's hand in his, as though that would somehow keep her with him.

'ECG reading, Flo?' Charlie asked.

'Still fluctuating pretty wildly, I'm afraid,' she replied, tight-lipped.

'Have you inserted a catheter to drain her bladder?' Elliot demanded. 'Emptied her stomach?'

Charlie nodded. 'Elliot, we're doing everything we can.'

Elliot knew that they were and put his hand softly to Nicole's cheek.

He remembered reading somewhere that Britain had one of the worst child fatality statistics in Europe. It had shocked him, but it had been the kind of shock he'd quickly forgotten because it hadn't been personal. It had just been an article. An article you shook your head sadly over, then turned the page.

But he couldn't turn the page on this accident. This was Nicole. His daughter. His child.

A sob welled in his throat. He couldn't lose her. OK, so he hadn't wanted her at first, hadn't wanted to be a father, hadn't wanted any child of Donna's, but if he lost her now…

Please, God, he prayed, don't take her from me. Don't let her die. She's so young, so very young. She has all her life waiting to be lived. If anyone should die, let it be me. Let me be the one who dies, not my daughter. Dear God,

I'll never ask you for anything ever again if you'll just let me keep her.

'Have we got a result back yet on Nicole's blood type?' Charlie demanded, seeing Richard appear at the cubicle curtains.

He nodded. 'It's ΛB, and on its way now. I've got the chest, leg, and head X-rays here if you want to take a look at them.'

'Elliot?'

Charlie was gazing enquiringly across at him but Elliot's eyes were fixed on Richard as though he didn't quite believe what he'd said.

'AB?' he repeated.

The junior doctor nodded again. 'Do you want to take a look at the X-rays, Elliot?'

He didn't answer. He simply turned back to the trolley, stared down at his daughter, then gently reached out and stroked her bloodstained hair.

'Jane, I think maybe you should take him out,' the SHO muttered. 'Delayed reaction—I've seen it happen before.'

So had she. 'I'll take him to one of the waiting rooms—'

'You'll take me nowhere!' Elliot suddenly exclaimed, swinging round to them. 'Let's take a look at these X-rays.'

Swiftly Richard snapped them up onto the board and hit the light to illuminate them.

Definite compound fractures of both tibias, Jane thought as she stared up at them, and it was three fractured ribs, not two. She could see the one which had punctured Nicole's left lung but luckily the endotracheal tube was in the right place.

'Head X-rays, Richard?' Elliot demanded, a tremor clear in his voice.

The junior doctor removed the first set of X-rays and replaced them with those of Nicole's skull.

'Slight hairline fracture, right side above her ear,' Charlie murmured, peering at the X-rays carefully. 'Anyone see anything else?'

'We'll need a CAT scan to be certain there's no other damage,' Elliot exclaimed. 'What's her CBC?'

'Twenty-five,' Floella replied.

It was getting dangerously close to the level when there wouldn't be enough blood to supply adequate oxygen to Nicole's brain and yet they were constantly pumping in blood.

'She's bleeding in her stomach,' Elliot said flatly.

'Not necessarily—'

'Cut the bull, Charlie,' Elliot exclaimed. 'She's bleeding in her stomach. How's her BP, pulse? Have you stabilised her enough for Theatre?'

Charlie glanced across at Floella.

'Both BP and pulse are still a little low,' she replied, 'but I agree with Elliot. I think we should send her to Theatre.'

She didn't add, Because I think we desperately need their skills, but they all thought it.

Swiftly Floella and Charlie wheeled Nicole out of the treatment room. Elliot and Jane followed them to the operating-theatre door, where one of the theatre staff firmly but kindly ushered them into a small waiting room. They heard the doors of the operating theatre clatter shut.

There was nothing to do now but wait. Wait and pray. Neither of them said very much—Elliot because he seemed to be lost in all his own private misery, and Jane because she didn't want to intrude on it.

What could she say anyway? she wondered. He wouldn't accept any of the platitudes they handed out daily to the relatives of the grievously ill patients they treated. He knew them all too well. Knew them for what they were

A desperate attempt to give hope when all too often there was none.

Oh, please, don't let her die, Jane prayed. Take anything else from me—I'll willingly give up anything else—but, please, let her be all right, because I don't think either of us will survive if she dies.

It was almost two hours before the door to the waiting room opened and Elliot immediately sprang to his feet when he recognised the paediatric surgical consultant.

'How…how is she?' he said raggedly.

'She'll make it, Elliot.' The consultant smiled. 'Now that we've repaired the damage to her stomach she's not leaking blood any more and her BP and pulse are going up. She's not out of the woods yet by any means, but her heart's strong, and she's a tough little girl.'

'There's no sign of shock, no indication of—?'

'Elliot, she'll be fine. I would stake my professional reputation on it. And before you ask,' the consultant continued, 'we did a CAT scan as well, and there's no sign of any brain damage.'

Elliot let out the breath he'd clearly been holding, then reached out and clasped the consultant's hand. 'Thank you. I know that's a totally inadequate thing to say, but thank you.'

'Hey, it's part and parcel of the St Stephen's service.' He grinned. 'We've transferred her to IC, so if you want to go up to see her one of my nurses will take you.'

Swiftly Jane and Elliot followed the nurse through the labyrinth of corridors towards Intensive Care, but when they reached the door, the nurse paused.

'You're going to see a lot of tubes and paraphernalia,' she said gently. 'It's standard procedure in a case like this so, please, don't get upset. And don't expect her to recognise you. She's been pretty heavily sedated.'

They both nodded, but even though Elliot was a special

registrar, accustomed to dealing daily with life-threatening cases, Jane knew that nothing had prepared him for the sight of his daughter wired and tubed, breathing through a ventilator.

'She's so small, Jane,' he said huskily. 'So very small.'

'And you heard what the consultant said,' she replied firmly. 'She's strong, and she's tough. She'll make it.'

He didn't answer, and she put her arm around his shoulders.

He looked awful, and she couldn't blame him. She'd felt quite sick herself when the nurse had led them into the unit and she'd seen Nicole, but for Elliot it was different. This was his daughter. The child he hadn't even known he'd had until a few weeks ago, and he'd grown to love her, to need her as much as she needed him.

'Elliot, I know she looks horrendous, but most of the damage is superficial,' she continued, willing him to believe her. 'OK, so she's sustained fractures, and it will take time for them and her stomach to heal, but they *will* heal.'

He didn't reply. He simply continued to stare down at his daughter as though he wasn't even seeing her. Shock, her professional mind diagnosed. It affected people in different ways. Some people couldn't stop talking, others retreated into silence.

'Elliot, she *will* be all right,' she repeated, putting her other arm round him and holding him tightly. 'Your daughter will be just fine.'

And this time he managed a crooked, lopsided smile. 'Yes, I know. My…my daughter will be just fine.'

They stayed in Intensive Care for over an hour, even though both the cardiology specialist and the paediatric consultant urged them to go home, to get some sleep. But Elliot wouldn't move, and no one had argued with him.

'Are you coming home now?' Jane asked after he'd

checked yet again with IC's night staff to make sure there was no change in Nicole's condition.

'I thought I might go down to A and E, thank Charlie and the rest of the team—'

'Elliot, they won't expect it,' she protested, 'and you're just about dead on your feet.'

'It won't take me a minute—'

'Then we'll go together—'

'No! I mean, you look completely shattered,' he continued as she gazed at him in surprise. 'I'll get you a taxi, and I won't be long, I promise.'

She debated arguing with him, then gave it up as a lost cause. 'OK, but keep that promise—no sneaking back up again to IC. You heard what the nurses said. Nicole's sleeping soundly, there are no complications, and what you need is sleep.'

He nodded but when he went down to A and E he didn't go into the treatment room but went instead into his own office where a duplicate set of the case notes of all the patients who had been treated that day were stored.

Slowly he sat down at his desk, picked up Nicole's file from the in-tray, and opened it.

The results of all the tests Charlie had ordered were there. The X-rays, the CBC, the blood tests. Each and every one of them was neatly typed now in black and white, and he stared at the words and figures, hoping he might have misheard Richard Connery, but knowing now that he hadn't.

Nicole's blood type was AB. His own was O, and Donna's had been A.

No matter how many times he might reread the notes, hoping that the evidence before him would somehow miraculously change, there was no way it was going to change. Nicole wasn't his daughter. There was no way on earth that the lovely little girl lying upstairs in Intensive Care could possibly be his.

CHAPTER NINE

'CHARLIE, are you trying to tell me you've somehow managed to lose a patient?' Jane demanded.

'Not lost, exactly, no.' The SHO grinned ruefully. 'More sort of temporarily mislaid.'

Jane shook her head. 'I'm sorry, but you're going to have to be a lot more specific than that. This patient you've temporarily mislaid…'

'I sent her off to the toilets over an hour ago to provide me with a urine sample, and I've just realised I haven't seen her since. Look, I've been really snowed under, OK?' he continued as Jane's eyebrows rose. 'There was that bloke with angina, the toddler who'd swallowed a battery—'

'OK, OK. What did she look like?'

'Huge—damn near 120 kilos—and suffering from what I very strongly suspect is a bad case of indigestion.'

'I remember.' She nodded. 'Have you looked in the ladies' loos to check if she's still in there?'

'Jane, I can hardly simply walk into the ladies' toilets—'

'Why not?' she protested. 'Good grief, Charlie, considering you've probably seen more of most women's private anatomies than their own husbands, I'd have thought going into one of their toilets would be a doddle.'

'But that's different,' he murmured uncomfortably. 'Look, couldn't you or one of the other nurses check it out for me?'

And she laughed, and shook her head, but she did.

'Goodness only knows how long the poor woman would have been stuck in that cubicle if Charlie hadn't asked me about her,' she told Elliot some time later. 'I feel so sorry for her. Jammed between the door and the toilet, far too embarrassed to call for help. She was absolutely mortified.'

'I'll bet,' he replied, his lips twitching. 'And it must have been even worse when you had to call out Maintenance to take the door off its hinges to get her out.'

'Elliot, it's not funny,' Jane chastised, desperately trying to suppress her own instincts to laugh. 'I doubt if she'll ever darken our doors again.'

'Not that particular door for sure,' he observed, his blue eyes dancing. 'According to Maintenance, it's only fit for firewood now.'

She bit down hard on her lip but it didn't help and a peal of laughter came from her.

He laughed, too, and a wave of love and tenderness welled up inside her when she saw it. It was so good to see him laugh. There'd been precious little laughter in his face during these last few weeks.

When Nicole had first been injured Elliot had haunted the IC unit, barely taking time to eat, far less sleep, and even now that she'd been transferred into the children's medical ward he still hadn't relaxed. He still looked as though he carried the worries of the world on his shoulders.

It was inevitable, of course. With Nicole improving daily, and no necessity to worry about her health any more, some form of reaction was bound to kick in. The realisation of how close he'd come to losing his daughter. The knowledge he now possessed of just how very fragile life was, and how easy it could be to lose someone you loved, especially a young, innocent child.

'Nicole was grumbling like mad when I dropped by to visit her this morning,' Jane commented, trying to keep the mood light. 'Apparently, she's decided hospitals are boring.'

He smiled. 'That's a good sign. Once a patient begins to find the hospital boring, it's a sure sign they're on the mend.'

'I know, but the trouble is, she really *does* think hospitals are boring,' Jane said, chuckling,' so I'm afraid it doesn't look as though she's going to be following in her father's footsteps when it comes to choosing a career.'

The smile faded from his eyes. 'She might. She might well follow exactly in her father's footsteps.'

There was a sadness about his face, a wistfulness she didn't understand, and gently she put her hand on his arm.

'Elliot, you do *know* that Nicole is going to be all right, don't you? Everybody's really pleased with her—the surgical reg, the medical reg, orthopaedics. She's made wonderful progress since her accident—'

'I know.'

Did he? Did he *really* know? Somehow she didn't think he did, and she tried again. 'Elliot, if there's something worrying you, something about Nicole—'

'Of course there's not,' he interrupted quickly. 'What on earth gave you that crazy idea?'

And perhaps she would have agreed with him—acknowledged that it was a crazy idea—if she hadn't seen, just for the merest second, a flicker of complete panic appear in his eyes.

But what in the world could Elliot possibly be so worried about? she wondered in confusion as a paramedic appeared with a young girl in a wheelchair, followed by what had to be the girl's white-faced parents. It didn't make any sense. It didn't make any sense at all.

'Her name's Louise,' the paramedic declared, guiding the wheelchair into cubicle 4. 'Eleven years old with what looks to be a fractured right arm and a very bad gash to her face. She was getting off a bus outside her home when she was knocked down by a car.'

'And it's the first time I've ever let her go anywhere on her own,' the girl's mother said tearfully. 'She wanted to go into town, you see, to buy one of those CD things for her birthday. She badgered and badgered me to let her go, and I thought she'd be all right—'

'Kelly, could you take Louise's parents through to one of our private waiting rooms, please?' Elliot interrupted smoothly, beckoning to the student nurse.

'And we made sure she went to all the road safety lessons, Doctor,' the girl's father continued, clutching his wife's hand as though it were a lifeline. 'We're not like some parents, letting her roam the streets to all hours. In fact—'

'Waiting room 2, please, Kelly,' Elliot said, and with obvious reluctance Louise's parents allowed the student nurse to usher them away.

'They panic a lot—my mum and dad,' Louise said, pulling a face the minute they were gone.

Elliot smiled. 'It goes with the job. How do you feel?'

'Sore,' she admitted as Jane carefully cut away her blouse. 'Sore and really, really stupid. I know I should have been watching out for traffic but I wanted to get home to try out my new CD player, and now it's wrecked— trashed. The car went right over it.'

'Better it than you,' Elliot observed, gazing critically at Louise's arm, which was not only very badly swollen but bent at an odd angle. Gently he lifted her hand and felt for her pulse. 'Can you move your fingers for me, please? Good…good. Now, can you feel that?' he added, lightly brushing her hand with his fingers.

'It tickles.' She chuckled.

He was relieved that it did. Her arm might be fractured, but at least the tendons that supplied function to her hand weren't damaged in any way, neither were the blood vessels nor nerves.

'I'm afraid it looks as though you've definitely fractured your arm,' Elliot declared when he'd finished his examination. 'We'll send you along to X-Ray to confirm it—'

'You mean I'm going to have to wear one of those plaster cast things?' the girl protested, only to groan as Elliot nodded. 'But they're *gross*.'

'Perhaps, but think of all the autographs and rude comments you can have written on it.' Jane smiled.

The girl brightened immediately. 'It'll drive my teachers nuts—and my mum and dad. Great.'

'Are you going to suture yourself?' Jane continued, glancing across at Elliot. 'Or would you like me to page Plastics?'

He lifted the girl's chin into the light and surveyed her face with a frown. 'Get Plastics. I've seen what can happen to wounds like this when all the dirt embedded in them isn't removed, and they're much more skilled than I am at dealing with facial cuts.'

'You mean I'm going to be scarred?' Louise exclaimed, tears suddenly welling in her eyes.

'Of course you're not,' Elliot assured her. 'You're going to be fine—just fine. And now I'm going to leave you in Sister Halden's capable hands while I go and put your parents' minds at rest.'

'Tell them I'm OK, will you?' the girl called after him. 'If you don't they'll ground me until I'm thirty!'

Fifty more like, Elliot thought with an inward smile when he went into the waiting room and Louise's parents rose in unison, fear plain on their faces.

'You're absolutely positive there's nothing else wrong with her?' Louise's mother queried when Elliot explained the situation.

'Completely positive.' He nodded. 'Her arm will have to stay in plaster for about six weeks and her face will be sore for quite a while, but apart from that she's fine.'

The mother let out a muffled sob. 'I've told her time and time again to watch what she's doing when she's crossing the road, but the minute she's out of my sight... It's in one ear and straight out the other.'

'Kids, eh, Doctor?' Louise's father exclaimed, trying for a laugh that didn't come off. 'You think you've got it sussed when you get them past the baby stage—that you can finally start to relax—but the minute they learn to walk... Well, I don't have to tell you about it, Doctor. The nurse told us you're a father yourself.'

Yes, he was a father, he thought with a jagged twist of pain as he left the waiting room, or at least he had been until three weeks ago. Until he'd discovered that Nicole wasn't his.

Why had Donna done this to him? She must have realised she wouldn't get away with it. She must have known he would find out eventually, so why had she told him he had a daughter, allowed him to grow to love her, knowing that one day the rug would be pulled out from under his feet?

Had she hated him so much that she'd wanted to get back at him, or was it simply that there'd been so many men in her life that she didn't actually know who Nicole's father was?

'Everything OK, Elliot?' Floella asked curiously as she passed him.

Desperately he swallowed the bitter tears clogging his throat, and nodded. All right? No, nothing was ever going to be 'all right' ever again.

And he'd have to tell Jane, he realised, seeing her coming out of cubicle 7. She'd have to know eventually, but what would she say? Would she insist he must track down this mystery man, that Nicole's real father had the right to be given the opportunity to make contact with her if he wanted?

No!

The word was wrenched from somewhere deep inside him.

The man had no rights. OK, so his sperm had created Nicole, given her life, but he wasn't her father. He hadn't been there for the bad times as well as the good. He hadn't hugged her, and dried her tears, and made sure she went to bed at a reasonable hour whether she wanted to or not.

He wouldn't tell Jane. He wouldn't tell anyone. Nicole was his. He couldn't give her up. He *couldn't*.

'Is Elliot OK?' Floella frowned as Jane joined her by the whiteboard to check on the name and details of her next patient. 'Nicole hasn't had a relapse, has she?'

Jane shook her head. 'She's doing really well. In fact, the medical reg reckons if she keeps on progressing like this we might be able to take her home at the end of next week.'

'Home?' Floella repeated, her eyes fixed on her thoughtfully. 'You consider Elliot's flat your home now, do you?'

A faint tinge of colour crept across Jane's cheeks. 'No, of course I don't—'

'Then why haven't you moved back into your own flat while Nicole is in hospital? I mean, there's no reason for you to be staying there at the moment, is there?'

There wasn't, Jane thought in dismay, and she should have thought of that if she hadn't wanted to set every tongue in the hospital wagging.

'I thought… I mean, Elliot and I decided…' What possible reason could she give that Floella would accept? 'The thing is, Flo—'

'The thing is that you and Elliot are living together,' the staff nurse sighed. 'And I mean *living* together.'

Jane blushed scarlet. 'Flo—'

'Look, I'm not going to blab it all over the hospital if

that's what you're frightened of. All I want to know is, are you happy? Are you sure this is right for you?'

Unconsciously Jane's lips curved into a tender smile. 'Oh, yes. Yes, I'm sure.'

And she was sure. More sure than she'd ever been about anything in her life. Just to look up from the breakfast table and find Elliot's eyes upon her, so warm and unbelievably gentle. Just to have him hold her in his bed at night, not even making love. It was right, so right.

'You've really got it bad, haven't you?' Floella said dryly, watching her. 'Well, all I can say is good luck to you.'

'You mean, you're not going to tell me I'm a fool, that I'll live to regret it?' Jane asked, but to her surprise Floella shook her head.

'You know his track record as well as I do, but if you think it's going to work, that Elliot's ready to settle down now, then, like I said, good luck to you.'

Luck didn't come into it, Jane decided. Elliot loved her. OK, so maybe he hadn't told her that yet, but he did—she just knew that he did—and she loved him, and nothing and no one was ever going to change that.

Not even Elliot himself when he spent the rest of their shift behaving like the original bear with a sore head.

'Boy, but is he a little ray of sunshine today.' Richard grimaced after he'd received the sharp edge of Elliot's tongue for the third time that day. 'Any idea what's wrong?'

'Your guess is as good as mine,' Jane replied, groaning inwardly as she heard the wail in the distance of what sounded like the imminent arrival of more than one ambulance. 'All I know for certain is that any thought we might have had of getting away on time tonight has just flown out the window.'

She was right. There'd been a multiple pile-up on one

of the roads leading into London and every A and E unit in the city had to take its share of the casualties.

'I wouldn't want your job for all the tea in China, Sister,' one of the road traffic policemen said, watching her as she dashed from casualty to casualty, assessing their level of priority.

'I suppose it's one way of keeping fit,' she said with a grin, but she didn't feel much like laughing by the time they'd treated all of the casualties who'd been brought in.

'What was the final count at the finish?' Charlie asked wearily when they finally managed to make their way to the staffroom. 'Three DOAs, five to Theatre with suspected abdominal injuries and four fractures?'

'Three fractures,' Floella corrected him. 'We can't really count that fourth guy.'

Charlie frowned. 'But he was involved in the accident, wasn't he?'

'Only indirectly. The little ghoul was trying to take photographs of the scene when he fell down the embankment.'

'If I'd known that, he could have hopped his way back out again,' Elliot said grimly. 'Lord, but I'm bushed. What's the time?'

'Would you believe it's only half past six?' Jane smiled. 'Some people would consider that a reasonable time to be finishing work.'

'So would I if I hadn't been on duty for twelve hours,' he groaned. 'OK, folks, let's hit the road. I, for one, just want to go home and put my feet up. Are you coming, Jane?'

She nodded, but as he reached for his coat Kelly suddenly let out an apologetic gasp. 'I'm sorry, Elliot, but I've just remembered something. You had a personal phone call earlier this afternoon, but I'm afraid it completely slipped my mind.'

'Tell me about it tomorrow,' he said dismissively, walking towards the door. 'Phone calls—personal or otherwise—are the least of my priorities at the moment. What I want is a hot bath, a—'

'But it was your sister-in-law.'

He stopped dead, and Jane saw his shoulders stiffen. 'My sister-in-law?'

'Your ex, I suppose I ought to have said.' Kelly smiled. 'Mrs Michelle Bouvier. She wanted to talk to you but you were busy with that young girl who'd fractured her arm.'

'I remember,' he said, and as he turned to face the student nurse Jane saw that his face had gone quite white. 'What did she want ?'

'She said she was in London for a few days and would like to come to see you and Nicole. I told her about Nicole's accident, and what ward she was in—'

'You *told* her what ward Nicole was in?' Elliot exclaimed, his face suddenly taut with fury, his eyes blazing.

'She asked me, and I didn't think it was a secret,' Kelly faltered. 'She said she would probably come in and visit her today around six o'clock. I'm sorry—I didn't think I was doing anything wrong. I mean, she's Nicole's aunt—'

'Of course you didn't do anything wrong,' Jane said soothingly, shooting daggers at Elliot. The student nurse was on the brink of tears and she would have been pretty near the edge herself if Elliot had been glowering at her the way he was glowering at Kelly. 'Mrs Bouvier has a perfect right to know which ward her niece is in.'

'Like hell she has!' Elliot exploded the minute the student nurse hurried away, white-faced and still tearful, and the rest of the staff had followed, throwing puzzled glances at Jane. 'Who the hell does she think she is—swanning back from Peru, or Iran, or wherever she's been, and demanding to see my daughter?'

'Elliot, this is ridiculous,' Jane protested. 'Michelle is Nicole's aunt, so it's only natural she would want to see her, especially as she's been in an accident. It's called family feeling.'

'Is it?'

'Of course it is! Elliot, this isn't like you,' she continued in confusion, seeing his expression. 'I know Donna hurt you very badly but, no matter what you might think of her, Michelle is the last direct link your daughter has with her mother, and I think you should be encouraging that link, not attempting to put up stupid and irrational barriers against it.'

He could see the disapproval and bewilderment in her eyes, but how to tell her he was frightened? Frightened that Donna might have told Michelle that Nicole wasn't his. Had she come to take her away from him, arguing she had more rights to the child than he did? And she did have more rights. She was Donna's sister, Nicole's aunt. He… He was nothing.

'Elliot…' The disapproval on Jane's face had turned to real concern. 'Elliot, what's wrong?'

It was the irony of the situation, he thought bleakly. The supreme, unutterable irony. He'd never wanted Nicole, would quite happily have palmed her off on Michelle a mere two months ago, but now…

His eyes caught sight of the treatment-room clock. It was a quarter to seven. Michelle would be there, in the medical ward, and swiftly he walked to the staffroom door.

'Where are you going?' Jane demanded.

'You said I ought to see Michelle,' he said grimly. 'Well, that's what I'm going to do!'

He'd liked Michelle the first time they'd met, Elliot remembered. He'd found her entertaining and witty, funny and kind. She hadn't changed a bit, and Nicole clearly liked her a lot, but now he discovered he didn't like her at all.

'Your daughter is quite charming, Elliot,' Michelle said as he and Jane led the way out of the medical ward, leaving Nicole surrounded by all the toys her aunt had brought her from Iran.

His daughter. He let out the breath he'd been holding from the minute he'd stepped into the medical ward, and sent up a silent prayer of thanks. She didn't know. Donna hadn't told her, and she didn't know.

'I confess it gave me quite a start to see how very like Donna she's become,' Michelle continued. 'My husband and I generally spent around six to eight months of every year on archaeological digs, you see,' she continued as Jane gazed at her in surprise, 'so I only ever saw Nicole occasionally, and it's amazing the difference six months can make to a child's appearance.'

'It is,' Jane agreed, heartily wishing Elliot would at least try to contribute to the conversation, instead of making it all too obvious that he wanted to leave. 'I'm sorry about your sister's death—'

'We were never very close,' Michelle interrupted, clearly seeing Jane's embarrassment. 'She had her world, and I had mine.'

'Quite,' Elliot declared tightly. 'And now if you'll excuse us, Michelle—'

'Elliot, I really would like to talk to you about Nicole,' she interrupted. 'Unfortunately I'm only going to be in London for a few days—Raoul is addressing an archaeological seminar in Paris on Thursday—so I wondered if I might come round to your flat later this evening—'

'It's been a long day, and I'm very tired, Michelle.'

'I appreciate that.' She nodded. 'It is not an easy job, being a doctor. In fact, I don't know how you manage to take care of Nicole—'

'I manage.'

The words were clipped, cold, and Michelle coloured.

Jane would have hit him if she'd been in Michelle's shoes.

OK, so his marriage to Donna had ended acrimoniously, but that didn't give him the right to be quite so unbelievably rude to her sister. She'd come with the very best of intentions, and a person would have had to be blind not to have noticed the way her eyes had stayed fixed on her niece throughout her visit, wistful and a little sad.

'Look, why don't you come round to the flat with us now?' she said quickly, and received a look from Elliot that would have killed. 'I'm afraid I can't promise you French cuisine, but it will give you and Elliot the opportunity to talk.'

'Oh, that would be lovely.' Michelle beamed. 'Thank you—thank you very much indeed.'

Jane didn't get any thanks from Elliot when they got back home. In fact, once Michelle was safely installed in the sitting room and Jane had gone into the kitchen to find something for them all to eat, he let fly with a number of comments about interfering women, and people taking too much upon themselves, which were no less effective from being hissed in an acid undertone in case Michelle should hear him.

'Elliot, I don't give a damn whether you're upset by the fact that I invited her or not,' Jane retorted as she slammed some meat into the microwave and took some ice cream out of the freezer. 'She didn't have to come all this way to see Nicole.'

'I don't know why she did.'

'*I* do,' she retorted. 'She came because she's clearly a very nice woman. She came because she wanted to see the only link she has left with her sister, and I'd have thought the very least you could have done was to be pleasant, and polite, and welcoming for one evening!'

She didn't know whether he took her comments to heart

or not. He was certainly less rude over dinner, but it wasn't by any stretch of the imagination a comfortable meal, and when it was finally over Jane got to her feet with relief.

'Why don't you both go through to the sitting room while I make some coffee?' she suggested.

'That would be very nice.' Michelle smiled, but Elliot, Jane noticed, didn't.

In fact, clear panic appeared in his eyes, but there was no way she was going to come to his rescue by suggesting he might like to help her with the coffee. Michelle had said she wanted to talk to him, and he was damn well going to talk to her whether he wanted to or not.

It wasn't the talking that bothered him, Elliot thought grimly when he obediently took Michelle through to the sitting room, it was what his ex-sister-in-law wanted to talk about. Something told him he wasn't going to like it, and it didn't take him long to discover that he'd been right.

'You've done a wonderful job with Nicole,' Michelle declared as soon as she sat down. 'Better than anyone could have expected in the circumstances.'

'I'm glad you think so,' he replied warily, knowing there was a 'but' to come, and there was.

'When the news finally reached me in Iran of Donna's death, I'm afraid it didn't come as any great surprise,' Michelle sighed. 'She always lived life in the fast lane, and a car crash... There was a certain inevitability about it. What did surprise me, however, was hearing she had entrusted Nicole into your care.'

'She is my daughter—'

'A daughter you knew nothing about until two months ago,' Michelle interrupted gently. 'A daughter who must have turned your life upside down.'

'She's made it livelier, certainly,' Elliot admitted, 'and I don't know how I would have managed without Jane—'

'Exactly,' Michelle said. 'You're a doctor, never knowing from one day to the next what emergency might come up, which is why Raoul and I have a suggestion to make. We'd like to take Nicole, give her a home.'

'No—no way!'

'Elliot, it makes sense,' Michelle insisted. 'It can't be easy for you, trying to juggle your work with taking care of a child.'

'It wouldn't be easy for you either,' he said. 'You and Raoul spend more than half of each year in the back of beyond. What would you do with Nicole then? Put her in a boarding school? No, Michelle, the answer's no.'

'Of course we wouldn't put her in a boarding school,' she protested. 'We'd take her with us. We could engage a tutor—'

'But—'

'Elliot, we've no children of our own—I can't have any,' Michelle said, her eyes fixed on him, large, pleading. 'We would love her, give her a good home. I know you're her father, but you're a single man, and as a single man you can't possibly give her the love and attention Raoul and I could.'

'Michelle—'

'She needs a mother, Elliot, and you're not asking me to believe that when you first heard of Nicole's existence you didn't wish there was somewhere else she could go rather than to you. Somewhere you knew she'd be loved and well taken care of.'

He had, but that had been then, this was now.

'It is very kind of you to be concerned about my daughter's welfare,' he said tightly as the sitting-room door opened and Jane came in, carrying a tray of coffee and biscuits, 'but there's no need for you to be. Yes, I'm a single man at the moment, but not for much longer.'

'You're getting married?' Michelle said faintly. 'To whom?'

Well, there was only logical answer to that. Only one woman in the world he would ever want to marry. 'To Jane, of course. Jane and I are getting married.'

'I see,' Michelle murmured, disappointment plain in her voice. 'Then I suppose congratulations are in order—to both of you.'

Elliot smiled, and if Jane looked completely stunned he wasn't surprised. He had rather sprung it on her.

'So when's the happy day?' Michelle continued.

'We haven't set a date yet but you can rest assured it will be soon. You were right when you said Nicole needed a mother. She does, and Jane's marvellous with children—the very best, in fact.'

'Is she?' Michelle said.

'Oh, absolutely.' Elliot nodded, then grinned across at Jane who was sitting silently in the corner of the room. 'Nicole adores her. In fact, even if I wanted to marry someone else I think she'd have one or two things to say about it!'

'I see. Well, it sounds like a very sensible arrangement all round,' Michelle said grudgingly.

'Doesn't it?' He beamed.

Michelle didn't stay long after that. She kissed Elliot and Jane on both cheeks, promised to visit them and Nicole when she was next in London and left.

'Thank God, that's over,' Elliot declared with relief, the minute she had gone. 'Let's hope she doesn't visit London very often.'

'Oh, I thought she was very informative,' Jane said evenly. 'In fact, I thought the whole evening was very informative.'

'Really?' he said in surprise. 'In what way?'

'The surprising news that you and I are getting married for a start,' she replied, her voice curiously cold.

A deep wash of colour flashed across his cheeks. 'Jane,

I'm sorry about that. I really should have asked you first, but—'

'You just assumed I'd say yes. You thought, Good old Janey, she always agrees to everything, so why not this, too?'

There wasn't a trace of amusement in her face, not a glimmer of a smile in her grey eyes, and the colour on his cheeks darkened to crimson.

'Of course I didn't think that. I intended to take you somewhere romantic to pop the question, but Michelle was hassling me—'

'She wasn't hassling you, Elliot, she was concerned about Nicole,' she interrupted, her face white, taut. 'Concerned that you might not be able to look after her properly.'

'She had no business to be concerned,' he said irritably. 'I love my daughter—'

'So much that you're prepared to do just about anything for her, including marrying me,' Jane finished for him, her voice breaking slightly.

'*No!*' he protested. 'Dammit, Jane, I want to marry you because I *love* you. You heard what I said to Michelle—'

'Oh, yes, I heard,' she replied, anger giving her strength. 'It would be so sensible to marry me. I'm marvellous with children, and Nicole likes me. You don't want a wife, Elliot. You want a surrogate mother for your daughter and, much as I love her, I think I deserve more from a marriage than that.'

'Jane, you've misunderstood, got hold of the wrong end of the stick—'

'I don't believe you.'

He looked into her face and it was cold and forbidding. Hiding all the pain and heartbreak that she felt.

'Jane—'

'You'd better answer that,' she declared as the phone began to ring. 'It could be important.'

'*This* is important,' he exclaimed. 'Jane, I love you, and I want to marry you.'

'It might be the hospital. Something to do with Nicole.'

He stared at her, indecision plain on his face, then walked quickly over to the phone and lifted it.

'It was one of the night staff,' he informed her when he'd taken the call. 'They need my help.'

'You'd better go, then, hadn't you?' she replied, turning on her heel, only to pause. 'I won't be here when you get back, Elliot. I'll pack my bags while you're away and leave tonight.'

'But you can't go!' he protested. 'What about me—what about Nicole?'

She hardened her heart, though it cost her everything. 'She's not my responsibility, Elliot. She's yours. She's your daughter.'

CHAPTER TEN

'BURNS case, Sister!' a paramedic called as he and his colleague slammed open the doors of the treatment room and wheeled their casualty into the first empty cubicle. 'Injuries to face, upper torso and arms. BP 90 over 70, cardiac output down thirty per cent, and you're never going to believe how the guy got himself in this state!'

'Go on—surprise me,' Jane sighed, beckoning to Floella for help.

'He was filling his lawnmower with petrol and smoking at the same time.'

'He was doing *what*?' Jane gasped in disbelief as she and Floella swiftly began cutting off the young man's charred and burnt clothing.

'I know, I know,' the paramedic said. 'You wouldn't believe how many idiots there are out there in the world, Sister.'

Oh, but she would, she thought sadly as she noticed Elliot striding towards them, and she had just joined their ranks.

No, not joined. She was so stupid she could probably have qualified as a founder member.

Floella had tried to warn her, but had she listened? Oh, no, not her. She'd known better. She'd known different. Just as she'd thought when he'd held her in the darkness of the night and told her she was beautiful, special, that he'd meant he loved her. Just as she'd believed when he'd said he'd never met anybody like her that he'd meant they would have a future together. But all the time he'd simply been thinking about Nicole.

And the wretched thing was that she had actually wanted him to grow to love his daughter. Had longed for him to see what a great gift he'd been given. But she couldn't marry him for Nicole. No matter how much she loved the little girl, to know that Elliot only wanted to marry her because of Nicole... No, she couldn't do it. She simply couldn't.

'Haemaccel drip, and lactated Ringer's solution to counteract shock,' Elliot ordered, taking in the situation at a glance.

Swiftly Jane set up the IV lines while Floella inserted a Foley catheter into the young man's bladder to check for signs of the presence of haemoglobin.

'Singed nasal hair indicative of inhalation burns, Elliot,' Floella announced.

'OK, get me a sputum sample, and I want a full colour check on the urine in that catheter. BP and pulse, Jane?' he continued, turning to her.

'Eighty-five over sixty, pulse fast. Respiration becoming very laboured.'

She was already holding out an endotracheal tube to him, but she wasn't looking at him. She hadn't looked him in the eye since the night she'd walked out of his flat almost two weeks ago, and it was driving him crazy.

Anger he could have dealt with, recriminations he thought he could have handled, but being ignored, being shut out of her life, gave him no weapons to fight back with. None at all.

'I want a chest X-ray, Jane,' he declared the minute he'd eased the tube past the young man's vocal cords and down into his trachea.

'Already organised.'

'And the burns unit—'

'I've paged them already.'

Of course she had. Jane was the consummate professional. Jane was the woman he loved, and he'd messed it up completely.

How could he have been so stupid? Taking it for granted that she must love him as much as he loved her, that she'd want to marry him. Yet he'd told Michelle they were getting married, so arrogant, so sure of himself and so desperate to ensure his ex sister-in-law could stake no claim on Nicole.

No wonder Jane had been angry. No wonder she'd turned him down flat. What woman would accept a proposal of marriage under those circumstances? A woman needed to know she was loved for herself. And he did love her, he thought, feeling his heart contract as he stared across at her white, drawn face. Loved her more than he could ever have believed possible, and yet now she would scarcely give him the time of day.

'Urine in the Foley catheter very dark, Elliot,' Floella reported.

'OK, give him a diuretic with mannitol to counteract it,' he ordered. 'We don't want his kidneys packing in. Not with fifteen per cent burns.'

'BP 90 over 60,' Jane murmured. 'IV's running smoothly, no signs yet of hypovolaemic shock.'

'Keep a check on the ECG reading,' he said. 'And let me know if it changes at all.'

He hadn't needed to give the order. Nothing escaped Jane's attention. Nothing to do with work, that was.

Somehow he had to get her to talk to him. Even more importantly, somehow he had to get her to listen. But how?

The only thing she would discuss with him was work, and even that was in clipped monosyllables. If she wouldn't talk to him, how could he convince her that he wanted to marry her because he loved her and not because he'd wanted a surrogate mother for his daughter?

'BP 95 over 60,' Jane observed. 'I think we could hand over to Burns now.'

She was right, they could.

'Good work, both of you,' Elliot said when the burns unit had ferried their casualty away.

Floella smiled, but for all the reaction Jane gave he might just as well have saved his breath. He gazed at her impotently.

What he wanted to do was stride across the cubicle, grab her by the shoulders and shake her senseless. What he actually did was clear his throat tentatively. 'It must be about time for a coffee-break. Care to join me, Jane?'

'Thank you, but I have requisition forms to fill in,' she replied, her voice even, neutral.

'Couldn't you leave them until later?' he asked, all too aware of the pleading note in his voice and that Floella was glancing thoughtfully from him to Jane and back again but no longer giving a damn. 'I'm sure you could do with a big dose of caffeine first.'

'Like I said, thank you, but I really must get on with the forms,' she replied, and walked away without a backward glance.

He didn't stand a chance, he thought as he stared after her, his eyes tracing the outline of her back, noticing that she had lost weight, that her uniform no longer fitted quite so snugly. Unless he could show her, prove to her, that she could trust him, that he loved her for herself and not simply for what he needed her to be, he didn't stand a chance.

'Why don't you just leave her alone?'

He turned to see Floella glaring up at him, and sighed. 'Flo, you don't understand—'

'Oh, I understand only too well,' she snapped. 'You just couldn't resist it, could you? Jane living in your flat, right under your nose. You just had to come on to her to see how far you could get.'

'Flo—'

'Well, you've had your fun, broken her heart, and now I want you to leave her alone,' she continued icily. 'If you don't… Well, all I can say is you're going to be sorry. Jane has a lot of friends at St Stephen's who won't take kindly to you messing her around.'

'Dammit, I am *not* messing her around!' Elliot raked his hands through his hair. 'Flo… Flo, I want to marry her. I've asked her to marry me, but she's turned me down flat.'

'You've asked her to… She's turned you down?' Floella gasped. 'But Jane—she loves you. Why in the world would she turn you down?'

His face tightened. 'I made a bit of a mess of my proposal.' That was the biggest understatement of the year, he thought, cringing inwardly as he remembered what he'd said. 'She misunderstood…got completely the wrong idea—'

'But how can you possibly mess up a proposal?' Flo interrupted, bewildered. 'Even an idiot could get that right.'

'Not this idiot, Flo,' he said grimly. 'This idiot really screwed it up, and now she won't even talk to me.'

Or answer any of my phone calls, he thought ruefully, and all the letters he'd sent had been returned unopened. In desperation he'd even gone round to her flat, but she'd shut the door on him, and when he'd point blank refused to go away she'd got one of her neighbours, a big burly guy with tattoos up his arms, who'd told him in no uncertain terms that if he didn't remove himself pretty sharpish his features would shortly be rearranged.

'What am I going to do, Flo?'

'You're asking me for advice?' She shook her head.

'You're the big charmer, Elliot, you figure it out. But figure it out soon. I hate to see Jane unhappy, so beg, plead—do whatever it takes—but sort it out.'

He sighed as he walked into cubicle 3. He would quite happily have begged and pleaded for all he was worth if he'd thought it would have got him anywhere, but he knew that it wouldn't.

He'd blown it. He'd met and fallen in love with the one girl in the world who could have made him happy, and he'd blown it good and proper. There was no way back now, and he was just going to have to live with it.

'I hear on the hospital grapevine that Nicole's being discharged next week,' Charlie commented as Jane binned the soiled swabs they'd used on their last patient, a nervous eighteen-year-old with a bad gash on his foot. 'That's great news.'

'It's wonderful, isn't it?' Jane smiled. 'We—that is, Elliot was hoping she'd be discharged last week, but she had a slight infection at the last minute and they decided to keep her in for just a few more days to be on the safe side.'

Charlie nodded, pulled off his surgical gloves, stared at them awkwardly for a moment, then clearly made up his mind. 'You'll be moving back in with Elliot again, then? I mean, I understand his mother's not due back from Canada for another two weeks.'

Jane closed the disposal unit with a bang. 'No, I won't be moving back in.'

Charlie eyed her sideways. 'But Nicole... Won't she need you there to look after her?'

'Whether she does or doesn't isn't really my concern,' she said, striving to sound dismissive and knowing she was failing quite miserably. 'I have my own life to lead, Charlie, and I can't be Nicole's nanny for ever.'

'Two weeks doesn't sound very much like for ever to me,' he pointed out.

'I have other commitments,' she declared, the redness of her cheeks betraying the lie. 'And I'm sure Elliot can hire a private nurse or a nanny for two weeks.'

'Yes, but—'

'Dammit, Charlie, why does everyone expect good old Janey to ride to the rescue every time?' she flared. 'I'm sick to death of being good old Janey! I want to be selfish, think-about-yourself-for-once Janey!'

The SHO gazed at her uncomfortably. 'And so you should. If anyone deserves some pampering, it's you. But I just thought... Nicole...'

'Charlie, she isn't my responsibility! I helped out for two months. Isn't that enough? Haven't...haven't I given enough?'

Her voice broke on not quite a sob, and Charlie put his hand out to her, his big, hearty face almost as red as hers. 'I'm sorry. I... Look, Jane, I didn't mean to... I wouldn't... I'm really sorry.'

She drew in a shuddering breath. 'I'm sorry, too. Sorry for yelling at you, but...'

'I understand.'

And he did, she thought as she stared up at him. He understood much more than she wanted him to.

'Does Nicole know you won't be there when she gets home?' he asked gently.

Jane shook her head, blinking away the tears that were forming in her eyes. She hadn't stopped visiting Elliot's daughter in Ward 12. She could no more have stopped than fly, but when Nicole had talked excitedly about the things the three of them would do when she got home she'd said nothing. It was cowardly, and she knew it, but she couldn't tell her. It was bad enough knowing she might never see her again, without having to answer questions she didn't want to answer.

'Jane… You and Elliot. There's no hope that you and he…?'

He didn't have to explain what he meant and she smiled a little tremulously. 'Not a hope in the world, Charlie.'

He sighed. 'That toast I made when Barbara and I took you out to dinner—when I wished you every happiness. It doesn't look much as though it's going to come true, does it?'

'Hey, worse things happen at sea,' she declared with a brightness that moved him more than he could say. 'And now we'd better get on. The waiting room's not getting any emptier while we stand around here chatting.'

It wasn't, Charlie thought as he watched her go, but he wished there was something he could do. It didn't seem fair for him and Barbara to be so happy, while Jane…

He sighed deeply as he saw her disappearing into cubicle 1. It wasn't fair but, then, life, as you very quickly discovered if you worked in A and E, was frequently very unfair.

Elliot didn't think life was particularly fair either when Charlie collared him outside cubicle 8 some time later.

'Charlie, I hardly think a fractured ankle is something requiring my expertise. If you can't see to it yourself—'

'Of course I can deal with it,' the SHO interrupted, 'but the guy says he thinks he knows you.'

Elliot frowned. 'What did you say his name was again?'

'Shaw. Adam Shaw.'

It rang no bells, but obediently Elliot followed Charlie into the cubicle, to be greeted by a wide smile of recognition from the red-haired man in his early thirties sitting awkwardly on the edge of the trolley.

'It *is* the same Elliot Mathieson,' he beamed, 'and looking twice as ugly as you did eight years ago!'

'I'm sorry, but—'

'Rawley Amateur Rugby Club,' Adam Shaw continued helpfully. 'I played prop forward and you were one of the flash boys on the wing. We did a lot of charity matches to raise money for one of the local hospices.'

Elliot grinned. 'I remember now. You borrowed my kit bag at the end of the last season and never gave it back, you thief.'

'Didn't I?' Adam Shaw frowned, then winked up at Charlie. 'Never try to put one over on this bloke. Memory like an elephant—never forgets anything.'

'I'll remember.' The SHO chuckled.

'How's that beautiful wife of yours?' Adam Shaw continued, turning to Elliot again. 'Bonnie, was it?'

The laughter disappeared from Elliot's face. 'Donna. Her name was Donna. We were divorced five years ago, and she was killed in a car crash three months ago.'

'Oh, hell, I'm sorry. I didn't know, never heard on the grapevine. Any family?'

'A daughter.'

'Then at least you have something to remember her by,' Adam replied.

Oh, he did, Elliot thought sadly, but not in the way the whole world would ever imagine.

'Are you married yourself?' he asked, anxious to change the subject.

'Married, and divorced, too, I'm afraid,' Adam replied ruefully. 'Bit of a disaster, actually. Brought it all on myself, of course. Never home, working all the hours God sent, trying to get ahead in my job. And the wife…she felt neglected, found someone else.'

'I'm sorry.'

'It happens. I see my kids occasionally, but it's not the

same. If you don't live with them, become just an occasional visitor, they move on, leave you behind.'

'I guess so,' Elliot murmured.

'Hold on to your kid,' Adam continued. 'Hold on to her, and if there's a girl in your life, hold on to her, too. I've learned the hard way that career, wealth, position, don't amount to anything if you haven't got a family to share it with.'

'He's got a point,' Charlie observed after Elliot had waved Adam goodbye with promises to keep in touch which they both knew would never be kept. 'In fact, it seems to me that you should have everything in your life now that any man could ever want. A lovely daughter, a girl like Jane.'

'Charlie—'

'She *is* a wonderful girl, you know,' the SHO continued doggedly. 'I don't think you could do better.'

'I'm sure you mean well, Charlie,' Elliot declared evenly, 'but my private life isn't really any of your business.'

He began to walk away but the SHO came after him. 'You're right, it isn't any of my business, but it seems to me that a man who's made a girl fall in love with him and then dumped her—'

'I haven't dumped her!'

'A man who's made a girl like Jane fall in love with him, and then dumped her—'

'Charlie, I *haven't* dumped her!'

'Is some kind of louse. I just wanted you to know that,' the SHO declared, 'and to let you know that I, for one, don't like it. I don't like it at all!'

And he swung round on his heel and walked away, leaving Elliot gazing after him, not knowing whether he wanted to laugh or go after the SHO and hit him.

Neither, he decided, as he saw Jane smiling at something

Floella had said, a smile that didn't reach her eyes, a smile that was a little wary and sad. He would do neither.

He would get her back, prove to her that he loved her, refuse to take no for an answer.

And what about Nicole? his mind whispered. Are you going to tell Jane that she's not yours?

One problem at a time, he told himself, noticing from the treatment-room clock that their shift was over. Tackle one problem at a time.

But his first problem was getting out of the door.

'Elliot, could I have a word?' Richard asked, waylaying him.

'Couldn't it wait until tomorrow?' Elliot replied, seeing Floella and Jane walk past him and out into the corridor, clearly making for the staffroom. 'I'm a little busy.'

'If I don't say this now I never will,' the junior doctor said firmly, then took a deep breath. 'Elliot, I know you're my boss, and I'm probably speaking out of turn here, but it's about Jane.'

'Why am I not surprised?' Elliot groaned. 'Go on, then, get it over with,' he continued as the junior doctor coloured. 'Tell me I'm the biggest louse of all time.'

'Well, frankly, I think you are, but that's not what I wanted to say to you,' Richard said determinedly. 'I just wanted to put you straight about something in case...well, in case you'd got hold of the wrong end of the stick. You might remember that I came round to your flat and Jane and I spent the whole evening in her bedroom.'

'Richard, could you please get to the point?' Elliot asked. 'Like I said, I'm in a hurry tonight.' And if I'm not fast, Jane will have left and another opportunity will have slipped through my fingers. 'Say what you want to say, and get it over with.'

To his frustration the junior doctor took another deep breath. 'I wanted you to know that nothing untoward occurred between Jane and me that night. I was feeling a bit down, and Jane volunteered to cheer me up, to listen to my moans and groans.'

'Is that it?' Elliot demanded. 'Is that the end of your revelations?'

Richard flushed scarlet. 'I just thought you should know. I couldn't have lived with myself if it was my fault—my being there that night—you dumped her.'

Elliot opened his mouth, closed it again, struggled with his temper and eventually managed a small, tight smile.

'Thank you for sharing that with me, Richard, and now, if there's nothing else?' The junior doctor shook his head. 'Good. Then I'll bid you a very good night.'

And before the junior doctor could reply Elliot was off and running through the treatment-room doors, down the corridor and into the staffroom.

'Where's the fire?' Jane couldn't help but laugh as he all but fell in the door, red-cheeked and breathless.

'I wanted to talk to you.'

Her laughter died in an instant, and she pulled on her coat and reached for her bag. 'I'm sorry, but anything you want to say to me will have to wait until tomorrow. I'm off duty now, and all I want to do is go home.'

'Jane, it's important—'

'So is the shopping I have to do before I can go home,' she replied, walking to the door.

'Jane, it's about Nicole.' That stopped her in her tracks as he'd known it would.

'What about Nicole? I saw her this afternoon and she seemed fine.'

'She *is* fine,' he reassured her, hating himself for worrying her unnecessarily, but desperate situations called for desperate measures. 'Jane, I need to ask you a favour.'

She stiffened immediately. 'If you're going to ask me

to move back in with you until your mother comes home—'

'No, I'm not going to ask you that,' he interrupted. 'It wouldn't be fair.'

Like it had been really fair of him to allow her to fall in love with him, to let her believe that he loved her, too?

But she didn't say that. Instead, she said, 'What's this favour, then?'

'To talk to you about Nicole. To see if together we can come up with some plausible reason for you not being there when she gets home.'

'Elliot—'

'Jane, she loves you—you know she does—and she's going to be heartbroken if you just disappear out of her life without a word of explanation.'

She stared at him for a long moment. He looked tired, weary, and surely those deep creases on his forehead hadn't been there two weeks ago?

'OK. All right.'

She put down her bag and began taking off her coat, but he shook his head.

'I thought maybe we could talk at the flat. Jane, anyone could walk in while we're talking,' he continued quickly as she opened her mouth, clearly intending to protest. 'And I really think our private lives should remain just that, don't you?'

No need to tell her that all of A and E seemed to know that they had been lovers. No need to reveal that the only thing left private about their relationship was why it had ended.

'Jane, please,' he continued when she said nothing. 'For half an hour, that's all.'

He held his breath as she thought about that, then to his relief she nodded. 'OK. For half an hour.'

*　　*　　*

It was strange to be back, Jane thought as Elliot ushered her into the sitting room. Strange and familiar at the same time. The seat where she'd always sat in the evening, the coffee-table she and Nicole had played Scrabble on. It had only been two weeks, and yet it felt like a lifetime.

'Would you like a coffee—tea—something stronger?' he asked awkward, eager.

'I don't want to put you to any trouble.'

'It would be no trouble.'

'Coffee, then.' She managed a smile. 'Thank you.'

'I won't be a minute,' he said heartily, too heartily. 'Take a seat, make yourself comfortable.'

She couldn't. There were too many memories associated with this room. Nicole like a little white ghost on that first night. Nicole laughing and giggling as her father tickled her. Michelle Bouvier…

She slipped off her coat, and couldn't prevent a wry smile from curving her lips as she looked around for somewhere to put it. A little over two months ago her heart had sunk when she'd first seen Elliot's home, so pristine, so elegant, so intimidating. Now there were toys on practically every seat, books left lying where they'd been dropped.

'I didn't tidy anything away,' he murmured, clearly reading her thoughts as he came back into the sitting room. 'I thought…if I did that it would be as though I was accepting she was never coming back. I kept the hairbrush you left in the bathroom for the same reason.'

She turned from him quickly, unable to bear the naked plea she could see in his eyes. God knows how much she loved this man, would never love anyone else the way she loved him, but she mustn't let him see it or he'd use it, use her again.

'Nicole… You said you wanted to talk about Nicole.'

'Aren't you going to sit down?' he said softly.

She did. It helped a little. Made her feel less shaky, less vulnerable, more in control.

'About Nicole,' she began firmly, taking the cup of coffee from his outstretched hand. 'I think it would be simpler if we just told her I had to go away on a nursing course.'

He sat down, planted his elbows on his knees and fixed his eyes on her face. 'And when you don't come back after two weeks, what, then?'

'She'll be with your mother in Hampshire.'

'I'm not sending her to my mother,' he said. 'I'm keeping her with me.'

'But how will you manage?' she gasped. 'When you work nights, the weekends?'

'I'll get a nanny—a succession of nannies if need be—but she's staying in London with me.'

He watched her take this in, digest it.

'Then if she's going to be staying with you,' she replied, 'all I can suggest is you tell her I've been looking for a place of my own for a while, and that I've found one.'

'She'll be hurt—upset.'

'Elliot, no one ever said this was going to be easy.'

His eyes caught and held hers. 'It could be, if you'd listen to sense, believe that I love you, and marry me.'

She got to her feet quickly and headed for the door. 'I have to go.'

'Jane, Nicole loves you very much, and I know that you love her—'

'Elliot, don't,' she pleaded, whirling back to him, her eyes large pools of pain and distress. 'Please, don't. What you're doing—it isn't fair. Yes, I love your daughter, and I'm delighted—more than delighted—to see how much you care for her, but I can't marry you simply to give your daughter a mother.'

Can't, not won't. Can't meant there might yet be a

chance for him, that she might love him as much as he loved her.

He took a jagged breath and stepped forward. 'Jane, as God is my witness, I love you. Not as a mother for Nicole—'

'I won't listen to this,' she cried, putting her hands over her ears. 'I won't let you do this to me. It's blackmail! Working on my feelings, knowing how much I care for your daughter!'

He pulled her hands down and held on to them. 'Jane—'

'No! Elliot, your daughter is a wonderful girl, a lovely girl—'

'And she isn't mine.'

She stared at him open-mouthed for a second, then shook her head. 'You're not making any sense. Of course she's yours. Donna—'

'Lied,' he interrupted harshly. 'When Nicole had the accident, and we needed to do all those blood tests… She's Donna's daughter, Jane, but I'm not her father.'

She couldn't take it in, couldn't believe it. 'But why would your wife lie? She must have known paternity could easily be established.'

'I guess she never figured on an accident—the need for blood tests,' he said, his face white, taut. 'She probably hoped Nicole would be all grown up and married before anybody found out.'

'But if you're not Nicole's father, then who…?'

'God alone knows,' he said grimly. 'Perhaps he was some one-night stand whose name she couldn't remember afterwards, or maybe she'd slept with so many men that month she didn't have a clue.'

She shook her head, still dazed, still confused. 'But why would she say she was yours?'

'Perhaps she wanted to do one good thing in her life, knowing that if anything ever happened to her Nicole would have security.' His mouth twisted bitterly. 'Or perhaps she wasn't that noble, and it was one last joke at my expense, dumping someone else's kid on me.'

She wrenched her hands free from his angrily. 'And is that how you feel? That Nicole was dumped on you?'

'*No*! She's my daughter, Jane. *Mine*. I don't give a damn about blood groups, she's *mine*.'

She stared up at him, frozen, stunned. He was crying. Cool, super-confident Elliot was crying, and she thought it was the most awful, heart-wrenching sound she had ever heard.

And suddenly she was crying, too, as hard as he was. Reaching for him, holding him tightly, trying to contain the sobs that racked his body.

'Why didn't you *tell* me? Oh, Elliot, why did you keep it to yourself? You should have *told* me, let me share it with you, let me help you!'

For a long time he couldn't answer, simply clung to her while she smoothed his hair back from his forehead and kissed him and murmured words that she hoped might give him some comfort, ease some of his pain.

'I didn't tell you because I thought you'd try to persuade me to track down Nicole's real father,' he said shakily at last. 'That you'd say it was the right thing to do.'

'Never!' she protested. 'Elliot, *you* are her father, the man she loves. Her real father could be anybody. Somebody horrible, somebody she would hate.'

'I couldn't give her up, Jane, not now,' he said, his voice cracking. 'Not now that I've grown to love her so much. She is my daughter, and always will be, even though we have no blood connection.'

'I know,' she whispered, holding on to him tightly, hot tears welling in her eyes again, only to feel dismay as he gently eased her away from him. 'Elliot...?'

'I know she will eventually have to be told the truth—

when she's older, a teenager—but I would like—I would very much hope—that we could both be there to tell her together.'

She wanted to say, yes, that she'd be there with him, but she couldn't.

'Elliot, I'm sorry—'

'Jane, even if you won't agree to marry me, even if all you'll ever let me have of you is what I have now—a shoulder to cry on—and not your love, I will still love you. I will *always* love you.'

'My love—you want *my* love?' she said, wanting to believe him, desperately wanting to believe him.

'Jane, I love you for the person you are, not because I want a mother for Nicole,' he said raggedly. 'I love you, and I love Nicole, and I don't want to lose either of you. And if that's selfish then, yes, I'm selfish, but I want both of you for the joy and happiness you've brought into my life.'

The tears in her eyes spilled over and down her cheeks. 'Oh, Elliot—'

'Jane, I love you so much that I'm trusting you with my future happiness. What I've just told you—you could use that knowledge, go to Michelle, tell her the truth, and that would mean I'd lose both of you. I'm putting all my future happiness in your hands.'

And he was, she realised, and it gave her the courage to say what she did.

'Elliot Mathieson, I have loved you since the first moment I set eyes on you.'

'You have?' he said, hope and uncertainty plain in his eyes.

She nodded.

'Then you'll marry me?' he said eagerly. 'You're saying, yes?'

'I'm saying yes, Elliot. I'm saying yes because I love you, and I love Nicole, and no matter what the future brings, we're in this together.'

SNOW EMERGENCY

BY
LAURA IDING

CHAPTER ONE

CHARGE Nurse Tess Ryerson battled a wave of nausea as the trauma team wheeled her patient into the Trauma Intensive Care Unit at Trinity Medical Center.

The female patient had crashed her snowmobile into a tree, suffering multiple broken bones and a lacerated spleen. Tess immediately connected her to a monitor.

"Blood pressure 77/34 with a pulse of 128. How much Dopamine do you have her on?" Tess asked, as the trauma team hurried about.

"Ten micrograms per kilo per minute." A familiar deep southern accent sent a ripple of awareness along Tess's nerves.

"I'm increasing her to fifteen." Tess ignored her response to the surprising—and not necessarily welcome—presence of Dr. Derek Walker, the trauma surgeon on call.

Plenty of time to be horribly mortified later.

She focused on the Emergency Department resident and nurse on the opposite side of the bed as she straightened out the spaghetti mess of IV tubing. Two units of blood were nearly empty.

"What's her hematocrit?" Tess asked the resident.

"Around 20. There's two units of O neg here and the blood bank is working on a type and cross-match for her now," Derek answered for the resident. Tess could feel his penetrating gaze urging her to acknowledge him.

She couldn't. "Good. Call the lab, tell them to rush the type and cross-match and send me another two units of blood."

"I thought it was my job to give orders?" Derek's curt tone forced her reluctant gaze to meet his.

She took a deep calming breath, so not in the mood for surgeon theatrics, and arched a brow. "Do you want her to get more blood?"

"Go ahead and give her the first two units, then check her hematocrit. If it's less than 30 give another," Derek confirmed.

Duh. No kidding. Tess bit back a snide retort. The sooner things were under control, the sooner they would all leave. "Fine," she said. "The fluid is in, her pressure is better, almost 90 systolic. We're making progress."

She continued to care for the patient as the ED nurse and resident left, leaving her and Derek alone. Tess kept busy, not bothering to give him more of her attention, just hoping he would leave. What was he doing here? She could feel her emotions stirring, but she tried to keep her face as blank as possible. Focus on the chart…

"You didn't return my phone calls." He spoke quietly, so no one else would overhear.

"No." Another wave of nausea caught her off guard and Tess leaned against the bed frame, praying she wouldn't throw up. She was busy and she knew she didn't have time to get into this with Derek. She gripped the patient's clipboard in her hand like a shield. "Anything else you want? Additional labs? Fluids?"

"Draw a basic chem panel when you get her next hematocrit."

She nodded and wrote the order, taking deep breaths as she hoped the nausea would pass. She'd felt sick for almost a week. Dear God, she couldn't believe all of this. The one and only time she'd indulged in a very selfish fling, it had backfired on her in spades. It was looking as if her one night of luxurious passion may have come with a steep price.

She suspected she might be pregnant.

Responsibility was her middle name. They'd used protection, but one of the condoms had broken. She hadn't worried so much at first, because she'd been on the pill. However, she'd forgotten about the meningitis patient she'd admitted a week earlier. Since she'd been exposed prior to the patient's diagnosis, the hospital had placed her on antibiotics as a precautionary measure.

Antibiotics and birth-control pills didn't mix. The first tended to negate the effects of the second. She was praying what she was feeling was due to a bug, that maybe it was the flu. She couldn't be sure until she took a pregnancy test.

Derek was still there, watching her. "I know you're busy, I'll find you later." As if reading her mind, he walked away, finally getting the hint and leaving her alone.

In the nick of time Tess raced to the bathroom, where she lost the entire contents of her stomach in a sickening lurch.

* * *

Derek couldn't believe he'd found her. Tess, *his* Tess, was a nurse in the Trauma ICU! A deluge of emotion swamped him.

He could remember their night together with absolute clarity. Every kiss. Every stroke of his fingers along her ivory skin. Every throaty sound she'd uttered when he'd slid deep inside her. His body tightened at the mere thought.

They'd met at a holiday party he'd attended at his boss's urging. The moment a laughing Tess had entered the room, she'd captivated him. His heart had somersaulted in his chest. He'd lost his breath, as if someone kicked him in the kidneys. He'd approached her and found, to his disbelief, that the instant attraction he'd felt was mutual. While it wasn't his style to take a woman home on the same night he'd met her, he'd felt deep down that they could potentially have so much more.

But the next morning he'd awoken to find she had disappeared while he'd been sleeping.

For a solid week he'd tried to find her, all the while getting acclimated to his new job as a trauma physician in Milwaukee—until his brother had phoned with the news of their mother's stroke. Without hesitation, he'd taken the first flight home, to South Carolina.

Thankfully, his boss, the Chief of Trauma Surgery, had granted his request to delay his start date by another month. A glitch in transferring his South Carolina MD license to Wisconsin had added another couple of weeks.

Until now. His first night on trauma call and he'd found Tess, the woman of his dreams.

His first instinct was to run, to get the hell out of dodge. Because somewhere deep inside, he knew with sinking certainty he'd just seen the woman he was destined to marry.

Hel-lo, reality check. Tess was not thrilled to see him. Too bad. He had no idea what he'd done to chase her away, but whatever it was, he was determined to set things right.

Halfway down to the ER, his pager went off. He retraced his steps to the ICU, answered the nurse's questions, then halted abruptly when Tess emerged from the bathroom, pale and shaken.

Derek again. Why couldn't he leave her alone? Didn't she have enough to deal with? Thoughts were racing through her head, spinning out of control. If she was pregnant, how on earth would she manage to work and raise a child all alone? Her hands trembled.

"Tess, are you all right?" He took her arm and steered her into the staff break room. She wanted to argue, but fatigue hit hard, and there were at least six more hours left in her shift.

"I'm fine." She sank gratefully into a chair. How ironic that all of this was hitting her at the same time that Derek showed up, she thought. If she was pregnant, Derek would be the father…

He immediately placed his palm on her forehead. The warm, male scent of him brought erotic memories she'd thought were buried deep, come rushing to the surface. "No fever. Thank heavens, for a minute I thought you were ill."

"I'm fine," she repeated.

He knelt on the floor before her, taking her clammy hands in his. "Tess, we need to talk."

They were alone in the break room. When she lifted her gaze to his, doubt assailed her. She had been avoiding him, but maybe he had a right to know the truth. She may not even been pregnant, she reminded herself. Should she confess her suspicions now? Or wait until after she'd done a pregnancy test to know for sure?

CHAPTER TWO

TESS gulped. Derek was right, they needed to talk. He deserved to know the truth about her possible pregnancy.

"Why did you run away that morning, without a word?" he asked.

She resisted the urge to bury her face in her hands. She didn't want to talk about their night together. She'd gone to the holiday party to escape her emotionally needy family. She didn't remember hearing that Derek was the new trauma physician, but she did recall the moment she saw him—the attraction was instant. She shamelessly flirted with him, then uncharacteristically spent the rest of the night wallowing in pure, sensual pleasure.

Why had that seemed like such a good idea at the time?

"I—" She shook her head, trying not to be drawn offtrack. "The reason isn't important."

"It is to me." Derek stared at her for a moment, then gruffly asked, "Did I hurt you?"

"No, of course not." Tess blew out a breath. His nervous concern softened her heart. It was now or never—the urge to chicken out, to avoiding telling him her suspicion was strong. There was no delicate way to break it to him. "I'm afraid I might be pregnant."

"Pregnant?" His jaw dropped.

"Tess!" Emma, one of the ICU nurses, dashed into the break room with wide eyes. "Did you hear? They're talking twelve to fourteen inches of snow. A blizzard!"

Good grief, could this night get any worse? The last thing she needed was to be snowed in. Tess jumped to her feet, bravely facing Derek. "Now you know the truth. I have to go."

And before he had a chance to stop her, Tess turned and headed out the door.

Derek could barely think with Tess's words reverberating in his head. Pregnant. Tess might be pregnant. Now that he thought about it, the signs were so clear. Her pale, drawn features, the way her hand was constantly pressed to her stomach, as if she might throw up.

Wait a minute, no reason to panic just yet. They were in the height of flu season and those same symptoms could be from nothing more than a nasty bug.

But if she was pregnant—

His pager sounded and he reluctantly read the message. Another trauma victim, actually two, were on the way. Every fiber of his being wanted to find Tess, to make sure she was really all right, but the trauma victims couldn't wait. Muttering a curse, he took the stairs down to the ED.

"What's the ETA?" he asked, entering the trauma room.

"Any minute." Steve Anderson, the resident on call greeted him. "One victim has been freed from the wreck; the other is still being extracted."

Within moments, the doors burst open.

"We have a 68 year-old male with a crushing chest

injury," the paramedic shouted over the din. "He's been in and out of V-tach. We had to shock him twice during the ride in."

"Call the cardio-thoracic team." Derek could see the patient had several other fractures, but his chest injury was the most life-threatening. "He'll need to go to the OR."

"I'll call them." Steve grabbed the closest phone.

Derek took control, rattling off a series of requests for X-rays, lab work and blood. They shocked the patient again, while waiting for the team. He couldn't let his personal life interfere with his work, but thoughts of Tess lingered in the back of his mind while he fought to keep the patient stable.

Fifteen minutes later, the patient was on his way to the OR for emergent open-heart surgery. Their second patient arrived—a younger man suffering severe hypo-thermia on top of his multiple fractures. A good hour passed before he was able to send the guy up to the Trauma ICU. He planned to follow, but made a quick detour to the supply room, grabbing a pregnancy kit and stuffing it in a brown paper bag.

He'd spent days wondering why Tess had run away, refusing to take his calls. Now there was a bigger reason to get to the bottom of her mysterious behavior. Tess might be pregnant.

Time to know one way or the other for certain.

In the break room, Tess laid her forehead on the cool glass of the window as the bright, glistening snow fell in deceptively innocent flakes.

The second shift hospital supervisor had, indeed,

declared a snow emergency. Third shift staff nurses had
flooded the switchboard with calls saying they couldn't
get in. No reason to be surprised to discover she wasn't
going anywhere.

No one was.

The supervisor had already turned empty resident call
rooms into sleep rooms for the nursing staff. Her job
would be to coordinate a sleep schedule for the ICU
nurses, in case they were stuck here for the next 24
hours. It didn't help to realize Derek was stuck here, too.
She couldn't avoid him. He'd wanted to talk, but what
possessed her to blab her secret?

"Tess."

Derek's deep southern accent had her spinning from
the window, the resulting dizziness nearly making her
fall. She put a steadying hand on the wall.

"Ah…if you're looking for your patient, he's in bed
twelve," she said, eyeing the brown paper bag in his hand.

"I'm looking for you, just like I did the morning
after you left."

A look of surprise passed along her face.

"I got your number through a friend but you didn't
answer my calls," he continued. "I couldn't find your
address—Trinity's security is tighter than the White
House—but I wanted to see you again."

Her heart gave a little pang and she desperately
wished things were less complicated. But they weren't.
"Look, Derek, we had a great time but let's just leave it
at that, all right?"

His gaze narrowed and she realized she'd ticked him
off. He couldn't know how badly she wanted to throw
herself into his arms. Why did he have to be so nice?

She'd learned the hard way not to date doctors, especially the ones you worked with.

Of course, she wasn't supposed to have hot, steamy, sexual flings with them, either.

"No, we're not going to just leave it at that—no matter what the results. Take this test." He handed her the bag. "I'll wait."

He'd brought her a pregnancy kit from the ED. They didn't stock them in the ICU, so she'd planned on going down herself, later. Her stomach flip-flopped as she wavered with indecision.

What was wrong with her? Normally, she was the most decisive person on the planet. She excelled at taking care of her crisis-laden family and being in charge here at work. What was she waiting for?

Without a word, she took the bag from him and disappeared into the bathroom. Swallowing hard, she stared at the package. Okay, she was stuck at work with relentless nausea. If this was the flu, she couldn't take anything to ease her symptoms, until she knew for sure. She took the test. As she waited for the results, the seconds seemed to take forever to tick by, and she could barely breathe.

She stared in silence at the results.

CHAPTER THREE

THE RED LINE on the test strip blurred, then sharpened into focus. She was absolutely, positively, undeniably pregnant.

A baby. *She was going to have a baby!*

Instead of the expected dismay, a thrill of excitement shimmered through her. Wow. She was going to be a mother! The thought overwhelmed her, making the room spin slightly.

That sentiment was quickly replaced with a sense of urgency—she needed to make plans! A new place to live, something with a nice fenced-in yard with plenty of neighborhood kids to play with, yet close to a good school…

She had completely forgotten about Derek, until he rapped on the door. "Tess? Are you okay in there?"

Tossing the kit in the garbage, she wiped her fantasy from her mind. She stood and opened the door.

"Well?" Tense, he stood, his dark, compelling gaze locked on hers. She had the strangest urge to walk into his arms, to bury her face in the comfort of his shoulder. To share the miracle of this tiny life they'd created.

The trauma ICU wasn't the place for this, especially

when she had a million things to do. Briskly, she nodded. "Yes."

"Oh God." His unexpected smile dazzled her. "I'm going to be a father."

"Shh, keep it down." Good grief, she hadn't even considered Derek's role in all of this. Or how she felt about him being back in her life. With a wince she glanced around to make sure no one had overheard him. "We'll have to discuss this later. I have patients to take care of."

She moved as if to go past him, but he caught her arm in his warm grip. "Tess, I'll be here for you. You're not going through this alone."

The prick of tears had to be from hormones, because she wasn't the sappy sort. She blinked them back and lifted her chin. "I appreciate the sentiment, but we barely know each other."

His grip on her arm tightened, then reluctantly slid away. As she turned to head toward the central nurse's station, she heard him say, "We will, Tess. Trust me, we will."

Two hours later, Derek found himself plenty busy when one of his trauma patients took a turn for the worse. But he couldn't help the goofy grin that wanted to break free, even as he ordered a fluid bolus in response to the man's low blood-pressure.

A baby. He and Tess were going to have a baby.

Not that she was especially thrilled with his reappearance in her life, and truthfully, that fact rankled. What was her problem? *We had a good time, let's leave it at that*. Like hell. She obviously had issues she wasn't sharing with him, but he wanted her, anyway.

Not just physically, although that attraction hadn't dimmed in the least. She was smart. He admired her nursing skill, the way she remained cool and calm in an emergency, multitasking like a pro.

Like now. "How much fluid have we given him?"

Tess hung an IV antibiotic, answering him over her shoulder. "Three liters, not counting the two units of blood. Urine output is marginal, his central venous pressure is up to 15."

See? She'd read his mind. "All right, back off on the fluids. If his pressure begins to drop again, we'll need to start him on epinephrine."

"Okay." She crossed to the supply cart and frowned. "Out of suction catheters? The second shift materials tech must not have come in. I'd better do an inventory."

She had yet to look at him, seeming to take every opportunity to remain distant. Briskly, she picked up her clipboard and headed toward the supply room.

Oh, no, he wasn't putting up with another of her infamous disappearing acts. Derek quickly followed. "I'll help."

She barely spared him a glance as she made her way down the hall. "Don't you have more important things to do?"

"No." His trauma pager had been blessedly silent and his patients were stable for the moment. "Stop avoiding me."

"Are you going to hound me like this for the whole nine months? Because if so, I'll go crazy." She went straight to the back of the room and began tallying supplies.

"No, you won't, You're a survivor." He grabbed her clipboard, tossed it aside then lightly clasped her arms.

"Tess, tell me what is really bothering you, besides being pregnant?"

The lights abruptly went out, enclosing the supply room in total darkness.

Tess held her breath, counting the seconds in her head. One, two, three…there, she heard the backup generator kick on.

But the supply room, not part of the critical power supply, remained shrouded in blackness.

Derek's hands pulled her close and his mouth captured hers in a startling kiss. Instantly, the weeks they'd spent apart faded. Desire flared, hot and quick and lethal.

Oh heavens, she wanted him. Here. Now. Hurry. No, not here, with boxes of gauze crinkling at her back, but in a bed. Naked.

His hands slid over the worn cotton of her scrubs making a mockery of the thin covering. Helplessly, she clutched his shoulders as he pressed an openmouthed kiss to her neck.

"God, Tess. I want you."

Okay. Yes. Here. Why not? She wanted him, too. She shifted and pressed closer, his hard, male body seemingly a perfect fit with hers. The rigid evidence of his arousal made her want to touch. She needed protection…

Wait a minute, this was exactly how she'd gotten pregnant! What was she doing? She shoved him away, breathing hard, searching desperately for her penlight.

With shaking fingers she turned the penlight on to see Derek. "Are you nuts? This can't happen. I want you to leave me alone."

"Really? You could have fooled me. I'd swear you enjoyed that kiss as much as I did." He crossed his arms over his chest. "Oh, I get it. You're running scared, just like you did the morning after the holiday party."

"I'm not running from anything," Tess scoffed.

"Yes you are, but what?" He leaned close and it took all her strength not to prove him right by bolting for the door. "Me? The baby? The way I make you feel? Tess, please…why won't you open up?"

CHAPTER FOUR

TESS hesitated, meeting Derek's intense gaze in the minimal illumination from her penlight. The dark supply room provided an aura of intimacy, isolating them from the rest of the world.

"You weren't supposed to be a doctor," she blurted, needing to tell him how she felt. "That's why I didn't return your calls. I don't date doctors. *Ever.*"

Confusion flashed in his eyes. "Someone hurt you."

"Yes." A wave of relief washed over her. Now he knew. "I learned the hard way not to date men I work with."

"Tess, I understand your logic. But think back to the night we first met. You didn't know me, and I didn't know you, but we clicked, instantly drawn to each other."

She couldn't lie to him. Not when their night together was forever seared into her memory. "I know."

"Are you honestly saying we can't move forward in our relationship because I'm a doctor?"

Stated so simply, her reasons for pushing him away did sound a bit lame. But her pregnancy complicated their relationship. Confused, she shook her head. "I don't know."

Derek's pager shrilled loudly, making her jump. "Damn," he muttered softly. "I have to go."

She nodded, unable to speak. He surprised her by pressing his mouth on hers for a quick kiss.

"We'll talk soon," he promised.

Alone in the supply room, she finished her inventory of the suction catheters via penlight. She didn't doubt Derek would find her later, but talking wouldn't change a thing.

He'd still be a doctor she worked with. And she was still pregnant with his baby. How could she ever trust Derek's feelings for her? And worst of all, what if they didn't last?

Derek hated leaving Tess, but the OR staff had paged him to let him know the trauma patient with the crushing chest injury was coming out of surgery. For the next couple of hours, he remained busy with the patient who'd undergone a coronary bypass surgery and a mitral-valve replacement.

Emma was the ICU nurse at the bedside. She was competent, but they didn't have the same synergy that he shared with Tess.

He sensed Tess coming up behind him. How had he grown so aware of her in such a short amount of time?

"Emma? I'm ready to take over for you." Tess consulted her clipboard. "You're scheduled for a four-hour rest period."

Concerned, he glanced at Tess. "Shouldn't you rest soon?"

She sent him an exasperated look. "I'm fine. As the Charge Nurse, I'm last to go."

"I'm okay, Tess, if you want to switch places," Emma offered as she hung an IV antibiotic.

"No, thanks. I'd rather stick to the schedule."

Derek appreciated Tess's organizational skills—clearly she preferred to do things according to plan. But what about making some exceptions once in a while? Couldn't she adapt her strict schedule for the sake of her health? For their baby?

He stepped back, listening as Emma gave Tess a detailed report on the patient's progress since returning from surgery. After fifteen minutes, Emma finally left them alone.

"His cardiac index is still low, and his pulse is tachy." Tess's tone was brisk and professional. "Did you want me to titrate the nipride and epinephrine drips?"

"Yes, until his cardiac index is at least 2.5 or better." Derek fought the urge to make her sit down. Not that she would appreciate his interference. "How are you feeling? Any nausea?"

"A little." She ignored him as she worked over his patient. "But I'm fine."

He glanced at the clock hanging on the wall above the patient's bed. Two o'clock in the morning. He'd pumped Emma on the length of their shifts. Tess couldn't be fine, not when they were already a good three hours past her normal eight hours. She was sick, pregnant and had just agreed to cover another four hours because of the mountain of snow piling up outside.

Did she think she was Wonder Woman?

A voice over the intercom interrupted his thoughts. "Tess, you have a call on line two."

"Excuse me." Tess swept past him to seek a phone

outside the patient's room. With unabashed curiosity, he blatantly listened to her side of the conversation.

"You have two extra nurses for us?" Tess's voice rose incredulously. "How did you manage that?" She paused, then nodded. "You bet I'll use them, thanks so much!" She hung up.

"Help is on the way?" he asked.

"Yes. Apparently, the house supervisor managed to get in touch with a couple of ICU nurses who live in the apartment complex across the highway." Her gaze slid from his and he immediately knew what she was thinking. The same apartment complex he lived in. The same place she'd snuck out of the morning after their night together. Tess cleared her throat, before continuing, "They walked here, despite the blizzard."

"Great. Now you can rest."

Her gaze narrowed then turned into a wince as she put a hand over her stomach.

"Maybe, at least for a little while."

"Dr. Walker!" One of the ICU nurses ran up to him. "Your patient in room twelve just went into V-fib."

"Call a Code Blue and get the defibrillator now!" Derek ran down to room twelve.

Damn. This was the guy who had been in the same car crash as the open-heart case. So much for being stable. "Charge the defibrillator to 200 joules and shock him."

Tess wheeled the defibrillator into the room and efficiently connected the patient to the defib pads. "Charged to 200 joules, all clear?" After making sure no staff members were touching the patient, she shocked him.

"Still in V-fib, shock again at 200," Derek commanded. "All clear?" Tess shocked him again

"Still in V-fib, shock again at 360 joules," Derek said. "All clear?" Tess gave the third electrical shock.

"Still v-fib, start CPR and give a miligram of epinephrine." Derek gave the orders calmly, although inside, he wanted to scream and shout. What had they missed? Why had this guy gone into a lethal cardiac rhythm? And could they save him?

Tess climbed up to kneel on the bed for chest compressions.

On a personal level, Derek wanted to yank her down, but her chest-compressions were excellent, giving the patient a reasonable blood pressure. Once they had given all the necessary medications, he called out, "Stop CPR, let's see what we have for a heart rhythm."

Tess halted her compressions.

Derek held his breath and there was a moment of complete silence as every person in the room stared at the monitor.

CHAPTER FIVE

"NORMAL sinus rhythm." Relief was evident in Tess's tone.

"All right, start him on amiodirone drip and send off a basic chem and cardiac injury panel," Derek instructed. They'd avoided further complications for the moment, but this guy's heart obviously needed a little help. "I'll call a Cardiology consult."

Most of the members of the code team dispersed from the room, leaving the patient's nurse to take over. Derek wrote a note in the patient's chart, then picked up the phone to call Cardiology.

After he placed the call, he took a few moments to think over what he would say to the patient's family— they also had to be notified. Although the patient was stabilized, his condition had just turned critical.

"Derek?" A warm hand on his shoulder brought him out of his morose thoughts. "Are you all right?"

Tess. Her concern warmed his heart. He wanted so badly to take her hand in his, but at the same time, he didn't want to undermine her professionalism while they were in the ICU.

He forced a smile. "Yeah, I'm fine. That was a close call, though."

"I know." Tess's expression mirrored his feelings. "You did a great job in there."

"Not just me, the whole team," he corrected. "Even if you did give me a moment of heart failure when you jumped up on the bed to do CPR. I'd feel better if you were off your feet, resting." He kept his voice low, so their conversation wouldn't carry.

Her cheeks reddened and her hand slipped from his shoulder. He instantly missed the physical connection. "Actually, that's exactly what I wanted to tell you. I'm on my way to rest in one of the call rooms. In case you need to find me."

"Good." Was there a hidden meaning in there? Man, he hoped so. She needed to take care of herself and he wished like heck he could go with her. His trauma pager was relatively quiet, but he couldn't risk leaving his patient just yet. "Get some sleep."

"I will. See you later."

Derek watched her walk away, wondering which call room she'd been assigned. Would she mind a little company, later? The thought gave him the spurt of energy he needed to finish his paperwork, then check on the remainder of his patients. The sooner he got things squared away in the ICU, the quicker he could find Tess.

Tess was physically exhausted, but emotionally too keyed up to sleep. Not unusual, the adrenaline rush of a code blue was enough to keep anyone awake.

She splayed her hand over her flat belly. For a few hours, the idea of having a baby had stayed in the dark recesses of her mind, but now the knowledge filled her head. Would it be a boy or a girl? Would he or she have straight dark hair like Derek or her riot red curls? She needed to think of a name…

A knock on her door brought her bolting upright. Groggily, she stared at the illuminated clock. She must have dozed, after all. Was her four-hour rest period over already?

"Tess? It's me, Derek."

Leaning over, she flicked on the small bedside lamp. She'd taken off her scrubs, so she wrapped a blanket around her nearly naked body and went to the door. She opened it just a crack, and peered out at him. "What's wrong?"

"Nothing's wrong." His lazy grin shot a tingle of awareness through her stomach.

"May I come in?"

Tess hesitated, knowing he wanted more than conversation. The memory of their kisses in the supply room reminded her of how close to the edge she teetered. He was a doctor, a trauma surgeon, no less. If she had a functioning brain cell left in her head, she'd run in the opposite direction.

But she didn't want to run, and not just because of the sexual chemistry between them. Derek was a sincere and compassionate doctor. There were no guarantees in life—the near-miss during the code blue proved that. And suddenly, looking at Derek, she realized just how much she was tempted to trust him.

It was a good feeling, she thought.

"Won't you give me a chance, Tess?" He edged closer to the door. "I promise I won't hurt you." He offered a smile.

Her resistance melted. How did he have the power

to make her act so differently than she usually would? With Derek she was another person, one who didn't care about the mistakes of the past, only the possibilities of the future.

"All right." She opened the door.

The relief in his gaze was comical. He came into the call room, then quickly closed and locked the door behind him. She opened her mouth to say something, but before she could formulate a coherent thought, he covered her mouth with his.

The room spun as Derek pulled her into his arms. With two steps he steered to the edge of the bed and gently set her down on the mattress. She clutched the blanket to her naked chest as Derek gazed down at her. He stroked a finger down her cheek.

"You're so beautiful. I can hardly believe I've found you after all these weeks." A ghost of a smile played across the hard planes of his face. "How did I get so lucky to be snowed in with you my first night on call?"

Her throat thick with emotion, Tess couldn't answer. Instead, she loosened her hold on the blanket and entwined her arms around his neck, then brought him closer for another kiss. Letting go of her old fears was much easier when he kissed her.

"I want you," Derek whispered. He made quick work of getting rid of his scrubs, then took his time divesting her of the lace she wore. He splayed his broad hand over her abdomen as his gaze feasted on her bare breasts. "Are you really up for this?"

"I'm fine." When his hand moved up to cup one of her breasts, she gasped. "Better than fine."

"Good."

He took his time exploring every inch of her, but his slow caresses were driving her mad—she wanted him to hurry. When he spread her legs to stroke her more intimately, she eagerly rose up to meet him.

"Derek, please," she clutched at him, urging him closer.

"Shh, let me look at you for a moment." He stroked the heart of her while pressing a kiss on her belly.

"Don't make me wait another minute." She threaded her hands into his hair and tugged him upward. The muscles of his arms bunched as he lifted up to cover her body with his, and thrust deep.

"Oh!" she cried out when he filled her so completely. Yes, finally—this was what she'd wanted! Maybe everything would work out between them, she thought... and then she couldn't think at all.

After several moments, all she heard was Derek's deep breaths. Then he pressed his forehead against hers.

"Tess, I think I'm falling in love with you."

She froze, her heart stumbling in her chest. The shrill ringing of the phone cut the silence of the room. Derek picked up the receiver and held it out for her to answer.

CHAPTER SIX

"TESS, we're declaring an all-clear. You're free to leave."

"All right." She barely heard her supervisor because Derek's words tumbled through her mind as she hung up the phone.

I think I'm falling in love with you.

"Is something wrong?" Derek asked. "You look pale."

"Yes. No, er…the snow emergency is over." She was all too aware of her nakedness beneath the sheets. What had she done? "I can go home."

Derek's dark brows pulled together. "I'd like to drive you home, but I can't leave until seven. Will you wait for me?"

"I can drive myself." She clutched the sheet, easing away. "I'm sure the plows have the major streets cleared by now."

"Tess." He put a hand on her arm, as if to stop her. "You're doing it again, running away from me. From us."

"I—need some time alone." Her voice sounded strange, distant, even to her own ears. "To think."

"I meant what I said." Derek tipped her chin up, forcing her to meet his gaze. "I'm falling in love with you."

Her eyes flashed and she jerked away from his touch. "We've only known each other a few days. How can you love me? You don't even know me." Fuming, she searched for her discarded scrubs.

"I knew from the moment I saw you, my life had changed. Our first night together, I discovered your great sense of humor. Your laugh was infectious." She didn't want to listen, but his voice tugged at her while she gathered her stuff. "After tonight, I know you're a warm, compassionate nurse who's been hurt in the past and I can only promise not to do the same."

"That's not enough." Her voice was soft, barely above a whisper as she clutched her clothes to her chest.

"I know you take responsibility seriously. And I know you're carrying my baby." Derek wouldn't give up. "All I'm asking is for you to give us a chance."

"I need time, Derek. This is just so much to take in all at once. I'd never keep you away from your child, but as far as a relationship goes—" she swallowed hard "—I'm just not sure."

The expression in his eyes was dark, tormented. She expected him to push harder, but he surprised her by nodding.

"I'll give you time, Tess." He stood. "But remember how hard I searched for you, after that first night. And how thrilled I was to find you, before you told me about the baby. From the moment I saw you, I was attracted to you. And making love again just now only reinforced how wonderful we are together."

She didn't have a response to that, so she slipped into the bathroom. As she leaned weakly against the door, she knew his words would follow her all the way home.

✳ ✳ ✳

Derek finished his shift and headed to his apartment across the street, wishing he dared go straight to Tess's place. But he'd promised to give her time.

And a few measly hours probably wasn't enough, damn it.

She was slipping through his fingers. Again. And he didn't know how to convince her that his feelings were real. Hell, they were so real they scared him to death.

When he'd found her in the ICU, he'd known their futures were irrevocably linked. But he hadn't anticipated the news of the baby.

At first he'd been ecstatic about being a father. Now he resented the very connection he'd once desired, because Tess hadn't believed him when he'd confessed he loved her. She thought he was handing her a line, because of the baby.

Nothing was further from the truth.

But how could he convince her?

Five excruciatingly long days passed before he saw Tess again. He'd called often, but she hadn't returned his messages. They kept missing each other at work, too.

When his buzzer sounded on Saturday morning, his heart leapt with hope. He used the intercom to answer. "Yes?"

"Derek? It's Tess. Do you have a minute?"

He had way more than a minute, but tried to remain calm. "Of course, come on up." He pressed the button to release the lock then went to open his apartment door to wait for her.

She looked wonderful, casually dressed in worn

jeans and a green wool sweater beneath her bulky coat. He could barely keep himself from hauling her into his arms and kissing her.

"I'm so glad you stopped by. You look wonderful. Do you want something to drink?" Cripes, was he babbling? He needed to get a grip.

"No, I'm fine." She shed her coat, then stood awkwardly in his living room. "I thought I should tell you in person."

His gut clenched at her solemn tone. "Tell me what?" She glanced away, but not before he saw the pain in her eyes. "I've had some bleeding."

"Oh, Tess, I'm sorry." Now he did cross over to pull her into his arms. "When? Why didn't you call me? I would have been there. There's no reason for you to go through this alone."

She didn't resist his embrace, but hid her face in the crook of his neck. "Do you really mean that?"

He was shaken by the news, already grieving for the baby that might no longer be, but he was more worried about Tess. How much blood had she lost? Was she really all right, emotionally?

"Of course I do. Nothing is more important than you, Tess."

She pulled away, enough to search out his gaze. "I want to believe you."

He squashed a wave of frustration but kept his tone calm. "I wish you could believe me, too. I'm not the one who hurt you. I wish I could take care of the guy who did."

She sighed and blew out a breath. "I guess I should explain. My dad was a doctor, Chief of Pediatric Surgery at Children's Memorial Hospital. He left us when I was a senior in high school. Afterwards, my Mom started taking sleeping pills. She was a mess, hardly able to cope. I was the oldest of five kids—I had to keep our family from falling apart."

Derek nodded, finally understanding what she'd gone through and why she had such a strong aversion to doctors. "I'm sorry."

"I'm usually the responsible one, until I met you." She placed a hand over her flat stomach. "I haven't lost the baby yet, but you need to know, it's a real possibility."

"I won't deny how sad I'd be if you lost the baby, but I meant what I said. Making sure you're healthy is my main concern." He brushed a kiss on her forehead. "It'll be okay, Tess. I'm here for you, no matter what."

She was quiet, then reluctantly pulled away. "You scared me when you said you were falling in love with me. Mostly because I've been feeling the same way. And I'm so afraid of ending up like my mother. My family is still pretty much in chaos."

"You're one of the strongest women I know." Derek hadn't met her mother, but he knew Tess. "I wish I could give you a guarantee, but I can't. All I can ask is for you to give me a chance to prove we're different. We are not your parents."

"I know." She raised her gaze to his. "I've been telling myself the same thing. I don't want to ruin what we have."

The tightness in his chest eased. Cautiously, he asked, "And what do we have?"

With a hesitant smile, she gently placed her hand over his heart. "I'm not exactly sure, but I'm anxious to find out."

Not an overwhelming proclamation of love, but he

was willing to take it. After all, they had the rest of their lives. He hauled her into his arms where she belonged.

"Me, too."

MILLS & BOON®

0806/03b

Live the emotion

_Medical
romance™

RESCUED BY MARRIAGE *by Dianne Drake*

Dr Della Riordan is in need of some luck – she
really needs to get her life back on track! The
practice on Redcliffe Island seems too good to be
true; with gorgeous Dr Sam Montgomery on hand
to help, Della begins to find her feet... But Sam is
hiding a secret that could well bring an end to
Della's dreams.

THE NURSE'S LONGED-FOR FAMILY
by Fiona Lowe

Jess Henderson is balancing her nursing job with
being mother to Woody, her two-year-old nephew.
Gorgeous Dr Alex Fitzwilliam manages to convince
her that there is always time for romance... But
Alex refuses to confront his feelings over the loss of
his own son. Alex must put his feelings aside if they
have any chance of becoming a family.

HER BABY'S SECRET FATHER
by Lynne Marshall

When Nurse Jaynie Winchester goes into premature
labour, no-one comes rushing to her side. Baby Tara
is delivered, and Jaynie is not the only one willing the
tiny mite to survive. Respiratory therapist Terrance
Zanderson finds himself getting involved with this
family, then Terrance realises who Tara's father is...

On sale 1st September 2006

*Available at WHSmith, Tesco, ASDA, Borders, Eason,
Sainsbury's and most bookshops*

www.millsandboon.co.uk

"I was fifteen when my mother finally told me the truth about my father. She didn't mean to. She meant to keep it a secret forever. If she'd succeeded it might have saved us all."

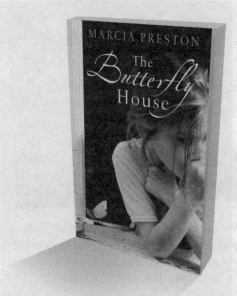

When a hauntingly familiar stranger knocks on Roberta Dutreau's door, she is compelled to begin a journey of self-discovery leading back to her childhood. But is she ready to know the truth about what happened to her, her best friend Cynthia and their mothers that tragic night ten years ago?

16th June 2006

MIRA